C000128007

FALLEN JESTER

USA TODAY BESTSELLING AUTHOR

DEVNEY PERRY

FALLEN JESTER

Copyright © 2021 by Devney Perry LLC

All rights reserved.

ISBN: 978-1-950692-83-5

No part of this book may be reproduced, distributed or transmitted in any form or by any means, including photocopying, recording or other electronic or mechanical methods, without the prior written permission of the author except in the case of brief quotations in a book review.

This is a work of fiction. Names, characters, places and incidents are the product of the author's imagination or are used fictitiously. Any resemblance to actual events, locales or persons, living or dead, is coincidental.

Editing & Proofreading:

Elizabeth Nover, Razor Sharp Editing

Julie Deaton, Deaton Author Services

Karen Lawson, The Proof is in the Reading

Judy Zweifel, Judy's Proofreading

Cover: Sarah Hansen © Okay Creations

OTHER TITLES

The Edens Series

Indigo Ridge

Juniper Hill

Garnet Flats

Jasper Vale

Crimson River

Sable Peak

Christmas in Quincy - Prequel

The Edens: A Legacy Short Story

Treasure State Wildcats Series

Coach

Blitz

Clifton Forge Series

Steel King

Riven Knight

Stone Princess

Noble Prince

Fallen Jester

Tin Queen

Calamity Montana Series

The Bribe

The Bluff

The Brazen

The Bully

The Brawl

The Brood

Jamison Valley Series

The Coppersmith Farmhouse

The Clover Chapel

The Lucky Heart

The Outpost

The Bitterroot Inn

The Candle Palace

Maysen Jar Series

The Birthday List

Letters to Molly

The Dandelion Diary

CONTENTS

PROLOGUE
CASSANDRA

The Betsy.

The notorious dive and biker bar.

I'd driven past here a dozen times. A hundred. A thousand. But tonight was the first time I'd stepped through its front door.

The smell hit me first—sweat, beer and stale cigarette smoke. Then there was the heat, like a furnace blast to the face. The music assaulted my ears, but at least I'd been expecting it. The punishing classic rock pounded so loudly that we'd heard it from the parking lot. We walked inside and were swallowed up by the sea of bodies, the noise of the crowd vibrating down to my bones.

"This place is epic!" Olive shouted above the music. Her smile—which had been firmly fixed in place since we'd started *getting pretty* earlier—widened. Then she threw her hands in the air. "Woohoo! To the bar."

"Aren't we in the bar?"

"What?" She cupped a hand behind her ear.

"I said, aren't we in the bar?"

"What?" She leaned in close enough I could smell the cinnamon on her breath from the piece of gum she'd popped in the car.

"Nothing." I waved her off.

"Come on." She grabbed my wrist and pulled me through the crush, sliding sideways and sidestepping the people dancing and drinking and groping.

Olive reached the bar and squeezed between two older men, each seated on stools. Both had gray beards, one of which was so long it brushed against the bar top itself.

A bartender appeared, waving Olive closer. When she stretched up on her toes to give our order, the man's gaze went straight to her chest.

I rolled my eyes. Did they teach that trick to men in bartending school? It was as obvious as the neon sign in the shape of a naked woman hanging above the ladies' room. Not that Olive cared when guys admired her breasts. She was on a mission to party—meaning get laid—and I was her reluctant accomplice. It was a role I typically avoided because our roommates were more than happy to go with her to the college bars in Missoula, searching for hookups of their own. But since we were in my hometown of Clifton Forge, Montana, the only one here for her to torture was me.

Olive believed in work hard, play hard. After a week spent in class and the library, Friday and Saturday nights were for cutting loose. *Drunked and fucked.* That was the saying she'd coined years ago in undergrad.

Such an imbecilic statement from a woman who was arguably one of the smartest I'd ever met. But Olive excelled at hiding her intelligence from the world, especially on nights like this. Unless we were on campus, Olive rarely spoke of school. If asked by a man what she did, she'd dodge the question, never boasting that she was getting her master's degree or that she was considered one of the brightest graduate students in our program.

Olive believed that men found intelligent women unattractive. Maybe she was right. I had no problems talking about school and it wasn't like I had a line of men beating down my door for a date.

Though if The Betsy was where she was fishing for men, maybe the topic of school would help drive the bottom-feeders away.

A man bumped into me, his eyes glassy as he looked down. "Ssoorrry," he slurred. He lifted an arm to steady himself, like he was going to put it on my shoulder. He missed and his fat beer belly dragged across my stomach as his equally fat hand landed on my boob.

"Don't touch me." I swatted him away.

He dropped his hand, his head bobbling on his too-thick neck, then he was gone, smashing into another unsuspecting female to my left.

When he grabbed her, she just laughed and gave him a hug, pinching his ruddy cheeks like they were best friends.

That woman belonged here.

I most certainly did not.

This weekend was supposed to be about studying. Olive and I had driven from Missoula to Clifton Forge just this morning, our books and laptops loaded, so we could spend a quiet weekend working away from the noise and distraction of our roommates.

My parents were off on one of their regular summer camping adventures. Starting at the end of May and lasting until late fall, they headed to the mountains as long as the weather was good. Camping was their escape from reality.

God, I'd kill for an escape at the moment. Why was I here? Why the hell had I let Olive talk me into this? I hated sweaty strangers rubbing up against me. I hated handsy men, and I hated loud, seedy bars.

The only time the girls got me to go out on a Saturday night in Missoula was when they promised it was to a local wine or martini bar. When they left to go clubbing, I called myself a cab and went home. Like Dad always said, nothing good happened after eleven o'clock.

Well, it was eleven thirteen and as per usual, Dad was right.

"Here." Olive spun away from the bar with two bottles of beer in hand.

I took one, let her clink the rim of hers to mine, then watched with wide eyes as she chugged hers half gone.

Her smile kept getting wider. "I love this place."

"Seriously?"

"Well, yeah. This place is fun! Loosen up, Cass. Let's have a good time." Her eyes darted over my head, taking it all in.

The dark walls were covered with neon beer signs. A jukebox sat in the corner, the lights blinking with the bass of the music. A set of deer antlers hung above it, the horns draped with bras.

Behind the bar were shelves upon shelves of liquor. Two bartenders, both tall, beefy men, filled drink orders. A song change came, and with the momentary respite of noise, the crack of a pool cue rang through the air.

"Let's go look around." Olive must have known I didn't want to because she clamped her hand around my wrist and hauled me toward the pool table. Every step, she'd look to the bar and to the bartender who'd checked her out earlier.

If she was still with me in an hour, I'd be surprised. She'd be *drunked and fucked* while I got ditched. "Super fun."

She didn't hear me over the music.

Damn it. I really should have told her no.

Olive had come up with this brilliant plan for a night out after we'd spent only two hours studying at my parents' dining room table. Just two hours and she'd been restless. I'd wanted to keep plugging away, then order pizza and curl up on the couch for a movie marathon. Not Olive. She wanted me to show her around Clifton Forge.

I'd indulged her, figuring after a quick drive down Central, she'd want to buckle down and work.

Wrong.

She'd spotted The Betsy on our small-town tour, then pelted me with question after question about the bar and the line of motorcycles parked out front. I should have known we'd end up here tonight. When Olive had that party gleam in her eye, there'd be no talking her out of it.

She'd worked her magic and convinced me that taking a break would actually make me more productive. I had been working hard—really hard. She'd planted words like *burnout* and *mental block* in my mind, warning me of students who never recovered.

Was I burned out? Maybe. Maybe not. But the doubt she'd planted had been enough to scare me into agreement.

So we'd stopped at a local store downtown and done some shopping. She'd bought the black, skintight halter top she was wearing. I'd found a scarlet, lace-trimmed camisole that Olive had promised made my coppery red hair look like waves of fire.

A sweet talker, this one, and I'd been putty in her skilled hands.

After shopping, there'd been more touring around town, then a quick stop for dinner. When we'd returned to Mom and Dad's, Olive had spent an hour in my childhood bathroom doing my hair and makeup.

Maybe I'd agreed to The Betsy because she'd made me look like a woman. A sexy woman.

I'd inherited Mom's delicate, youthful features and her auburn hair, which I normally wore in a ponytail. Whenever I tried to buy wine at the grocery store, the clerks thought my ID was a fake. At twenty-four, I could easily pass for a high school sophomore.

But tonight, I was a woman. A grown woman who was entirely out of her element.

"Let's try to get those stools at the bar when they leave," Olive said into my ear, her cheek brushing mine. She nodded at two women dressed even more scantily than us in midriff-baring tops and miniskirts.

The women giggled together, their eyes darting past us toward the pool tables, as they waited for their drinks.

I turned, curious who they were staring at, and gasped at the sight.

The Tin Kings.

The former motorcycle club was as infamous in Clifton Forge as The Betsy. As were their members.

"Whoa." Olive whistled. "Is that them? The bikers you were telling me about earlier?"

"Yes." I elbowed her in the ribs and nodded to the seats just as the other two women received their drinks and left, but it was too late to distract her.

When Olive sat down, she didn't face the bar or her bartender. No, she faced the pool table.

I followed her gaze—she'd locked it on her target. And he stared right back.

"Did you not hear what I told you earlier?" I asked. "They have reputations."

"Good. That means I'm guaranteed an orgasm."

"Olive—"

She was already gone, disappearing through the crowd only to end up beside none other than Emmett Stone.

Ditched. In record time. I spun around to the bar and my beer.

I couldn't even be mad at her. Yes, the Tin Kings had reputations as womanizers and criminals, but they were hot as hell. One in particular had played a role in my teenage fantasies, back in the days when I'd lived in Clifton Forge and seen him around town on his motorcycle.

But I wasn't Olive. She only had to make eye contact with a man to have him hooked. Meanwhile I'd sit here with a beer I wouldn't enjoy and wish I weren't quite so forgettable.

"Why am I so boring?" I didn't want to be dull. Really. I just . . . Olive had told me to loosen up and the truth was, I didn't have a damn clue how.

"Boring?" A deep, rugged voice sent shivers down my spine. "Nah. Not boring. Not with hair like that."

My heart stopped beating.

Because sliding onto Olive's vacant stool was Leo Winter.

The Leo Winter.

Arguably the most handsome man on earth with his disheveled blond hair, pale gray-green eyes and devilish grin that made panties combust.

Leo Winter.

Former motorcycle club member.

Current playboy.

I doubted there was a female who'd graduated from Clifton Forge High School in the last decade who hadn't dreamed about Leo once or twice. When he rolled past you on the street riding his Harley, you stared. When he stopped for gas, you stopped too, just for a closer glimpse, even if your tank was full. One of my friends had stalked him through six aisles at the grocery store, snapping over fifty pictures along the way.

He was the older, unattainable bad boy all the girls wanted to tame. A legend.

A legend who was quite clear that he didn't touch *girls*.

Oh, but he'd had his share of women. That reputation I was sure he'd earned.

Sex appeal hugged his body like a second skin, swirling with the colorful tattoos that decorated his strong arms. His white T-shirt pulled around his broad chest and the defined muscles of his back. His faded jeans molded to bulky thighs and tapered to scuffed motorcycle boots.

The way he sat on the stool, utterly at ease and in control . . . And tall. Even seated, he towered over me. It was impossible not to stare as he made himself comfortable, leaning his forearms on the bar while one hand brought an amber bottle to his sinful lips.

He didn't speak. He didn't so much as look my way. He just sat there, seemingly content to sip his beer and watch the bartenders fill drinks.

Was I supposed to do something? Say something? Because my mouth had gone dry. Never in my life had I sat this close to a man so blindingly attractive. Flirting was Olive's area of expertise, not mine.

Or maybe . . .

Maybe I was not on the Leo Winter spectrum. Maybe he'd sat down simply because the seat had been empty.

Ouch. Here was a man in search of an available *woman* and I looked like a dolled-up teenager.

"Heeeey, youuu." The brush of a stomach on my arm was the first signal that Belly Man from earlier was back. He propped himself on the bar at my other side. Then his finger swiped for a lock of my hair. "Red."

"Remember what I said." I swatted his chubby fingers away. "Don't touch."

"I like you, Red," he slurred.

"Original," I deadpanned, shifting to the farthest edge of my stool before taking a long drink from my beer.

Olive and I had come to the bar in my car, planning on taking a cab home if we drank too much. But the cab wouldn't be necessary because unless she came back in the next five minutes, I was out of here. She could call a cab of her own or have Emmett drop her at my parents' place.

"Wuz yur name?"

I ignored him.

"Red. I'll juss call you Red."

Ugh. I pushed my beer away, ready to make a break for it, when Leo's smooth voice stopped me.

"Get lost, Bobby. You're interrupting."

He was? What exactly was he interrupting?

Without another word, Bobby disappeared. The open space at the bar next to me was quickly swallowed up by a woman who looked past my shoulder at Leo. But he didn't pay her a lick of attention.

He'd turned sideways to face me. His gaze raked across

my profile, hot and lazy like the sun moving across the afternoon sky.

Shit. Breathe, Cass.

"What should we call you?" he asked, the timbre soaking deep into my bones, melting the marrow.

"W-what do you mean?" Oh, hell. A stutter. *Really?* I was officially the lamest female in this bar.

"A nickname. I'm not calling you Red. How about"—Leo snapped his fingers—"Firecracker?"

Any other man and I would have scoffed. But that word, firecracker, was as explosive as the object itself. The flame in my cheeks burned hot as I fought a girlish smile. "I'm, um . . . I'm not much for fireworks. Boring, remember?"

He grinned. "Maybe you haven't met anyone who knows how to light the fuse."

A siren sounded in the back of my mind, screaming, *Danger, danger. This man is not in your league.* But I stole a play from Olive's book and hit the off switch.

Tonight, I wasn't the geek. I wasn't the good girl who loved old books and early bedtimes. I wasn't the girl who did everything that everyone expected her to do. Tonight, I was a sexy woman who saw the fantasy within her reach and stretched for it.

"How would you light the fuse?" By some miracle, my voice was steady.

Leo leaned in close, his piercing pale eyes darkening. "With my tongue."

CHAPTER ONE

CASSANDRA

S *ix weeks later . . .*
    "Hey, it's me," Olive said in her voicemail. "We
were thinking of going out for some beers tonight at that new
brewery, so this is your five-hour warning. You've been holed
up in the library all weekend. Did you even come home last
night? Close the books. Come home for a nap. Then get
ready for some fun."

I shoved the phone into my pocket and stared out the
door's glass window to the driveway.

Olive didn't know that I was in Clifton Forge. I hadn't
told her or anyone when I'd left Missoula before dawn
yesterday. She thought I was off studying, when really, my
entire world had come to a screeching halt and I'd come
home.

But there was a lot I'd hidden from my friends lately, like
the fact that I'd been kidnapped and held captive by a motorcycle gang. And that according to the pregnancy test I'd
taken three days ago, I was pregnant with an asshole's baby.

"Cassie?"

I jerked, startled by my mom's voice, then turned away from the door where I'd been standing for ten minutes. Stuck.

"I thought you left already," she said, drying her hands on a dish towel.

"Forgot my notebook." I lifted the object in my hand. I hadn't forgotten it, but I didn't want to admit that simply leaving the house and walking to the driveway took every ounce of courage I had these days.

"Honey, you can ask us to walk you outside," she said, coming closer. Mom was like a bloodhound when it came to sniffing out a lie.

"I'm fine." If fine meant scared, humiliated and pathetic.

The fact that I was standing at all was a miracle. Most of me wanted to curl up in a ball and never leave my bed again.

"I'm sorry the barbeque didn't go well." Mom put her hand on my arm, motioning me in for a hug, and like I had a million times, I fell into her embrace.

Mom's hugs worked wonders. They made me feel safe and loved and warm. These hugs, and the ones from Dad, were the reason I wasn't comatose or in a constant state of tears.

"Why don't you stay here and rest?" she asked. "You can watch movies all day on the couch. I'll buzz to the store and buy the ingredients for that spinach and artichoke dip you love so much."

I gagged. The mention of artichokes threatened to send me racing to the bathroom for another session with my head in the toilet. "Movies later. I think it will be good for me to get out of the house."

This trip to the coffee shop was a test. I was challenging myself to do something normal. To prove the bastards who'd snatched me from the very driveway I'd been staring at hadn't beaten me.

"Okay." Mom rubbed my back, then let me go. "I'm here if you want to talk."

There was a plea in her voice, the same one that had been there since the kidnapping. But I didn't want to talk about that day or about the pregnancy. Not yet.

Not until I could make sense of it myself.

Normally, Mom was on the receiving end of the flood-gates. When I needed to rant about a course or professor or classmate, I called Mom. When I celebrated a good grade, I called Mom. When I'd sat in the bathroom of my house in Missoula, holding a positive pregnancy test, I'd called Mom.

But the kidnapping . . . I wasn't ready to unload that one. Not on her. My mother's shoulders could carry a lot, but that was a weight I wouldn't add.

Besides, the pregnancy was enough. For now, that had to be the focus.

At least it had been easy to track down the father. I'd been prepared to go to The Betsy and ask around about Leo. Turns out, all I'd had to do was cross the street.

"Do you think it'll stop being embarrassing?" I whispered.

"Oh, Cassie." Mom's expression softened.

"I feel so stupid, Mom. I mean . . . safe sex isn't rocket science."

"And you hate feeling stupid."

More than anything else in the world, I hated looking like an idiot.

And Leo Winter had made me a fool.

I'd spared Mom the erotic details, but she knew that I'd hooked up with a guy here in town the weekend I'd come to study with Olive. I'd confessed to going to The Betsy and though she'd tried to hide it, there'd been a hint of disappointment in her face. Then she'd asked about the father.

If not for the kidnapping, I wouldn't have hesitated in telling her about Leo.

But...

Leo was a Tin King.

And for now, he was my secret.

After the kidnapping, Dad had been in a constant rage toward anyone who rode motorcycles. Even older couples who rode recreationally he now considered *criminals*. My kidnappers had belonged to the Arrowhead Warriors—a notorious gang from Ashton, a town three hours away and nowhere near Clifton Forge—but my parents wouldn't be able to separate them from the Tin Kings. They blamed the Kings for bringing trouble to our street.

They weren't entirely wrong, though I didn't want them to hold a grudge against Scarlett.

She hadn't meant for me to get dragged into this disaster.

The Warriors had come to Clifton Forge, searching for Scarlett. She'd been hiding across the street at the chief of police's house. The details of why she'd left Luke's were hazy but when she'd come out of the front door, I'd been in the driveway, home for another weekend of study—sans Olive.

The Warriors had taken her, and I'd been in the wrong place at the wrong time. Before I'd been able to call the cops, they'd nabbed me too.

It wasn't her fault. It wasn't Leo's fault.

It was mine.

I shouldn't have gone to The Betsy.

"One mistake, Mom. One. And I threw my future in the garbage. What was I thinking?"

"Sweetie, your future is not in the garbage. It is possible to go to school and have a baby at the same time. Fall semester will be done by Christmas. You can take the spring off, and after the baby, we'll be there to help. We can move to Missoula if we need to."

"No." I sighed. "I can't ask you to move. You love Clifton Forge. It's home."

Both of my parents had grown up here. They were high school sweethearts and not once had I ever heard them mention moving.

Besides, Leo was here. If he did want to be involved in the baby's life, wouldn't it be better if we lived in the same town?

That was a big if, especially given yesterday's confrontation.

I really, really shouldn't have gone to that barbeque.

"We love you more." Mom touched a lock of my hair, the coppery-red color nearly the same as hers.

"I love you too. I'm going to go." I raised my notebook, steeled my spine and turned for the door.

The only reason I managed to turn the knob was because she was behind me. Then, one foot in front of the other, I stepped outside. It was a beautiful summer day, the sun shining bright on green lawns. The sound of children playing in their yards echoed through the block. Three doors down, a Subaru Outback pulled into the driveway and a family piled out, each member dressed in their Sunday best.

With my car keys clutched in one hand, I scanned the sidewalks, looking for any sign of danger. My head was spinning as I moved toward my car. Dragging in a breath, I held in the clean air that smelled like freshly mowed grass.

It's okay. This was a safe street. I forced my feet forward, eyes glued to the blue of my car. *Don't look.*

I looked.

First, to the place where the Warriors had shoved me into the back of a van. Next, to Luke and Scarlett's house.

Yesterday, after I'd arrived at home, Scarlett had texted and invited me to their place for a barbeque. I'd been avoiding her since the kidnapping and the guilt had driven me to accept. If I was moving home, I couldn't avoid her forever, right?

I'd been so freaked out about crossing the street and seeing her again that I hadn't noticed Leo's bike parked outside, gleaming red and orange in the sun.

Today, I made it a point to look carefully and it was nowhere in sight.

It was for the best. Leo and I needed to have a conversation, preferably without the cursing and shouting this time, but first, I needed a plan. Hence, my notebook.

I tucked it under my arm, hitting the locks on the car, but as I opened the door, another door opened.

Scarlett emerged from her front door with Luke standing behind her, alert and watchful.

"Cass!" She waved as she jogged across her yard and the street.

"Hey." I tossed my notebook and keys into the seat of my Toyota, the gift my parents had bought me after high school graduation. The car I'd once loved.

Mom and Dad would be heartbroken if they knew the Warriors had ruined their gift. Trading it in wasn't an option either because I didn't have the money for an upgrade, and they'd know something was wrong if I downgraded.

Another secret. Another symptom.

"Hey." She smiled, tucking a lock of her long, light blond hair behind an ear.

Across the street, Luke hovered in the doorway at their house, keeping watch. It was nice that he stayed there, giving her that security. It was nice that I wasn't the only one scared to walk across their driveway.

"About yesterday, I'm so, so sorry," she said.

"It's okay. How would you know?"

"It's not okay. Leo was an asshole."

Yes, he was. "You heard everything?"

"Um . . ." She cringed and nodded.

"Great," I murmured. The exact words that I'd yelled yesterday escaped me now, but I did remember calling him a son of a bitch and telling him that he'd ruined my life. When would the humiliation end? "Not my finest moment."

"Don't even worry about it." She gave me a sad smile. "Really. You were only reacting to him. And we're all entitled to lose it from time to time."

"Oh, I lost it all right." For a woman who prided herself on staying relatively levelheaded, yesterday had been a display of sheer emotional chaos.

The barbeque had been a disaster. First, I'd cried on Scarlett's shoulder. Maybe it had been just seeing her face or having it all hit me at once, but I'd stepped through her door and the tears had sprung free. She'd been gracious enough to let me cry on her shoulder while I'd blurted that I was pregnant.

That I could have recovered from, except moments later, Leo had come through their patio doors.

The thin composure I'd reconstructed had crumbled to dust.

At least he'd recognized my face. That was the only ray

of hope. Yes, he'd forgotten my name—or I hadn't told him my name at The Betsy. He hadn't connected me to the woman who'd been kidnapped with Scarlett. But he'd recognized my face. That was something, right?

I'd asked him for a moment and without any fanfare, I'd told him I was pregnant.

He'd called me a fucking liar.

Our conversation had nosedived after that until the epic explosion when he'd stormed out and ridden off on his bike and I'd marched home.

"I'm sorry," Scarlett repeated.

"Don't be."

"I don't know Leo very well, but everyone says he's not like that usually. An asshole."

"That doesn't make it right."

"No, it doesn't."

Even after he'd called me a liar, I'd tried to stay calm. I'd reminded him that my name was Cassandra Cline and that we'd hooked up six weeks ago.

He'd stared at me like I was one of many forgettable fucks. I probably was. So I'd plunged into detail, blushing furiously as I'd replayed the details of our night at The Betsy, hoping to spark more than just faint recognition.

I'd told him how we'd talked until our beers were empty. How he'd taken my hand and led me to the parking lot. How he'd screwed me against a car.

"Pick a car, Firecracker."

"What?" I giggled.

"Pick a car."

"Why?"

"Just pick one."

I scanned the parking lot. A shiny black sports car caught my eye in the back row, its clean paint catching the orange and blue glow from the bar's sign. "That one."

He'd fucked me against that car. In the dark of night, where anyone who came out could stumble on us, I'd let Leo inside. After that, we'd piled into my car and I'd followed his directions to his house, where I'd spent the night in his bed before leaving early the next morning to pick up Olive from Emmett's.

But no matter how many details I'd thrown at him, Leo had balked and sworn he'd used protection. That it couldn't possibly be his and I needed to check with the other men I'd been fucking.

Conversation had degraded quickly from there.

Leo had basically called me a whore.

I'd definitely called him a bastard.

In all my life, I'd never been called a skank or a bitch. At least, to my face. I'd also never told anyone they could rot in hell.

Yesterday had been a day of ugly firsts.

"Anyway, I just . . . I'm sorry," Scarlett said.

"You don't have to keep apologizing. It's not your fault."

"I wish we could have talked yesterday. You said you were quitting school and moving home. Maybe we'll have time now."

"Yeah." My shoulders sagged. "I'm withdrawing from my summer classes. I haven't told anyone besides my parents that I'm not going back for fall semester." Not even my roommates.

Academics were my life. School was my passion. I wanted to get my doctorate and teach for a while. Once I was established, I'd write books or work in a museum.

My dreams were circling the drain with the contents of my stomach from the latest bout of morning sickness.

"I was actually going to head to the coffee shop." I pointed to my notebook in the car. "When I get stressed, I have to think. Make a plan."

"Really? I'm meeting my sister at the coffee shop." Her eyes lit up. So much for time alone. "Would you like to go together? I'd really like to catch up. We don't have to talk about anything serious. Leo or . . . you know."

The kidnapping.

"Sure." I nodded. If I was moving home, it would be nice to have a friend. And maybe she could give me Leo's number. Eventually, he and I had to talk this through.

"I'll still drive," I said. "If that's okay. I might stay there for a while."

"Of course." Scarlett smiled and backed away, rushing to her house, like if she didn't hurry, I'd change my mind.

I got in my car and closed the door, instantly hitting the locks. Then I reversed out of the driveway, waiting along the sidewalk for Scarlett. Less than thirty seconds later, her garage door opened and Luke's police truck backed out. They led the way to the best coffee shop on Central. Luke came inside with Scarlett and ordered a black coffee, then he kissed her and returned to his truck, leaving us alone to visit.

The instant we were settled at a table with four chairs, the door chimed open and an identical version of Scarlett rushed inside.

"Hi." Presley hugged her sister and smiled at me as she took her seat. Her hair was short, cut in a style that I could never pull off. "Hey, Cassandra. Sorry I missed you yesterday."

Yesterday. The barbeque. Of course she'd been there and heard everything. "Yeah. So . . . this is embarrassing."

"Don't be embarrassed." Presley put her hand on mine. "Yesterday was on Leo. He acted like an ass."

"To be fair, I delivered quite the piece of news." Wait, why was I defending him? He *had* been acting like an ass.

"Let's not talk about him," Scarlett said. "How are you feeling?"

"I'm fine." If fine meant nauseous, exhausted and stressed. "How are you? I should have told you yesterday, but congratulations. Mom and Dad told me you and Luke got married."

Scarlett smiled and toyed with the diamond ring on her left hand. "It was a no-fuss ordeal but sort of perfect too."

"It was perfect," Presley said, just as a rumble sounded from outside.

Our faces turned to the glass. We all knew what machine made that sound.

No. Don't let it be him. I wasn't ready yet. I didn't have my plan. Leaving the house had been a horrible idea. I should have let Mom make me spinach and artichoke dip, even if the idea made my stomach roll.

The rumble turned to thunder right before a streak of red and orange and black pulled into the open space in front of Luke's truck and came to an abrupt stop.

"Oh, no." Scarlett turned to me, then looked at Presley. "Did you . . ."

Presley shook her head. "No. I didn't call him."

My eyes tracked Leo as he swung off the bike and strode toward the door, shoving a pair of mirrored sunglasses into his messy dark-blond hair.

The front door chimed and there he was, handsome and

totally oblivious to the three of us sitting at the corner table, watching him stride to the counter.

"It's not even ten." Presley checked the time on her phone. "Usually he's in bed until after noon."

I stared, speechless, as he walked to the counter. The swagger that had lured me into the parking lot of The Betsy was working on the barista.

She was practically drooling with hearts in her eyes as he approached. She toyed with the end of her ponytail as her cheeks flushed while he placed his order. She giggled at whatever he said before writing a note on the paper to-go cup. The coy smile on her face told me exactly what she'd written.

"I'm going to go." I scrambled to collect my notebook, phone and keys.

"No." Scarlett put her hand on my arm. "*He* can leave."

"I don't want to cause a scene." The barbeque had been more drama than I'd had in a year. Well, except for the kidnapping.

"Stay," Presley said. "I know Leo was an asshole yesterday, but that's not who he is. You terrified him. Pregnant is not a word he'd react well to. Give him a chance to show you that he's a good guy."

A good guy? I hoped he was a good guy. Really, truly hoped. My dad was the best man I knew, and I'd always imagined marrying a man like him. A man who'd love me and cherish our children. If Leo turned out to be cruel . . . I couldn't fathom that at the moment. So I took Presley on her word.

"All right."

We waited, the three of us holding our breaths, until bootsteps sounded on the shop's wooden floor.

Leo spotted Presley first. His mouth turned up. Then he noticed me and whatever smile was there vanished.

Did good guys glare like that? Because *wow*. My heart was racing but I refused to cower as he came to our table, stopping by its edge.

He set the coffee cup in his hand down and there was the barista's number doodled inside a heart. He smelled like wind and a masculine spice that was all Leo. A scent I'd washed from my skin weeks ago.

I had to tip my chin back to lock my gaze with a pair of angry gray-green irises. Since our night at The Betsy, he'd grown a goatee. Stubble dusted the sharp corners of his jaw. Leo crossed his arms over his chest, the black T-shirt he was wearing straining at his tattooed biceps.

He stared, his lips set in a firm line.

Did he really think I was going to speak first? I could barely breathe. And if he was truly a good guy, then he could prove it. An apology would be the right place to start.

"I want a paternity test."

My nostrils flared. So much for my apology. "Fine."

"No." Presley sat straighter in her chair and the glare she sent Leo was hot enough to bring his coffee to a boil. "She's telling the truth. Stop acting like this."

"A lot of women would say shit—"

"Does Cass look like one of your typical *women*?" Presley cut him off. "Her clothes actually cover her body and the longest word in her vocabulary is more than four letters."

"A paternity test." His jaw ticked. "I want one."

Presley opened her mouth, but I held up a hand. As much as I appreciated her standing up for me, this was my battle to fight.

"I'll give you a paternity test. Anything else?"

He shook his head. "When I prove you're a liar, you'll be out of my life. And Pres, you know the reason she's lying? Because I always wrap it up. Always."

"Except when you can't wait, right? That's what you told me. *I can't wait.* That I was so beautiful, you just wanted a few strokes bare, then you'd put on a condom before you came. I'm not exactly experienced and had to hit up Google to learn about the dangers of pre-cum."

Leo's bravado faltered and his arms dropped to his sides.

The other patrons in the coffee shop were staring. The barista leaned across the counter to hear. Maybe this would be a lesson for her, and I could save her some heartache.

"If you want a paternity test to prove that we're both idiots, fine," I said. "But it's not going to change the fact that I'm pregnant. And you're the father. Like it or not, your life is now tied to the one growing inside me."

Fear flashed across his face. True, unabashed fear.

I'd been so angry that I'd missed it yesterday. But Presley was right. I saw it clear as the Montana summer sky.

Leo was terrified.

Didn't he realize that I was too?

"What do you want from me?" he asked.

"Nothing." This wasn't a trap. I wasn't out to steal his freedom or money or whatever it was he was so desperately trying to protect.

"Good. Because nothing is all you're going to get."

My heart cracked. I was sure it carried to my face.

Without a backward glance, he turned and strode out the door.

The illusion of Leo Winter shattered as he climbed on his motorcycle and roared away.

CHAPTER TWO

LEO

"Fuck," I clipped, picking up speed as I rode away from the coffee shop. My coffee had been left behind, forgotten on the table, and damn it, I needed that coffee. I was hungover and hadn't slept for shit.

Nothing good came from waking up before ten.

The wind whipped across my face as I headed toward the highway. Without caffeine, there was only one thing that might stop the pounding in my head.

A long, fast ride.

The moment my tires hit the highway, I raced, willing my lungs to open up with each mile. I hadn't been able to breathe since the barbeque yesterday. Since Cass.

Fuck, but I wanted to deny it. I wanted to forget about her because this pregnancy scare was total bullshit. Probably a trap. But Presley had been right. Cass wasn't like the women I normally hooked up with.

That was what had drawn me to her in the first place.

She'd sat at that stool at The Betsy and for a minute, I'd thought she was too young. Too sweet. Too shy.

Except she hadn't been shy. Just . . . out of her element.

We'd started talking and there'd been a spark in her eyes that had drawn me in for more. She was smart. Sexy without flaunting it. Witty. A firecracker.

And that's how I'd remembered her.

Firecracker.

Not Cassandra or Cass. Firecracker. I might have forgotten her name, but I hadn't forgotten her face. Yesterday at the barbeque, it had taken me a minute to put it together because she'd been out of place. But I'd know that hair anywhere and when the pieces had come together—that she was the one who'd been kidnapped with Scarlett—I'd been speechless.

Then she'd steeled her spine and announced that she was pregnant.

Boom. One shot fired, close range to the chest. I was dead on arrival.

What a fucking disaster.

I always used a condom. A girl wanted to fuck, I suited up. No exceptions. And yesterday, last night, this morning, I would have told Cass just that. But then she'd thrown my own goddamn words in my face.

I can't wait.

You're so beautiful, let me go bare.

Just a few strokes.

What the fuck? I knew better. I'd known better since high school when my best friend had been caught in a pregnancy scare.

We'd been seventeen, both reckless and pissed off at the world. His girl had come up to his locker, announced she was pregnant and wasn't sure who the father was. He'd turned his back on her and walked away. One week later, she'd returned and said she'd gone to a clinic to get an abortion.

That kid would have been fifteen. Not a lot younger than when I'd started hanging out at the Tin King clubhouse.

After that and seeing how it had scared the shit out of him, I'd vowed no more inexperienced women, which hadn't been a problem at the clubhouse. I might have been young, but I'd had a strong body and the women hadn't minded my age. The guys never kicked me out, even though I was just a kid, so it worked. Unlimited access to booze and women. What more could a seventeen-year-old want?

That I even finished high school was a miracle, but Draven threatened that if I didn't get my diploma, he'd toss me out. The minute I graduated, I prospected the club.

And life. Got. Good.

There was nothing I wanted more than to be a Tin King. To be a part of the brotherhood and defend it with my life. I did whatever was necessary for the club. Without question. Without hesitation.

Then everything turned to shit and . . . it ended. To this day, I couldn't believe it. Disbanding the club sure as hell wasn't what I wanted, but my wishes didn't matter. And when it was time to vote, I did what was best for my brothers.

I stood beside them. Draven. Dash. Emmett. I voted the way they'd asked me to vote because we might not wear the patches, but they'd always have my loyalty.

Other members left to join different clubs. Some scattered to the wind, starting over in new towns and new states.

Should I have left Clifton Forge? It wasn't the first time I'd doubted my decision to stay. My brothers had moved on. And I was trapped, longing for the past.

Draven was dead. Dash had a wife and kids. Emmett

might not have settled down, but he had business interests to keep him occupied and not once had he mentioned how much he missed the club life.

If not for the shit with the Arrowhead Warriors these last few years, there wouldn't even be a semblance of our club left.

After the kidnapping, the feds had shut the Warriors down and most of their members were facing prison time. Their president, Tucker Talbot, was on trial for a laundry list of charges and if there was any justice in our country's legal system, that son of a bitch wouldn't see beyond the walls of a prison cell for the rest of his miserable life.

How fucked up was it that a part of me hoped he'd get out?

Really fucked up.

The Warriors had killed my brothers. They'd killed Draven. They'd murdered Emmett's dad. They'd hurt my friends. They'd kidnapped Scarlett and Cass.

But without them, without an enemy, who was I fighting?

Who was I?

Not a father, that was for damn sure.

I had no business having a child.

Too late.

Cass was telling the truth. She was pregnant and I was the father.

I was having a baby.

The truth slammed into me like being tossed from my bike to the pavement going ninety miles per hour.

My lungs squeezed, unable to get any air, and I took my hand off the accelerator, slowing the bike before I actually crashed my new Harley. Just two months ago, I'd finished the custom mods and added my own paint.

The orange and red suddenly reminded me of Cass's hair. That color, like strands of copper and fire, was burned into my brain.

I pulled off the road, parked and ran my hands over my face. "Fuck."

This wasn't happening. No child deserved to have me as its father. The best thing for Cass would be to forget about me now. What kind of father would I make?

Probably one a lot like my own. And I wouldn't do that to a kid.

I gave myself a minute, dragging in some air, then I turned around and rode toward town. My head was still pounding. My lungs weren't working right. My arms and legs felt weak. For the first time in years, a ride hadn't calmed my nerves. The last time I'd had this kind of anxiety had been after Draven's funeral.

So like I'd done that day, when nothing else would work, I aimed my tires at the Clifton Forge Garage.

It was a Sunday, meaning the place would be all mine. I'd lose myself in the paint booth for a while, hopefully long enough to get my head wrapped around this situation with Cass. It was a good plan until I pulled into the lot and spotted two bikes parked in front of an open bay door.

"Hell," I muttered, parking beside Dash's new Road King.

Not two seconds after I killed my engine, he came walking out of the garage with Emmett at his side. "Hey."

"Hey." I jerked up my chin and shoved my sunglasses off my face. "You guys working on something today?"

Emmett had a grease rag in his hand but he shook his head. "Figured you'd show up here eventually."

"I'm that predictable, huh?" After years of friendship, Emmett seemed to have this sixth sense about where he could find me. Like last night, when he'd tracked me down to a bar about five miles out of town. I'd needed to get drunk but hadn't wanted to go to The Betsy—the scene of the crime.

"Want a beer?" Dash asked.

"Yeah." Maybe it would help me through this hangover. I followed Dash and Emmett into the garage, welcomed by the scent of metal and oil. After the club had disbanded, this garage had become a second home. It was all the real family I had left.

"I'll grab 'em." Dash strode through the shop, disappearing through the door that led to the office where we kept a fridge.

"Thanks for the ride last night," I told Emmett.

"No problem." He clapped one of his large hands on my shoulder and gave it a squeeze.

Dash returned with three bottles, and after twisting off the top and chugging a long swallow, he settled on one of the rolling stools.

I walked to the far wall, leaning against a tool bench. My first sip of beer tasted like piss, but that was to be expected given how much I'd had last night. After ten, I'd stopped counting.

Emmett had found me by that point. He hadn't asked any questions about Cass. He'd simply stood by my side while I'd proceeded to get hammered.

"How'd you get my bike to my place?" I asked Emmett.

"The blonde. She drove my truck. I rode your bike."

"Ah. Again, thanks." I lifted my beer in a salute, then took another drink. "What are you guys up to today?"

"Talking," Dash answered.

"About the Warriors?"

He shook his head. "About you."

"Spare me a lecture today, all right, Dash?" I shoved off the workbench. Maybe the garage wasn't the right spot for me today. I'd go home and find something to paint there instead.

"Wait." He held up a hand.

I glanced at the open bay door but stayed put. As much as I didn't want to hear this, it was either now or at work tomorrow. And if I waited until tomorrow, Presley would be here too. After the exchange at the coffee shop, she'd shred me to ribbons.

Her lectures about spending less time at The Betsy and avoiding hookups with *randoms* were getting old. She didn't realize that I'd slowed down with the women, not because of her lecturing but because meaningless sex had gotten old. Not something I felt like explaining—she was like a sister and my sex life was none of her business.

Pres meant well, but that didn't make her lectures less exhausting to hear. Especially since Dash seemed to take her side more often than not.

Did he forget that not too long ago, before he'd met Bryce, he'd been on the barstool next to mine? Who the hell was he to judge?

It hadn't been a problem when we'd all been in the club. Grown men, older than me, had partied every night at the clubhouse. There had been more booze and more women too. Why was it an issue when it was at The Betsy?

"We're on your side, Leo," Dash said.

"Are you?"

"You know we are." He frowned and took a drink of his beer. "Just worried."

"Don't be. I'm good."

He opened his mouth, like he was going to say something else, but Emmett spoke first. "About Cass."

"I don't want to talk about it." I raised the bottle to my lips.

"You two had a hell of a blowout last night."

"Yeah," I grumbled. I'd lost my fucking mind and forgotten that everyone had been listening from Luke and Scarlett's deck.

"How'd you leave things?" Dash asked.

Not well. "Ran into her at the coffee shop this morning. Told her I wanted a paternity test."

Dash and Emmett both cringed.

"Put yourself in my shoes. You'd want one too. Why is everyone so sure she's telling the truth?"

"Maybe because she is," Emmett muttered.

I flipped him off.

"You need to talk to her, Leo," Dash said. "After the kidnapping, she went back to Missoula. I figured she'd stay there. Luke said she's going to school. But it sounds like she's moving home."

Because she was *pregnant*. That word was the reason I was hungover. "I'll figure it out."

"She's tied to you now," Emmett said. "Which makes her tied to the club."

"There is no club."

Dash's glare was like a flamethrower. "We're still brothers."

"What's your point?" I pinched the bridge of my nose.

This headache was going nowhere.

"You need to keep an eye out for her. Like we talked about yesterday, before she showed at the barbeque, the Warriors might still be a threat. We have no idea if and how they'll retaliate."

Christ. This just got more and more complicated.

After Scarlett and Cass had been kidnapped, the FBI had raided the Warrior clubhouse in Ashton. Between the kidnapping and a video that Scarlett had captured on her phone when she'd spent some time at the Warrior clubhouse with an ex, the feds had gathered enough to obtain a warrant.

The Warriors were finished. Most faced prison sentences, even a few members who'd once been Kings. Traitors. Some of the minor players had been released on bond, but none of them had the balls to call the shots.

It was unlikely that we'd ever hear from them again.

But . . . there was a chance. And we had family members on the line. We wouldn't drop our guard and risk a wife getting hurt. Or a child.

I had a new stake in this game, didn't I?

My head began to swim, and I set my beer aside as the world tipped upside down. The air was too thin and my pulse roared in my ears.

"Leo."

Emmett's voice was wrong. Muted. Distant.

"Breathe." A strong hand landed on my shoulder, forcing me to bend. "Head between your knees. Breathe."

I closed my eyes and dragged in a breath. Then another. Then another. Over and over until the floor righted itself and the white spots cleared from my vision.

When I looked up, Dash's hand was still on my shoulder

and the understanding in his eyes made me feel like a fucking tool.

"I can't have a kid," I whispered, then dropped to my ass, leaning against the drawers of the tool chest and raking my hands through my hair.

Dash crouched in front of me. "You can. You are."

"I'm not made for this."

"I get it. I went through the same damn thing when Bryce got pregnant."

"What do I do?"

"Talk to Cass. She's probably as freaked as you are, if yesterday's fight was anything to go by."

I nodded and gulped more air.

Then Emmett was there, at my side and handing me my beer. "Let's work on something for a while. Hit the booth or tinker on a bike. Enjoy a Sunday at the shop, just the three of us. Like old times."

"There's that '73 Firebird in the back lot," Dash said. "It's just sitting there. We could roll it in and see what she's gonna take."

Dash had bought the car at an auction in Great Falls. He'd met a collector who'd fallen on hard times and been forced by his bank to liquidate some of his holdings. He'd kept his restored cars, but the partial projects and junkers had been hocked. Dash had scored the Firebird for a steal.

"I'm game," I said. "That's a sweet car."

Or it would be.

First, it would need an overhaul. The old, rusted body parts would need to be cut away and replacements refabricated. It probably needed a new engine and a whole list of other upgrades, but when it was done, I saw it in a fiery red-orange.

The color of Cass's hair.

Firecracker.

What the actual hell had I been thinking? Going bare?

"I'm a fucking idiot. With Cass. And I should have put it together that she'd been taken with Scarlett, but I didn't." That night at The Betsy, had she even told me her name? In my head, she'd been Firecracker. And after the kidnapping, she'd gone immediately from Ashton to Missoula, so I hadn't seen her.

Smart woman. She'd gotten the fuck out of Dodge.

"At least you remembered her face," Emmett said. "Pretty sure I hooked up with her friend and I can't remember her name or her face."

Dash just shook his head and chuckled. "Let's never tell my wife that we're having this conversation. She'd castrate me in my sleep."

"Come on." Emmett held out a hand to help me to my feet. Then I followed him and Dash to the back field, where we kept old parts and old cars.

It took us an hour to make space for the Firebird in the shop and get it hauled inside. We did a cursory assessment of the remodel, taking in the wear and tear on the shell and interior. The engine block was cracked and would be trashed. Dash made a list of the repairs while I sketched out the design.

"This is going to be a badass ride." Emmett took my drawing and held it up.

"Hell yeah." It would be the car I'd want one day. For the times when I couldn't ride my bike but wanted to drive in style.

Emmett took his empty beer bottle to the garbage can, tossing it inside. "All right, I'm outta here. I promised Mom

I'd swing by and say hi. Hopefully I can beg lunch off her."

"I'd better get home too." Dash took his bottle and mine to toss out. "We're going to take the boys to buy fireworks for the Fourth."

We were supposed to have a big get-together at their place. Burgers. Beers. Fireworks after dark. A party I'd normally look forward to. As it was, I didn't feel like being around all the wives and kids.

Maybe I'd skip out this year and head to The Betsy instead.

"I'll lock up," I told the guys, shaking their hands and waiting until the rumble of their bikes disappeared down the road.

Then I took another look at the Firebird.

I'd sketched it in black and white, but I couldn't get that bright, flaming color out of my head.

"Fuck." I ran a hand over my jaw. My headache was gone, and I was hungry for the first time all day. But I didn't want to go home. Not only because the fridge was empty, but because I'd be empty there too.

So I locked up the garage, climbed on my bike and went to the place where I didn't have to think. Where I didn't have to be anything but fun.

The parking lot at The Betsy was empty. I didn't dare drive around back because I knew exactly what I'd see. A shining black car with a pair of skintight jeans and lace panties beside a tire. Locks of red hair spread over a glossy hood. And a pair of caramel eyes that had been my undoing.

It was twenty minutes before they officially opened at one, but it wouldn't be the first time I'd come early, pounded on the door and someone had let me in.

Why did that suddenly feel so pathetic?

Before I realized where I was going, I put The Betsy behind me and drove across town toward Cass's house. I parked in front of Luke and Scarlett's place, then crossed the street for her door with my heart in my throat.

Now that last night's drunken, angry haze had cleared, I knew this feeling. I fucking hated this feeling.

Fear.

Dash and Emmett had been right to warn me. To push me to talk to Cass.

Swallowing hard, I pressed the doorbell and when Cass opened it too soon, I still wasn't ready to face her. Maybe I'd never be ready.

Her caramel gaze flared. Her face was pale, too pale, but there was a spark there—fury. Her cheekbones seemed too sharp in her face, but she was beautiful, especially with that auburn hair that shone copper under the sun.

Beautiful? How did I get that thought out of my head? Because I needed it gone to do what I was here to do.

"Peephole." I pointed to the door.

"Huh?"

"You were kidnapped a month ago. Have a shred of self-preservation and check the goddamn peephole before you open the door."

Her lip curled. "How do you know I didn't?"

"Because you opened the door with a smile on your face." That smile wouldn't have been for me.

"My parents went for a walk. I locked the door behind them. I thought they were back."

Whatever the reason, she needed to be more careful. This world was a dangerous place. The biggest hazard? *Me.* The man currently standing on her front porch.

"What are you doing here, Leo?" She crossed her arms over her chest.

Cass was too good for a man like me. For the brand of trouble I'd bring to her life.

What was I doing here? I was here to scare her off. To chase her the fuck out of Clifton Forge for good.

"Can we talk?"

CHAPTER THREE

CASSANDRA

L eo wanted to talk. I wasn't sure what surprised me
more—him on my doorstep or the fact that he was
asking for a conversation. After the coffee shop, I'd been
certain he wouldn't speak to me until I had a paternity test to
prove I wasn't lying.

"Um . . . sure?" It came out like a question because
talking was, well . . . questionable. Yelling, no problem. But a
civil conversation? I wouldn't hold my breath.

I looked over Leo's shoulder. A walk around the neighborhood would be best. We'd be less likely to cuss and
scream at one another if there were people outside. But four
houses down I spotted my parents. They'd gone on a walk
themselves, likely to talk about me.

Thank God, Leo had parked his bike across the street at
Luke and Scarlett's.

Leaving now wasn't an option. Mom and Dad would see
us and there'd be questions. Lots of questions. The ones I'd
escaped so far because my parents were taking it easy on me.

But if they saw Leo, those questions would be much more pointed and impossible to ignore.

"Uh, come on in." *Shit.* I was going to have to hide him in my room.

He nodded and shoved his hands in his jeans pockets, then followed me inside.

The moment I closed the door behind him, my house felt too small and too hot.

He was wearing the same black T-shirt he'd been in at the coffee shop. The same jeans draped down those long legs to a pair of scuffed black boots. Simple. Casual. There were guys at school who wore variations of the same, but the way those clothes looked on him gave off an entirely different edge.

Leo was temptation personified, rugged sex appeal entangled with the thrill of the forbidden. He was the flame I'd known would burn but I'd touched it anyway.

I hated that I didn't hate him. How he'd treated me in the past twenty-four hours deserved nothing less than loathing, but one long look at his handsome face and I was dragged back to our night together. A night when he'd treated me like a goddess and made me feel desired. Erotic. Special.

He'd flashed me his straight, white teeth in a perfect smile and I'd fallen under his spell. Leo had a way of smiling that made me feel like it was only mine. That he'd never looked at another person the way he looked at me.

I guess I *was* special. I was the woman having his baby. Unless there were others.

Oh, God. Were there others? When was I going to stop being so naïve? I'd been played. Perfectly and beautifully played, but played nonetheless.

"Cass?"

I blinked and tore my eyes away from his shirt. "Sorry. I'm . . . I'm a mess."

I'd told Scarlett the same thing yesterday. A mess. That four-letter word was too small for what I was feeling, and for a woman who had an extensive vocabulary, it was too inconsequential. But mess . . . that was the right word.

"Admitting it sounds like an excuse. It makes me feel like a failure. But never in my life have I looked into the future and not known what it looked like. It's . . . unsettling. Maybe I'm a mess because I haven't ever *not* known what I wanted."

The future had always been this crystal-clear picture since the day I'd picked up my first copy of *The Diary of a Young Girl* by Anne Frank. Or maybe it was *The Hiding Place* by Corrie ten Boom. I'd read both books when I was twelve and though heartbreaking, they'd both made such an impact that history had become my future. I'd wanted to learn more about true stories.

Leo studied my face, his eyebrows coming together.

"I don't know why I just told you that."

He ran a hand over his jaw and goatee, drawing it to a sharp point at his chin. "Do you want to go somewhere?"

"Oh." Right. He'd come here to talk. And my parents would be here any minute. "Um . . . let's go to my room."

We passed the living room and walked down the hallway toward my bedroom. The walls were lined with pictures of our family. Camping trips. High school graduation. There was more than one photo of me with a book tucked under my arm or resting on my lap.

Most people slowed when they saw the photos. When Olive had been here, she'd inspected each and every one, and there were fifty-three. Mom loved her pictures.

But not Leo. He walked faster, like the last thing in the world he wanted to do was catch a glimpse into my life. I didn't have much of an ego, next to none really, but he kept slicing the tiny pieces. Maybe when he was done with me, I'd be able to hate him.

I wanted to hate him.

I should hate him.

I didn't.

We reached my bedroom and I stepped inside just as the front door opened and my parents' voices drifted down the hallway.

"I'll be right back," I told Leo, waving him into my room, then shut him inside.

I sucked in a deep breath, then hurried to meet my parents.

"I thought you were going to keep the door locked," Dad said.

"Oh, I saw you guys coming down the block."

He frowned, then walked over and put his hands on my shoulders, bending to kiss my forehead. "How are you feeling?"

Raw. Bruised. Scared.

"Fine. And hungry," I lied. "Mom mentioned my favorite spinach and artichoke dip earlier. It sounds pretty good." It sounded awful, but I'd rather force down some dip than have my parents realize that Leo was in my bedroom.

"Then we'll go to the store." She nodded, coming to stand behind Dad. "What else do you want?"

"Whatever sounds good to you guys. Maybe some ginger ale."

"I'll get some more saltine crackers too for tomorrow morning."

"Thanks. I might take a nap."

"Good idea, Buttercup." Dad pulled me into a hug. "We'll be back. There's a motorcycle at Luke's place, probably one of those Tin Kings, so you stay inside, okay?"

"Okay." If only he knew who that motorcycle belonged to and why it was on the block.

Soon. I'd tell them soon. But in this moment, I dragged in a long breath, inhaling Dad's woodsy cologne, the one Mom bought him every birthday, and letting it soothe a few fears. My life was falling apart, but at least I had amazing parents.

Though they had to be disappointed. If I was disappointed in myself, then they had to be ashamed. What would they tell their friends and our extended family? How would I face anyone at the next Cline family reunion?

God, I'd messed up. How could I have been so foolish? Tears threatened but I blinked them away.

Dad let me go and held out his arm for Mom. "Come on, Rose Petal. I have a hankering for an iced coffee on the way."

Mom took his arm, smiled at me, then let Dad escort her to the garage. I waited, listening until they backed the car out and the door came down behind them. Then I swallowed the lump in my throat and went to my bedroom, finding Leo standing in the middle of the room.

He didn't move when I came in. He stared at the corkboard above my small desk, the one where I'd pinned notecards and photos.

"What is this?" he asked.

"A vision board."

"What's a vision board?"

I walked to the bed, collapsing on the edge, too tired to have this conversation standing. I hadn't been sleeping for obvious reasons, and I'd spent my energy reserves this morning. "It's a way to organize goals. Get my PhD. That's why there's a photo of the graduation hat. Quotes from people I find interesting. People I'd write books about."

"You write books?"

"No, I go to school. Or . . . I did. I am—was—getting my master's degree in history. I have a meeting on Tuesday morning with my thesis advisor to drop out of the program." Not a conversation I wanted to have.

Leo backed away from the corkboard and I followed his gaze as it traveled around the room.

Not much had changed in here from when I was a teen. There was a shelf above the small TV positioned at the foot of the bed that held my once-beloved trinkets. A hand-painted teacup and saucer that my grandmother had given me before she passed. A dried corsage from my senior prom. A friendship bracelet from a friend who I hadn't spoken to since undergrad.

Beside the shelf was a row of necklace hooks where I'd once hung my jewelry. It was mostly empty now because most of my necklaces were on a similar set of hooks at my house in Missoula.

There was a poster of a glitter butterfly beside my window. Beside me was the ragged teddy bear that I'd had since I was little.

Tomorrow, I'd probably be mortified that Leo Winter was standing in my high school bedroom, but at the moment, I didn't have the energy for it.

"Did you grow up here?" he asked, stuffing his hands into the pockets of his jeans as he stayed in the center of the open space. Tension radiated off his muscular frame, making the air heavy and cold.

"Sort of. Mom and Dad were the first to build on this

street when the development was new. We moved in my junior year. Before that, we lived by the elementary school. What about you?"

"Yeah, I grew up here. Lived in the trailer park off Sundale Road."

I nodded, not sure what to say or where to look. I decided to keep my mouth shut and stare at the plush cream carpet. Mom would freak if she knew Leo was in here wearing his scuffed boots. She had a strict no-shoes-on-the-carpet policy.

"How old are you?" he asked.

"Twenty-four. You?"

"Thirty-two."

Why did this feel like a job interview?

"So you're quitting school."

"Yes." I choked on the word. Acknowledging it, admitting it, was enough to fill my eyes with tears. "It makes the most sense. I need to move home. It's more affordable here and with my parents around, it will be easier when the baby—"

That word was like a ticking bomb in the room. If Leo had been tense before, now he was practically vibrating.

"Anyway . . . yes, I'll quit school," I said, clearing my throat. "One summer session and a fall semester away from my thesis. But there's no way I can work and go to school. I'm surviving on student loans as it is. My scholarship . . ." I glanced up only to find Leo staring at a wall with a blank expression in his eyes. "Never mind."

He didn't care that there was a chance I'd have to pay back my scholarships. And given the job market for history majors in Clifton Forge, I doubted the jobs I could get would be enough for me to afford anything extra besides rent, food and childcare.

"When?" He waved a hand toward my belly.

"I don't know exactly. I haven't been to the doctor yet. I literally found out three days ago. But my guess is March."

He nodded and dropped his gaze to the carpet. Mom had vacuumed while I'd been at the coffee shop and Leo's boots left footprints in the soft pile.

"Has this—" The question died on my lips. Why was it so hard to talk to him? It hadn't been, that night at The Betsy. At first, I'd been nervous, but then as he'd started to flirt with me, seduce me, I'd relaxed and just been myself.

"Has this what?"

"Has this happened to you before?" I couldn't bring myself to look at his face.

"You mean do I have kids?"

I nodded.

"No."

"And a, um . . . wife?"

A low growl came from his throat. "No."

The air rushed from my lungs. That was something positive. Not a lot, but something.

Leo shifted and crossed his arms over his chest. "Listen, there's some trouble. That's what I wanted to talk to you about."

I sat up straighter. "What trouble?"

"With the Warriors."

One word and my heart stopped. "What do you mean? I thought they were in jail."

"Most of them are. Some of them aren't. But even in jail, that doesn't mean they aren't a threat."

"A threat to who? Me?"

"Maybe. There's a long history of violence between the Kings and the Warriors."

My stomach did a nasty somersault. "What are you saying?"

"I'm saying that now you're tied to me. Unless you want to get rid of . . ." He waved a hand at my belly.

Maybe I'd asked the wrong question. Maybe I shouldn't have asked if he had kids or a wife but how many women had come to him with a pregnancy.

"If the Warriors find out you're having my kid, it paints a target on your back."

Was he threatening me? Was he trying to scare me into an abortion? "Is this trouble with the Warriors real or is it your way of pushing me toward the outcome that you want?"

"It's real," he clipped.

I opened my mouth, ready to argue, but then the image of Luke standing in his doorway earlier while Scarlett had come outside to talk to me popped in my head. "That's why Luke was watching us."

"What?"

"Earlier today, before the coffee shop, Scarlett came over. Luke watched us. I thought it was because she's scared to be on the street alone, like I am, but that's not the reason." And he'd come with us to the coffee shop. He'd stayed outside, but he'd been there the whole time.

"You're scared to be on the street alone?"

"Oh, um . . ." Damn it. I hadn't meant to let that slip. I looked up, surprised by the concern on Leo's face. "Okay, so the Warriors might come after me again. That's what you're here to talk about."

"Yep."

So much for discussing the baby. "Okay," I drawled. "And . . ."

"And don't go broadcasting the news."

"Y-you don't want me to tell anyone?" My heart actually cracked when he nodded. Wow, I was a stupid, stupid woman. I'd never felt more insignificant in my life. A surge of anger scorched my veins, and I fisted the comforter at my side, wringing it in my grip. "Worried that I'll ruin your chances with women if they find out you have a *baby* on the way with one of your one-night stands?"

He flinched at the word baby and in that moment, I'd never wanted to slap a person more in my life. "That's not what I'm saying."

"Then what are you saying?"

"Be careful. Check the damn peephole." He threw an arm toward the door. "Avoid going out on your own."

"Consider your warning heard. Anything else?"

"Call me if you see something suspicious."

"I would but I don't have your number," I said through gritted teeth, digging out my phone and when he rattled it off, I entered it in and sent his phone a text, hearing it ding in his pocket. "Should I plan to call you for anything else? You know, like when I have your child?"

Leo's jaw ticked.

"You haven't asked me yet if I'm keeping it. Why?"

"Because I figure I don't have a damn say in the matter."

"You don't."

He drew in a long breath. "What are you going to do?"

"I don't know," I answered, maybe out of habit.

Except I did know.

Since the moment I'd taken that pregnancy test, my mind had immediately jumped to changing my plans. I wasn't sure what those plans looked like yet, but not once had I considered an abortion. That option hadn't crossed my mind. Instead, I was a mess over how to bring a baby into this world and do a good job as a single mother.

"I'm going to keep it. The baby. Do you want to be involved?"

He didn't answer.

And that was answer enough.

This was, hands down, the most painful experience of my life. Sitting there, I watched a man who I'd once fantasized about, who'd given me one unforgettable night, shrink before my very eyes.

All because of fear.

It rolled off his body in waves, pulsing between us. What I'd seen on his face at the coffee shop paled next to this expression. The crease between Leo's eyebrows deepened. Worry lines marred his forehead. His perfect mouth turned down.

He stood, paralyzed, scared to death. Leo had been nothing but an asshole since I'd come back this weekend, but in this moment, all I wanted to do was hug him. To show him a little bit of comfort.

Before I could rationalize that need, I stood from the bed, crossed the floor in my bare feet and wrapped my arms around his waist.

He stiffened.

I didn't let go.

Why? Why was I hugging him? The answer eluded me, but I held on tight regardless, drawing in his incredible scent. I inhaled him, holding the wind, spice and cedar scent in my nose for a long moment. I held him, pretending that we were back in his bed, weeks ago, with the moonlight streaming through the window. Back when I was just a girl living a dream and he was the man making it come true.

Maybe this hug wasn't about Leo at all.

"What are you doing?" He settled one hand on my hip, but he didn't push me away.

"I'm scared too," I confessed.

His body stiffened again, stringing impossibly tight. Then suddenly it sagged. His arms came around me, pulling me so hard into his chest that it was difficult to breathe.

It was like Leo was trying to envelop me. Like if he pulled hard enough, the two of us would be strong enough to turn back time.

I closed my eyes and held on harder, listening to his heart race beneath my ear.

We stood there, fused together, as the heartbeats passed until Leo finally loosened his hold.

It took an effort to unwrap my arms and inch my feet away.

Leo stared down at me, his pale-green eyes searching mine for answers I wished I could give him but simply didn't have. He looked as vulnerable as I felt.

That was to be expected, right? All parents probably had a shock at the beginning. We had months to deal with this and come up with answers. To start, we needed to call a truce.

"I'm sorry for springing this on you," I said. "At the barbeque yesterday. I didn't expect to see you there and I could have done that better."

My apology snapped him out of his own head. He blinked. Then the wall slammed down between us.

And I was the enemy again.

"You should finish school," he said, clearing his throat. "Do your next semester. Leave Clifton Forge."

I inched away. "You want me to leave?"

"Yeah, I do." He might as well have punched me in the stomach. "Look, Cass, I've got nothing for you. For this kid. I was looking for a good time, not a commitment or responsibility."

"You had sex with me. You realize how babies are made, right?"

He sighed. "I fucked up."

"No, you fucked me."

Leo faced the door, giving me his profile. Before he could make an excuse to bolt, I gave him the out he so clearly desired.

"Go," I snapped. "Please. I don't want my parents to see you here and they should be back soon."

That got his attention. He turned to me with his eyes narrowed. "They don't know."

"They know I'm pregnant. They don't know that you're the father." And with the way things were going, I doubted they ever would. The last thing I needed was my dad going into a rage and doing something stupid, like picking a fight with a former motorcycle club member.

Leo huffed. "Of course they don't. *Buttercup.*"

He'd been listening to me talk to my parents. My temper raged and my God, it was refreshing. Because this was better. Hating Leo was so much better than feeling this deep, pathetic longing.

I was not the woman who'd tame the bad boy. This was not the fantasy where he realized the woman he'd been searching for all along was me.

This was real life and I hated . . . hate I could do.

"You don't get to do that," I said, my voice steady but full of fire. "You don't get to mock a wonderful father for giving his daughter a nickname. Because as far as fathers go, you're failing miserably."

"I don't *want* to be a father."

"Then you won't be." I pointed to the door. "Goodbye, Leo."

Without another word, he strode out of my room.

The front door slammed so loudly the entire house rattled. Then the windows shook with the rumble of Leo's Harley as he thundered away from my house.

Out of my life.

Tears welled in my eyes and I swiped at my cheeks furiously trying to keep them from falling. Tears wouldn't make Leo a better man. Tears wouldn't fix the past. This baby—my baby—didn't need tears. What he or she needed was a mother strong enough to stand on her own two feet.

Minutes later the garage door opened, and I hurried to the bathroom to splash water on my face. My cheeks were still splotchy but hopefully Mom and Dad would think I'd just woken up. I met my parents at the door with a forced smile and helped them haul in a load of groceries.

"I've been doing some thinking," I said as we all bustled around the kitchen, putting things away.

"You wouldn't be you if you weren't thinking," Dad teased.

"I'm going to head out. Drive back to Missoula."

Mom froze beside the fridge, a gallon of milk in her hand. "Today?"

I nodded. "I have a class tomorrow morning."

"But . . ." Mom looked to Dad.

"I need to finish school. It was an impulse to think I had to quit." And shame.

There were seven of us in the program. I'd be the only pregnant one, and there would no doubt be questions and odd looks. Part of the reason I'd decided to quit was to save myself a bit of that embarrassment. But I'd rather deal with my classmates than be within fifty miles of Leo Winter.

"I haven't told my advisor yet," I said. "I'll cancel my meeting with her and just go back to normal. Then I'll work hard and do my thesis this fall. Graduate before the baby is born."

"Are you sure, Cassie?" Dad asked. Normally, I was Buttercup. He only ever called me Cassie when he was worried or mad.

"I'm sure. I don't know what will happen after next semester, but I've got time to figure it out."

Mom unglued her feet and put the milk away. Then she came to me and pulled me into a hug. "Drive careful."

No questions. No arguments. They trusted me behind the steering wheel of my own life.

Someday, sooner than I'd planned, I hoped to be a parent like them.

Only I'd be doing it alone.

CHAPTER FOUR

LEO

S ix months later . . .
    "Leo," Isaiah called from the doorway to the paint booth. "You in here?"

"Yeah." I came walking out of the storage room, a can of paint in one hand and a stir stick in the other. "Just mixing up a new color for that Road Glide. Check it out."

I held up the stick, letting the paint drip off the tip and into the can. Under the light, the cinnamon color shone with flecks of gold and caramel. Two shades that reminded me of a pair of eyes I hadn't seen in months.

Eyes that belonged to a woman I didn't let myself think about.

"Perfect color," Isaiah said. "That'll look awesome."

"I think so. I'll add some black pinstripes along the tank and the fairing spoiler. But she's gonna shine."

"Mind if I come in and mess around later?"

"Not at all." I took the can back to the storage room, popping on the lid, then rejoined Isaiah.

He was inspecting a side panel that I'd primed yesterday

for a custom job Dash had brought in a month ago. "Are you going to paint this today?"

"Yeah. Wanna help?"

"If you don't mind." Isaiah had been a mechanic here for years, and during that time, he'd always been hungry to learn. When he'd started, he'd stuck to the routine jobs, oil changes and tune-ups, but over time, he'd expanded his skill set. He could do nearly every aspect of a custom rebuild and restoration these days, from metal fabrication to engine work. Lately, he'd been learning to paint.

The Clifton Forge Garage did it all, from oil changes to custom bikes and classic cars. Draven had built one hell of a business and when he'd retired, he'd passed it down to Dash.

Nick, Dash's older brother, ran his own garage in Prescott, Montana. Between the two brothers, the reputation they'd built was impeccable. You couldn't go to a car show in the Pacific Northwest and not hear the Slater name dropped in conversation.

If Draven could see them now, he'd be damn proud.

Customers from across the country brought their cars to Montana to be restored. Even with two shops, Nick and Dash had to turn work down and the waiting list was eighteen months long.

It was the reason why that Firebird was in the lot behind the shop again. There was no space for it in the garage. With two bays we kept open for regular maintenance jobs, the other two were on the board for whatever projects were on the docket.

So the Firebird sat, unfinished, under a blanket of snow.

"Appreciate you teaching me how to do this," Isaiah said, running a hand over his short hair. "One day, I want to build something all on my own. Every step. Have it to pass down to the kids."

Kids. Everyone was always talking about their kids. "Yeah, no problem."

He'd been shadowing me for about a month in the booth. He'd come in and mess around with the air gun, a lot like I'd done early on.

Those days had been all about the art. I'd loved painting pinup girls or a crazy skull. On a wall of my room at the clubhouse, I'd painted a version of the Tin King patch. Then I'd brought a sketch of the same to my tattoo guy and had him put the piece on a shoulder blade.

Half of the skull was silver, made to look like metal. Behind it was a riot of fire, its orange, yellow and red-tipped flames dipping over my shoulder and tickling my ribs.

The other half of the skull was a simple white, adorned with a head wrap and different bohemian pieces. It was a symphony of color and some thin stitching of sorts around the eye socket and teeth.

The words that had sat below the skull on my cut weren't on my shoulder but instead wrapped around a bicep.

Live to Ride

Wander Free

The Tin King patch was a work of art. It showed two sides to many complicated men. Violence and love. Fear and spirit.

Emmett had a tattoo of the same. So did Dash but in the years since he'd met Bryce and they'd had their two boys, there were new tattoos on his body that held more significance. His kids' names and their birthdates. His wife's name on his calf.

But for me, that skull was the most significant ink on my skin.

Always would be.

Isaiah walked to the wall, studying the sketch I'd tacked up of the Firebird I'd done months ago.

The day she'd been in town.

The day I'd chased her away.

"Presley's ordering lunch," Isaiah said. "She wants to know what you'd like."

I scoffed. "She couldn't come in here and ask me herself?"

Isaiah held up a hand. "I'm staying out of it."

"Yeah," I muttered.

When I was working on a car, I usually had a partner, either Dash, Emmett or Isaiah. But when I was in the booth, I was alone. Maybe that was why I'd spent so much time in here lately. It was rare that I had company, especially company from Presley.

She should give lessons on delivering a cold shoulder. I'd been enduring the freeze for months.

Isaiah led the way out of the booth, and as soon as we were in the garage, the sound of a pretty voice drifted across the space. It instantly caught his ear and for a guy who didn't smile a lot, the grin that stretched across his face was easy.

"Hi." Genevieve came waddling over, her pregnant belly leading the way and her heels clicking on the concrete floor. She was wearing a pair of black slacks and a fitted sweater with her hair twisted up, probably having come from the law office where she worked as a lawyer.

"Hey." Isaiah put his hands on her belly, then bent to kiss his wife. "Everything go okay today?"

"Just a normal morning." She sighed. "Had to draft up a

57

will for a young couple and that's always emotional these days. I'm glad to be done early today. When my brother showed up to follow me here, I couldn't close my laptop fast enough."

It had been months since the FBI had raided the Warrior clubhouse, but we were all still taking precautions, especially for the wives. The women rarely went anywhere alone. When Bryce needed to go to the newspaper office while Dash was working, I'd tag along with her and make sure she got there safely. When Presley had errands to run over the lunch hour, Emmett would ride shotgun. When Genevieve came here from her law office, Dash or Isaiah would tail her.

"Did you go to daycare already?" Isaiah asked.

She nodded, just as the office door opened and Dash came out with his one-year-old niece on a hip. Amelia had one hand in his mouth and the other latched on to an ear, tugging hard.

I turned away. I should have stayed in the paint booth. Christ, there were a lot of kids and pregnant women these days.

Genevieve. Presley. Scarlett.

I was fucking surrounded by swollen bellies. It was like they'd all conspired against me so that just one look and I'd feel like a miserable son of a bitch.

Well, the joke was on them because I didn't need their help to feel like a piece of shit. I could do that all on my own.

Dash didn't work on Fridays normally, which was part of the reason I'd been working every Friday. He was my brother. My boss. My friend. Maybe I was imagining the judgment in his gaze, but even now, when I looked up, I swore it was there.

At least he didn't talk about it. About her.

No one talked about her.

"Da da." Amelia spotted Isaiah and instantly Dash was forgotten. She launched herself into Isaiah's arms, earning a kiss on the cheek and a toss in the air.

"Pres is ordering lunch," Dash said, jerking his thumb toward the adjoining office door.

"I heard." I gave him a nod, then left them for the office, escaping one pregnant woman for another.

Presley was stationed behind her desk, the phone sandwiched between her ear and shoulder. "We'll see you tomorrow at eleven. Bye."

The smile on her face for the customer flattened when she saw me.

Whatever.

"You're ordering lunch?"

She nodded and picked up a pen, the ballpoint hovering over a sticky note as she stared at me, waiting.

"Where are you ordering from?"

"The deli."

"Hot ham and swiss."

She scribbled it on her note, then picked up the phone, dialing the number to the deli that she'd memorized years ago when this shop-wide Friday lunch had become a thing.

While Presley talked on the phone, as sweet as can be to everyone but me, the door chimed. Bryce came in with Emmett on her heels.

"Hi." She smiled brightly. Her dark hair was tied up in a ponytail and her neck wrapped in a scarf. January was cold as fuck this year and the blast from the parking lot swept into the office.

"Hey." I took a chair along the wall, relieved when she came to sit beside me.

Bryce was the one person over the past six months who hadn't mentioned Cass or looked at me like I was a complete fucking failure. She was also the only female who wasn't pregnant, making her my current favorite.

"How's life at the *Clifton Forge Tribune* today?" I asked, spotting a bunch of notepads in Bryce's purse.

"Quiet. Other than the fight in the parking lot of The Betsy on New Year's Eve, all we've got are birth announcements and obituaries."

"I was there for that fight," I said, giving her a grin. "Need an eyewitness report?"

"Do you have anything new to tell me other than the big guy with the beard swung first, and then the big guy without the beard swung back?"

"Nah." I chuckled. "That about covers it. Not even an exciting fight. No weapons. No broken beer bottles. Tame, really. The bartenders didn't even have to break it up. Bearded big guy took a hard hit to the gut and started puking. Fight over."

Bryce rolled her eyes but smiled. "I knew I should have just called you instead of going down there to talk to Paul. I could have saved myself the trip."

"Of course he was there," Presley scoffed. While I'd been talking to Bryce, she'd ended her call to the deli. "We should look into changing your address so your mail can be delivered there and you can skip going home altogether."

"So what if I like The Betsy?" I should have kept my mouth shut but the question came out too quickly. "I have friends there."

"Friends," she deadpanned. "Right. Is that what you're calling your harem these days? A group of *friends* who will spread their legs for you?"

"Can we just . . . not do this?" I ran a hand over my face, suddenly not so hungry for a sandwich.

"Sure," she clipped.

The air in the office went still and too quiet. The conversation in the waiting room even seemed to dull.

"Do you have to go every night?" she quipped.

"So much for dropping it," I muttered.

This argument between Presley and me had been brewing for months.

Six, to be exact.

There was a gleam in Pres's blue eyes, a look I knew too well. She was in a mood and whatever hold she'd kept on her tongue was about to break free.

"Are we really going to do this? Now?"

Pres's eyes narrowed.

"How long until lunch gets here?" I asked.

"Thirty minutes."

Without another word, I stood from my chair and walked into Dash's office. He was using it more and more these days, spending less and less time in the shop. Pres did most of the office work as the manager, but with her maternity leave coming up, he was stepping in to cover while she was gone. His desk was scattered with papers, and a cup of cold coffee sat beside his keyboard.

Presley marched into the office behind me, slamming the door so hard that the hanging photo of Draven, Nick and Dash shook against the wall.

I steadied it, taking a long look at his face while I made sure it was straight. The photo was from not long before he'd died, and his dark eyes smiled as he stood between his sons. There was a dusting of silver stubble on his jaw as he grinned. Some days, I swore I could still smell him in this office, the hint of mint and Old Spice lingering to tell me he was still here.

Presley walked behind Dash's desk and sat down in his chair, her shoulders rigid.

I stayed standing. "Say what you want to say."

"Why are you acting like this?" She launched right in because she was pregnant and lunch was coming.

"Acting like what?"

"Like nothing has changed." She threw up a hand. "Like life is grand. Going to The Betsy every night. Partying. Drinking. Whoring."

It always came down to the women. I hadn't had a woman since Cass, not that I was going to share that fact with Presley. If I told her I'd slowed down, that I'd limited the hookups even before Cass, then Pres would ask why. And I didn't want to get into the why. I didn't want to explain to my friend that I felt lost, and meaningless sex wasn't helping.

Besides, Pres had already made up her mind about what I did at The Betsy.

She had Shaw to go home to. I had nothing but an empty house and my demons to keep me company. No, thanks. So I went to socialize and have a couple of beers. Most nights, I'd play pool and bullshit with the other regulars.

But I hadn't touched a woman.

Not. One.

I was too preoccupied by the woman stuck in my goddamn head.

And Cass had been stuck there for far too long, ever since I'd taken her home and seen her hair spread across my white pillows.

After that night, I'd had other women come up to me,

but I'd pushed them away, hoping that Firecracker would show up for round two. Then the kidnapping had happened a couple weeks later and everything had been a fucking train wreck. I'd been on alert, avoiding the bars in case the Warriors had decided to retaliate.

Then the barbeque.

Then Cass.

I hadn't touched a woman since she'd told me about the baby, not only because I was terrified of sex at the moment but because no one had appealed. When I went to The Betsy every night, it wasn't to find a hookup. Alcohol, yes. But women? Fuck no.

"What else?" I asked, my give-a-shit for this conversation dried up. I loved Pres, but I was miserable, and she was too busy being angry at me to care.

"Grow up, Leo."

"Sure."

She shook her head. "I don't even know you."

"Yeah, you do. This is who I've always been." I wasn't the relationship type. I sure as fuck wasn't a father figure.

"No. This is not you."

"Yes, it is. I'm doing the right thing."

"I actually think you believe that." Her voice gentled and her shoulders slumped. "Leo, you will regret this."

I shook my head. "This is the right thing, Pres. She's better off."

"Then you really aren't getting it. I'm so mad at you. So, so mad." She reached her arms into the air, like she was going to strangle me from her seat. "But if you actually think Cass and your child are better off without you in their lives, then you have no idea what kind of man you are."

"Wrong. I know exactly the kind of man I am."

"And the fact that you don't see what I see breaks my heart," she whispered. Then she stood from the chair and crossed the room, returning to the main area of the office without another word.

Fuck. Presley didn't have any clue what she was talking about. She didn't know the things I'd done. My hands fisted at my sides and I closed my eyes, wishing we still ran the underground fights from back in the club days.

I could use a few hours in the ring, throwing punches, taking hits and getting lost in the blood and adrenaline. The cash I used to walk away with from those fights would have been a nice bonus—I'd bet on myself and rarely lost—but it had always been about the release. Those fights had been a place to channel my frustration with the world, my real family and whatever the fuck else was going on in my head.

Maybe after work I'd go home and pummel the heavy bag in the home gym I'd set up in my basement.

Or maybe I'd go to The Betsy and raise my first beer in a toast to Pres.

First, I had to survive lunch and finish up work. So I took a long breath and returned to the office.

Bryce looked between Presley and me, her eyebrows pulled together. "That's it? I was expecting . . . well, something much louder."

I shrugged and returned to my seat beside her, grateful she was here to cut the tension.

Presley wouldn't look at me from behind her desk. As the office filled with people and lunch arrived, she didn't so much as glance my way.

Amelia was a constant source of entertainment, crawling and toddling between adults, and as the others talked and laughed, I couldn't eat my sandwich fast enough. The second the last bite was in my mouth, I gave the room a wave and retreated to the shop.

"Fuck." I picked up a rag from the workbench in the paint booth and threw it against the wall. Then I took out my phone, pulling up the contact I'd saved months ago.

Firecracker.

Cass hadn't called or texted since she'd left Clifton Forge. I'd gotten exactly what I'd asked for.

Nothing.

So why the hell did it feel so empty?

I shoved my phone away and raked a hand through my hair. Then I put in my earbuds, cranked up some music and went to work. But no amount of painting could get her off my mind.

Six months and she plagued me daily. Hourly. Was she okay? Was the baby? Did I care?

Yes.

But as long as she was safe and out of Clifton Forge, it was for the best. The Warriors had no reason to go after her and as long as they didn't know about the baby, Cass would be forgotten.

And eventually, she'd forget about me too.

Most people did.

What Cass needed most was to move on with her life. Find a decent guy with a straitlaced nine-to-five who'd treat her like a queen. Who'd treat my kid like a miracle.

My kid.

If it was a boy, would he look like me? If it was a girl, would she have blond hair or her mother's red? My stomach twisted. That kid wasn't mine.

This was my choice. It was the right thing. The Warriors could bring more trouble to Cass's life, but more than that, it was me. She was a good woman with a bright future. I was a reformed thug who'd probably screw up and break her heart.

I was the danger.

Yet she'd hugged me.

That day in her room, the way her arms had wrapped around me, so tight I could still feel them. *Christ.* I'd never been hugged like that. Not fucking once.

Why? Why had she hugged me? I'd been a total prick to her from the moment she'd told me she was pregnant, and she'd hugged me.

After months of replaying that day and our conversation, I still couldn't figure out why.

I checked the doorway, making sure none of the guys were near the booth, then I hit pause on the music and pulled up my voicemail, replaying the message from this morning.

"Hey, Leo. Bruce Ponds calling from Dallas Customs. Just checking in to see if you've given any thought to our conversation last week. Give me a call when you get a chance."

I listened to the message twice and with each repeat, the pit in my gut got deeper.

Last week, Bruce had called and given me a hell of a proposition to consider. He'd been a fan of my work for a while, having seen some of my stuff at a car show in Denver. When he'd called the office and asked for my number, I doubted Presley had realized it was to extend me a job offer.

Bruce ran a custom shop in Dallas with a reputation similar to the one Dash had here in Montana. One of his guys had quit, leaving a hole in their crew, and he wanted the best.

Apparently, the best was me.

The pay was comparable to what I made here. I doubted I'd have as much flexibility as Dash gave me—I worked whenever I felt like it and he never questioned me the days when I skipped coming in altogether. Bruce could be a pain in the ass micromanager who'd drive me insane and require me to punch a clock.

But the job was in Dallas. The opposite end of the country.

Far away from Cassandra Cline.

Cass had been gone from Clifton Forge for six months. She'd stayed in Missoula for the holidays and rumor had it her parents had gone there for Christmas. I was glad they'd made the trip because spending Christmas alone was depressing—that's how I'd spent mine. I'd declined my invitation to Dash and Bryce's place because they'd hosted a huge get-together and there were too many happy pregnancies.

Avoiding it would only last so long if I stayed in town. Eventually, Cass would come back to visit. Her family was here too. As much as I loved Clifton Forge, my home and my history here, Cass had the same.

I couldn't take that from her.

In this small town, it was inevitable that I'd bump into her and our kid. That was not an experience I cared to have. Just the idea made my chest squeeze too tight.

So Dallas. I was moving to Dallas. I'd all but made the decision after I'd hung up the phone with Bruce, but since my impulse decisions usually landed me in a heap of shit, I'd chosen to sit on it for a week.

My mind hadn't changed.

I'd tell Dash and Emmett first, then I'd accept Bruce's

offer and pack my things. I'd say goodbye to Montana and start fresh.

My stomach was in a knot by the time I finished up work. This time of year, the days were short and by six o'clock, it was dark outside. I found Emmett with the current remodel project and a grinder in his hand, cutting out a rusted piece of the door panel to refabricate.

"I was going to head to Stockyard's and grab a burger," I said. "Want to join me?"

"Sounds good." He tore off his face guard, setting it and the grinder aside. "I'm about done for today anyway."

I grabbed my coat from the hook on the wall while he stripped off his coveralls, then the two of us washed up. We headed out, each driving our own rigs toward Central.

My nerves were on high, my hands shaking and my heart beating too fast when we arrived. As soon as we sat at a tall table in the middle of the bar and restaurant, my foot started bouncing on the stool's footrail. Thankfully, the room was dimly lit and there was already a decent-sized dinner crew to fill the room and draw attention.

Unlike those of us who went to The Betsy, Stockyard's regular clientele wasn't here for the drinks and the party. There was always standing room, though at dinner, it was usually busy because their greasy burgers and salty fries were unbeatable.

"We should see if they get a game going," Emmett said, nodding to the poker table at the back. "I'd be up to play for a while."

"Yeah." After my announcement, I suspected that would change.

The waitress came over and took our orders. I waited

until she'd delivered our beers but before I could speak, Emmett beat me to it.

"Presley finally broke the silence, huh?"

I nodded. "Yeah. Figured she'd rip me up one side and down the other, but she actually didn't have much to say."

Though the few words she'd said had slashed to the core.

Leo, you will regret this.

I'd regret being a shitty father more than I'd regret being absent. Especially if that meant giving Cass a chance, free and clear, to find a guy who'd be a good dad.

For a man who'd spent plenty of years wreaking havoc, my motto when it came to Cass was *do no harm.*

"Have you heard from her?"

"No."

"You can't ignore her forever."

"Watch me." I lifted my beer and chugged half the pint glass. When I set it down, I expected to see a scowl on Emmett's face. Instead, he looked . . . amused. Was he trying not to laugh? "What?"

He pointed over my shoulder toward the door.

I turned just in time to see her walk through the door, followed by her parents.

And son of a bitch, I nearly fell off my stool.

The auburn hair caught my eye first. It draped around her face, a contrast to her soft, creamy skin. Her cheeks were flushed, a peach color the same natural shade as her lips. Cass wore a black parka but she hadn't zipped it up and her belly stretched her green sweater.

I wasn't sure what I expected when her eyes scanned the room, but when they landed on me, the glare she sent me sure wasn't it. Meanwhile I stared at her with my goddamn mouth hanging open.

What was she doing here?

This was why I had to get the hell out of Montana. Because seeing her, the first thought in my brain was how beautiful she looked. Even glaring, she was breathtaking.

I was the cause of that rage and I hated myself for it. I hated that the sweet, quietly sexy woman who'd ensnared me at the bar months and months ago looked at me with ice in her veins.

I'd done that to her. I'd hardened her.

Cass lifted her chin, dismissed me, then glanced over her shoulder at her parents coming into the bar, and the three of them crossed the room to an empty table.

I didn't exist.

I was nothing.

She might as well have shoved a knife into my side. Christ, it shouldn't hurt but damn did it ever.

I swallowed hard and swiveled to the table, my focus entirely on my beer.

Emmett still had that shit-eating grin on his face. "Oh, this is going to be so much fun to watch."

"Fuck off."

A throat cleared from over my shoulder. "Well, hello to you too, Leo."

CHAPTER FIVE

CASSANDRA

W hy did he always have to look so good? It wasn't fair.

Here I was, a baby whale, and Leo was, well . . . Leo. One day I fully expected to be driving along Central and spot a statue of him, erected by the town council so the female population of Clifton Forge could pay homage to his gorgeous face.

His hair was longer than it had been in the summer. His jaw was as roughhewn as always but his goatee was fuller. Even his shoulders seemed bigger, either from working out or because I'd forgotten just how tall and muscular he was.

And then there were his eyes, the same piercing gray-green that visited me in my dreams.

I should have thought of this. When we'd driven by Stockyard's and there hadn't been a motorcycle in sight, I'd thought it was safe to suggest a dinner out to save Mom some time cooking. But it was winter. Of course he wouldn't be riding around town. There wasn't much snow and the streets were clear but the January temperatures were bitter cold.

Stupid, Cass. It was like I crossed the Clifton Forge town limits and became a moron. That, or it was pregnancy brain.

Thankfully, that lovely *fuck off* comment had snapped me out of any delusions that this encounter would be anything but antagonistic.

"I didn't mean you," Leo said, nodding at Emmett. "He can fuck off."

I stayed quiet.

Why had I even walked over here? Right. To talk. I should have stayed at the table with my parents and pretended Leo didn't exist. But my feet, and that damn pregnancy brain, had brought me over. The temptation had been too strong to resist.

Maybe he'd changed.

"So, you're, uh, back?" He rubbed the back of his neck.

My heart was in my throat, but I stayed still, standing and staring. It was nice to see him off-kilter. "Yes."

It took all my effort to deliver that single word without inflection, but I refused to show him my emotions. Anger. Hurt. Fear. Anxiety. The list of what I'd felt in the past six months went on and on, but he wouldn't get that from me.

I was in control here.

This time around, I was calling the shots and I was going to get through a single conversation with Leo where my emotions didn't take charge. Six months had done me wonders to pull myself together and no man, especially Leo, was going to throw me off.

Leo swallowed hard. "For how long?"

"For a while."

The color drained from his face but he nodded. "Good. That's good. Since your family is here."

I studied his face, waiting for a sign. An acknowledgment that I was visibly carrying his child. A hint of feeling. An indication that maybe after six months, the idea of having a baby would have made him willing to participate.

Nope. Fear was still running the show.

My temper spiked and the rage that I'd tamped down came to a blazing roar. So maybe I didn't have quite as firm a grip on it as I'd thought.

"Cassie?" Mom came up behind me, putting her hand on my shoulder.

Her features were frozen with shock. Behind her, Dad looked just as surprised but also wary and ready to throw punches. They both knew who Leo and Emmett were.

When we'd come in, they'd each taken a chair at the table, but I'd set my purse down, then excused myself to see Leo. There was no point in asking for a conversation. He hadn't changed. Even if he did want to talk, I doubted I'd want to hear a word he had to say.

"I'm not all that hungry after all," I told Mom. "How about we get an order to go and head home?"

"Um, sure. If that's what you want."

"What's going on, Cassandra?" Dad asked, crossing his arms over his chest.

I couldn't remember the last time Dad had called me Cassandra. It was either Cassie or Buttercup.

For months they'd been asking me—not often, but enough—about the baby's father. I think both assumed it was someone from school. Mom had pulled me aside on their visit to Missoula for Thanksgiving and asked me if I'd been raped during the kidnapping by the Warriors.

I hadn't realized that them not knowing had caused so much stress.

I'd assured her that it hadn't been rape but that I wasn't

ready to talk about the father. I'd asked Scarlett to keep it between us as well, just in case Mom and Dad crossed the street and I came up in conversation.

Leo was my secret.

And I was tired of keeping it. So damn tired. Avoiding the truth had been easier in Missoula, but now that the semester was over and I was looking at the next chapter of my life in Clifton Forge, I couldn't keep this secret.

When we got home, I'd tell them the truth.

"They're friends with Scarlett," I told Dad. "Just stopping by to say hello."

Dad gave me a sideways glance, then shook it off. "I'll get our order in."

Mom stayed behind me, her gaze alternating between Leo and me. When her eyes settled on my face, I realized that I wouldn't have to tell her about Leo. She already knew.

I gave her a small nod.

Her eyes closed and her sigh of disappointment was like having the wind knocked out of me. She turned without a word to join Dad.

"They still don't know it's me," Leo said quietly.

I shook my head. "Why would I tell anyone? You told me not to."

He flinched and my silly, tender heart softened toward that look of pain. Maybe one day, I'd turn that heart into steel where Leo was concerned. I'd need more time to practice because at the moment, damn it, I wanted to hug him again.

"Cass—"

"See you around, Leo." I spun away and found Mom and Dad at the bar. I told them I was going to wait in the car, then collected my purse and hurried outside.

The well of tears that flooded my eyes the moment I was in the car only made me mad. I swiped them away, then stroked my belly, feeling a little flutter from the baby. "He doesn't matter. And we don't need him."

I believed that statement, body and soul.

It didn't take long for Mom to join me in the car with the keys so we could turn on the heat. I wasn't surprised that she'd left Dad to wait for the food. "Your dad is going to struggle with this."

"I know." I sighed. "I'm sorry."

"When did it happen?"

"Before the kidnapping. That weekend you guys were camping and I brought Olive home to study. We went out to The Betsy and . . . I made a bad choice."

I refused to say mistake. Never would I associate the word mistake with my child.

After months of growing her in my womb, months of talking to her and feeling her and loving her, she was my child. She was no mistake. The fears from early on in my pregnancy had vanished, replaced by excitement for a new future. A new life.

"Oh, honey." Mom shook her head.

"Leo knows," I said. "He's made his decision to walk away."

"He can't walk away." She spun around in her seat, her mouth hanging open. "You're moving here. He won't be able to avoid you."

I shrugged. "That's his problem, not mine. He'll miss out on an amazing little girl. I've got my plan and it isn't going to change."

She faced forward, glaring daggers at the Stockyard's door like she could send her invisible knives through the walls and into Leo's face. "Part of me wants to let your father go berserk. Any other guy and I'd let him. But . . ."

"Oh, I know. Dad's a lover, not a fighter." Despite his broad, tall frame and the fact that he was in better shape than most men half his age, I couldn't picture Dad throwing a punch. Leo, on the other hand . . . "I highly doubt Leo would ever hit Dad."

"Better not test that theory."

"Don't worry. Leo will do his best to avoid me completely."

She blew out a long breath. "We should have moved. Your dad and I talked about it for months and we should have just done it. Then you wouldn't have to worry about seeing him around town. The three of us—four of us—could have started fresh."

"No, Mom. You're both so close to retirement. You've got the house. You can't start over. I wouldn't have let you."

"You and the baby are more important to me than our jobs and our home."

I stretched forward to put a hand on her shoulder. "This will be okay. Let's stick to the plan."

She covered my knuckles with her palm. "Your dad called you Cassandra."

"I know," I groaned. "I'm in trouble. Think he knows about Leo?"

"I think we don't give your father enough credit. He might not have put it together yet, but he's got all the pieces lined up."

"I'll tell him as soon as we get home."

An hour later, the cheeseburgers we'd ordered were cold and Dad hadn't stopped pacing the living room. Mom had been right. We hadn't given him enough credit.

From the moment he'd walked out of Stockyard's, Dad's anger had been palpable. The drive home had been silent and the moment we'd walked inside the house, he'd told me to get my butt to the living room.

That was where Dad always convened the uncomfortable discussions.

"I'll kill that son of a bitch. I'll run him down in the car, leave him to bleed out in a ditch somewhere."

Mom rolled her eyes. "Dale. Enough."

That was the seventh death threat in a row, though not as gruesome and violent as its predecessors. The worst was when Dad had described how he'd slice off Leo's penis.

"I told you, Claudia. I told you those Tin Kings should all be in prison. What kind of man walks away from his child? What kind of man doesn't take responsibility for this?" Dad's arm swung toward my belly.

"Dad, it's going to be fine."

He shot me a glare.

"Okay, never mind," I muttered. Apparently, this was not a conversation for my participation.

Dad stopped pacing abruptly. Mom and I shared a look as Dad stood there. Then, before either of us could stop him, he was stalking toward the door that led to the garage.

"Dad! No!"

"Dale!" Beside me, Mom shot off the couch, something that was impossible for me to do at this point. "Where do you think you're going?"

"I've got some things to say to that son of a bitch."

"Language," Mom snapped, maneuvering in front of him to block his path. "You are not going anywhere. You are going to calm down and remember that this isn't your problem to solve."

"She's right." I came up behind him and put a hand on his elbow. "You can't blame this entirely on Leo. I was there too."

"Please." He cringed. "Don't say another word about . . . that. Ever."

"Sorry." I fought a smile.

Dad's shoulders slumped and he turned, pulling me into his arms. "You deserve only the best."

"That's why I have you."

He held me tighter, dropping his cheek to my head. "I still want to chop his dick off."

"Eww." I giggled. "I'm sorry for not telling you."

"I understand why you didn't." He let me go, but put his hands on my shoulders, holding me in place. "After the kidnapping—"

"I'm starving." I stepped out of his hold, retreating down the hallway for the kitchen.

The kidnapping wasn't something I wanted to discuss, tonight or any night. I thought of it daily, but considering it used to be hourly, we were moving in the right direction. Avoiding it was working and that was exactly what I'd continue to do.

The cheeseburgers from Stockyard's were cold, but I took mine out anyway and brought it to the dining room. Mom and Dad weren't far behind me with their own burgers. Any further discussion of Leo died as we dove in, eating in silence. I was about done with my meal when the doorbell rang.

"I'll get it." Dad shoved his last bite in his mouth, then got up for the door.

"It's late," Mom said. "I wonder who it is."

I shrugged. "Maybe a neighbor?"

"What the hell do you think you're doing here, you motherfucker?" Dad's voice bellowed through the house.

Mom's eyes went wide.

My heart stopped.

Not a neighbor.

We both knew who the *motherfucker* was.

"Oh, shit." I shoved out of my chair and hurried to the entryway, Mom right behind me.

I got there in time to see Dad's fist connect with Leo's cheek.

"Dad! No!"

Leo grunted and took a step back, but he didn't so much as lose his balance.

"Dale!" Mom gasped.

"Get the fuck out of here," Dad commanded, his finger pointing to the street.

"Stop." I shoved past him, putting myself between the men.

Leo had a hand on his jaw, rubbing where Dad had hit him, but there was no anger or retribution in his eyes. We all knew he'd deserved that punch.

"What are you doing here?" I asked.

"Came to talk to you."

"Fine." I reached past Dad for the coat hook and pulled off my parka, then I shrugged it on.

"Cassandra," Dad warned.

I ignored him and pulled the door closed behind me.

"Let's go." I strode past Leo and down the driveway, not waiting for him as I hit the sidewalk and marched onward.

"Are you warm enough?" Leo asked, falling into step beside me with his long strides.

"Yep," I clipped, walking faster. Warm? I was burning. "What do you want?"

"You caught me by surprise at the bar."

"No kidding." My breath billowed in a white cloud as I spoke, streaming past my shoulder.

"We don't have to walk."

"I walk every night," I said. "Or I did in Missoula."

"Alone?"

"No. One of my roommates always came with me." And now that I was home, Mom or Dad would gladly volunteer.

Leo's warning from months ago that the Warriors might come for revenge had stuck and I rarely went anywhere alone. That, and I'd been kidnapped by those bastards, so his warning hadn't really been necessary, had it?

"When did you come to town?" he asked.

"We got in this morning. My parents came to Missoula to help me pack my things." All of my belongings from the house where I'd lived with my grad school friends were in the garage. My parents had come for Christmas and stayed through New Year's to help me pack.

Leo didn't respond, just kept pace.

"Was this all you wanted? To ask me questions?" I asked, risking a glance up at his profile. It was a bright moon tonight and the light from the winter sky seemed to highlight every perfection on his face. The high cheekbones. The soft lips. The slight bump on the bridge of his nose where it had probably been broken once.

"No." He looked down at me and there it was. That urge to hug him again.

What the hell? That really, *really* needed to stop. "Then what do you want?"

"I'm moving."

"Oh." My feet stuttered a bit, and though I wasn't going to fall, Leo's hand was there, taking my arm to make sure I didn't crash. "I'm good."

He let me go in a snap.

"You're moving?"

"Yeah. I just don't want you to worry that we'll run into each other. Few weeks, I'll be gone."

My heart twisted. It shouldn't have, but it did. Because no matter what plans I made, no matter how often I told myself that we didn't need him, a part of me had hoped that he'd come around. Not for me, but for his daughter's sake.

A part of me had hoped that when the questions about her father came, years from now, I wouldn't have to tell her that I'd made a bad choice.

"Okay." I swallowed the lump in my throat and kept walking.

And Leo stayed with me, step for step, as we weaved through the blocks of my neighborhood. There were still Christmas lights up around the neighborhood, brightening the sidewalks and making the night seem cheerier than it was.

Finally, when my nose was cold and my lips stiff from the chill, he spoke. "What is, uh . . . your plan?"

"Find a place to rent. That's the priority right now. I love my parents, but I won't live with them and subject them to a newborn's schedule."

"I figured you'd stay here. Have some help."

"No. I'm an adult and can stand on my own two feet." Sure, maybe I looked like I belonged on an episode of *16 and Pregnant*, but I was a grown woman and could do this on my own.

He nodded. "Got it."

"I have a job lined up as a transcriptionist. It's free-lance so I can have a flexible schedule after the baby is born."

He nodded again.

"Why did you ask me a question when you don't want to know the answer?"

"I don't know," he confessed.

"It's a girl."

This time, his footsteps faltered but I didn't reach for his arm. He could steady himself.

"You probably didn't care about that either."

His jaw clenched and his eyes stayed forward, my parents' house getting closer every second. His truck, older than I would have expected, was parked in the driveway. "Didn't expect your dad to hit me."

"He loves me. And you deserved it."

Leo didn't argue.

"So you came here to tell me you're moving. Anything else?"

"Are you okay? Healthy, I mean. You and . . . you know."

"The baby," I finished for him. He couldn't even say it. That fear was so pungent it chased away the cold, fresh crisp in the air. "Are you asking because you care or because you think you should ask?"

"I care."

I stopped walking.

Leo took another step but, when he realized I wasn't moving, spun back.

"You care?" I asked.

"Yeah."

"I don't understand you." I threw up my hands.

He tipped his head to the sky, his breath like a plume of

smoke. When he faced me again, there was raw honesty in his expression. "I don't want to be a father."

"But you are." I motioned to my belly, stretching the midsection of my coat. "There's no undoing this. I'm not ready to be a mother but what we want isn't part of the equation anymore. It's not about you or me. It's about her."

His shoulders fell. "Fair enough."

"You're the most confusing man in the world. You want me to leave, I leave. You want me to keep this quiet, I do. But you keep coming here to find me. What do you want, Leo? What?"

"I don't know." He raked a hand through his hair. "I don't fucking know."

Yes, he did. I saw it now, just like the fear. I saw the truth. "You don't want to walk away."

"What?"

God, why hadn't I recognized this months ago? I was glad that I hadn't because otherwise I wouldn't have gone back to Missoula and finished my thesis. I wouldn't have earned my degree.

But it was right there, written all over his handsome face.

He didn't want to walk away.

"You keep showing up at my door. Why? So that I'll tell you to go? So you can push me away? You could have let me walk away at Stockyard's. You could have moved away without another word. Instead, you came here to tell me about it."

"I just wanted you to know that you could stay. I'll go." He scowled. "You can stay and you won't have to worry about me bumping into you or something."

Scarlett could have delivered that message. But the same day I'd come back to Clifton Forge, he'd decided to deliver it himself. "Okay. Then move. Disappear. Do whatever you want. We don't need you."

We didn't need him.

That statement was brimming with so much truth that it spilled onto the frozen sidewalk and crept across the cracks, soaking Leo's boots.

We didn't need him.

"But we'll have you," I whispered. "If you want this, we will have you."

All he had to do was choose to be a part of this child's life.

"I'm moving," he repeated.

"So you keep on saying." I took a step past him and walked toward my house.

Leo didn't follow.

I left him standing there with my words to consider. I was done playing this game. The baby was coming in two months.

It was time for him to figure out what he wanted.

CHAPTER SIX

LEO

We will have you. Cass's words ran on repeat. Everything she'd said kept bouncing through my mind like a silver pinball through its machine. For hours I'd been driving around, and those words wouldn't go away.

Damn if she wasn't right. I'd said I was leaving, that she'd get nothing from me, but I hadn't walked away. I was all talk with no follow-through. Cass hadn't reached out to me in months, but the day she'd returned, I'd gone to her.

I was drawn to her, more than I was willing to admit.

"Fuck me." I pounded a fist on the steering wheel as I drove toward home.

What I really wanted was to get on my bike and hit the road. To get some air and clear my head. Except it was cold and I preferred not to freeze my ears, nose and balls off.

My house, as always, was dark and empty when I pulled into the driveway. I'd walk through the door and behind it there'd be nothing but lonely rooms and too much silent space to avoid thinking.

Lately, on nights like this when I knew I wouldn't be able to shut my brain off, I'd go to the basement and beat the shit out of a heavy bag until I was physically exhausted enough to sleep. But a brutal workout didn't appeal tonight.

Why had I bought such a big place? A year ago, I'd bought this home when everyone else was getting married and growing up.

It was Emmett's fault. While I was at The Betsy most nights, Emmett was becoming this businessman, with properties and investments all over town. He'd built his own house in the mountain foothills, wanting land of his own. He'd said something to me one day about putting his money to work for him and I'd got to thinking maybe I should be doing the same. Making an investment instead of keeping a load of cash in the bank.

Everyone around me was bragging about their acreage and interest rates and equity value, so I'd decided it was time to spend some of the money I'd stashed away. Years of being with the club had set me up for life. That money hadn't been made legally so it was locked in my safe to spend as cash around town—I didn't need much to exist on. What I earned from the garage had gone to the bank.

My realtor had shown me this place first. I'd liked it. I'd bought it.

The street was quiet and there was distance between me and the neighbors, part of the reason I hadn't done much searching around town. I could go to the detached shop and crank up the music, work on my bike or whatever project I felt like, and no one complained about the noise.

But as I stared at the black windows, covered with blinds Scarlett had chosen for me a few months ago, I realized it was all a damn mistake. I should have stayed in my shitty duplex where at least the neighbor's lights were usually on.

I'd lived at the duplex in town for over a decade, even back in the day when I'd spent most of my nights at the clubhouse. The duplex was cheap. The guy next door was quiet. I wasn't home much, especially in the summers when the days were longer.

But it was a crash pad. That was where I'd taken women to fuck, never to my own home.

Except Cass.

She'd been the only one I'd brought here. She'd been . . . special. Extraordinary. Phenomenal in bed, letting me have my control and so damn responsive.

"Fuck me." Now I was hard. I rubbed my hands over my face.

Go inside.

Walk away.

Move to Dallas and forget this goddamn place.

The truck sat idling in the driveway and I couldn't bring myself to shut it off. Why had I gone to Cass's house when I should be inside packing?

I opened my mouth, testing my jaw where her dad had punched me. It would be sore for a few days. He'd hit me square and solid. *Good for him.* Cass deserved a guy like that watching over her. Keeping the assholes like me at bay.

Maybe he'd do that for the baby too.

It's a girl.

A girl.

My curiosity was making me insane. I shouldn't care. But the image of a little girl with Cass's red hair was stuck in my brain. Maybe she'd have my eyes, not that I'd find out.

Except I could.

All I had to do was stay.

My ribs felt too tight, squeezing so hard I couldn't draw in a long breath. Cold as it was, I rolled down the window and gulped the freezing air.

Why wasn't I gone already? My own father had walked away without a backward glance. It should have been easy for me to follow in those footsteps. Hell, it was in my DNA.

Go inside, Leo.

I shoved the truck in reverse.

Without thinking, I drove to the place where I used to find my answers.

The clubhouse.

The garage was dark except for exterior lights that cast yellow circles onto the frozen pavement. I passed it and rolled down the lot to the building swathed in shadow.

There used to be so much life here. Now the clubhouse looked like a skeleton. Most days, I didn't let myself even glance this direction. It was too hard to see it abandoned and without a line of bikes parked out front.

The trees around the clubhouse had grown taller, their limbs bare and their leaves scattered at their snow-covered roots. More skeletons. How many times had I puked in those trees after too much to drink? How many women had I taken into the grove for a quick fuck?

Those had been the good times, right?

The windows were all boarded up from the inside. It was a task that Dash, Emmett and I had done after the Kings had disbanded. Screwing the sheets of plywood up had been like driving nails into my own coffin. But I'd done it, mouth closed, because that was what the brotherhood had decided.

The front doors were locked with a thick chain and padlock. I had a key. I could go inside.

But it would be even emptier than my house. The last time we'd gone in, the smell had bothered me the most. Instead of leather and tobacco, it had smelled like dust and putrid, stale air.

The scent of dead memories.

What do I do? Silence. Empty, crushing silence.

There were no answers here.

I hated that I knew exactly where I'd find them.

"Son of a bitch." I flipped the truck around and aimed its tires toward the opposite end of town. Every cell in my body seemed to rattle the closer and closer I got to Cass's place until my muscles were practically vibrating.

Her street wasn't as dark as mine, a combination of porch lights and Christmas decorations still hanging from eaves. They cast her neighborhood in a soft, yellow glow. One of the nice features of an old-model truck like mine was that you could shut the lights off, where with the newer models everything ran on auto controls. I flipped mine off and crept toward Cass's driveway, parking against the sidewalk.

The clock on the dash showed it was just past midnight. No doubt her dad would shoot me if he knew I was here at this hour. So as quietly as possible, I shut off the truck and opened the door, pressing it closed with a muted click. Then I crossed the lawn, the frozen grass crunching beneath my boots. When I made it to the house, I inched along the side toward the farthest corner.

Then I pulled out my phone and texted the number I'd memorized months ago but never dialed.

I'm outside.

Once it was sent, I rapped my knuckles on her window.

The light flipped on a moment later, then the curtains rustled as she pulled them back. Despite her heavy eyelids, there was a scowl on Cass's face. Her hair was pulled into a ponytail and she was wearing a pair of pale gray pajamas, the sleeves so long they draped to her fingertips.

From my angle below her, all I could see was belly. That was my kid in there. *It's a girl.*

Why was I here?

Cass unlocked the window and slid it open. "It's midnight."

"Sorry."

Cass sighed. "What do you want, Leo?"

"I don't know," I admitted. I really, truly didn't know why I couldn't leave her alone.

"Front door." She pointed that direction. "Please be quiet."

I nodded as she relatched the window, then made my way to the front. She had the door open by the time I made it to the stoop. I took off my boots, leaving them outside. They'd be cold but no way I was risking waking her parents.

We walked silently, slowly, down the hallway to her bedroom. When I stepped inside, she closed the door behind me and went to the edge of the bed.

I went to her desk, taking the chair and leaning forward on my elbows.

"How's your face?" she asked.

"Hurts."

"Good."

"You probably don't even realize how lucky you are to have a dad who'd do that for you."

"Yes, I do. I know exactly how lucky I am."

I met those caramel eyes and drowned. Would she hold out a hand to haul me to the surface? "I feel lost."

What had she done to earn my confessions? But here I was, throwing them at her like candy at a parade.

Cass shifted on the bed, tucking her feet beneath the fluffy comforter. Then she took a pillow, cuddling it to her chest as she lay down. But her eyes never wavered from mine. She was just getting comfortable to listen.

"The club . . . that was my center for a long time. We broke it apart and I hated every second. That's not something I've ever told anyone. I voted for it because it was best for my brothers. But I didn't want it."

"What was it like? The club?"

"A family. A bond. We worked together. We fought together." We'd killed together.

"What were you fighting? The Warriors?"

I nodded. "Sometimes. Not always."

The club had been involved in a number of illegal activities. The most lucrative and dangerous had been providing protection for drug runners. We'd handled some private security for a few local businesses, basically acting as local thugs. And there'd been the underground fighting ring, which was now nothing more than a boxing club at one of the local gyms. Much too tame for my taste.

"Why were you fighting?"

"Simple answer? Our livelihood and way of life. Money. Power."

Her forehead furrowed and curiosity filled her expression.

So I continued before she could ask questions that I wouldn't answer. "We were on one side of the law. You grew up here. I'm sure you've heard rumors over the years." Most of which were bullshit but there was some truth at their core. "We weren't good men."

"You were a criminal."

"Yes." There was no point in hiding the truth from her. She deserved to know. "I've done things I'm not proud of. I've done things I am proud of but would land me in prison."

"Have you ever hurt an innocent person?"

"No." Nothing like the kidnapping that had happened to her.

Maybe that was why we'd justified our actions. Killers killing other killers. Thieves stealing from other thieves. But every man I'd gone after had had as much blood on his hands as I had.

"Not all of the brothers can probably say that. We weren't Boy Scouts."

"But you never hurt someone who was innocent."

"Not that I know of."

"All right," she said. "Do you miss it? The crime?"

"Nah."

"You miss the camaraderie."

"And I miss Draven." Another confession. I missed him more than anyone knew. My own father had abandoned me a long time ago, and Draven had filled his shoes. But I wasn't his son, and grieving him had become something I'd done in silence. Alone.

"Who's Draven?"

"Dash and Genevieve's dad. He was the president of the club for a long time. He offered up his life to the Warriors to protect his kids."

Cass's eyes widened. "I remember reading about his death in the paper. They reported that he committed suicide."

"He didn't," I said through gritted teeth. One of the greatest injustices was that the world thought Draven had committed suicide to avoid a prison sentence when really, he'd made the ultimate sacrifice.

"Oh. I must have missed that in the news."

Christ, maybe I shouldn't have said that. "It's not public knowledge. Maybe keep that to yourself."

"Sure," she agreed and somehow I knew whatever I said tonight would stay between us.

"Bryce puts as much truth in the paper as she can but leaves out a lot when it comes to the club." She'd protect Dash's secrets—our secrets—forever.

"Ah." Cass nodded. "What about Marcus Wagner? The old police chief? Was that story true?"

"Yeah. He killed Genevieve's mom and tried to frame Draven for it." That son of a bitch would never see the free world again, but prison seemed too good. I'd rather see him in hell.

"Mom and Dad talked about it for months whenever they'd call me because of the movie crew last year. They saw the director and actors around town every now and then."

"Presley is married to Shaw Valance." Maybe she knew that already. I wasn't sure how much contact she'd had with anyone here in the past six months. Regardless, there wasn't much news around town that didn't spread like wildfire and Presley marrying a famous actor had burned through the streets in days.

"I know. Dad teases Mom because she has a crush on Shaw. They see him now and then whenever they come to see Scarlett. Mom texts me every time."

"Shaw's a good guy. Good for Pres."

Cass shifted, rubbing her side.

"You okay?"

"It's fine. Things are beginning to get a little bit cramped in there." There was joy on her face as she took in her belly.

It was hard to see so I dropped my gaze to the carpet. It was too difficult to see her excitement and deny that there wasn't something—not excitement, but a curiosity of my own—buried deep.

The room smelled like her, like citrus and sweet pears. Fresh and soothing. The night we'd been together, I'd buried myself inside her and my face in her hair to breathe in that scent while I'd made us both come.

My cock jerked beneath my zipper. Fucking hell.

"You said you were lost," she said, bringing me back to the conversation.

"Yeah. I guess I haven't known what direction to go since the club."

"Is that why you're moving?"

I shook my head. "No."

"Then you're moving because of me."

"Do you really want to run into me around town like what happened tonight at Stockyard's?"

"There are people in the world who manage to have a child together and coexist in the same town. I'm sure we can figure it out."

"It'll be easier if I go."

"Easier on who?"

"You." I met her gaze. "It'll be easier on you."

"And not you?"

"No." Leaving Clifton Forge would be brutal. Saying goodbye to Dash and Emmett and Isaiah and Presley, everyone, would cut deep. With the club gone, they were the only family I had left.

"Do you want to know why I think you came here tonight?"

"Clue me in because I'm not exactly sure." Just like I wasn't exactly sure how magnets worked. That was how I felt about Cass, pulled toward her, but I couldn't articulate why.

Her eyes softened. "Whether you're ready to be a father or not, this baby is yours. You belong to her like she belongs to you. The loyalty you had to your brothers, to your club, is in your blood. And it's searching for a new connection. It's screaming at you to find a new place to channel it. That place is here. With her."

Thank fuck for the chair beneath my ass because if I'd been standing, I would have dropped to my knees.

How did that make so much sense?

"Draven always warned me to be careful around smart women. His wife was smart. He loved her completely, but he always said his life would have been easier if she hadn't been smarter than he was."

Cass's soft lips spread into a smile. "You loved him, didn't you?"

"He was the father I never had."

"I'm sorry you lost him."

"Me too."

"And your real father?"

"Not in the picture. Never has been."

"I'm sorry, Leo."

She could have taken that fact and run with it. Most women in her position would have thrown it in my face because I'd done no better. But Cass wasn't like most women. I'd known it the night we'd met. She kept reminding me with each conversation.

I shrugged. "Don't pity me."

"Why not? My father punched you in the face tonight because he loves me so much. Every kid, no matter how old, should have a guardian. He's mine. My mom too."

Cass would be that guardian to the baby.

Maybe . . . maybe I didn't want her to carry that load alone.

"I don't know what I expected when I came here tonight, but it wasn't this." Sharing my past. Talking about the club.

"That's because you're too busy trying to fit me into the mold of the women you normally hook up with to realize that I'm nothing like them."

"You never say what I expect."

"Good." A smile toyed on her mouth as she stroked her belly. "That makes me feel mysterious and a little bit sexy, which is far from how I actually feel at the moment."

Oh, she was a damn mystery. That was a fact. And if she thought she was anything but sexy, she needed a new mirror.

Cass was the most alluring, captivating woman I'd ever met. It was the reason I'd sat beside her at the bar. One glance at that hair and those eyes and I'd been entranced, addicted and desperate for a touch.

One night hadn't been enough.

Goddamn, but I wanted to kiss her. I wanted to push her into that bed and kiss her breathless.

This was not the direction my thoughts should be headed, again, so I stood from the chair and paced to the closet, the farthest possible space in the room from Cass on her bed.

"I haven't told anyone I'm moving," I said. "I haven't even officially accepted my job offer." I'd wanted to tell Dash and Emmett first before calling Bruce in Dallas.

Maybe because I wanted them to talk me out of it.

"That's because you don't want to move." Cass voiced the truth I wouldn't.

I don't. Texas wasn't where I belonged. And if I stayed here, I didn't want to run into my kid at the store one day and have her look at me like I was a stranger.

I took a deep breath. "You said you'd have me."

She nodded. "We will."

"I don't know what I have to give but . . . I'd like to be part of this." I wasn't even sure where those words were coming from but they were honest.

"Okay," Cass said.

"That's it? No argument? No punishment for my behavior?"

"My dad hit you in the face tonight. It was oddly satisfying to watch."

I chuckled and rubbed my jaw. "Glad you got to see it then."

"Me too." Her hand drew another circle on her stomach. "She's not just mine, Leo. I might be an only child, but I'm very good at sharing. But we're going to need to move these conversations to the daylight hours."

"What are you doing tomorrow?"

"Apartment hunting." She yawned. "I've got an appointment at nine to meet a landlord."

"How about you cancel it? Sleep in."

"I sort of need a roof over my head."

"Then take mine." The words hurled past my lips.

"Huh?" She pushed herself up to a seat.

I gulped. Christ, what was I doing? "I've got a big house with three extra rooms. You could stay there for a while. Save some money. We could get to know each other."

Cass blinked as her eyebrows knitted together.

"Yeah, I can't believe I just said that either." This woman was scrambling my brain.

"Want to take it back?"

"No," I said without hesitation. "I mean it. If you want to save up, not live alone, you're welcome at my place. You can check it out first if you want. Tomorrow."

She continued to stare at me, her head tilting to the side as she tried to figure me out. When she did, I hoped she'd share the wealth.

I held my breath, not sure if I wanted her to say yes or no. Yes. No.

Yes. She was going to say no. I could feel it.

"Okay," she whispered.

"Really?"

"Change your mind already?"

"No. Just . . . you never say what I think you're going to say."

She smiled. "You'll get used to it."

I hoped so. Not just because it was unnerving as hell but because I wanted to know her. "I'll get out of your hair. I'm home all day tomorrow. Text me whenever you want to come over."

"I will." She shoved off the bed and followed me to the front door, hovering in the frame as I pulled on my ice-cold boots.

"Night." I waved and started for my truck but she stopped me.

"Leo."

I turned. "Yeah?"

"If you hurt me or my daughter, I will cut you out of our lives faster than you can blink."

There was the guardian. There was the fire.

"Fair enough." I dipped my chin. "Good night, Firecracker."

Her breath hitched.

Maybe she wasn't the only one who could shock the other.

CHAPTER SEVEN

CASSANDRA

"I don't like this."

"I know, Dad. You've mentioned it once or twice."
Or seventeen times.

"There's no rush, Cassie," Mom said from the backseat. "Why don't you wait a week or two?"

"I want to get settled." The feeling that I was running out of time was constant these days. "The baby will be here soon. And I guess . . . I'd rather get to know Leo before she's born. This isn't permanent. I still have my plans, but I can save some money on rent."

"It's not like we're charging you." Dad whacked the turn signal too hard, following my directions toward Leo's house.

I'd only been to his home once and though I knew exactly where he lived, Leo had sent the address over this morning.

"Don't worry. It will be fine." Maybe. Hopefully. Though the knot in my stomach betrayed my outward confidence.

Why had I agreed to this? Obviously, I was losing my

ever-loving mind. But no matter how many doubts raced through my mind, they hadn't stopped me from packing this morning. It was like my body just moved on autopilot, loading clothes and toiletries and books. Luckily, most of my belongings were still in boxes and a suitcase from when I'd left Missoula.

Dad's shoulders were hunched forward as he gripped the steering wheel with too much force. Mom was worrying her lip between her teeth and her knees were bouncing.

"It will be okay." Was I telling them? Or myself?

Leo had looked so sincere last night. For the first time, he'd admitted his fears. He'd dropped that guard, and when he'd offered to let me stay with him, he'd looked so . . . fragile. Desperate.

My *okay* had just slipped out.

Yes, I was still angry at him for how he'd treated me but last night's conversation had taken us a long way in what I hoped was the right direction. My foolish heart had melted when he'd stood outside my window, like he couldn't wait to see me until morning.

When he'd confessed to being lost, I'd had to bite the inside of my cheek to keep from crying. His words had been so honest, and in the end, that was all I wanted. His honesty.

I had hope for Leo. And for this baby, I wouldn't give up on him.

Not yet.

If he failed me, us, then I'd cut him loose. Just thinking of walking away made my chest ache, but I'd do what needed to be done.

Moving into his house would give me a chance to assess if he could be a part of our lives. It was only for a week or two. How hard could it be?

Dad took another turn, and I scanned the homes, taking in the details I'd missed the dark night I'd spent with Leo and the morning after. The neighborhood wasn't new to Clifton Forge, but it was new to me. None of my friends from school had lived here.

"This is a nice neighborhood," Mom said, forcing cheer into her voice. Her knees bounced faster.

"Yeah." I swallowed the lump in my throat.

God, maybe this was stupid. Leo had worked his way into my tender heart last night and here I was, moving into his home.

My phone dinged—a text from Olive.

Hey, mama! Just checking in.

I quickly typed out a reply that I'd call her later, then tucked the phone away.

Olive was the only one of my roommates from Missoula who I'd heard from since Christmas. All of the girls had gone to their respective homes to visit their families for the holidays and enjoy the break from school. Two of them would be back, having not graduated yet. Olive had moved to Seattle to start a doctoral program at the University of Washington.

I expected she'd be the only one I'd keep in touch with. Even then, she'd be busy soon with school as she settled into the program and made new friends. Meanwhile, I'd be adjusting to life with a newborn.

Drifting apart was inevitable. I could feel it coming like a bad grade on an exam.

My friends from high school no longer lived in Clifton Forge, and though there were familiar faces here and there, I didn't have friends in town. True friends. None who I could confide in about my fears of becoming a mother. None who I could call when I was low. None who I'd trust with details about my predicament with Leo.

I loved my parents, but they were my parents. Right now, I was staying strong for them. Telling them about my anxieties would only make them worry more and they had plenty to worry about as it was.

Loneliness as cold as the January air crawled into my bones.

Maybe that was why I was moving here.

Because last night I'd recognized the loneliness on Leo's face too.

Dad slowed the car—my car. They'd be dropping me off, then bringing it back after it was unpacked. They'd refused to drive separately today, probably because Dad wanted any excuse to return and check on me. Numerous times.

"This is it?" Mom's eyes widened. "It's . . ."

"Nice," I finished for her, my heart beating faster as Dad pulled into the driveway beside Leo's truck.

The night we'd met, after the car in the parking lot of The Betsy, he'd asked me to come home with him. I'd expected a cramped bachelor pad with an unkempt yard. But his home was charming.

The rancher stretched across the wide lot, leaving room for the driveway and a detached garage. The house itself was brick and had been painted a navy blue. With the honey-colored posts and shutters on each window, it was surprisingly feminine. The porch was decorated with two white pots, each with a pruned topiary tree.

"Is this it?" Dad squinted at the front door and the numbers beside it.

I didn't have to answer him because that very door opened, and Leo came striding outside.

His long-sleeved T-shirt was pushed up at the forearms, revealing those colorful tattoos I was coming to find familiar. Maybe he'd tell me about them and satisfy my curiosity. His faded jeans molded around his strong thighs with every long step, falling to those scuffed boots he'd insisted on taking off last night.

If Mom knew that he cared about her carpet, she'd probably kiss him on the mouth.

A low growl came from Dad's chest as he watched Leo come to my door.

"I love you, Dad."

His hands strangled the wheel. "I love you too, Buttercup."

"I know." It was the reason he was here, because he loved me enough to let me make my own mistakes. I gave him a small smile as Leo opened my door. Then I swung my legs out and took his hand, joining him in the cold. "Hi."

"Hey." His eyes were greener this morning. "You sure about this?"

"Are you?"

"I'm not sure about anything anymore."

These confessions of his were going to be my undoing. "Let's start with unloading a few bags. Then we'll go from there."

Mom and Dad climbed out of the car and both stared at Leo. If awkward were a sweater, this one fit like a scratchy wool turtleneck that choked and stifled.

Mom looked Leo up and down. Twice. She looked at the home, then back at the man who owned it, and after a slight headshake, like she couldn't marry the two together, she walked to the trunk.

Dad stood beside his door, looking over the roof of the

car at Leo. He crossed his arms over his chest. "I'll hit you again if I need to. I'll hit you a million times if you hurt her. I don't like you."

Oh, Dad. I swallowed a groan.

"Dale," Mom hissed.

"There's no point in anything but brutal honesty here, Rose Petal. I can't stand him. I don't trust him. And he's not good enough for Cassie."

Ouch. I braced, waiting for Leo's reaction.

But he simply nodded. "Understood."

As Dad continued to glare at him, Leo stood there and endured every second. He didn't raise his chin or puff out his chest like my wonderful, maddening father. Leo took every moment of Dad's scorn and had the sense to look remorseful.

Maybe he really was.

Mom noticed because when I met her gaze, that glare of hers had faded. She gave me a sad smile, then said, "Dale, it's cold. Pop the trunk."

Dad obeyed and joined us all at the back. Leo reached for a bag but Dad snatched it up first.

Leo's jaw clenched but he didn't say a word. He simply chose two other bags, hefted them out and led the way to the door.

"Okay, you guys have to leave." I took a backpack out and slung it over my shoulder. "Right now."

Dad's face whipped my way. "What? We're not—"

"Yes, you are." I took the bag from his hand, wishing I had thought of this earlier. When they'd insisted on coming along, I should have put my foot down. "You can come inside when you bring the car back, but for right this minute, you need to go. I can't play referee and deal with everything else at the same time."

"Cassie—"

"Okay." Mom cut him off. "How long would you like?"

"Give me an hour or two."

Dad shook his head. "No. I don't trust him."

"Leo's not going to hurt me, Dad. He's going to show me around the house and let me get settled into a guest room. Please, trust me to make the right decision."

He closed his eyes and blew out a deep breath. Maybe the reason he hesitated was because he didn't trust me. Or maybe he didn't trust the world. Not that I blamed him. In the past year, I'd gotten pregnant and kidnapped. One was a result of my own choices, but the kidnapping had changed Dad.

It had changed us all.

"We'll be back." Mom kissed me on the cheek.

Her hair, the same shade as mine, was pulled into a knot today. In the winter sun, she looked older. Another side effect of the past year. Mom and Dad had both aged. Dad's hair was more white than blond and the crinkles around his eyes had deepened.

"Thank you," I said as Dad hauled out two boxes and a suitcase, setting them on the driveway. Then with a kiss to my forehead, he and Mom returned to the car and left.

They were barely onto the street when Leo rejoined me. "They left."

"I asked them to." I stared at the taillights. "They worry about me. Too much. I need to do better figuring out my life so they can get back to living theirs."

Going back to school had helped. Mom and Dad knew how much I'd loved school and how set I'd been on achieving my goals. But school was over now and this next step was a big one.

A shiver raced over my shoulders as the chill air sank past my thin tee. Not exactly winter wear.

I'd gotten hot earlier, emptying out my drawers. I'd only put on a gray tee with a pair of olive cargo pants. My black baseball cap was hiding the fact that I hadn't washed my hair today and my Converse were barely tied because reaching my feet took effort.

"Come on." Leo collected the suitcase at my feet, then slipped the backpack from my shoulder to put over his own.

With one last glance at my parents driving away, I followed Leo to the front door and inside. The scent of furniture polish and Pine-Sol hit me first. "You didn't have to clean."

"Yeah, I did." He grinned over his shoulder and a flutter stirred in my belly.

Maybe after we spent more time together those flutters would go away. Maybe the allure of his handsome face and sexy grin would wear off.

I was banking on a lot of *maybes* these days.

Rather than drool over his tall, sculpted body or get lost in his pale eyes, I studied his house, something I hadn't done the first time I'd been here. "Your home is lovely."

"Don't give me any credit. The previous owners remodeled before they put it on the market. And Scarlett decorated."

"She did? Oh. I didn't realize she was a decorator."

Scarlett and I had texted some while I'd been at school in Missoula. We never chatted for long and after she'd told me that she was expecting too, our conversations had centered around comparing pregnancy complaints. Never, ever about the kidnapping. We didn't know each other well, but now that I was back, I hoped that would change. Scarlett had a spark that I admired.

"It's unofficial," Leo said. "She's going to an online school and wanted to practice. She was pissed at me for . . . you know." *Me.* "She told me that if I let her decorate my place, she'd hate me a little less."

"Sounds like her." I smiled.

"I don't know her as well as Pres," Leo said. "But they've got the same sass. They've aimed it at me a few times this year and it's got a bite."

"Your suffering shouldn't make me happy, but it does."

He chuckled. "Make yourself at home, okay? I mean it."

"Thank you." I wouldn't, but he didn't need to know. This was a trial and I'd treat it as such. I hoped he'd come through but I had a backup plan in case.

He rushed outside, leaving me in the entryway, standing beside my things while he went outside for the last of the boxes. They joined the backpacks and suitcases on the floor as he closed the door and nodded for me to follow him deeper into the house.

"Let me give you the tour. Then I'll haul everything to your room."

"Okay." I tucked my hands into my pockets, hiding my nerves.

When he'd brought me here after The Betsy, we'd been a fumbling mess of lips and hands and discarded clothes. I hadn't even paid attention to his bedroom. And the morning after, I'd rushed out the door, not exactly a walk of shame, but more that I'd wanted to leave before he could ask me to leave.

Now I was living here.

Oh my God. I was living with Leo.

"You okay?" he asked.

"Great." I nodded. "I love these floors."

They were done in a soft walnut that made the white trim and doors pop. That white was the only bright shade to be seen. The walls in the entryway were rich charcoal gray and the living room was a shade bolder.

Oddly enough, the deep colors worked. It was very different from the neutral beiges and taupes of my mother's style, but it was warm and moody. Cozy.

The colorful area rug brightened the space. The furniture in the living room was camel leather, worn and scratched in some places, each piece facing the TV above the stone fireplace. Charming, but it was the artwork that stole my attention.

Every piece was small and framed. They clustered in the free wall space around the room. Some were colorful, like the mountain ridge in shades of blue that dripped color from the bottom. Or the pine tree outlined in black but accentuated with shades of forest green and lime and shamrock.

I walked closer to another piece on the wall, larger than the others. It was a raven, black as night with shattering wings. Beneath it was the faintest hint of blood-red. Spooky, yet stunning.

"Those are my tattoos." Leo came up beside me. "Or these are the drawings I did for the tattoo artist."

"You did these?"

He nodded and shoved up the sleeve of his shirt, showing me the underside of his forearm with the tree. Its tip tickled the inside of his elbow and the trunk was so long it stretched to his wrist.

My fingers reached up, skimming his skin. I had no idea

why I did it. Temptation. Pregnancy brain. But the jolt that raced up my arm made me snatch my hand back. "Sorry."

"Not like you haven't touched me before, Cass."

"Right." I'd touched him *everywhere*. My cheeks had to be the color of my hair. Guaranteed.

We might have touched then, but this was now. Touching was a bad, bad idea. Standing beside him was temptation enough without adding anything physical into the mix. The point of me being here was not to intimately reacquaint myself with Leo.

This was a test.

I suspected that his awful behavior from months ago had been driven by fear. He'd freaked and lashed out. I wouldn't hold a few bad days against him forever. Leo had one more chance to prove himself the man I suspected he actually was.

This test didn't require any touching. None.

I took a step backward. "You're an amazing artist."

"This is just for fun." He lifted a shoulder. "It's not what pays the bills."

"You work at the garage, right?" I asked but already knew the answer.

"Yeah. I'm a mechanic and do all of the painting."

As a woman who knew nothing about cars, even I'd heard of the Clifton Forge Garage. Probably because before the kidnapping, Dad had bragged about them a few times. He'd thought it was cool that our small town had a nationally renowned garage.

I knew what Leo did there. In a moment of desperation months ago, when the hormones had been storming and the upcoming-single-mother blues had set in, I'd gone on to social media and searched for Leo, expecting to find him living his best life while I was growing his child.

But Leo didn't have any social media accounts. Not one. The garage had an Instagram account and I'd memorized every photo that included his face. I'd read the articles, scouring every line for just the mention of his name or another photo of him beside a gleaming classic car.

It had satisfied my initial curiosity, but now that I was in his house, I wanted to know more.

I wanted to know everything.

Was he still the town playboy? Was he spending his nights at The Betsy while I'd been at home alone?

I guess I'd find out soon enough.

"The kitchen is this way." Leo walked down the hallway toward the back of the house, where the kitchen split the place in two. Unlike the living room, here, the white cabinets were bright, and the large window over the sink gave the room an airy feel.

"My bedroom is down that hallway." He pointed as he spoke. "It used to be the garage but the previous owners turned it into the master when they put up the detached garage. Laundry is across from my room. Door to the basement is at the end of the hallway. Not much down there but my weights and gym stuff."

"I won't be needing those." I rubbed my stomach, covering up my belly button that had popped out a couple of weeks ago like the button on a turkey.

Leo's gaze followed the movement. He extended a hand, almost touching, then pulled it away, up and through that blond hair.

"Go ahead. I don't mind."

"Um . . . nah."

Random women in the grocery store would rush up to

me and put their hands on my belly without asking. Not Leo. I pretended like it didn't sting.

He cleared his throat and headed down another hallway that ran in the opposite direction of the one to his room. He paused outside the second door we reached, waving me inside. "This is you."

The bedroom was painted the same navy blue as the exterior of the house. The sprawling white bed in the center of the room looked like a fluffy cloud floating through a midnight sky. "It's beautiful."

"Scarlett. She picked it all out. The previous owners had a thing for dark walls, I guess. I didn't feel like painting. Cars? Yes. Walls? No. So I told Scarlett to try and make it work."

"I'd say she was successful." I walked toward the bed, my feet sinking into the thick carpet.

"Bathroom's through there." He hovered at the doorway, motioning to the en suite. "Closet's empty. Room beside yours is empty too. So is the one across the hall. This whole side of the house is yours."

"This is a big house." I went to the window, pushing back the pale gray curtains. "I don't need this much space. Really."

"Not like I'm using it."

No, it wasn't. Why had he left it so empty? Why hadn't he put anything in these rooms?

I stared outside and around the street. The lots on this block were large, allowing for decent yards between homes, but Leo's seemed remote.

"You're sort of set apart from the neighborhood."

"Yeah. Part of why I bought it. This was the first plot in the development when it was built in the eighties. Not long after, they rezoned because I guess the developer got himself into a tight spot financially and by cutting down on the lot size and dropping the price, he could sell them easier. I don't know. That's just what my realtor told me. So this is basically two lots with the house in the middle. I don't have anyone breathing down my neck."

For a man who confessed to feeling lost, he sure had isolated himself. "Well, thank you for letting me stay. I promise not to breathe down your neck."

"I didn't mean you."

"I know." I gave him a little smile as I moved away from the window. "Your house is beautiful. I didn't tell you the first time I was here, but it's quite unexpected."

"What were you expecting?" he asked, leaning against the doorframe.

"Trashy bachelor pad."

He chuckled. "A few years ago, yeah. That was me."

"Thank you for letting me stay here."

"Glad you are." He pushed off the doorframe. "I'll get your stuff."

He'd delivered only one suitcase to the bedroom when the doorbell rang.

"It's probably my parents," I said, following him to the entryway. Sure enough, when he opened the door, my dad was standing with his arms crossed behind my mother.

"Here are your keys." She peeked inside, waiting for an invitation. But today was not the day for guests so I plucked the keys from her hand.

"Thanks, Mom. I'll call you later."

"But—okay." She frowned and looked up at Leo standing behind me. "If she has any contractions or labor pains, you call us. Even if she tells you not to."

"Yes, ma'am."

Mom crossed the threshold, pulling me into a hug and whispering in my ear, "I hope you know what you're doing."

"Me too."

She held on tight, not letting me go.

I patted her shoulder. "Okay, Mom."

She didn't budge.

"Mom."

"Rose Petal." Dad's gentle voice and a hand on her shoulder was what pulled her away. He took her place, hugging me close, then ushered her to the driveway.

I waved, waiting until they were both in their car, then closed the door.

Reality came crashing down. I'd moved in with Leo. Alone. Two strangers under one roof.

Please, let this work.

"Your mom's name is Rose Petal?" he asked.

"No." I shook my head. "It's Claudia. Dad calls her Rose Petal. To everyone. So much so that some people actually think it's her name."

"I thought maybe she'd been raised by hippies or something."

"No." I laughed. "My granddad is retired but he and Grandma still live here and they are the opposite of hippie. He was a businessman. She was a housewife, like June Cleaver. My grandma loves to read true stories. She was the one who turned me on to them in the first place and got me interested in studying history."

Leo nodded. "And your dad's name?"

We hadn't done introductions, had we? Things were moving so fast I was struggling to keep up. "His name is Dale."

"Dale," he repeated. "And he calls you Buttercup."

"That or Cassie. My friends called me Cass, but Mom and Dad have always called me Cassie."

"What about Cassandra? Anyone call you that?"

"Professors. Dad when I'm in trouble."

He nodded and didn't move. Instead he stood there, trapping me in the entryway as his gaze raked over my face. He'd done the same thing at The Betsy all those months ago.

Leo stared, unabashedly.

Maybe it was to unnerve people.

Maybe he liked what he was seeing.

That would move us into dangerous territory, so I pointed toward my side of the house. "I, um . . . think I'll spend some time unpacking."

"Yeah." He blinked, shaking the look off his face, and picked up my bags. When I went to grab my backpack, he waved me off. "I'll get it."

"Okay. Thanks." I ducked my chin, hiding under the brim of my hat, then went to the bedroom.

While he brought in my bags and boxes, I gave him a wide berth, then said another thank-you before he left me alone.

Was this a mistake? That question looped through my mind as I set folded tops and panties into drawers. While I hung sweaters and stowed jeans.

Temporary. This was temporary. This was a way for Leo to get to know me and realize I wasn't his enemy, then once we were on common ground, once he'd adjusted to the idea of fatherhood, I'd find a new place. Maybe in my time here we'd come to a sort of friendship.

Unpacking didn't take long, but by the time I was done, hunger drove me from the bedroom. I went in search of Leo to tell him I'd go to the grocery store and found him in the living room, relaxed on the couch, watching a basketball game on TV.

"Hey." I hated this part of adjusting to new roommates. It was why I'd lived with the same three girls for so long. We might not be best friends, but we knew how to coexist. I missed Olive and the familiarity we'd had after five years together. "I was going to go to the grocery store."

"There's food here. Help yourself."

"I—" Before I could finish my sentence, his forehead furrowed and he shoved off the couch, walking to the bay window that overlooked the front yard. He sighed and raked a hand through his hair. "Shit."

"What?" I went to his side, expecting to see my parents back for another visit.

Instead, the glass began to vibrate, and the sound of distant thunder filled the air. Leo must have heard it, knowing the sound, because one minute we were alone.

And the next, the Tin Kings were parking in his driveway.

CHAPTER EIGHT

CASSANDRA

"When are you due?" Genevieve asked as she popped the top off a plastic container filled with chocolate chip cookies.

"March eleventh."

Leo's eyes shot to mine. He hadn't asked my due date. Now he had it.

I suspected he'd learned more about my pregnancy in the past fifteen minutes than he had since conception. His kitchen was full of people and everyone was curious about me. Question after question, comparison after comparison, I'd never been around this many pregnant women.

Genevieve smiled. "I'm due in May."

"We're both due in March too." Scarlett smiled at Presley, both of whom had bellies about the size of mine. "Crazy how that worked out."

"I think it's perfect." Bryce tore off the lid to a tray of veggies and ranch dip. "This is going to satisfy my baby cravings so I don't get any ideas of quitting my birth control."

"There will be no such ideas." Dash came walking into

the room with a three-year-old Zeke hanging over his shoulder. Or maybe that was Xander?

Introductions had been done in a rush, and the boys looked so similar that I might have mixed them up. Not to mention they were both miniature versions of Dash with their dark hair and mischievous smiles.

"Zeke, where's your brother?" Bryce asked.

Zeke. That one was Zeke.

He looked up and squirmed until Dash put him down. "Downstairs."

"Is there anything fragile down there?" Bryce asked Leo.

He shook his head. "Nah. Nothing they can ruin."

"Stay out of trouble," Bryce warned her son. "Or I'm kicking you outside."

Zeke nodded and sidled up to Genevieve's side. "Can I have a cookie?"

"No," Genevieve and Bryce answered in unison at the same time Dash said, "Sure."

The only word Zeke heard was his father's, of course, and he snatched two cookies and disappeared before his mother and aunt could stop him.

"Sorry." Dash shrugged and grabbed a cookie of his own, winking at Genevieve before throwing a hand around his wife's shoulders and hauling her into his side.

Dash, of course, I'd known of because, like Emmett and Leo, he had a reputation around town. Presley was easy to pick out because she was Scarlett's twin. I was still struggling to wrap my head around the fact that Shaw Valance—*the* Shaw Valance, who I'd seen in countless movies—was sitting at Leo's dining room table, drinking a beer.

He was the only guy who hadn't rolled in on a Harley today. Dash, Emmett and Isaiah had all ridden their bikes while the women had come in a succession of SUVs. Scarlett had ridden with Presley and Shaw because Luke had gotten called into the station.

With them had come enough food to last a week. I hadn't needed to go to the store after all. And no one had been shy about admitting the reason they were all here. *Me.*

Leo had told Emmett that I'd moved in today and word had traveled quickly. This impromptu gathering was likely to size me up.

"Incoming, V," Isaiah called into the kitchen from where he was sitting with Shaw and Emmett at the table.

Amelia had a bright smile on her little face as she crawled toward her mother's legs. The little girl had enthralled me from the moment Isaiah had carried her into the house. Maybe because she was the only girl and the boys were so wild that it was hard to pin them down.

Genevieve swept her up from the floor and kissed her cheek, then snatched a carrot out of the tray for her daughter.

"How old is she?" I asked.

"She'll be one next month," Genevieve answered as her daughter launched herself toward Dash.

He popped the rest of the cookie in his mouth, then took his niece and blew a raspberry on her neck, making her giggle. Handsome men with little kids were mesmerizing.

My gaze moved to Leo.

He was visibly ignoring Dash and Amelia, totally focused on sipping his beer from where he stood against the counter in the corner of the kitchen. Did he not like kids? Because he was going to need to get over that. By March eleventh.

Dash stole another cookie, then took Amelia into the dining room. The moment they were out of sight, Leo relaxed and took in the activity in the kitchen. Everyone seemed to know their way around. Everyone but me. To them, this was probably a normal Saturday get-together with friends.

No, not friends. Family.

This was his family. And he would have left them behind because he'd been scared to bump into me in town.

"Hey," Scarlett whispered, inching closer to where I stood against the counter.

The kitchen was U-shaped with a pass-through to the living room on one end and the dining room. We'd all crammed into this space and I'd hung at the far end of the counter.

"Hey." I smiled.

"This is probably overwhelming."

"A bit," I admitted. These were likely all of the faces I would have seen at her barbeque months ago.

"Sorry."

"Don't be. It's good to see you."

"You too. I'm glad you're back. How was school?"

"School was . . . hard. In a good way. I'm glad I was able to finish and earn my degree. Having that achievement under my belt has made moving home feel less like a failure and more like the next chapter."

"Congratulations." She clinked her glass of water to mine. "What's next?"

"Work for a bit. Save up some money. I'm going to do some freelance transcriptionist work. I actually got a lead on it from one of my professors."

Authors dictated their books and then a transcriptionist, me, took the audio files and transcribed them. The pay was decent and the hours flexible.

"Leo said you were going to school," I said. When we'd been in the Warriors' basement, she'd told me that she wanted to go to school.

"Just online." She shrugged. "I want to get my degree in interior design."

"Good for you. I love what you've done here."

"Thanks." She laughed. "It was fun, and Leo was so gracious about it."

Down the room, he was still in the same place, watching the room but not really participating in any one conversation.

That was, until Presley walked over to him and wrapped her arms around his middle.

"What is this for?" he asked, settling one of his arms around her shoulders.

"I'm not mad at you today."

He chuckled and dropped a kiss to her short blond hair. Something about their embrace bothered me. Not that I thought they were any more than friends. Maybe it was because I doubted he'd ever be so easy with me. So open.

"She's been pissed off at him for months," Scarlett said.

I tore my eyes away from Leo and Presley. "He told me."

"Leo's a good man. How he's been acting, well . . . she's disappointed in him."

Presley had moved up the list of people I wanted to know better. I appreciated her loyalty, though I wasn't sure what I'd done to deserve it.

The doorbell rang and Scarlett straightened but she didn't go to answer it alone. She waited, following behind Leo, as he strode through the house. When they came back, Luke was with her, their hands locked.

"Hey, guys." He raised his free hand to greet the group.

"Want a beer?" Bryce asked, already going to the fridge.

"Please." He nodded, bringing Scarlett's knuckles to his lips. "Sorry that took so long."

"It's fine." She waved it away. Being the chief of police's wife probably meant she dealt with a lot of strange weekend and evening calls.

"Hi, Cass." Luke grinned at me. "Welcome back to town."

"Thanks. It's good to be home."

There was nothing but truth in my statement. Home. Clifton Forge. There wasn't a place on earth where I wanted to have my daughter born but here. Even if this temporary roommate situation didn't work out with Leo, even if he ultimately decided to walk away, this town would always be home.

"Should we eat or talk business first?" Dash asked, coming back into the kitchen, Amelia still in his arms.

Business. What business?

Leo shoved off the counter and came to my side. "Business. Let's sit at the table."

He nodded for me to follow him and when we walked into the room, Emmett, Shaw and Isaiah vacated their seats to let the women sit.

Leo stood behind me, his hands resting on the back of my chair as everyone looked at Dash to start the conversation. He handed Amelia to Isaiah, then took his place behind Bryce's chair.

"We're glad to have you here, Cass," he said.

"Why do I feel like there's a *but* coming?"

"No but." Bryce shook her head. "There's an *and*."

"And"—Dash put a hand on his wife's shoulder—"now that you're back, we want to make sure you're safe."

My stomach dropped. This was not something I wanted to discuss. Today or ever. It had been six months since Leo's warning the last time I'd been in Clifton Forge. Wasn't this over? "The Warriors, you mean. Agent Brown called me a few months ago and said they were all in jail. She told me not to worry."

"Most are in custody," Luke answered. "The major players at least. Tucker Talbot's trial is underway. Same with some of his lieutenants. But . . ."

"There it is," I muttered.

Luke gave me a sad smile. "While the leaders are in custody, some of the Warriors have been released on bond. They're expected to stay in Ashton."

"But they might not," I finished for Luke. "I did nothing to them. *They* kidnapped *me.*" And I'd done my best to forget it.

"You didn't do anything." Leo shifted, coming out from behind my chair to stand at my side so I could see his face. "We did."

The Tin Kings.

"So you're telling me I'm in danger. Still."

"Yeah. They might retaliate and try to take their revenge." There was genuine worry in Leo's eyes and the concern made my heart sink.

Had coming home been a mistake after all? I didn't want to move away from my parents, not now. But if that was what it would take to secure my daughter's safety, I would. "Should I leave again?"

"Let's explain the situation. Then you can decide." He was supposed to say no. Maybe we hadn't made as much progress as I'd hoped.

"All right." I nodded and waited.

"It's complicated," Emmett said. "We have a lot of history with the Warriors and it's likely they blame us for their incarceration."

"Or me," Scarlett said.

Because she'd had a video. I remembered it from the basement. The details from that night were hazy, probably because I refused to relive them, but she'd had a video of the Warriors and had tried to blackmail them. For what, I wasn't sure. Maybe her safety.

I assumed the history Emmett had mentioned was the same that Leo had told me about last night, but I couldn't be sure. I struggled to see how one end of the string connected to the other, but with this many new faces aimed my way, I stayed quiet.

I'd let them explain, then I'd formulate my questions. Whether they liked it or not, I was going to ask questions. It was in my nature. Making decisions based on CliffsNotes was not my style.

"The Warriors fucked up and opened the door for the FBI to walk inside their clubhouse," Dash said.

"By kidnapping us?"

He nodded. "Partially. And killing a federal agent. That was the catalyst for the raid. But any rage that Tucker Talbot has toward us will be aimed at those of us who used to wear a patch. Too much happened in the past. Too much blood was spilled. It's not on you, Scarlett. Or you, Cass. The reason we're talking about this is to make sure we all stay safe."

"What exactly does staying safe entail?" Clearly the rest of them had discussed it and I was being pulled into the loop.

"Try not to go anywhere alone," Dash said. "We're all here for you. If Leo's busy, call one of us. Watch for anyone suspicious. If someone makes you uncomfortable, tell Leo."

"When you're home alone, keep the alarm on," Leo said. "Doors locked."

I nodded. "And my parents?"

"Should be fine," Luke said. "We're right across the street."

"No offense, but I was taken on that street."

"Fair point," he said. "But I doubt they're in any danger. I doubt you are either. This is simply a precaution."

Then why didn't I feel better? "It's been months. Has anything happened?"

"No," Dash said. "There hasn't been any sign of the Warriors in town. Chances are, it's over. For good. But we're not about taking chances these days."

I swallowed the lump in my throat. "What about the FBI? Can they help?"

My contact with the FBI had been infrequent at best. Every month or so, Agent Brown would call to check in on me. I'd dodged the last two calls and ignored her voicemails.

Maybe I should have taken those calls after all.

"I keep in touch with her," Luke said. "And the reason she didn't warn you is because I doubt she realizes that you're still connected to us."

That's right. This wasn't really about the kidnapping. It was about the baby. Leo's baby. I looked up and found his eyes waiting.

"You're part of the King circle now," he said. "Like it or not."

The jury was still out.

But hours later, after adjourning the *business* discussion, after dinner and a conversation considerably lighter, I decided that maybe the Tin King circle wasn't necessarily a bad place to be.

"Call me, soon." Scarlett hugged me as we stood in the entryway. "Let's go to lunch or something."

"I'd like that."

"I'm glad you're back. I hope we didn't freak you out too much earlier. We just want you to be safe. Both of you."

"Thanks."

With another hug, she let Luke escort her outside while Leo and I said goodbye to the others. It was dark and cold outside, but Dash and Isaiah didn't seem to mind climbing on their bikes to drive home.

Bryce wrangled her boys, who'd been wild but entertaining, into their SUV as Genevieve loaded in a sleeping Amelia and waved goodbye.

Emmett was the last to leave. He slapped Leo on the shoulder. "I'm going to grab a beer."

"'Kay."

Emmett jerked up his chin. "Night, Cass."

"Good night." I waved.

Leo waited until Emmett was on his bike, then he closed the door, leaving the two of us alone for that awkward moment I'd avoided earlier.

"I, um . . . I think I might crash." I pointed toward my end of the house.

Leo ran a hand over his jaw. "Call me if you need anything."

I nodded and, before it could get awkward, disappeared to my bedroom. Pulling off my hat, I found an elastic tie and twisted up my hair into a top knot. Then I sank down to the edge of the bed and kicked off my shoes.

Tonight had been fun. And interesting.

A potential threat from the Warriors made me nervous,

but what had really piqued my curiosity tonight was the way Leo had acted around me.

He'd stayed close, always in the same room. While the guys had discussed projects at the garage and the latest football game, he'd been in and out of their conversation depending on where I was. If I was in the kitchen, talking to the women, then he was in the kitchen.

Bryce and Dash's sons had challenged all of the guys to an arm-wrestling contest and when we'd gone into the living room to watch the event—Xander and Zeke had tied as undefeated winners—Leo had stood by my side except to participate.

And he'd laughed.

We'd all laughed. Somehow, in a single night, his friends had filled a void I hadn't realized was so deep. I missed my own friends. I missed Olive, my roommates and my classmates. But tonight, the loss had been a little less, thanks to a group of bikers and their beautiful wives.

"Hey." Leo knocked on my open door.

"Hey." I stood from the bed. "What's up?"

"Wanted to give you these." He held out a key and a sticky note with a code to the alarm on it. "The garage is full of my shit right now but I'll get it cleaned out so you can park in there."

"The driveway is fine," I said. "I have remote start for the days when it's cold. I don't mind."

"You good?" he asked as I set the key and note on the dresser. "With everything we talked about?"

"I don't know. Ask me tomorrow."

He hooked a thumb over his shoulder. "We can hit the grocery store tomorrow if you want."

"Sure."

"My Sundays are pretty chill. Whenever you want is good with me."

"All right. Thanks again, for letting me stay."

"You don't have to thank me. I didn't earn it." He backed away for the door, but I stopped him.

"Leo? Was the danger from the Warriors the reason you were so mean to me? Because you wanted me to leave town?" This would all be easier if he'd done it for my protection. He'd told me that he didn't want to be a father but maybe that had been a lie.

He sighed. "I wish I could say yes."

Damn. But at least he was being honest. "Good night."

"Night, Cassandra."

Cassandra. My name sounded like a dream in that gravelly tone.

As he disappeared down the hallway, I replayed the day. It hadn't gone horribly. That was something, right? We'd managed a day together without argument. Though his friends had instigated the baby questions, he now knew my due date, that heartburn was making my nights miserable and that just the mention of bananas would send my stomach into a nasty roll.

Living together could work. This could be our chance to break down the walls and get to know each other. Domestic trips to the grocery store. Evenings spent eating together and watching TV.

I closed the door, changed into my thick pajamas and was about to head to the bathroom to brush my teeth and wash my face when a loud rumble echoed outside. Crossing the room, I reached the window just as a single headlight reversed away from the garage.

Leo was on his bike. And before I could make sense of it, he roared down the street.

Emmett. He'd told Leo he was going for a beer. Probably to The Betsy. Then Leo had told me to call him if I needed anything. I'd assumed that call would be through the house, not that I'd have to literally call him on the phone.

He'd told me to call because he wouldn't be here.

"I'm such a fool." As the sound of his bike drifted away, I closed my eyes. My first night here and he'd left me alone.

Saturday nights weren't for staying home with the mother of his child.

Saturday nights were for The Betsy.

I really hated that bar.

CHAPTER NINE

LEO

"Morning." I yawned.

Cass looked up from her seat at the dining room table, her fingers hovering over the keys of her laptop. "Afternoon."

I glanced at the microwave. It was after noon. "Guess it is."

Last night had been a late one. I'd rolled in around six this morning and crashed hard.

After work yesterday, I'd gone to The Betsy for a beer. I'd got caught up at the pool table, playing and bullshitting with a group of guys who were in town for a weekend of snowmobiling in the mountains. They'd rented a house, and after the bar had closed at two, they'd invited me over to check out their machines. I'd slept on a couch, woken up sober and called a cab to drive me back to my truck at The Betsy.

When I'd gotten home, still tired, I'd planned to rest for a couple hours. Guess I'd been more tired than I'd thought.

I took a chair beside Cass, rubbing a hand over my face to clear the fog of sleep.

In the past two weeks, I hadn't actually seen her much. Mostly, our paths would cross whatever time I climbed out of bed, usually in this exact spot, then we wouldn't see each other until the next day.

It was working for us. I stayed out of her way. She stayed out of mine. Whatever worries I'd had that living together might be awkward were pointless. This was easy coexistence. We could do this. No sweat.

Other than the fact that I wanted to kiss her every time I saw her, this was easy.

Don't kiss her. If I did, I doubted I'd ever stop.

"How's it going?" I motioned to her computer, forcing my thoughts away from her mouth.

"Fine." Her eyes darted to my bare chest before she looked to her screen.

I'd climbed out of bed and only bothered tugging on a pair of sweatpants. "How's your work going?"

"Fine."

Fine. I'd been around Presley long enough to know that fine didn't mean fine.

"Sorry if I woke you up when I got home." I'd tried to be quiet but the keypad on the alarm was loud and maybe she'd heard it when I'd disarmed it.

"It's fine." She waved it off, then closed the lid on her laptop. "I'm going to take off. I've got a couple of meetings this afternoon."

"What meetings? Are you going alone?"

"I have a showing with a landlord in fifteen minutes. My mom is meeting me there. Then I have a doctor's appointment at one thirty. I'll be going there alone."

Landlord. "What landlord?"

She sighed. "Leo, this isn't working."

"What do you mean?" This was working exactly like it should. She was living here to save some money.

Cass leaned her forearms on the table. "I moved in here because I'd hoped we'd get to know each other. And I thought . . . never mind what I thought. It's difficult to get to know someone when you spend five minutes a day with them."

"Just trying to stay out of your way."

"No, you're just living your own life." Her nostrils flared for a moment before she shook her head and plastered on a tight smile. "It was always going to be temporary. The baby is coming soon, and I want to get settled. For good."

"And you can't get settled here?"

She stood from the table, having to use the armrest to shove herself to her feet. "No, I can't. We tested it out. And failed. Now we know."

Without another word, she gathered up her laptop, phone and earbuds, then disappeared to her bedroom while I sat stuck in my chair.

What the fuck? How was this not working? I stayed clear. I did my own thing. She had the run of the house. Hadn't I told her she could do whatever she wanted? To make herself at home?

Before I could catch up, the front door opened and closed. I shoved off my chair and raced for the door, but she was already backing out of the driveway and easing down the street.

Alone.

My fists clenched at my sides. She wasn't supposed to be going anywhere alone. And whatever place she was seeing wasn't going to be as safe as here. I had a state-of-the-art security system and lived in a safe neighborhood.

"Fuck." I shoved away from the living room window and hurried to my bedroom, taking a shower to wash off the beer-and-bar smell from last night. Dressed in a pair of jeans, my boots and a long-sleeved T-shirt under my lined flannel coat, I swiped a granola bar from the pantry—Cass must have bought them, because I hadn't.

My truck was in the driveway, the windows frosted. One of these days, I'd get a newer truck with remote start like Cass's car, but today was not that day, so while my breath billowed around me, I ran the ice scraper across the glass. Then I got inside, shivering at the cold air that didn't warm until I was five blocks away from the garage.

There'd be no bikes in the parking lot for the foreseeable future. We'd gotten a heavy snow a few days ago and it didn't look to be leaving until spring. The roads were for shit. And Cass was out driving alone.

"Son of a bitch." How had we gotten here? What was wrong with my house? I parked and marched inside the office, wanting some coffee.

Presley was behind her desk and she raised an eyebrow as I walked inside. "Afternoon."

"So I've been told."

"I wasn't sure you'd even make it in today."

"Don't start, Pres." I disappeared into the waiting room. It was Draven's old office that had been converted into a common area for customers because neither Dash nor Presley could bring themselves to take up his old space.

Not that I would have been able to either. Hell, it was hard enough coming in here and getting coffee without remembering how it used to be. How it should have been if not for the fucking Warriors.

I filled up a mug and turned, ready to escape into the paint booth for a while, but a pregnant woman was blocking my escape.

"What?" I snapped at Presley.

She crossed her arms over her chest, her forearms resting on her belly. "Are you okay?"

"No," I admitted.

"Is it Cass?"

"Yeah. She's moving out." And I wasn't exactly sure why that made me so goddamn mad. Two weeks. Why had she moved in at all if she was just going to leave after two weeks? Why bother?

"Do you want her to move out?"

"No. I wanted her to save some money. Not have to worry about shit on her own." And if she needed something, I'd be there. Or . . . I could be there. Cass was right, it was hard to get to know someone when you rarely saw them. Maybe I'd been spending too much time away.

"Then ask her to stay." Presley shoved off the doorway and waddled to the office, resettling in her chair and forcing me to follow. "Put some effort in, Leo. Stop going to the bar every night and get to know the woman who is having your baby."

I frowned. Not this shit about The Betsy again. "I'm trying to stay out of her way."

"No, you're doing you. Cass moved in to give you a chance that, let's be honest, you didn't deserve. Then she sits there alone, in a stranger's house, when she could have been with her parents or in her own space. While you, what, go out and party all night? I'm guessing that's the reason you're rolling in after noon. Because you found something, or some-one, to entertain you last night."

"I wasn't with a woman." I hadn't been with a woman for fucking months. Not since Cass.

Presley gave me that look, one that I hadn't missed for the past two weeks. The look of sheer disappointment. She was pissed at me again.

But I needed her. So I swallowed my pride, gritted my teeth and asked, "What do I do?"

"You have to figure it out on your own."

Christ. Why wouldn't she just tell me? "I don't want her to move out. It's safer at my place, and I'm there if she needs me."

"Don't tell me. Tell Cass."

Unless it was already too late. "Do you know what doctor she goes to?"

"Dr. Tan," Presley said. "She's my OB too. Her office is in the hospital annex."

"I'll be back later." I set my mug down on the corner of her desk, then strode for the door. As I backed out of the lot in my truck, Presley stood at the window in the office with a shit-eating grin on her face.

I ignored it and drove away.

It was almost one, so instead of attempting to hunt down Cass at whatever rental place she'd been scoping, I drove to the hospital. It took me a minute to navigate the maze that was their hallways, but I finally found the right door and scanned the small waiting room. There was another couple in the back corner, both of them on their phones. No Cass.

"Can I help you?" the receptionist asked.

"Cassandra Cline. She—we—have an appointment at one thirty."

"She hasn't checked in yet. You're welcome to wait."

"Thanks." I strode over to a chair, sitting down and bracing my forearms on my thighs. Then I counted the minutes until the door opened and a brilliant flash of beauty walked inside.

Cass didn't notice me. She went to the window, a smile on her face, and greeted the receptionist. "Hi. Cassandra Cline to see Dr. Tan."

The receptionist rattled off a list of questions and took Cass's insurance card, then motioned to me.

Cass followed the woman's gaze and when she spotted me, her eyes widened.

"Hi." I stood and met her by the desk.

"H-hi."

"Here you go, Ms. Cline." The receptionist slid a clipboard across the counter, a pen attached to the top with a thin chain. "Fill that out and give it to the nurse when they call you back."

"Sure." Cass gave her a quick smile, collected the paperwork and walked to the chairs. "How'd you know this was my doctor?"

"Presley."

She nodded and stripped off her parka before taking a chair, shifting and twisting, trying to find a place to set the clipboard down to fill out the answers. She couldn't reach the side table, so she reclined deep into the chair and tried to use her belly. "I should have done this at the counter," she muttered, her pen strokes shaky.

"Here." I took the board and the pen, setting them on my thighs. "I'll write."

Cass studied my profile as the pen hovered above the page.

"What?"

"Why are you here, Leo?"

"I don't want you to move out."

"So you came to my doctor's appointment?"

I shrugged. "It's where you are."

She blew out a long breath. "Well, you're in luck. The place I looked at was overpriced and smelled like smoke."

"There's no point in you moving out. You were right. I heard you. I'll be around more. We'll get to know each other."

"Starting with my medical history." She tapped the clipboard, then began dictating answers as I wrote them down for her. Mostly, I checked a lot of boxes *no*.

Cass signed the few places required, finishing just as a nurse opened a door and called, "Cassandra."

She pushed out of the chair, collecting her purse and coat.

"Can I, um . . . come in there?" I jerked my chin toward the nurse.

"Sure."

Cass took a step but I didn't move. Why couldn't I move? She looked back, her gaze softening, then reached for my hand.

One touch and I unglued my feet. Her fingers stayed in mine until we were in the exam room.

The nurse had her sit in a chair, then took her blood pressure and reviewed the clipboard before handing her a small cup. "Bathroom's next door."

"Thanks." Cass stood. "I'll be back."

"Where are you going?"

"One of the joys of doctor's visits when you're pregnant.

Regular pee tests." She shook the cup. "You can just sit here."

Sit? Not a chance. The minute she was gone I stood and paced the small room, keeping my eyes away from the posters on the wall of the pregnant female anatomy, until the door opened again and Cass returned.

She climbed onto the exam room table, the paper crinkling beneath her. "You don't have to stay if you're uncomfortable."

"I'm good."

"This is my first visit with this doctor." Cass rubbed her belly, the silence stretching between us, until a knock came and the doctor walked inside.

I was basically shoved to the side, taking up the space by Cass's head as the doctor started in on a litany of questions.

"How have you been feeling?"

"Great."

"Any concerns?"

"Nope."

"Do you have names picked out?"

"Not yet." Cass glanced my way. "I have a short list."

"Whatever you want. I don't care."

Wrong answer. She closed her eyes and her lips pursed tight.

What? Her choices were probably fine and I didn't care what the baby's name was. Except Dale. I didn't really want my kid named after her dad. Dale wasn't my favorite name. So if she had a preference, that was fine.

"And you're the father?" Dr. Tan asked.

"Uh, yeah."

She looked between the two of us, probably wondering what the hell a woman like Cass, smart and classy and polished, was doing with me. The doctor must have realized this pregnancy hadn't been planned because after a quick assessment, I was dismissed, and she gave Cass a smile that looked a lot like pity. "Let's have a listen."

Cass scooted farther onto the table until she could lean back against the paper-covered pillow. Then she pulled up the hem of her sweater, revealing her belly. Her skin was flawless, stretched over her bump. Seeing it bare suddenly made this very, very real.

My heart started to race as the doctor grabbed a white bottle and pulled a machine over.

"This will be cold." Dr. Tan squirted a glob of clear liquid on Cass's belly, then took a wand and ran it over the goo.

A dull echo filled the room, a whoosh and then a *whomp, whomp.*

A heartbeat.

Cass looked up. "Cool, right?"

The sound grew louder and louder with every pulse until my own heart seemed to match the same rhythm. Every beat was like a hammer, slamming the reality of this into my skull. The baby wasn't a concept anymore. It—*she*—was real. This was real and happening too fast.

I wasn't ready.

All this time while I'd been in denial or losing my shit, Cass had been solid as a rock. A rock I was going to lean on for a moment.

The blood drained from my face and I bent over the bed, using it to hold me up. My knees were seconds away from buckling. My forehead dropped to Cass's shoulder and I inhaled the sweet citrus scent of her hair, concentrating on how damn good she smelled as the volume of the baby's heartbeat began to quiet in my ears.

Cass's hand slid down the table and found mine. I clutched it tight, stealing from her strength until I could stand up straight.

"Is this your first time hearing it?" Dr. Tan asked.

I managed a nod.

The doctor pulled the wand away and the sound disappeared from the room. A good thing, right? Then why did I want to hear it again?

Dr. Tan grabbed a cloth to wipe Cass's belly clean. "Strong heartbeat. I've got the records from your doctor in Missoula and unless you have any concerns, everything looks to be progressing nicely. We'll start appointments every week going forward. I'd like to get a blood test next week too."

"Sure thing." Cass nodded.

"Then we're all set. Take your time. You can schedule your next appointments on your way out or just give us a call. It was nice to meet you, Cassandra. And . . ." Dr. Tan waited for my name.

"Leo," Cass answered for me.

"Leo. We'll put that in your chart."

"Thank you," Cass said as the doctor slipped out of the room.

Neither Cass nor I moved. I couldn't and she stayed still, waiting for my reaction.

"That was . . ." I cleared my throat. "Not what I was expecting today."

Cass righted her sweater and pushed herself up to a seat. Then she climbed off the table and reached for her jacket on the chair behind me.

I snapped into action, grabbing the coat for her and holding it out for her to put on. "Thanks for letting me stay."

"You're welcome in all of this, Leo. To come to the appointments. To pick out names. She's as much yours as she is mine."

"I'm still getting used to the concept of *she*. Today . . . made it more real."

Cass reached for my hand, taking it in hers. Fire flickered up my skin, the same fire that always spread when we touched. It was part of the reason I hadn't looked at another woman since her.

I burned for her. Only her.

Her touch was delicate but firm as she pulled my palm to her belly and pressed it against the swell. Then she let me go, leaving my hand exactly where it was.

I tensed, about to pull away, but there was a look on Cass's face, like this was a test. I'd failed enough of them that I didn't move. Every second I touched her belly, it became easier. Ten. Thirty. Sixty. I stayed frozen until the fear I hadn't acknowledged began to fade.

Cass's eyes were waiting when I met her pretty gaze.

A touch. A connection. I stayed locked with her as our night together from months ago came rushing back. How I'd held her. I never held women. How I'd slid inside her, slow and lazy. I never went slow. How I'd had her in my bed.

Only her.

It wasn't just the baby who terrified me. Her mother scared me too.

If she left, I'd lose her. "Don't move out."

Cass dropped her chin and a lock of that silky hair dropped into her face. I reached up and tucked it away. "I feel like a fool," she said.

"Why? Because you're pregnant?"

She looked up and shook her head. "I hate feeling stupid. More than anything. Being at your house while you're out with other women . . . I feel like a fool. I feel pathetic. I can't be at your home while you're out all night with—"

"A bunch of guys."

"Huh?"

"Last night, these guys were in town to go snowmobiling. They were at The Betsy and invited me to their place to check out their machines. It was late and I'd been drinking. I slept on a couch and waited until I could drive home. Not a woman in sight."

"Oh." Her shoulders sagged. "Still . . ."

"I haven't been with a woman since you."

Cass's mouth fell open.

I hooked my index finger under her chin and pushed it closed. It was that or kiss her. "Don't look so surprised."

"Are you serious?"

"Have I ever lied to you?"

"No."

"I'm not going to start today, Firecracker."

She studied me with that slight tilt of her head, like she'd done in her bedroom weeks ago. And, like she had that night, she whispered, "Okay."

"Okay, you'll stay?"

"I'll stay."

"Thank you." A wash of relief cascaded over my shoulders. "Then let's get out of here. The uterus and vagina posters are making me uncomfortable."

She giggled and let me take her hand. I wasn't sure why I wanted it, but since she'd arrived at the doctor's office, we'd touched. I didn't want to stop.

I didn't let her go, using the snow and ice in the parking lot as an excuse to hold it tight. When we got to her car, I opened her door. "I'll follow you home."

"All right."

I waited until she locked the door before I left her and walked to my truck a few rows back. Then I met her at the mouth of the parking lot and followed her through town.

The roads were for shit, even worse than they'd been an hour ago. The snow was falling again and with traffic, it compacted into slick tracks. At the first stop to turn onto the highway, I touched the brake, and the back of my truck began to fishtail. There was no grip on my tires. I pumped them twice but just kept sliding. "Damn it."

Cass turned, moving out of the way so I didn't bother stopping. I just turned and caught up to her until the turn-off to our neighborhood. Then the same damn thing happened as we weaved through the side streets toward home. Either it was too icy for my bald tires or my brakes were failing. Maybe both.

When we made it home, I hopped out of the truck and immediately bent to look at the undercarriage.

"Everything okay?" Cass asked.

"Yeah." I scanned the driveway for a leak. No brake fluid.

If the line was broken, the brake pedal would have gone to the floorboards and stayed there, so the hydraulic fluid was catching, but didn't have enough pressure. Maybe the hoses were corroded and cracked.

I stood and brushed off my jeans. "This truck is temperamental. I've had it since high school. I bought it to fix up but that never really happened."

The black 1985 Chevy wasn't much to look at on the

outside or under the hood. Probably because I rarely drove it. I chose my bike unless we were in the dead of winter, like today.

"Want to take my car?" Cass held out her keys.

"Nah. I'll get this to the garage and check it out. Better order some new tires too."

"Okay. I'm going to head in. Get a little more work done."

"I'll see you tonight."

She nodded and took a step away, then turned back. "When you say tonight, do you mean before or after midnight?"

I chuckled. "How about dinner?"

"Dinner would be great."

"Want a burger from Stockyard's?"

"Sure."

"Want to go there?"

"Um . . . okay." The surprise on her face made me feel like a complete asshole.

While I'd been out living my life, she'd been stuck here. Alone. Maybe she thought I was hiding her. That I was ashamed to be seen with her.

Really, it was the other way around. The only thing I'd do for Cass's image was tarnish it. But like it or not, people around town were going to find out. Hell, they probably already knew. I only hoped the gossips would take it easy on her. Dinner together might make it worse, but it might also shut them up. Who knew? I'd stopped caring what people in Clifton Forge thought about me a long time ago.

Not for Cass. For her, I cared.

"I'll pick you up around six."

"Bye." She made her way to the door, using her key to

unlock it. Before she went inside, she turned back and gave me a smile that stopped my heart.

I rubbed my sternum as she disappeared inside and tried a deep breath. My lungs wouldn't quite fill. Probably the cold. I got in the truck and drove away, but the twist in my chest didn't stop. Every block I'd see that beautiful smile and ache, worrying that having it in my life was fleeting. That soon she'd come to her senses and that smile would be gone.

She'd called us temporary earlier. It bothered me then and it bothered me now.

I didn't want to be temporary. We'd spent so little time together, but with each minute she snuck deeper into my shattered soul.

Draven had told me once that he'd considered his wife the light of his life. Not just the love, but the light. And that after Chrissy had died, the world had gone gray.

Cass promised redemption. She was young, pure and golden light.

If I let myself fall into her, I wasn't sure I'd survive it when she left. I shoved those thoughts away as I approached downtown and the stop light on Central. The brakes had been touchy but had worked. I tapped the pedal.

Nothing. I touched it again and whatever pressure it had given me earlier snapped. The pedal dropped to the floor, no tension, and I was on my way into the busy intersection.

There were no cars in front of me at the light so I took a gamble. I let the truck coast, my foot over the gas, ready to slide into the road and hope like fuck no one was coming because I wasn't stopping.

"Fuck." My heart raced as the light got closer. I leaned forward, checking for traffic. "Goddamn it."

The flash of headlights caught my eye. I was fifty feet from the light and there was a semi coming down Central.

Thirty feet.

I reached for the window, rolling it down with the crank handle. I managed to get my arm out and waved the truck away.

Twenty feet.

He didn't see me.

Ten feet.

I downshifted and stomped on the emergency brake. My wheels jerked but the tires were like figure skates on the ice.

Oh, fuck.

This was going to hurt.

CHAPTER TEN

CASSANDRA

"The doctor's appointment was good," I told Mom. "No concerns."

"I should have gone with you."

"Actually, Leo came." I smiled as I spoke the words. "He was there when I got to the hospital. And he asked me not to move out."

"You're kidding." Mom's shock rang loud through the phone.

"Nope."

"What are you going to do?"

I sat down on the couch and stared out the window. "Well, it's not like I found an apartment today, so I guess I'll stay."

"Cassie, I . . . oh, never mind."

"What?"

"Your dad and I were talking. Even if the place today hadn't been a total bust, we would really like it if you'd come home."

"Mom, we've talked about this."

"I know you want your independence. Moving home doesn't make you a failure, honey. And it's not forever. You said staying with Leo was temporary. So why not be temporarily here, where you have two people who go to bed by nine o'clock, have no desire to set foot in The Betsy and can be here to help with the baby?"

I sighed, wishing that very thought hadn't crossed my mind as I'd driven to the hospital earlier, before Leo had asked me to stay. Life at home would be easier and Mom would certainly be more help with the baby than Leo.

Unless he had a magical personality change in the upcoming weeks, there was no sign of him embracing fatherhood.

But what if he stepped up? What if he stopped partying every night and was here? Something had clicked today at the doctor's office. There'd been a change in Leo, maybe the beginning of a bond. If not with the baby, at least with me.

Deep in my heart, I knew Leo could be a good father. Maybe it was my imagination, but today when he'd heard the baby's heartbeat, I'd seen reverence in his face. He'd come around. He would. We needed more time.

"Let me give it another week," I told Mom. "I've still got time and if it doesn't work out, then yes, I'll move home."

"Okay." She blew out a long breath.

"Thank you. For always being there."

"I'm your mama. Where else would I be? You'll understand that soon enough."

I was beginning to already.

Leo was getting yet another chance, but those chances would run out. The minute this little girl was born, she was my priority.

"I'd better get back to work," Mom said. "Give me a call later."

"I will. Bye." I ended the call and set my phone aside, then ran my hands over my belly. "What do you think? Was he telling the truth earlier?"

The baby kicked my ribs and I laughed. "I'll take that as a yes."

I'd had a string of sleepless nights since moving in. I'd toss and turn, knowing Leo was out and wondering if he was with another woman. Last night I'd barely slept an hour because unlike the other nights when he'd gone to The Betsy, he hadn't come home.

My mind had run away with itself and I'd pictured him in another bed. I'd convinced myself he was actually dating someone, and I was his dirty little secret. The first thing I'd done this morning was search the classifieds for open rentals. I wouldn't be the woman he'd already used and left behind while he sowed more of his oats.

But if what he'd said was true, if there hadn't been anyone since me, then that changed everything, didn't it?

Did he want to get together? Did I? Falling for Leo would be as reckless as the Greeks opening their gates to the Trojan horse. Yet the attraction between us was as obvious as my swollen ankles. Touching him today had been precious, sweet relief. The hormones were pumping and God, I would kill for a decent orgasm. A Leo orgasm, because that man knew how to deliver.

My phone rang and I picked it up, Presley's name on the screen. "Hey."

"Hey. I need you to come to the hospital."

"What?" I shot off the couch as fast as a pregnant woman could shoot out of any seat. "Are you okay?"

"It's Leo."

My heart dropped. Was it the Warriors? Had they finally come for their revenge? "What happened?"

"He was in an accident."

His brakes. My stomach plummeted. "Is he all right?"

"They won't let us see him. I'm here with Emmett and Luke. The doctor hasn't told us anything, but Luke said his truck is in bad shape. We're at the emergency room."

"I'm on my way." I moved for the door, hanging up the phone before grabbing my keys and purse. I slung my coat on, then hustled outside, careful not to slip on the sidewalk. The roads were slow and though I wanted to rush, I forced myself to drive under the speed limit across town.

Emmett was standing outside of the emergency room entrance when I pulled into the parking lot. I found the closest spot and before I'd even shut off the car, he was there, opening my door and offering an arm to help me inside.

"Did the doctor come and talk to you?"

"No. When we get in there, tell them you're family. Then they'll let you go back or at least get you an update."

I nodded. I was losing control of my body. My heart was beating too hard. My limbs were shaking. I dragged in a breath, then squared my shoulders as we walked through the ER's sliding glass doors.

"Leo Winter," I said, planting my arms on the nurses' station counter. "He was in an accident."

"And you are?"

"His fiancée." The lie rolled smoothly off my tongue—a miracle for a woman who'd had few reasons to lie.

The nurse looked me up and down, probably wondering why someone so young was claiming to be Leo's fiancée. If not for my belly, I think she would have called me on my lie. "Have a seat. I'll let his doctor know you're here."

"Thanks," I breathed, then let Emmett escort me to the chairs where Luke and Presley were waiting.

"Hi," Presley said as I sat beside her.

"Any word?"

"No." Luke took the chair across from ours, leaning forward to speak quietly. Emmett stayed standing, hovering behind my seat.

"What happened?"

"Best I can tell, he slid through an intersection and got T-boned by a semi."

My knees started bouncing. "Did you see him?"

Luke shook his head. "I got there just as the ambulance was leaving. But the officers on the scene said it wasn't that bad."

Presley's hand found mine and I clutched it tight. "He was having trouble with his brakes. I offered him my car but he was going to check out his truck at the garage. That's where he was going."

"The truck's not in great shape, but I talked to the driver who hit him. Leo must have thrown it in reverse or hit the e-brake at the last second because the trucker said he was sure he was going to hit straight on. Whatever Leo did, it put his truck at enough of an angle that when the semi hit, it spun him. Plus the ice. From the witness reports, sounds like it could have been a lot worse."

"He'll be okay." I swallowed hard, not believing my own words. "Is there anyone else we should call? I don't know about his family."

"We're his family," Emmett said. "Dash is on his way.

Isaiah is covering the garage and as soon as the last job is done, he'll lock it up and come down too."

How long did they think we were going to be here?

A door opened behind Luke and a man wearing a pair of teal scrubs and a white lab coat came out. "Leo Winter."

"That's me." I raised my hand and stood, leaving everyone behind as I followed the doctor deeper into the emergency room. The sterile smell burned my nostrils. My tennis shoes squeaked on the waxy floor. They wouldn't let me back here if it was bad, right? "Is he okay?"

"Considering what the EMTs told me his truck looked like? Yes. He'll be fine. Bumps, scrapes and bruises." The doctor stopped beside a curtain. "See for yourself. I'll give you a minute."

"Thanks." I gulped and pulled back the curtain, the air rushing from my lungs.

Leo rested on the narrow bed with his eyes closed. Two legs. Two arms. And that handsome face, as perfect as it had been hours ago except for the butterfly bandage above his left eyebrow.

He cracked his eyes open. "Hi, babe."

"Hi." My entire frame sagged as I rushed to the bed. "Are you all right?"

"I'm good. Doc gave me some pain meds."

I lifted a hand, my fingertips hovering above the bandage on his forehead. There was a smaller cut at his hairline covered with a glossy ointment. "What happened?"

"Those fucking brakes." He sighed. "And my tires. I thought they'd hold till I got to the shop. Turns out, they didn't."

I closed my eyes and rested my hand on his shoulder. "You could have been killed."

"Nah. Just a wreck. At least I wasn't on my bike."

"Then you would have been killed."

"My bike's in a lot better shape than my truck."

"Especially now."

He chuckled and winced. "Ow. Damn."

"What? What is it?"

"Just a tender rib, according to the doctor. Couple of cuts from when the window shattered. Nothing that won't heal fast. Hell, I've had worse at bar fights and they sure as hell didn't bring me here when the cops showed up."

"You don't have to downplay this."

He took my hand in his. "You look worried."

"I am worried."

"Don't be." He brought my hand to his heart. "I got lucky. I hit the e-brake and managed to spin myself mostly out of the way when the semi hit."

If not for Leo's fast thinking, this might have ended differently. The surge of relief made me dizzy and I twisted to sit on the edge of Leo's bed just as the doctor came into the room.

"How are you feeling?" the doctor asked him.

"Fine. Wouldn't mind getting out of here though."

"Now that your fiancée is here, I'm sure we can get you discharged and on your way home."

"My wha—"

"That would be great," I interrupted and squeezed Leo's hand. I'd explain our fake engagement later.

"How's your pain?" the doctor asked him.

"Not that bad."

"I think you'll be fine alternating Tylenol and ibuprofen. If it gets worse, call me and I'll write you a prescription. Want me to wrap your ribs?"

"No, I can do it if I need to."

"Rest," the doctor said with a pointed look. "Don't let him drive. Or ride."

"Of course."

"Thanks, Doc," Leo said.

"You owe me a beer the next time I stop by The Betsy."

Leo nodded. "I'll buy you two."

"The nurse will be in with your paperwork. Take care, Leo." He closed the curtain on the way out.

"The doctor goes to The Betsy and you know him?"

"The bar's not only for vagrants and criminals." He sat up and swung his legs over the bed's edge. "You came there."

"True." My eyes landed on his chest. "There's blood on your shirt."

"It'll wash."

My eyes welled with tears and I wiped them away furiously before they could fall. "Gah. Stupid hormones and adrenaline."

"Hey." Leo tugged me close enough to frame my face and pull my forehead to his. "I'm fine."

"I should have made you take my car."

"Made me?"

"Yes. Made you."

"What's this about a fiancée?"

I stepped out of his hold and picked up the coat that someone had draped over the back of a chair. "It was Emmett's idea. They wouldn't let anyone but family back here to see you."

"Ah." He stood from the table, closing his eyes for a second as he swayed. Then he shrugged on his jacket.

A nurse came in with some paperwork, then showed us to

the exit for the waiting room. Dash had arrived and we found him pacing. The moment he spotted us, his entire frame relaxed and he clapped Leo on the shoulder. Emmett did the same. Luke assured Leo that the trucker was fine and hadn't received any injuries. And Presley hugged Leo so hard that he winced.

"Sorry. You scared me," she whispered.

Me too.

"We'll let you get home." Presley released Leo. "Expect a visit tomorrow."

With that, we all made our way to the parking lot. The sky was nearly dark, the nights of mid-January coming early. Leo took my arm, whether to hold me up or so I could hold him up, I didn't know, and we walked to my car. I drove us home, bypassing Stockyard's on the way.

"Sorry about dinner," Leo murmured, his head against the rest.

"It's okay. I'll make us something."

"We could order in."

"Whatever you want."

He hummed and closed his eyes. By the time we made it home, he'd fallen asleep. It was impossible not to stare at his profile when I parked in the driveway. To appreciate that sharp jawline and those soft lips. Did he realize how good looking he was? *Probably.*

And he'd been mine. I'd been the last. Me. A man who didn't have to work to get a woman into his bed hadn't wanted any after me.

He stirred, his eyelids heavy as they opened. "Hey."

"Hi," I said. "We're home."

"'Kay." He reached for the door, shoving it open.

I hurried out and to his side so we could go in together.

Then I flipped on the lights as we walked toward his bedroom.

I hadn't spent much time on this side of the house. Other than venturing here for laundry, I'd stayed behind the invisible boundary that separated his half from my half.

Even now, I hovered back at the mouth of the hallway.

"Can I get you anything?"

"Water. Couple of pain killers."

"Are you hungry?"

"Not really. Sorry. But you should eat."

"I'll be quick. You go lie down. I'll be there in a second."

"Thanks."

I hurried to the kitchen and got his water and pills. Now that the panic from the hospital was gone, my stomach growled. I dove for the fridge, scarfing a leftover bowl of pasta from yesterday and chasing it down with my own glass of water. Then I ventured toward his bedroom.

Leo's scent clung to the air, spice and cedar and that masculine undercurrent I couldn't inhale fast enough.

I peeked inside his bedroom, hesitant to just barge in. The bed was in the center of the room, facing a TV on a wide stand. Leo had turned it on and the screen cast a muted glow over the dark room.

Like the rest of the house, the walls were painted a bold color, nearly black in the dim light. Unlike my white bed to contrast, his was nearly as dark as the walls. He rested on top of a thick quilt, either gray or green or navy, I couldn't tell. He'd propped his head up on a couple of pillows covered in the same color.

His eyes were closed as I tiptoed to his nightstand and set the glass down beside his alarm clock.

"I'm awake," he murmured, opening his eyes.

"Here." I placed the pills in his palm, then handed him the water. "Can I get you anything else?"

He shook his head and swallowed the pills, then set the glass aside.

"Get some rest." I ached to run my hands through his hair, like I had once months ago. To feel it and reassure myself he was fine. But I backed away, ready to retreat to my side of the house.

"Sit with me." He reached out, faster than I'd expected, and snatched my hand. "Please."

I nodded and rounded the bed, climbing onto the other side and using the extra pillows for support.

Leo tossed me the remote. "Your pick."

"You might regret that. I live for the History Channel."

Those pale eyes caught a flicker of light and my breath caught. "Whatever you want, babe."

Babe. That was the second time he'd called me that today, both when he wasn't entirely awake. Maybe that was what he called all women. An endearment for when he couldn't remember a name.

Or maybe it was just for me. It wasn't Firecracker, but babe was a close second.

I picked up the remote from beside his hip and flipped through the guide on the TV until I found a rerun of a John Adams miniseries. "Is this okay?"

Leo hummed his agreement.

"I've seen it before. It's got some Hollywood embellishment but for the most part, it's fairly accurate. The book was better."

Leo's breath evened out and when I glanced over, his eyes were closed again.

So I relaxed on his bed with my hands splayed on my

belly to feel the baby's kicks. She went wild for half of an episode, then settled down. My eyes were tired. My pajamas were calling. But I couldn't bring myself to get off of Leo's bed. It was hypnotic, listening to his breathing and being in his space. His bed was as soft and plush as I remembered.

A dream.

I stirred awake when a pair of fingertips brushed a lock of hair from my forehead.

Leo hovered beside me, his fingers diving deeper into my hair. "You fell asleep."

"Sorry," I whispered.

"It's okay." His breath caressed my cheek. He didn't move away.

Neither did I.

Leo's gaze ensnared me, holding me so tight I couldn't think. His fingers continued their exploration of my hair, threading through the locks that drifted over the pillow. Then his eyes dropped to my mouth.

I mimicked the movement, taking in his pink lips and remembering once how they'd felt on my skin. Then they were there, no longer a memory.

Leo kissed me deliberately, one press of his mouth to mine.

And I lay there, fighting the urge to surrender.

"Cass," he whispered against my lips. "Kiss me back."

"No."

"Why?"

"Because what if you regret me in the morning?" I voiced the biggest insecurity I had when it came to this man.

We'd spent the night together and just two weeks later, my entire world had been turned upside down. Then I'd seen him at Scarlett's barbeque and though there'd been recognition on his face, he hadn't remembered my name.

Maybe I'd never told him. Maybe he wasn't to blame at all.

But that didn't erase the sting. In Leo's past, I was one of many. A nameless girl.

"If I hadn't gotten pregnant, you would have forgotten about me."

"Maybe you're right." Leo's eyes closed and he dropped his forehead to mine. "But that's not where we are, Cassandra."

Damn him. That honesty was so . . . endearing. The walls fell away, the anger and frustration I'd had with him for weeks simply disappearing.

My reckless, foolish, unguarded heart was putty in his calloused hands.

I leaned forward and pressed my lips to his. I hit mute on the fears echoing at the back of my mind and kissed the man I craved.

Leo's hand came to my face, cupping my jaw as he deepened the kiss. His tongue slipped between my lips, the tip tickling mine. Then I opened for him completely and whatever hesitancy we'd had evaporated. Our tongues twisted and twined as I clung to his chest, pulling him closer.

My chest heaved when he tore his lips away.

"God, Cass." He groaned as his hard body pressed into mine. "You taste so good."

His eyes drifted down my breasts, his hands following the motion until he hit the swell of my belly.

A blast of panic ran through my body when he froze. His eyes. His hand.

I held my breath, waiting for him to pull away when his fears beat him once more.

But he didn't pull away. He splayed his hand on my belly, spreading those long fingers wide. "I want you. But I don't want to hurt you."

"You won't."

He met my gaze. "What do you want?"

What I'd always wanted. "You."

He surged, his lips finding mine again as we fumbled, shoving clothes, baring skin. Leo broke away to sit up and reach behind his head, yanking his shirt away and tossing it to the floor. He was off the bed in a flash, shoving away his jeans and the black boxer briefs beneath.

The man was built for pleasure. His broad shoulders were roped with strong muscle. His washboard stomach and the deep-cut V at his hips pulled my gaze to his thick, hard cock.

One look and I was trembling, throbbing and aching for a release.

I reached for the elastic on my leggings, but Leo shook his head. "Let me."

He walked, with purposeful, tortuously slow strides, to the foot of the bed, where he planted a knee and came onto the mattress, his skilled hands sliding under the hem of my sweater to find the elastic waistband.

It shouldn't have been sexy. I felt exactly the opposite of attractive at the moment. But watching the lust in his eyes, the appreciation, as he stripped me out of my clothes made my breath hitch. His eyes appreciated every inch of my bare skin.

"Sit up." Leo stretched out a hand to take mine, helping me up enough so he could push my sweater up and drag it over my head. Then with a quick flick, he unclasped my bra and tossed it to the floor.

"Lie back."

I obeyed, my hair spilling around my shoulders.

Whatever insecurities I had about my pregnant body vanished under his rough touch as his fingers moved up my thighs.

This was the Leo I remembered—the lover. Not the asshole who'd yelled at me or the man who'd asked me to leave town. This was my Leo, the bossy, seductive man who was in complete control.

He showed more gentleness tonight than our time before. He kissed me deeper. He caressed and toyed, letting his hands explore with agonizing patience.

Maybe one day I'd stop comparing this to the time before. Maybe not. That night had been branded onto my memory.

Leo tore his lips from mine, letting them trail across my cheek to my ear. He took the lobe between his teeth, giving it a nip before dropping his mouth to my neck. He sucked, hard. He licked and kissed, and tomorrow I'd have a mark.

His hands came to my swollen breasts, cupping them in his hands as he shifted, sitting up and kneeling between my legs. The movement forced my thighs apart and exposed my center. It brought my belly between us.

We couldn't ignore it. *He* couldn't ignore it.

Leo stared at it, letting his hands glide over the curve. "I didn't expect this."

"Expect what?" The baby?

His hands came to my thighs. "You're beautiful. So fucking beautiful, Cass. I have wanted this for so damn long."

Before I could even make sense of those words, Leo positioned himself at my entrance. Then, bare, he slid deep.

"Oh, God." My back arched and a mewl escaped my lips. The stretch, the sensitivity. This was definitely not like the time before. I was close to coming apart and we'd barely started.

"Fuck, you feel good, Firecracker."

I relaxed into the pillow, loving the feel of Leo's hands gripping my hips and tilting them to the right angle. His fingers dug in so hard, he might leave bruises.

That snapped me out of my haze and my eyes flew to his. "You're hurt."

He shook his head, pulled out and glided inside, this time going impossibly deep. "This is the best I've felt in months."

A lock of blond hair fell forward as he moved with every measured stroke. If he was in pain, he didn't show it. There was nothing but desire and heat and ecstasy. Pure ecstasy as he brought us together, thrust after thrust. There was just enough force behind his hips to make me gasp when the root of his cock brushed against my clit.

My breasts swayed, bouncing slightly with his rhythm. My hands fisted the comforter beneath my back. The build seemed to double each time Leo's cock hit the right spot, until there was nothing I could do but surrender.

"Leo," I cried as wave after wave crashed over me. White stars broke behind my eyes. My toes curled and my limbs trembled.

Pulse after pulse, he held on to me, not letting up until the aftershocks eased and I dared to open my eyes. This had to be a dream.

A fantasy. I soaked it in, watching in rapture as Leo

fucked me. His tattoos were nearly colorless in the dark. With his unkempt hair and that sexy goatee, he was like my own personal devil, here to corrupt me and sweep me away. He hissed as he moved, taking his lower lip between his teeth. Then his shoulders went taut, his hands gripped tighter, and he slammed into me once more, pouring his release inside as he came with a rumbled groan.

Neither of us moved as we regained our breaths. Leo dragged a hand through his hair, shoving the strands out of his face.

"That was . . ." He pulled out and collapsed by my side. Then he tossed an arm over my chest, hauling my back into his front. "Was I too rough?"

"No." I sank into his embrace.

"Good." He kissed my bare shoulder, and with me tucked into his arms, he fell asleep.

I fell soon after.

Maybe, despite my better judgment, I'd fallen months ago.

CHAPTER ELEVEN

LEO

A horn beeped outside, and I looked up from my project to see Bryce and Dash's SUV in the driveway.

I grabbed the cleaning cloth I'd been using to wipe down the top of the desk and shoved it in my back pocket, then headed for the front door. The air bit into my arms as I met Cass by the rear side door and helped her out.

"How was it?" I asked.

"Wonderful." She smiled. "You have incredible friends."

"We're your friends too." Bryce climbed out and shot me a smirk. "We like Cass more than you. We took a vote at the shower. It was unanimous."

"I voted with the women," Dash said.

"Incredible friends," I deadpanned with a grin. "Do we need to bring anything in?"

"A lot," Cass said. "Too much."

"Pfft." Bryce scoffed. "This is your first baby. It's part of the deal to get swamped with gifts at your baby shower."

"Thank you."

"It's our pleasure."

Cass started for the back of the rig, but I caught her elbow. "Head on in. I'll get this."

The sweet smile she gave me was one I'd seen a lot in the past two weeks. Normally, I'd kiss her for it. Except with Bryce and Dash here, that kiss would have to wait. Cass and I had landed on an unspoken agreement.

We didn't talk about the sex. With each other and certainly not with others.

Though there had been a lot of sex. A lot. It had been the best damn time I'd ever had with a woman.

Cass had been working long hours, trying to finish up on a transcription project before the baby was born. I'd come home from the garage and usually find her typing at her laptop. She'd put it away and we'd have dinner together. Darkness would fall and we'd disappear into my bedroom, spending hours worshiping each other's bodies until she fell asleep.

She always fell asleep first. Maybe it was the pregnancy, but by nine o'clock, she'd be conked out.

For too many years, my nights had started at nine, so while she slept, I'd watch TV and wonder what was happening at The Betsy. Except last night, when I'd started on a project for Cass.

Dash passed me with his arms loaded with gift bags all in varying shades of pink.

"Holy shit," I said, joining Bryce at the back of the SUV. "Overboard much?"

"Shut it. There were a lot of people there, which means a lot of gifts. Kids require stuff. Something you'll figure out soon enough."

Along with Bryce, Genevieve, Presley and Scarlett, Cass had invited her aunts and cousins to the shower. Claudia, of course, had helped with the planning and she'd invited a few friends who'd known Cass since she was a kid.

I hadn't realized until Cass had shown me her invite list just how much family she had in Clifton Forge. Who knew what they all thought of me—probably nothing good.

The Clines ran with one crowd in town. I ran with another. Cass was the bridge between those worlds, and if I were a better man, I'd burn that bridge to the ground and set her free.

"How are you doing?" Bryce asked as we each began looping bags over our arms.

"Good."

"How are things with Cass?"

"Also good."

She gave me a small smile. "She's sweet. She's young but not naïve. She's got a little fire to her too."

"Yes, she does." Bryce had no idea. I'd been stoking that fire with my bare hands the past two weeks.

"Has she talked about the Warriors at all? The kidnapping?"

"No. Why?"

"Claudia pulled me aside today. She's worried. Cass hasn't talked about it with anyone. She's trying not to press but . . . Scarlett told me what happened. Talking from experience here, being taken from your home messes with your head."

Bryce had been kidnapped years ago by Marcus Wagner. It had been part of his scheme to ruin Draven's life. Marcus had taken Genevieve too, planning to kill them both in the mountains to start a war between us and the Warriors.

"She can't keep that inside, Leo. It will haunt her."

I blew out a deep breath and nodded. "I'll talk to her."

"Thanks." Bryce took her load to the house and I followed behind.

It took us one more trip to empty out the SUV and pile everything into the living room. "That's a lot of pink."

"I'm so glad I had boys." Dash clapped me on the shoulder. "We'll get out of here. I'm going to The Betsy for a beer tonight."

"Oh, you are?" Bryce raised an eyebrow.

"Baby, I earned it. Did you hear a peep from me or the boys today during your party?"

"You left. You took them to the garage."

"Exactly."

She rolled her eyes and laughed, then went to hug Cass goodbye.

"Assume I'll see you tonight?" Dash asked as I walked him to the door.

"Uh . . . yeah." Why not? I hadn't been out in weeks. Cass would fall asleep and I could go have a beer. Play pool. Catch up.

"Thank you, again," Cass told Bryce as they came to the entryway.

"You're welcome. See you soon." Bryce smiled, then took Dash's hand to leave for home.

Cass sagged against the wall as I shut the door. "That was fun, but I'm so tired. My cheeks hurt from smiling."

I walked over and put my palms on her face, gently rubbing her jaw with my thumbs. "Glad you had a good time."

"Your friends really are special. They went all out with the food and mocktails and gifts."

"Like it or not, you're with the Kings now. We're pretty tight and we keep it that way."

"I like it." She smiled and closed her eyes. "I think I'm going to take a nap."

"'Kay. Want to show you something first." I took her hand and pulled her toward the empty room beside hers.

Though it was no longer empty.

The second Dash and Bryce had come over to pick her up, I'd gotten to work, assembling the bookshelves and hauling in the desk that I'd stashed in the garage last week.

I tugged Cass to the doorway and nodded for her to take a look inside. "So you don't have to work at the table."

"Leo." Her hands came to her open mouth as she took it all in. She walked past me to the desk, running her hands over the smooth wooden surface and the waterfall edges. The walls in this room were a deep green so I'd gone for a whitewashed wood to brighten it up.

Scarlett's chatter about decorating had sunk in.

"I can't believe you did this." Cass's eyes flooded and tears dripped down her beautiful face.

"Hey." I crossed the room and wrapped her in my arms. "Why the tears?"

"Because I'm hormonal." She buried her face in my shoulder, taking a moment to pull it together. Then she sniffled and stood straight. "Sorry."

"Don't be." I tucked a lock of hair behind her ear and dropped my lips to hers.

She leaned in, sucking my tongue into her mouth. Her fingers threaded through my hair, tugging hard. Then I took over, diving in for what was mine.

I kissed her exactly the way she deserved to be kissed— with everything a man had.

Cass was breathless by the time we broke apart and that nap time would have to wait. I picked her up and set her on the desk, then planted a hand over her heart and eased her onto her back.

"Did I tell you I like this dress?"

She shook her head, a smile at the corner of her mouth as her thick, silky hair spread behind her. "Why do you like it?"

I grinned and slipped my hands under the hem to tug off her panties. "Easy access."

She laughed and looked toward the window. "Are you going to shut the blinds?"

"Nope. I'm going to fuck you on your new desk and if the neighbors happen to look across the street, then they'll get a show."

"Oh my God." She laughed and put her hands over her face. "You know that my parents know one of the couples who live on this street."

"Babe, don't talk about your parents when I'm hard."

She laughed again but the second I slipped a finger through her glistening folds, the time for joking around was over. Cass whimpered as I plunged in, circling her twice before pulling out. Then I unbuckled my belt and unzipped my jeans, taking out my cock to drag through her center.

"Leo," she moaned, arching to get closer.

I shoved her dress up higher as I eased inside with a slow stroke, planting myself deep. "Fuck, you feel good."

"Move."

I gave myself another moment to savor the flutter of her inner walls, then I eased out only to slam in again.

Cass gasped and a visible shudder ran down her arms.

It was never enough. Being inside her never lasted long enough.

I craved more. She demanded it.

This was my firecracker. This was the woman who came

alive in my hands. She might tease, but she didn't give a shit if the windows were uncovered because all she wanted was me.

"Hold on."

She nodded and gripped the edge of the desk. Then I pounded into her, the slapping of our skin echoing in the room. Her whimpers and moans only drove me on faster as I held her thighs apart, pinning her at just the right angle until her body trembled and her head pressed into the wood at her back, arching her throat as she came on a cry.

I squeezed my eyes shut and let go, pouring inside of her until I was wrung out. After the white spots cleared, I glanced at the window. As I suspected, an empty street. But I covered her up anyway, draping the dress over her legs and sliding out to tuck myself away.

"Come here." I held out a hand and helped her up.

Her hair was everywhere, draped down her shoulders and the sleeves of her black dress. I combed it away as she relaxed into my touch, sated and sleepy.

With her hair pulled away, I let my hands drift to her ribs, splaying across her belly.

It was easier now, touching her. I'd even felt the baby kick a few nights ago and if Cass had been awake, she would have seen me have a moment of amazement followed by one of sheer panic.

I wasn't ready to be a father. That hadn't changed. I didn't know what the fuck I was doing. Maybe most fathers didn't, and they were just better at pretending than I was.

Instead of dealing with it, trying to figure it out, I focused on what I knew.

Sex.

Sex was easy. Sex was uncomplicated. Sex was fun. Sex with Cass was out of this damn world.

Getting lost in her was natural, like falling asleep. The rest . . . I'd deal with it next month. The baby wasn't coming until March. I had time, right?

"Want that nap?" I asked.

"Not yet. I think I'll move some books in here and try to make it until seven. Then just crash for the night."

"I'll help."

We spent the next few hours setting up her office. Over the past month since she'd moved in, more and more things had appeared. Mostly deliveries from her parents. I was rarely here for those. Dale and Claudia usually came over when I was at work, on their respective lunch breaks or at five, when I was usually still at the garage.

Avoiding them was better. They didn't like or trust me—not that I blamed them. They didn't want Cass living here, and I doubted they had any idea that we were having sex. Dale would have lost his shit over that.

We'd have to figure it all out eventually. When the baby came, we couldn't keep dodging each other, but again . . . I'd deal with it next month.

"We need to pick a room for the nursery," Cass said as we returned to the living room and the sea of pink gifts.

I'd forgotten about the mess. "Wherever you want."

"You don't have an opinion."

"Not really."

"Okay," she drawled. "Then probably across from my room so it's easy for me to get there in the middle of the night."

Meaning she wouldn't be sleeping in my bed after the baby came. "What is all of this stuff? Do you need so much?"

"Yes, according to my Google research and what most of the women told me at the shower today. Bottles. Diapers. Towels. Clothes. My mom bought us a car seat and my aunts all chipped in for the crib and changing table I wanted. They're getting delivered tomorrow. Those are the necessities."

"The kid needs her own trash can?"

"I guess it helps contain the smell."

"Fucking great," I muttered. How the hell did you even change a diaper?

Cass frowned. "You don't have to help. I'll take care of this. Just like I'll take care of *the kid*."

And now she was pissed. *Christ.* "Sorry."

She waved me away. "It's fine."

God, I hated that word. Why couldn't she see how hard I was trying? Why couldn't she see that I was walking blind here? Before I got pissed, it was time to go. The last thing I wanted was a fight.

"I'm going to go meet Dash for a beer."

Shock flashed on her face for a second, then she blinked and nodded. "Fine."

Another fine.

"Why don't you come too?"

"To the bar?"

"Well . . . yeah." It wasn't like she hadn't gone there before.

Cass stared at me like I'd just asked her to fly to the moon. "No, thanks."

"Fine." That damn word was rubbing off. I brushed a kiss to her cheek and headed for the door. "See ya later."

The air was cold as I jogged to my truck, in such a hurry to escape the explosion of all things baby and an argument with Cass that I'd grabbed my keys but not a coat. Lucky for me, my new truck had heated seats.

After the accident, it hadn't taken me long to heal up from the minor bruises. I'd gone to a dealership two days later and bought the newest model Chevy on the lot, complete with all the embellishments. Chrome running boards. Custom stereo system. Tinted windows so dark they weren't exactly street legal. The exterior was black as midnight, and it had the best engine on the market.

My bike was top of the line. My truck should be too. The old one, shit brakes and all, was now scrap metal. I'd sent it straight from the towing company who'd collected it after the accident to the local junkyard.

I sat behind the wheel, staring at the house. A light turned on from Cass's side, not her bedroom but the other room. My hand hovered over the ignition.

Inside was a beautiful woman who had dealt with a lot of my shit. I didn't know how to stop screwing up. Maybe Dash would have some advice.

The drive to The Betsy seemed different than it had two weeks ago, and it had nothing to do with the new truck. It was guilt. Every mile, every turn of the wheels, and I knew I was heading in the wrong direction.

"Goddamn it."

Cass was at home, unpacking and setting up a nursery for the baby—our baby—and I was off to the bar. But she could have come along. We could have had a little fun, then come home and the baby shit could have waited until tomorrow.

It was probably for the best. The crowd on a Saturday could get wild and Cass was tired. I'd go have some beers. Spend time with Dash and call Emmett down. Then I'd come home after Cass had fallen asleep, and tomorrow, hopefully, she wouldn't be pissed.

The parking lot wasn't full when I got to the bar, but it was still early. Most Saturdays didn't get started until eight or nine. But I spotted two familiar trucks—Dash's and Emmett's. They were the only company I needed.

"Is that Leo Winter?" Paul squinted, pretending to make out my face. "We'd thought you died."

I chuckled and strode to the bar to shake my favorite bartender's hand. "Still alive."

"How's it going?" he asked.

"Not bad. Been busy."

"Beer or whiskey?"

"Tequila," Emmett answered for me, coming up to my side and handing over a pool cue. "We're getting drunk tonight."

"Sounds good to me." Maybe after a few shots the guilt of leaving Cass behind would disappear.

"Think Cass will be our DD tonight? Or do we call Pres?"

"I'm sure as hell not calling Cass to drive here and pick my drunk ass up."

Emmett nodded. "And I'm scared of Pres these days. She almost bit my head off yesterday when I didn't rinse out the sink after dumping the last swig of my coffee."

"Cab." Dash came over. "We're all getting drunk and calling cabs."

Paul lined up six shot glasses on the bar and poured his finest tequila into each. "You guys want to cash out each time or start a tab?"

"Tab," the three of us answered in unison, picking up a shot.

"Cheers, boys." I raised my glass, then tipped it to my lips.

By the time the bar was full of people laughing and drinking and dancing to the loud music, I'd lost count of how many shots I'd taken.

"I'm out." Dash slid off his stool at the table where the three of us had been sitting for hours after giving up on pool. "I'm leaving while I can still stand up and get it up. The boys should be in bed by now. I've got a woman at home who needs an orgasm or two."

Guilt pinched hard in my chest. No matter how many shots I'd had, it just wouldn't go away.

This wasn't where I was supposed to be. I'd fucked up. I should be at home with Cass.

"I'd better go too," I said but before I could stand up, Emmett put his hand on my shoulder.

"What? It's not even nine o'clock. One more drink. Then we can share a cab."

I sighed. "'Kay. One more."

He stood and went to the bar as Dash walked for the door, giving me a wave before disappearing outside to call a cab or flag the ones that hung close to The Betsy on Saturday nights.

A delicate hand snaked up my shoulder.

I flinched away from the touch, turning.

A brunette was at my side. She'd been eyeing me from her own table for the past hour—apparently not taking the hint that I wasn't interested. "Hey, Leo."

"Hey." I shifted my shoulder, trying to dislodge her hand.

But instead of moving away, she took it as an opening to move in closer, squeezing in between me and the table and pressing her hip against my thigh. "Having fun tonight?"

"Yeah." I focused on her face, trying to figure out if I'd hooked up with her before. She was familiar but I'd had a lot to drink and her features were a bit fuzzy. She looked like every other woman. Not Cass.

"Here you go." Emmett put four shots on the table just as a blonde latched herself to his side.

These chicks must have been waiting for Dash to leave, probably because he would have told them to fuck off.

"Hey, baby," the blonde purred to Emmett.

"Hey." He shot me a smirk and put his arm around her shoulder. "What's your name again?"

She stood on her toes, motioning him closer. Whatever it was that she whispered in his ear made him laugh. He drained two of the shots, one after the other, then sealed his lips over hers.

"So much for sharing a cab," I called to his back as he steered the blonde toward the door.

"I guess it's just the two of us." The brunette ran her long fingernails up my thigh, going for my zipper.

I clamped a hand over hers, stopping it before she could touch my cock.

She took it the wrong way because when I turned to tell her to get lost, she pressed her mouth to mine, dragging her tongue across my lower lip. She pulled away before I could stop her, then leaned in toward my ear. "I'll share your cab."

"Nah. Sorry, sweetheart." I shoved her hand away. "Not interested tonight."

"Aw." She pouted and took the stool where Emmett had been sitting. "Buy me a drink at least?"

"Knock yourself out." I motioned toward the shots, then

dug out my phone to call for a cab, seeing a missed call on the screen.

Cass had called just a few minutes ago and I breathed a long sigh. She couldn't be that pissed if she'd called me, right? The music and noise from the crowd were deafening but the second I walked outside, I'd call her back.

"Take yours too," the brunette whined, sliding the other shot glass closer.

"Huh?" I looked up.

She motioned to the shot. "Your drink."

I set my phone aside and frowned, but took the glass, clicked the rim to hers and swallowed the tequila in a gulp. "Thanks. Have a good night."

Before she could stop me, I shoved away from the table and walked for the door. Three feet away, a thick, flabby arm came around my shoulders.

"Leo! Come here a sec." Bobby hauled me to where he was talking to a group of guys I knew because they all worked at the fire department.

We shook hands and bullshitted for a while, but then Bobby began to grate on my nerves. He was one of the loud and boisterous regulars who I played pool with often. A good guy when he wasn't smashed, which was not tonight.

He leaned in too close as he spoke, and I eased back, stumbling on a crack in the floor. My head was spinning too fast. My eyes crossed as I tried to focus on his face. *Shit.* How many shots had we had? I must have lost count if I was this drunk.

"I gotta go, Bobby." I walked away. Maybe some air would clear my head.

It didn't. One step into the parking lot and I nearly dropped to my knees. The strength in my legs was gone. My eyes struggled to focus and I was seeing double, but I managed to set my feet on a path to my truck.

I'd crash inside. I'd call a cab when I sobered up a bit. Where was my phone?

I didn't remember reaching the truck's door. I didn't remember crawling inside.

All I remembered was staring through the windshield as my truck rolled down the road, wondering what the fuck had been in that last shot.

And who the fuck was driving me.

CHAPTER TWELVE

LEO

I flinched awake and winced at the pain in my skull. "Fuck."

Squeezing my eyes shut, I brought my hands to my temples and pressed hard.

The bed moved at my side. Despite the pain, I forced my eyes open, expecting Cass.

Not Cass.

The brunette from last night smiled into her pillow. "Morning."

No. No, no, no. This wasn't fucking happening.

I shot out of bed, swaying at the sudden movement, then I took in the strange room. "Where are we?"

"My place, baby."

The air skated over my naked body. Where were my clothes? My eyes weren't working right as I searched the floor. They were fuzzy and heavy, like I was crawling out of a nightmare. But I found one of my boots and with them, my jeans. I swiped them up and shoved them on.

"How'd I get here?"

"I drove us." She propped up on an elbow, baring a breast. "Come back to bed."

Where was my shirt? I spotted it beside my other boot and boxers.

I shoved the boxers in the back pocket of my jeans and pulled on my T-shirt. "Where are my keys?"

She sat up and pouted, this time letting both of her tits free of the sheets. "Do you really need your keys this minute? Let's have some fun first."

"Bitch, where are my keys?" I roared.

She jerked before pointing to the nightstand.

I swiped them up and moved to pull on my boots, doing my best to balance even though the whole world seemed to be spinning in the wrong direction. Then I strode for the door, but I stopped myself before leaving, facing the woman as my heart beat so hard it was like someone was taking a baseball bat to my chest.

"Did we fuck?"

She shot me a glare and pulled the sheet up to cover herself, but she didn't answer.

"Did we fuck?" I repeated.

She jutted out her chin.

"Answer the question." I walked toward the bed, looming over the foot. "This is not the time to play games with me, understand? Did. We. Fuck?"

She dropped her gaze to the cream quilt and shook her head. "No."

A wave of relief nearly dropped me to the floor. "How'd I get undressed?"

"I helped you inside and took off your clothes. You passed out."

"Where's my truck?"

"In the driveway."

With that, I marched out of her house, only taking one wrong turn before I found the front door and walked out into the blinding sunshine.

"Christ." I was going to vomit. And I did. I shuffled to a snowbank off the woman's driveway and emptied the limited contents of my stomach. Wiping my mouth dry, I stood straight and went to my truck, climbing inside.

The doors were unlocked. My wallet was in the passenger seat along with my phone.

I swiped it up and checked the screen. Seven missed calls this morning. Two from Dash. Two from Emmett. Three from Presley, plus a text.

Fix this.

"Shit."

No need to call her and find out what I needed to fix. I tossed the phone aside and turned on the truck. It was almost noon. *Son of a bitch.* Cass was going to rip my balls off, and I was going to let her.

The drive home was painful, not just because my heart was still pounding in sync with my head. This wasn't just drunk and hungover. My arms were too heavy. My legs too numb. I was sluggish and stuck in a haze. Last night had been a complete blackout.

I hadn't blacked out since the clubhouse days. That had been in my early twenties when some of the brothers had bought laced weed and we'd had a hell of a party. The next morning I'd woken up with two women in my bed.

"Fuck. Fuck. Fuck."

How could I have been so goddamn stupid? Why hadn't I just gone home? Why had I left in the first place? I rolled the window down, needing some air, otherwise I'd be puking again.

This was the worst morning of my life. Hands down. In all my years, I'd never felt so ashamed. Even the time I'd woken up in jail because I'd gotten into a bar fight with a sixty-something-year-old man who'd kicked my ass at pool and—after I'd run my mouth—just kicked my ass, period.

What the hell had I been thinking last night? At least I hadn't gotten behind the wheel and killed someone else or myself. A damn miracle. That, and the fact that I hadn't screwed that woman.

I wouldn't have been able to live with myself, let alone face Cass.

Turning down my street, I sucked in a deep breath as the house came into view. Cass's car wasn't in the driveway. *Shit.* That would at least give me a chance to take a quick shower and wash off that woman's scent. It clung to my skin like a gray film.

The house was eerily quiet when I walked inside and punched in the code on the alarm panel. It smelled like Cass, fresh and sweet and . . . home.

Shower. Then groveling. Weeks of groveling.

I hurried to my bedroom, stripping my clothes. They'd go in the trash, not the hamper. I'd never wear those jeans or T-shirt again. Then I went to the master bathroom and turned on the shower to a punishing temperature. My skin was raw and red by the time I stepped out and toweled off. I dressed and went to the kitchen for an energy drink, still not feeling like myself but more alert than I had been before the shower.

The first gulp from the can burned but I chugged it anyway, only stopping when a note on the counter caught my eye. I picked it up, my stomach plummeting as I took in Cass's neat handwriting.

I read it once. Then twice. Then the energy drink went sailing across the room, crashing into a wall and splattering its greenish-yellow liquid over my floor.

"Fuck!" I shouted, my throat burning as I mentally replayed her written words.

THIS IS HARDER *than I thought it would be. I need some space. I need some distance. I need to decide how you're going to fit into our lives. I'll be staying with my parents until the baby is born. My dad will come and get the rest of my things. I'll call you when I go into labor in case you want to be at the hospital. But until then, please respect my decision. Please give me time to think.*

SHE WANTED to think about how I fit into her life. All this time, she'd left the door wide open. She'd given me time to get my head around this, and whatever I wanted, she'd never once said no. Until now.

Cass had slammed the door closed just when I'd finally been ready to walk inside. When I'd figured out it was time to pull my shit together. When I'd realized that the only woman I wanted was her.

I took the note with me as I walked toward her bedroom. My footsteps were heavy and the knot in my gut twisted as I approached the door. One glance inside and I wanted to vomit again.

The closet was open and empty. The nightstand was

missing her phone charger and green apple lip balm. The candle on the dresser was gone.

I shoved off the doorframe and went to the office. Her books were still on their shelves from where we'd put them yesterday, but her laptop was nowhere to be seen.

"Damn it." I closed my eyes and ran a hand over my face. She had to come back for the books, right? And what about the baby's stuff?

The nursery. I spun around, going for the room across the hallway.

Cass had unpacked the gifts last night after I'd left for The Betsy. The new trash can was in the corner. The car seat was set beside a wall. There were piles of folded clothes and baby blankets on the carpet.

She'd taken her own things but had left everything for the baby. What did that mean? When had she left?

I looked at the note clutched in my hand and read it again, one word jumping off the page. *Space.* She wanted space.

"Fuck it." She wasn't getting space or distance or time. She didn't get to make this decision on her own. She needed to hear my apology, and I wanted to understand why she'd stayed to unpack, only to leave awhile later. Was it because I hadn't come home?

With my keys in hand and that note crumpled in a fist, I stormed out of the house and to my truck. I sped down the block, only pausing long enough at the stop sign to pull up Emmett's name.

"Hey," he answered. "Tried calling you. Suspect you know this, but I guess Cass moved out."

"I know." I gritted my teeth. "Found out when I got home. How'd you hear?"

"Scarlett. She saw Cass pull up with her car loaded this morning, then called Pres, who called Bryce, who called Genevieve."

Fix it. These women were going to drive me insane.

"Goddamn it." I didn't need them in the middle of this.

"Look, I need to know. Did you black out last night?"

"Black out? No."

"I think that bitch who was talking to me put something in my drink."

"What the fuck? Are you serious?"

"Yeah. I don't remember anything. After you left, she took one of the shots you bought and I took the other. I got up and talked to Bobby and some of the guys at the fire department for a while, then got dizzy. Went outside to get in the truck and sleep it off. Woke up this morning naked in that chick's bed."

"Shit."

"Yeah. Nothing happened. Still." First, I had to convince Cass that it was the truth. There'd been no evidence of sex on my body when I'd climbed into the shower, so I was choosing to believe the brunette that we hadn't had sex. Next, I had to get Cass to forgive me for being an epic dumbass.

"She drove my truck to her place, and I passed out," I said. "We didn't have that much to drink, right?"

"No way. I've seen you drink three times as many shots in a night and still walk through your front door."

Then she had drugged me. "I gotta go."

"What are you going to do about the woman?"

"Before I do anything, I need to talk to Cass. Then I'll deal with the woman."

"Don't get thrown in jail."

185

"No promises," I said, ending the call.

I'd never hit a woman in my life and before today, I'd never had the urge. Not that I'd cross that line, but that brunette was going to pay for this. She was going to pay for hurting Cass and fucking up the good thing we'd had going. The blame started with me. But the brunette had played her part and she'd be dealt with.

The trip across town was spent trying to keep my rage in check. It would do me no good to show up at Dale and Claudia's place pissed off.

Cass's car was in front of the garage and I parked behind it, then got out and hustled to the front porch.

I didn't even get the chance to knock or ring the bell when the door flung open and a furious Dale came at me with his fist raised.

"Whoa." I held up my hands and backed up. I wasn't in the mood to take another punch from Cass's father, though I deserved it. "I just want to see Cass."

"Get the fuck off my property."

"Dale." I sucked in a breath. "You're misunderstanding this."

"Am I?" He dropped his arm by his side. "Because the way I understand it is that you're too busy screwing around to treat my daughter with the respect she deserves."

"I haven't been screwing around."

"And you're a liar."

My fists balled at my sides. "Let me just talk to Cass and explain this. Five minutes." That was all the time I needed to apologize and tell her that I'd been fucking drugged last night.

"No." He crossed his arms over his chest. "She doesn't want to see you."

186

"Please." I didn't beg. Ever. But for Cass, I'd swallow my pride. "I care about your daughter."

"You have a funny way of showing it, leaving her each night for The Betsy."

It hadn't been each night, but I wasn't going to argue details. "Dale, please."

He didn't budge. Seconds ticked by and all he did was breathe. Then he uncrossed his arms. His shoulders slumped. And the anger on his face faded, leaving only worry. Worry for his daughter because she was tied up with me.

"You're not good enough for my daughter."

"I know," I whispered.

"My granddaughter deserves better than you."

On second thought, I wish he had punched me. The truth hit harder and deeper than any physical blow. That baby girl deserved a fuck of a lot better than me as her father.

"I can't walk away." I'd tried. I knew I should let them go, but I couldn't walk away.

"She doesn't want to talk to you. She gave you a second chance that you hadn't earned, but my Cassie has a big heart. You blew it."

"I know that too."

"This is her decision. If she wants to talk, she knows where to find you. Don't come back here until she invites you. Or I'll kill you myself."

I'd been threatened with death before. I recognized the difference between the men who idly tossed those words around and the men who had the spine to see it through. Dale meant it.

"Will you tell her that I'm sorry?"

Dale's expression hardened to stone.

"I am sorry." I never should have left home last night.

He stepped back and slammed the door in my face.

I waited, giving myself a minute to hope that Cass would show, but the door stayed closed. The winter chill was ice against my skin, leaving me no choice but to get in my truck and drive away.

Dale was right. About all of it. None of this would have happened if I hadn't gotten spooked by the idea of a nursery. Cass would still be where she belonged, at home, if I had manned the fuck up and dealt with this.

Grow up, Leo.

Presley's voice sounded a lot like my own in the back of my head.

Yeah, it was time to grow up. No more living life one day at a time, working when I wanted the money or was bored. No more cutting out of town on a long ride when I needed freedom. No more partying to fill in the blanks.

There was too much blank.

The Tin King Motorcycle Club had been my purpose for so many years, now that they were gone, now that Draven was gone, there was too much blank.

Until Cass.

The past two weeks with her, the hole in my life where the club had once been hadn't felt so vast. She'd filled it with that pretty smile. With her eyes. Her laugh. Her body. Her heart.

My body ached as I drove across town. The Betsy was calling and it would be so easy to hit the bar and get piss drunk today. But vengeance was top of mind. I'd take it first, then get wasted.

Growing up would have to wait until tomorrow.

The drive toward the brunette's house took ten minutes.

It was a damn miracle I'd been paying enough attention this morning to remember which neighborhood and house was hers. If not for the snowbank where I'd puked, I might have gotten the wrong place since every home on the street was sided in nearly the same shade of tan.

I pounded on her door and rang the doorbell. Twice.

Her footsteps sounded and when she opened it, she kept the safety chain locked. "Uh . . . hey, Leo. What are you doing here?"

"Can't find my wallet," I lied.

"Oh." She closed the door and the chain slid free before she waved me inside. "Come on in."

I shook my head. "What did you put in my drink?"

Her face paled and she tried to shut the door again, but I shoved my boot in the way. "I'll call the cops."

"You do that. We can all sit down and have a nice chat about how I ended up blacked out in your bed."

She pulled her bottom lip between her teeth, then the resolve on her face crumpled. "It was only supposed to loosen you up."

Damn. I fucking knew it. "You did it so I'd have sex with you?"

"No. I was talking to this guy at the bar. He had a vial of G and said he'd pay me five hundred bucks to slip it in your drink."

Motherfucker. Rage, as hot as molten lava, spread through my veins.

"It was only supposed to relax you." The brunette had the decency to look sorry. "I followed you outside when you left. You got in your truck and it looked like you were going to drive home, but I talked you into letting me drive instead. And I brought us here."

Where she'd stripped me naked. Was that the goal? To get me into bed with another woman so Cass would run out on me? That made no sense. No one knew about Cass and me. We'd kept that quiet. And the only person I knew who hated me enough to try and shove me into another woman's arms was Dale.

As much as he hated me, I couldn't see Cass's dad hiring this woman to drug me at The Betsy.

"Why? Why would he pay you to do this?"

"You'll have to ask him." She shrugged. "All I know is that I can make my rent this month."

"Who is he?"

"I don't know. Some guy."

I clenched my jaw. "Then what did he look like?"

"Not as tall as you. Not as big. Brown hair."

"That's it?"

She lifted a shoulder. "It was dark, and I was more interested in his money than the color of his eyes, okay? Are we done now?"

"Not yet." I pulled my phone from my back pocket and before she could turn away, I snapped a picture of her face. "Now we're done."

"Asshole." The moment I moved my foot, she slammed the door, but I was already gone.

I strode to my truck, then headed for The Betsy. My plan to get drunk was on hold until I had some answers. Who would want me drugged? The Warriors?

If they wanted me dead, there were a lot better ways to do it than roofie a drink. This didn't seem direct enough for them. It was too . . . slick. If Tucker Talbot was seeking revenge, he'd want us to know it was him.

This was too subtle.

"Hey," Paul greeted me when I walked through the door at the bar. "Good timing. I just opened and was about to turn on a game. Beer?"

"No, thanks, man. I actually need some help." I dug out my phone and pulled up the photo I'd taken of the brunette. "Recognize her?"

He leaned forward, narrowing his eyes. "I think she was here last night. Her and a blond friend."

That was the great thing about Paul. He worked here nearly every weekend and his memory was as sharp as cut glass. He might play the easygoing bartender, but he was actually buying the owner out. Not many people knew that Paul was a savvy businessman too.

And he paid attention to what went on in his bar.

"About last night . . ." I slid onto a stool and recanted what the brunette had told me.

Paul's jaw ticked. "I don't want that shit in my bar."

"Any chance you saw her talking to a guy last night? She doesn't know who it was who paid her. She said he had brown hair and wasn't quite as tall or big as me."

He shook his head. "It was busy last night. I did my best to keep an eye on what was happening, but you know how it goes."

"Any chance you had the cameras on?" I pointed to the camera in the corner of the room above the jukebox.

"No. They haven't been working lately so we just left them off. The ones in the parking lot are working. They might have caught something."

"Mind if I take a look?"

"Not at all. Give me some time to pull footage."

"Appreciate it." I knocked on the bar, then left, the desire to get drunk gone completely. Instead, I drove home, hating that it would be empty. Hating that I'd driven Cass away.

As much as I wanted to go to her house and beg her to come back to mine, I stayed the course. If someone had drugged me, for whatever reason, then it might not be safe for her with me at the moment.

I'd leave her alone, not only to respect her wishes, but also because until we dug through the security footage and found the bastard who'd messed with me last night, Cass was better off with her parents.

The moment I was parked in the driveway, I pulled out my phone and sent Cass a text.

I'm sorry.

Maybe Dale would deliver my message. Maybe not. I wasn't taking the chance.

Holding my breath, I stared at the screen, praying those little moving dots would appear. That she'd text me back. I waited five minutes and finally gave up.

There were two huge boxes stacked beside the door when I walked to the house. According to the labels on the cardboard, a changing table and a crib.

The gifts from Cass's aunts.

Since I didn't have anything else to do today, I hauled them inside.

And assembled them in the nursery.

CHAPTER THIRTEEN

CASSANDRA

I'm sorry.

"Sorry." I huffed and shoved a sweater onto a hanger. "He's sorry."

I'd gone through the entire gauntlet of ugly emotions in the past day. Shock. Embarrassment. Heartache. But after Leo's text, I'd landed firmly on anger. There was no sign of that storm blowing over.

"He doesn't get to be sorry." I hung up the sweater and went for another.

Yesterday, after I'd gotten to my parents' house, I hadn't had the energy to unpack my bags. Still in the embarrassment-slash-heartache phase, I'd curled up on the couch and cried for a solid hour. Then Leo had shown up and because Dad had left the door open when he'd gone out and threatened Leo's life—when would the humiliation end?—I'd heard their entire conversation. Leo sure brought out a violent streak in my father.

But death threats aside, everyone in Clifton Forge knew Dale Cline was harmless. Leo could have easily fought his way inside. Dad would have let him pass and deliver that apology in person. Instead, he'd left and I'd received that cop-out of a text an hour later.

I'm sorry.

Did that apology encompass all of his screwups? Was he sorry for going to the bar instead of staying home and helping with the nursery? Or was he sorry that he'd kissed another woman and spent the night with her? It had to be the former because he didn't know I'd seen him with that brunette.

Was this how it had been for months? Had I believed him, blindly, when he'd said I was his only one simply because I'd wanted so badly for it to be true?

I am a stupid woman.

My chin quivered and my eyes flooded. I tightened my hold on the fury before the embarrassment and heartache returned for a second unwelcome visit.

I'd fallen.

I'd fallen for Leo.

I'd fallen for his lies.

This was The Betsy's fault. Aiming my anger at the bar helped me get the tears under control as I reached for another shirt from my suitcase resting on the bed.

After Leo had left on Saturday, I'd started unpacking the gifts from the baby shower. Even then, I hadn't been angry at him. Disappointed, yes. But not angry. Yet another in the long, long line of second, third, fourth, twentieth chances I'd given Leo.

I'd unpacked gifts, the entire time making mental excuses for him.

Leo didn't hesitate to touch my belly anymore. That was something, right? Granted it was always during sex, but still. A touch meant something, didn't it?

He'd come to every one of my checkups and every time he heard the drum of the baby's heartbeat, his eyes softened. When I'd hung an ultrasound photo on the fridge, he hadn't asked me to take it down.

Progress. Baby steps.

So what if he wasn't quite ready to decorate a nursery? A baby's room, in his home, was a concept I'd give him time to accept because it meant she was no longer growing inside of me.

Soon, she'd be her own person with her own belongings who'd depend on us for everything. Thinking of that sort of responsibility was a lot for me to deal with, let alone Leo.

He wasn't ready.

But we had time to get him there.

It was the reason I'd delayed setting up the nursery in the first place. I'd known he wasn't ready. But time was passing quickly and she'd be here soon. If I was going to live at Leo's, then it was time to settle in and give the baby a room. And a name.

That was another topic I hadn't forced on Leo.

Another second chance.

Rather than tell Leo to grow up, I'd made excuses for his behavior.

After going through the gifts yesterday, I'd sat down in the living room to call Olive. She hadn't been able to make the shower, but she'd sent the cutest outfit for the baby. We'd ended up spending an hour talking about her doctoral program.

Olive's classes were a challenge. Her professors were brilliant. Her new roommates were fun and friendly. It was impossible not to feel a twinge of jealousy and longing. That was the life I'd had. The life I missed.

Olive was living my dream.

Maybe that was the reason I'd entertained her suggestion to go to The Betsy two nights ago.

I'd been honest with her about Leo and how we'd started sleeping together. Then I'd told her that he'd left for that damn bar for a night of fun.

Show him you're fun too. Show him he can have you and a social life.

Silly me. I'd thought he'd want me as part of his social life. At the very least, I could drive him home. Leo had invited me, after all. What use was a pregnant girlfriend if she didn't play the designated driver?

Except I wasn't his girlfriend.

Turns out, he didn't want me as part of his social life, and his invitation had been just another lie.

Olive's encouragement had worked, and I'd gone to The Betsy. It had taken me five minutes in the parking lot to work up the courage to walk inside. I'd been on my way in when Emmett had walked out with a blonde tucked under his arm. He hadn't noticed me.

I'd pushed through the door and scanned the crowd only to find Leo with another woman.

I couldn't get that brunette's face out of my mind. I couldn't stop seeing her kiss him. Seeing her hand on his leg and her body pressed against his.

"Ugh." I squeezed my eyes shut and pressed my fingers to my temple, willing that mental picture away.

"Hey. Are you okay?" Mom knocked and came into my room.

"Just a headache," I lied, opening my eyes and forcing a smile.

She came over and put her hand on my shoulder. "How are you?"

"Mad."

"Good."

Mom knew about Leo and the other woman. She also knew I'd been sleeping with him. There were aspects I'd keep from my father, but when Mom had come into my bedroom last night and asked for the truth, I hadn't held back a single detail.

"Your dad and I were talking last night. Over our lunch hour today, we'll go over to Leo's and get the baby's stuff from the nursery and whatever else you left behind."

I sighed and walked to the bed, slumping on the edge. My feet hurt. My back hurt. The heartburn felt permanent and Tums had become as necessary as peeing every five minutes. What I needed was a good night's rest.

I doubted I'd get one for a while.

In our short weeks together, my body had become accustomed to Leo's bed. It was soft and plush and warm, especially in his arms. Last night, brittle loneliness had settled into my bones and kept me awake.

"I don't want to be here." Damn those tears. Why wouldn't they go away? I swiped at my cheeks as Mom sat beside me, putting her arm around my back.

"I know."

"Why wasn't I enough?" I whispered.

"Oh, Cassie." She pulled me closer so I could rest my head on her shoulder. Then I stopped fighting the tears and let them fall.

Why did Leo need another woman? Why wasn't I enough? Was I too young for him? Was I not experienced enough in the bedroom? I'd thought the sex had been other-worldly but what did I know?

My experience with men was limited at best. I'd dated a couple of guys in college. I'd lost my virginity to my boyfriend freshman year of undergrad. We'd broken up two months later and the next day I'd seen him coming out of the dorm room across the hallway from mine.

It hadn't really bothered me because classwork had been my primary companion. My priority. Any guy who'd tried to get my attention hadn't really stood a chance. My studies were demanding, and I liked it that way. Structure and routine had been the foundation for my academic success.

Then Leo.

I'd fooled myself into thinking I was special. I wasn't. I was simply the girl who'd trapped him on accident.

"I wish I had answers for you, honey," Mom said. "I don't understand how he couldn't look at you and realize he'd found a treasure. I hate him for it."

"Don't hate him." The defense slipped out so fast I couldn't stop it. Here I was, protecting him again. When was I going to learn? Tigers like Leo didn't change their stripes.

"For the baby's sake, I won't." She kissed my hair. "I'm proud of you."

"Proud? What for? Having a one-night stand with a playboy biker, getting pregnant and throwing my dreams in the trash? I should have known better. I should have stayed focused. Stayed home."

"You're young. You wanted a night of fun. That's completely understandable. No one would blame you for that, especially given how hard you work."

"I miss school." I sighed. "This can't be the life you planned for me."

"No, it's not, but life doesn't always go as planned. Despite our best efforts. I'm proud of you for finding balance in the middle of a tornado. It will be okay."

"I hope you're right."

"I'm always right. Just ask your father," she teased.

"There's only a month left, maybe less if this little one comes early. Everything's about to change." And Leo wasn't the only one who was scared. "There are many single parents out there, but Mom, I don't know if I can do this on my own."

"Something tells me you won't have to."

Wait. Was she talking about Leo? How could she have faith in him after everything I'd told her yesterday? Maybe because, despite my best efforts, I couldn't smother that hope for him too.

Mom shifted and I sat up straight. "Why don't you give me the key to his house and the alarm code? I assume he's working today."

"Yeah, but he doesn't go in until later." Who knew how late he'd stayed out last night? Maybe he wasn't even home yet. Had he stayed with the brunette again?

"Well, if he's still home at noon, then he'll just have to deal with us being there too."

I put my hands on my belly, feeling the baby shift. We'd need her things. The diapers and creams and clothes. So why wasn't I digging through my purse this very second to give Mom the key?

Irrational, foolish hope.

"I appreciate that you'd go over there," I said. "Let's give it a few days first. That will give me time to make space here."

The truth was, I couldn't bring myself to make a clean

break.

For me. And the baby.

"I understand why you want to wait, but Cassie, you can't delay too long." Of course Mom would realize that this had nothing to do with shifting furniture or clearing out space in the house.

"If I'm not there, pushing him past his fears, they'll conquer him. He'll forget he has a daughter." He'd forget about me.

"Your dad doesn't think Leo deserves you."

"I know. I heard yesterday, remember?" I'd also heard Leo agree.

"Want to know what I think? He probably doesn't deserve you, not after all the mistakes he's made. The man sure isn't making it easy. But deserve you or not, Leo needs you. He just hasn't realized it yet."

"What if he never does?"

"You're not walking away from this empty-handed, honey." Mom placed her hand on my belly just in time to feel the baby shove an elbow or a knee or a foot into my side.

I smiled. "You always know what to say. Thanks."

"You're welcome." She kissed my hair again, then as I sat up straight, she stood. "I've got a bunch of meetings today but call me if you need anything."

"I will. I'm going to spend the day working too." The distraction of a task would keep my mind off Leo.

Waiting until Mom and Dad each left for work, I found my laptop and settled at the dining room table. I hadn't even had the chance to use the desk Leo had bought for me—for work.

Why would he go to that trouble for me but not help me set up the nursery for the baby? Why would he spend all day creating a space I could call my own, then go to the bar and score a hookup?

None of it made sense.

And after the day spent working, I still hadn't righted any of it in my mind.

The book I was transcribing was for an author I hadn't read before. It was only her second story, but it was engrossing and her writing, even dictated, was impeccable. At one point, I'd gotten so lost in her voice and tale that I hadn't realized my fingers had stopped moving over the keyboard.

Her story was about a nurse in the Civil War, living in Virginia. The nurse, Ester, was charged with attending to injured soldiers after General Robert E. Lee had surrendered his Confederate troops to the Union in 1865.

Ester's home burned down in the war and her only living relatives, a brother and father, had both been killed. Having had enough blood and death, she used what money she'd saved and the money her father had stowed in the family graveyard to leave Virginia. She set out West, hoping to find a new life in California after the Gold Rush.

The book was fiction but infused with history, the events accurate, the narrative addictive and the settings so descriptive I could close my eyes and be on the journey, sitting beside Ester in the covered wagon as it bounced and bumped along the California trail.

My plan for years had been to graduate with my PhD, then teach. One day, maybe I'd write nonfiction. Books that others might one day use when they were embarking on their own studies.

Yet with every paragraph of this addictive story, a longing for something new bloomed in my heart. Nonfiction in my field typically required a doctorate. But historical fiction did not.

What if I wrote a book like this?

The idea came to me so quickly that it startled me. I wouldn't need to pay for school or move to a college town, juggling a baby and my education.

What if I just . . . wrote a book?

As enthralled with Ester's story as I was, I put the transcription aside and spent the rest of my afternoon researching the various ways to publish a book.

Maybe that was putting the cart before the horse, but the urgency to explore this was so overwhelming that I couldn't concentrate on anything else. I was so busy making lists and jotting down follow-up questions that I nearly missed Leo's text message just after five o'clock.

All thoughts of writing and publishing vanished as I read the words on my phone.

I hate this.

My jaw dropped and the anger from earlier came back with a vengeance.

He hated this? Was he trying to make me feel guilty? Like I was the one to blame here? My fingers flew across the screen and before I could think better of it, I sent my reply.

What exactly do you hate? Me not being there to warm your bed at night? Don't you have a brunette for that?

Instead of replying, his name flashed with an incoming call.

"Leo, I asked you for space," I answered.

"Cassandra." His gravelly voice, full of remorse, went straight to my soul.

Damn it. I shouldn't have answered the phone. "What do you want?"

"We have a lot to talk about, babe. I don't want to do it over the phone. I'm sorry I went to the bar. I should have stayed and helped with the nursery. Just know I didn't betray you. I didn't cheat."

Lies. "You told me that you haven't been with anyone but me since the first time. I believed you then. I don't now." Not when I could see that woman's face so clearly. When I could see her lips pressed to his.

He blew out a long breath, the whoosh so loud I could practically feel his breath on my cheek. "I've never lied to you."

God, I wanted that to be true. But what I'd written to Leo in my note had been the truth. I needed time to think about the future and what would be best for this baby. I needed space to collect the pieces of my heart.

"Please . . . let me be," I whispered.

He was quiet on the other end of the line. The clock in the kitchen ticked louder and louder with every passing second. Until finally, he spoke. "I'll respect your decision. For now."

It took effort to pull the phone from my ear and end the call. Then I squeezed my eyes shut so I wouldn't cry. Because I really, *really* wanted to cry.

He'd respect my decision. He'd leave me alone.

He might be sorry. He might hate this.

But he hadn't asked me to come back home.

CHAPTER FOURTEEN

LEO

"Find out anything last night?" Emmett asked.

"Nothing." I swiped up a rag, wiping at the grease on my fingers.

I'd been working on the Firebird all day, enjoying a solo project and some time out of the paint booth for a change of pace. We'd brought it in from the back lot a few days ago and since, she'd had my focus. The car was going to be a beauty, especially now that she was getting some attention.

The list of jobs lined up on the board was long, but we had a small window while we waited on parts and payments and customers to make decisions, and when Dash had suggested the Firebird, I'd jumped at the chance to get my hands on her again.

I skimmed my finger over the side panel, imagining it in flaming orange. There were projects where the color in my mind's eye changed as we worked. I'd see the car differently as it was transformed. But not this one. It had to be that orange.

And if I had my way, this car would be mine too.

A gift to Cass.

It had been a month since she'd moved. An agonizing month. The only reason I hadn't insisted—begged—she come home was because we still hadn't figured out who the bastard was who'd paid that bitch to drug me. Or why. Though it hadn't been for lack of trying.

I'd gone to The Betsy nearly every night in the past month. It was the best way to find the guy and without Cass, it was too lonely to stay home. Each time I went to the bar, I'd have a few beers, ensuring each and every one of them was opened by Paul or the other bartenders in my sight. I'd play pool and pretend like it was just another night, meanwhile keeping watch in case the brunette came in again or anyone eyed me suspiciously.

The brunette hadn't shown. And for a month it had been nothing but familiar faces.

Emmett had scoured the security camera footage from the night I'd been drugged. He'd found Cass coming to the bar and racing away. Otherwise, there hadn't been anyone who'd matched the brunette's description that he or I hadn't already known.

Whoever had drugged me had snuck in and out without notice.

Or . . . the brunette had lied to me.

"Been thinking . . . maybe the brunette did it on her own." I sighed. "I don't think there was a guy who paid her." She'd seemed scared when I confronted her but hell, maybe she was a good actress.

"Yeah." Emmett rubbed at his beard. "I'm leaning toward that conclusion too. Still best to stay vigilant. Keep an eye on your drinks. We'll all do the same."

There'd be no need to watch my drinks. Any desire I had

to go to The Betsy had died a month ago. The only reason I'd kept showing was to find answers. And if there was any danger, to make sure Cass wouldn't suffer from the fallout.

It had to be a case of a crazy bitch who'd crossed a line. End of story. Time to move on.

The baby was due any day now, and the second she was born, I was bringing Cass home.

"Any word from Cass?" Emmett asked, picking up a wrench from the stack of tools I'd brought over earlier. Today I'd been taking out the interior of the Firebird, stripping out the old seats and nasty carpet.

"I texted her last night." I'd sent her a picture of the crib and changing table in the nursery.

I'd assembled it the day she'd moved out but hadn't shown her yet. Maybe because I'd hoped that she would come home and see it for herself. But her due date was in three days and she still hadn't collected the baby's things.

I was taking it as a good sign I could convince her to move back.

It was unlike Cass to not have things settled. Even in the short time we'd known one another, I could tell she was a planner. She made grocery lists and meal plans. I missed the sticky notes of daily to-dos beside her laptop.

For her to leave the baby's things might mean that she'd gotten new ones at her parents' place. Or maybe she hadn't completely given up on me.

For a month I hadn't broached the subject with her for fear that she'd act and leave for good. But last night, while I'd had dinner alone at the dining room table, I'd wanted her to know that she still had a place. That the baby had a place.

So I'd texted the picture and asked how she was feeling.

She hadn't replied. She rarely did. But I'd texted all the same.

Despite her request for space, I hadn't been able to go more than three days without sending her a note. The texts weren't for her, but myself. I craved that connection to her. I wanted her to know that she was on my mind.

"Is she going to move back in?" Emmett asked.

I sighed. "I don't know, and I haven't asked. Treading lightly these days."

"Do you want her to?"

"Yeah." Badly. Something I didn't want to tell Cass via text.

God, I missed her face. I missed her eyes and her smell and her taste. Going this long without seeing her had turned me into a moody asshole. If not for work, I would have crawled out of my skin.

The reason we had this small window on the job schedule was because of how much time I'd been spending at the garage. With Dash, Emmett, Isaiah and me all working on the remodels, they'd gone quicker than anticipated.

One morning I'd shown up at eight and Presley had threatened to drive me to the hospital because clearly, if I was in before ten, I must be feverish. So I'd shown up three days in a row at eight just to see the look on her face.

I would have seen it again today, but Pres had taken the day off. Emmett, Isaiah and I were all taking turns covering the office phones. Isaiah was in there now, the poor bastard. Office work was boring and my shift in there later would be painful.

"Can I ask you something?" I knelt beside the passenger seat and took a utility knife from my pocket, beginning to cut the old carpet away. "I think I want to buy this from Dash."

"It'll be a sweet ride when it's done. Good investment."

"I thought maybe Cass might like it."

Emmett blinked. "You're giving this to Cass?"

"Why not?" I shrugged. "It wouldn't be to drive every day. There's not a lot of room in the back for a car seat, but she could take it out for fun. Drive it in the summer."

Emmett stared at me, unspeaking.

"What?"

He shook his head. "I didn't realize . . ."

"Realize what?"

"That you were in love with her."

The knife slipped from my hand.

I wasn't in love with Cass, was I? Sure, I missed her company. I respected the hell out of her. She was the smartest woman I'd ever met and braver than most too. But love?

"The color just drained from your face." Emmett chuckled. "Change of subject?"

"Please," I choked out.

I didn't love Cass. We were . . . what the fuck were we? Former lovers? Friendly? I doubted she'd call me a friend. Soon-to-be co-parents?

Those labels were all wrong. And they weren't the labels I wanted. Not anymore.

There was a hole in my life. I'd known it for a long time. That hole had been there as a kid who'd needed a father. A kid whose mother loved him, maybe, but hadn't understood him. The hole had filled some when I'd joined the club. Then it had grown, expanding exponentially when the Tin Kings had disbanded, doubling again after Draven had died.

Hole upon hole. And the only time it hadn't felt soul-deep had been with Cass.

"She deserves better than me."

Emmett's gaze narrowed. "You really think that?"

"It's the truth. I've got nothing to offer her but baggage."

He scoffed. "It's a good thing Draven is in the ground. He'd kick your ass for a comment like that. And you'd deserve it." Without another word, he threw down the wrench so hard it bounced on the car's floor. Then he stood and strode away, leaving me beside the Firebird.

Why was he pissed? I didn't have an education. For years I'd used my fists to make extra cash in the boxing ring. I drank too much. I'd had too many women. Like Dale had said, Cass deserved better.

Before I could make sense of Emmett's reaction, my phone rang in my pocket. I stood and dug it out, Cass's name on the screen.

My heart jumped into my throat. For a month, I'd wished for this. I'd wished for her to call. Now she was and because it had been a month, I was scared to answer.

But I did it anyway. "Hey, babe."

"Hello, Leo," Claudia said.

"Oh . . . hi. Sorry, thought you were Cass."

"She's getting checked in at the hospital."

"What?" I swayed on my feet. "She's—the baby—"

"Get down here, Leo."

I swallowed hard. "Yes, ma'am."

It took me a moment after she ended the call to find my balance. My boots seemed stuck to the floor while my head spun like a top. I planted a hand on top of the Firebird, closing my eyes until I was steady. Then I couldn't move fast enough.

I ran toward the sink in the corner, turning on the water and scrubbing my hands with fury. But the grease was stuck to my skin and the water was cold. "Come off. Fucking come on."

I had to get my hands clean. I couldn't go to the hospital with greasy hands.

"Hey, man. You okay?" Isaiah came out of the office and to my side.

I shook my head. "I gotta get this grease off."

"Might work better if you use some soap?" He picked up a bottle of orange liquid and squirted some onto my palm.

"Right." I scrubbed more, letting it lather, and finally, the grease began to break itself free from my fingers.

"What's going on?"

"Cass." *Scrub.* "Hospital." *Scrub.* "Baby."

"Deep breath."

I obeyed, sucking in a long breath as I washed.

"Here." Isaiah handed me the brush we used to get the grease out of our cuticles and from underneath our nails. Then he gave me one more squirt of soap and went to the office door to holler inside. "Cass is at the hospital."

"You're kidding." Emmett appeared in the doorway. "Presley just texted me from the hospital."

I didn't hear much of what he said to Isaiah. Something about Presley being with Scarlett and Scarlett having contractions. None of that mattered when there were black smudges on my hands.

My knuckles were red beneath the faucet, the water having warmed to a scalding temperature, but still, I scrubbed. I would not walk into that hospital with grease on my damn fingers. There wasn't much I could control in this, but my hands would be clean.

For once in my fucking life, I wanted clean hands.

"You're good." Isaiah reached in front of me and shut off the water. "You're clean."

My hands were practically raw, but that didn't mean they were clean. *I* wasn't clean.

The violence we'd committed. The laws we'd broken. The lives we'd ended. Cass, our child, shouldn't have my ghosts haunt their lives.

"No, I'm not." My voice was hoarse.

Emmett walked over and put his hand on my shoulder. "It's in the past, brother."

How could it be in the past when I thought about the club each and every day?

"You've got a choice," Isaiah said, tossing me a towel to dry my hands. "Let that past ruin your future. Or learn from it and vow never to let it happen again."

"Easy as that?"

"No, man." He shook his head. "It's never easy. You fight every day. You work your ass off to be better than you were. And you show up, especially on the bad days, because they make you want to keep fighting."

I closed my eyes and let his words sink in.

Isaiah had his own demons, ones he'd battled on his own. While I'd always had the club, my brothers, Isaiah had lived a solitary life. He'd lost a woman in a car accident and had gone to prison because he'd been the driver behind the wheel.

When he'd moved to Clifton Forge and come to work at the garage, he hadn't spoken much. He'd been closest to Presley. But then Draven had been framed. Isaiah had found himself in the middle of our mess and he'd walked away with the ultimate prize. Genevieve. He wasn't fighting alone these days.

Fight.

"I gotta go." I nodded at the guys, then strode for the door. One set of bootsteps echoed behind.

Emmett caught up quickly and kept pace toward our bikes parked against the chain-link fence. March had come and with it, the spring weather. My truck had been abandoned in the driveway at home.

"You don't have to come," I told Emmett as I straddled my bike.

"And take your shift in the office? No, thanks. I'd rather wait at the hospital."

"Thanks, brother."

He answered by putting on a pair of shades and starting his bike.

The hospital was on the other end of town, close to the Missouri River, which ran along the edge of Clifton Forge. There were a few patches of ice at the water's edge, but for the most part, it had all melted. The same was true with the snowbanks, now gone from streets and yards.

The air was fresh and crisp as it whipped over my face. Thank God for it. I needed the minute on the bike, to feel the road and the vibration of the machine. To think. To fight.

Cass didn't deserve me, but I wouldn't leave her alone. I simply couldn't.

Emmett and I parked in the visitor lot, and I forced my steps to remain even as we trekked to the hospital's entrance. My knees were shaking. My limbs felt like rubber. But I walked, one foot in front of the other, through the sliding glass doors and along the hallways marked with arrows toward the maternity unit.

A nurse dressed in purple floral-print scrubs greeted me from behind a counter. "Can I help you?"

"Cassandra Cline."

"And you are?" Her gaze shifted between Emmett and me.

I swallowed hard. A good goddamn question. Who was I?

Thankfully, I didn't have to answer. Dale came walking down a hallway, his face pale and etched with worry. "Leo."

I pushed off the counter to meet him beside a wheelchair. "Is she okay? Can I see her?"

"Room one ten." He pointed down the hallway. "Last one on the left."

"Thanks," I said, surprised he'd tell me.

"I'll hang in the waiting area," Emmett said. "Holler if you need anything."

I nodded and took off, walking toward Cass's room. I knocked and eased the door open. The oxygen rushed from my lungs the moment my gaze landed on her dressed in a faded blue gown and propped up on a bed in the center of the room.

She looked beautiful. Breathtaking. Fuck, but I had missed her.

Even though her belly was covered with a white blanket, I could see how she'd grown. Her hair was spread out across the pillows behind her back. The smooth skin of her cheeks was flushed and dewy. When her gaze turned to me and I met those caramel irises, I was done.

Without thinking, I strode to the bed and put my hands on her face. Then I pressed my lips to hers and gave myself a second to soak her in before pulling back. "Hi."

"Hi," she whispered as I dropped my forehead to hers.

"You okay?"

"Ask me again in a minute." She squeezed her eyes shut and her hands went to her side as her entire body tensed.

I stood straight, watching with wide eyes as she gritted her teeth and winced.

"Breathe through it." Claudia rushed to Cass's side, taking her daughter's hand. She met my gaze from the other side of the bed and gave me a pained smile.

I hadn't noticed her when I'd come in, too consumed with Cass.

"That's it." Claudia rubbed the back of Cass's hand, twisting to look at the monitor next to an IV stand. "Almost done."

The spike on the monitor's screen was going down.

"Ouch." Cass collapsed into the pillows, her eyes still closed.

"Are you sure you don't want the epidural?" Claudia asked.

"I don't know." Cass looked to her mother. "Yes. No."

"Does it hurt that bad?"

Both women shot me a glare.

"Sorry." I held up my hands. "Should I go?"

"No, you stay." Claudia bent and kissed Cass's forehead, making the decision for me. Then she swept out of the room, leaving us alone.

"Are you sure she should leave? I don't know what I'm doing," I admitted.

"Neither do I. That's what the nurses are for. And I've read books."

Of course she had. She was prepared. All I'd done was build a damn crib.

"I like the crib," she whispered.

"It's a nice piece. Sturdy. Took me a few hours to build."

214

"Last night?"

I shook my head. "The day you moved out."

"Leo." Her gaze softened. "Why?"

"Because it's so big that your dad can't fit it through the door without spending three hours taking it apart."

She giggled. "So you did it to punish Dad?"

"No, I did it because I hoped you'd come back."

"We have a lot to talk about."

I sat on the edge of the bed and took her hand. "I know."

"But not right now." A twist of pain crossed her gorgeous face.

My eyes shot to the monitor and the line that was shooting up. Fuck. Where was Claudia? What had she said? "Breathe."

Cass nodded, hissing out a breath as her hand gripped mine like a vise.

The contraction seemed to go on forever until finally, Cass unclenched her teeth and sank into the pillow. "Ooof, that hurts."

Ooof, that hurts soon turned into *damn it, that hurts.* Damn it became hell. Hell became shit. Shit became fuck.

Tears streamed down Cass's face as Dr. Tan swept into the room.

"How are we doing?" she asked, going to the foot of the bed and flipping up the covers.

I focused on Cass, pushing a lock of hair off her sweaty forehead. "What can I do?"

"Say something," Cass said. "Distract me before the next one comes."

The contractions were right on top of each other now. "Scarlett is here. Pretty sure she's in labor too."

"Really?" A smile whispered across her face. "Our babies might have the same birthday."

It was getting close to midnight according to the clock on the wall. "If not the same birthday, damn close."

"I'd say you're having this baby today." Dr. Tan stood and smiled. "Ready to try pushing?"

"Like right now?" Cass's eyes widened.

"Yep." Dr. Tan and the nurses buzzed around the room, the doctor suiting up in a blue covering as one nurse went to the other side of the bed. "Okay, Leo. Grab a leg."

"Huh?"

"Hold her leg, just like this." The nurse smiled at me like she thought I'd been waiting all day to be honored with this task.

"Or you can come down here and watch." The dare gleamed in Dr. Tan's eyes.

I dove for Cass's leg. "I'm good."

I'd expected Cass to scream as she pushed. I'd expected her to yell and shout, maybe throw a few well-earned insults and *fuck yous* my way. But every time the doctor told her to push, she clamped down her teeth and pushed.

Four in total.

Then came the wail.

A wail from a pair of newborn lungs. A wail from a red-faced baby girl. A wail that changed everything.

Not long after, the smiley nurse shoved a pair of scissors in my hand and told me where to snip the cord. Then they whisked the baby to a tray, where she was cleaned and wrapped, then returned to Cass to rest on her bare chest, giving us a few minutes alone before they'd come back to help Cass clean up.

There were new tears down her cheeks now. My hands acted on instinct and brushed them away.

Fuck, she was tough. Tougher than me a million times over.

"Do you want to hold her?" Cass asked.

"I don't know how." Even with my friends and their kids, I'd never held a baby before. I waited until they were at least two and a lot less breakable.

A new tear fell from Cass's cheek as I sat down and held out my arms.

She reached out, placing the baby's head in the crook of my elbow and her tiny body along my forearm.

What was I doing here? How was I ever going to make this work? But even when the nurses came in and helped Cass to the shower, I refused to let the baby go.

The nurses helped Cass change into a pair of her own pajamas before getting her into a wheelchair. Then one of them stole the baby from my arms.

"Are we going somewhere?"

"This is just a delivery room," a nurse answered. "We'll get you settled into a recovery room for the night."

I nodded and since the nurse pushed the baby in her cart crib, I slung Cass's bag over a shoulder and pushed her wheelchair down the hallway toward the opposite end of the unit to a smaller, dimly lit room with a full-sized bed.

Cass took the baby, baring a breast for an attempt at nursing, while the staff came in and out of the room, bringing water and pamphlets and instructions.

"Will you go find my parents?" Cass winced as the baby latched on to a nipple. "My mom texted that they found a quiet waiting room on the second floor."

"Sure." I backed away and the moment I was in the

hallway and out of sight, I planted my hands on my thighs and put my head between my knees.

Oh, shit. Oh, shit. The delivery had taken hours but it had still happened too fast.

The sound of a door opening and closing had me standing straight. Dale and Claudia appeared, having come from the stairwell.

Awesome. Dale had just seen me close to passing out.

I pointed to Cass's door, too freaked to be embarrassed.

Neither of them spoke as they rushed past me and to their daughter.

I shuffled down the hallway, my hands shoved into my pockets to hide their shaking, not exactly sure where I was going until a familiar voice caught my ear and I steered myself toward the closest waiting room.

There were people in the chairs. My people. Presley was asleep against Shaw's shoulder. Dash was a couple seats down, stretched out with his eyes closed. Emmett was standing beside Luke.

They stared at me as I walked over.

"Everything okay?" Luke asked.

Okay? She was so little. How did you take care of someone that small? How did I change her diaper or teach her to ride a bike or help her with math homework? I wasn't equipped to do any of those things.

But I would. Because she was . . . mine. Forever, she was mine.

"I have a daughter." I blinked and raked a hand through my hair. "Holy fuck, I have a daughter."

CHAPTER FIFTEEN

CASSANDRA

"Call if you need anything." The nurse wrote her name —Sophie—on the whiteboard in the room.

"Thanks." I gave her a sleepy smile, then dropped my eyes to the baby.

I couldn't stop looking at her. I couldn't believe she was here and so perfect. I'd loved her when she was growing inside of me, but now, holding her in my arms . . . I hadn't realized that I'd love her even more.

A consuming type of love. The type where I'd sacrifice anything for her—money, happiness, life. She was the axis around which my world would spin.

"What do you want from the cafeteria?" Leo asked, flipping through the small menu that the nurse had handed him. His legs were stretched out long beside me, his feet bare.

I hadn't expected the large bed when they'd brought us to the recovery room. I'd thought it would be another single like in the delivery room, but I guess for parents who both spent the night, the extra bed space was nice.

Leo had been reluctant at first, giving me space and

trying to get comfortable on the stiff two-seat bench beneath the room's window. Then after my parents had left for the night, I'd taken pity on him and told him to come to bed.

He hadn't left my side since.

"Some fruit. And a ham and cheese omelet."

We'd eaten last night after we'd settled into the room. Mom and Dad had run out to get us some sandwiches since the hospital's cafeteria had been closed. That had been only four hours ago. Still, after all the energy I'd expended yesterday and the lack of sleep, I was starved.

Leo reached for the phone on the side table and called in our breakfast. It was just after six in the morning and I suspected my parents wouldn't stay home for long. The baby was sleeping, which meant this was my window for an overdue conversation.

"I'm mad at you."

He sighed. "Can I explain?"

I looked at the baby and nodded.

"I went to the bar to hang with Dash and Emmett. And because . . . I got spooked when you started talking about the nursery."

At least he could admit it. "Why did that scare you?"

"Look at her." He leaned closer, staring at our daughter. "Doesn't she scare the hell out of you? She's *ours*. She's mine. What if I fu—mess her up?"

Why did he think that? He hadn't told me about his parents and upbringing, but that conversation was also overdue.

"Yes, the responsibility scares me," I admitted. "But not enough to run away and miss everything good she'll bring with her."

"Yeah, because deep down, you know you won't mess her up. I can't say the same, Cass."

My heart twisted. This man had so much to give her. When would he see that?

"The nursery . . . made it all real. It was easier when it was just you and me."

"It was never just you and me."

"Up here, it was." He tapped his temple. "Let's just pray she got your brain, not mine."

I gave him a small smile. Maybe she would get my brain, but I hoped that her deep blue eyes, the ones she'd flashed me for the briefest moment this morning, would eventually fade to Leo's pale green.

"I wasn't looking for a score at The Betsy," he said. "And nothing happened."

Jealousy and anger and betrayal and humiliation bubbled up from the pocket where I'd stuffed them this past month. I blinked and saw that woman hanging off of him. I blinked and saw his lips pressed to hers. Nothing to him was not nothing to me. "Who was she?"

"A bitch who slipped drugs into my drink."

I jerked, making the baby stir. Leo and I both held our breath as we waited to see if she would sleep or wake. Thankfully, it was the former because I had questions. A lot of questions. "You were drugged?"

He nodded. "Yeah. She admitted it. Said a man paid her to do it."

"Who?"

"No idea. I've spent the last month going to The Betsy trying to find out who he was, but even after Emmett scoured the parking lot's security footage, we have no idea."

"Why would someone drug you?"

"I'm thinking there was no guy and after I shoved her away from me, her ego got bruised. So she figured she could get me into her bed a different way. I passed out in the truck. She drove it to her house. Somehow got my ass inside. Took off my clothes. The next morning after I woke up, she made a play and I shoved her away. Again. I swear, Cass, I didn't touch her. The only reason I slept there was because I had blacked out from the drugs she'd slipped me."

My molars clenched so hard there was a chance I'd crack a filling loose. Now *this* was angry. I was furious at the woman. At myself. If I'd listened to Leo, if I'd let him explain, maybe we wouldn't have spent a month apart. If I'd had the guts to walk up to him at The Betsy and shove that brunette away.

She'd put her hands, her lips, on what was *mine*. "That. Cunt."

Leo arched an eyebrow and glanced at our daughter.

I sucked in a deep breath, closing my eyes for a moment as the angry tide ebbed. Then I looked at our daughter and said, "Pretend I didn't say that."

Leo chuckled and turned sideways, propping up on an elbow to look at her and face me. "You came to the bar that night. Why?"

"Because I wanted you to think I was fun. That you didn't have to leave me to have a good time."

"I think you're fun."

"No, you don't."

"I wouldn't have invited you to come with me if I didn't think you were fun. Me going to the bar was never about you. It's my own shit."

This wasn't news. The problem was I didn't know how to fix it. Forcing the pregnancy on Leo hadn't worked.

Invading his home hadn't worked. Spending time away from him hadn't worked. What else did I try?

The little bundle in my arms needed me to make the right choice.

"Come home, Cass. Please."

"I don't know if that's a good idea, Leo." I wanted to. For me. But . . . "Maybe if we were something."

"We are something." There was such intensity in his hypnotic eyes. Such honesty. It was Leo's truths that had always been my undoing.

"What?" I whispered. "What are we?"

"Beats the hell out of me. I've never done this before."

"Had a baby?"

"Had a Cassandra."

Leo spoke my name like a wish upon the wind.

"I miss seeing you at the dining room table with that crease between your eyebrows as you type," he said. "I miss watching you stand in front of the open fridge, letting all the cold air out because you can't decide what you want to eat. I miss knowing you'll be there when I get home. I miss you, Firecracker."

Oh, these goddamn hormones. Clearly, having the baby hadn't dulled them in the slightest. My eyes flooded and I buried my chin to hide them as best I could.

It was silly to try. Leo hooked a finger under my chin and tipped up my face toward his. "One more chance. Give me one more. I screw this one up, you stay. And I'll go."

There was such conviction in his voice. I had no doubt that if we imploded, he'd hand over the keys to his house and walk out the door. "It hurt. That night. And at the barbeque when it took you a minute to place me."

"Cass, I—"

"Let me finish." I needed to say this while I could. "You were this sexy, unattainable force. The minute you sat down beside me, I knew I was so out of my element. The guys I'd dated before would have killed for a shred of your charisma. They were nice and academic and . . . boring. Sitting beside you was like seeing the stars for the first time. You were out of my universe. And when you left me behind last month, it was a reminder that I wasn't enough."

"No." Understanding and regret crossed his face. "Cass, you've got it all wrong."

"Do I?"

"You're in a universe of your own." He reached for me, threading his fingers behind my neck as his palms warmed my skin. "You don't even realize it. You drew me in that night. One look at you and I couldn't get to that stool beside yours fast enough. I would have fought any man in the bar for you. One look and you were mine."

I closed my eyes before more tears could fall.

"I'm sorry. I'll say it until you believe it. I'm sorry."

I sighed. "Okay."

"Okay, you believe me?"

I shook my head. "Okay, I'll come home."

His entire body sagged in relief as he pressed his forehead to mine. "We're gonna figure this out."

The baby squirmed and scrunched up her nose before giving a small, cute pout. "She's going to use that pout against us."

"And get whatever she wants."

"Every time."

A knock came at the door and a woman entered with our breakfasts. Leo ate first, scarfing his own omelet while I nursed the baby.

"She needs a name."

He nodded and reached for his phone on the table. "I've got a list."

"You do?" Who was this Leo and what had he done with the Leo I was intimately acquainted with?

"I couldn't sleep last night. You were wiped and she squirmed in her crib-cart thing, so I held her and started looking up names."

"You were holding her when I woke up."

He shrugged. "I held her all night."

Oh. My. God. Now I was going to freaking cry again. Why couldn't he have been this sweet from the start? How much time had we missed?

I shifted the baby to the other breast, the movement giving me an excuse to hide my face. The nurse had helped me last night but so far, breastfeeding was not easy. As the baby took hold of my tender nipple, I dragged in a deep breath and got my emotions under control.

"Want my favorite or least favorite first?" Leo asked.

"Favorite."

"Seraphina. It means fire, because I hope she gets your hair."

"Damn it." The tears were impossible to stop now. They erupted out of my eyes like water from a hose, dripping down my face and onto the baby's blanket.

"What? Is she hurting you?"

I shook my head, using my free hand to swipe at my cheeks. It was no use. The tears just kept falling.

Leo, oblivious to the fact that he was the cause here, swiped up a napkin and dabbed my face.

"You're making it worse."

"How?"

"By being . . . this guy. Who are you?"

A wash of guilt clouded his handsome features. "Just a guy trying to deserve you."

"Stop." A sob escaped. "I'm hormonal and exhausted and hungry. Unless you want me to cry through breakfast, I need you to stop being that guy for a minute. Be the other Leo."

He leaned in, pressing a kiss to my temple. "Your tits are fucking huge."

I laughed. "Thank you."

"Welcome."

He stayed close, leaving one arm around my shoulders as my tears dried up. Then he fumbled to get a burp rag over his shoulder, shifting and adjusting the cloth until it was just right, before taking the baby from my arms to pat her back while I inhaled my food.

"Want the rest of my list of names?" he asked.

"Why? Her name's Seraphina."

The smile that spread across his face, so full of pride, stole my breath.

"Seraphina Winter," he whispered. "I like it. Does she need a middle name?"

"Betsy." The name blurted past my lips before I could stop it.

Leo laughed. "That's the sleep deprivation talking."

"I have no idea where that came from. But . . . it fits. That's where she started."

"Seraphina Betsy Winter." His hand engulfed her entire body as he leaned her away to look at her face. "What do you think, little?"

Little. "Leo, I'm about to cry again."

"Seriously, babe. Your tits are magnificent right now."

I snorted, smiling as I rested my head on his shoulder. "Much better."

"Forgot to tell you last night. I saw Luke in the waiting room while your parents came in to visit."

In the chaos of today, I'd forgotten Scarlett was here too. I abandoned Leo, easing off the bed. My entire body was tender and sore, something the nurses had promised was normal. I walked to my bag, which was sitting on a chair, and dug out my phone from the pocket where Leo had stowed it last night before I'd fallen asleep.

There were text messages to read and voicemails to listen to, but I went straight to my recent calls and hit Scarlett's name.

She answered on the first ring. "We're in room one thirty."

"We're on our way."

"We are?" Leo asked as I hung up the phone and dug out the kimono robe Mom had bought me two weeks ago.

"Yes." I tied the robe as he eased off the bed one leg at a time, testing the floor for its strength before he stood, the baby held in the cradle of his arms. "Can you carry her? Or do you want to roll the crib?"

There was a flash of fear on his face, that maybe he'd drop her, but whatever faith he lacked in himself, I had it in that same pocket where I kept all things Leo. He wouldn't hurt her. He had one last chance to realize that himself.

We'd come home and he'd have one last chance.

"I'll, uh . . . I can carry her."

"Okay." I gave him a small smile, then led the way, our progress slow. Not only because of me but Leo, who was still in bare feet, moved an inch at a time toward Scarlett's room.

I knocked and pressed the door open, finding her and

Luke on a bed identical to the one in our room. In Scarlett's arms was another pink bundle.

"A girl?" I clapped my hands together. She'd told me last week that she'd been secretly hoping for a girl.

"Meet Mary." She smiled, looking as beautiful and happy as ever. Then her eyes widened as Leo came in behind me, still taking turtle steps.

"Come sit." Luke sprang off the bed, making a space for me.

I took his place, then held out my arms for Leo to make the transfer. "This is Seraphina."

"Gah. Great name," Scarlett said. "That wasn't on your list."

"Leo came up with it."

She gave him a sideways glance. "You did?"

"I did." He nodded, his face full of pride as he shook Luke's hand. "Congrats, man."

"Same to you."

"When do you get to go home?" Scarlett asked.

"Probably not until tomorrow. She was born just shy of midnight and they want to keep us the full twenty-four hours." It wasn't the time to tell her that when we left, we'd be going to Leo's. First, I needed to brave that conversation with my parents. "What about you?"

"Probably in the morning too. Which means I suspect we'll get a ton of visitors today."

Leo leaned against the wall and yawned. "There was quite the crew here last night."

"Who?"

"Presley, Shaw. Emmett and Dash. I bet they'll all be back before noon. If Bryce lets Dash sleep that late."

"I see epic birthday parties in our future." Scarlett laughed, leaning in to look at Seraphina. "She's perfect."

"So is Mary."

"It's fitting, don't you think? You and me, coming out of that basement together at the Warrior clubhouse. Now we've got these girls. It's like our reward."

My chest tightened as I nodded, pretending like just the mention of that basement didn't make me want to crawl out of my skin.

In the weeks since I'd moved home, Scarlett and I had spent a lot of time together. One morning, about two days after Leo's *visit* with Dad, she'd come over with a decaf latte. We'd been having coffee every morning since.

Scarlett rarely brought up the kidnapping, and I was quick to change the subject whenever she did. She'd let me. But I could feel Leo's scrutiny on my face and when I looked up, he was staring at me, his expression serious.

"Good?" he mouthed.

I forced a smile.

"We've got some other news." Luke leaned forward from his seat in the corner chair. "I got a call from Agent Maria Brown yesterday."

I sat up straighter. "Why?"

Leo pushed off the wall, his shoulders tensing. "Tucker."

"Yeah," Luke said. "Three consecutive life sentences."

The air rushed from my lungs.

Leo's frame deflated. "Thank fuck. Do the others know?"

"Not yet. Figured I'd tell them when they came to visit today."

"News on the other Warriors?" Leo asked.

"Nothing you don't already know. The federal prosecutor pushed hard for Tucker's trial first. It sets a precedence for the other Warriors. But Maria warned me that there's a long way to go. So far, the shortest sentence is five years."

"So that's it?" I asked. "The danger is over?"

Luke sighed. "Not quite. There are fifty-seven Warriors being sent through the system. They've got men on murder charges, drug trafficking, kidnapping, assault and a slew of lesser crimes. Some copped pleas for a reduced sentence and are already in prison. Some are awaiting trial. But not a single power player in their club is walking free. And with Tucker in a cell for the rest of his miserable life, it's a good sign this all dies with him."

I closed my eyes and breathed. Then I prayed. *Please. Please, don't let the Warriors taint Seraphina's life.*

"It'll be okay." Scarlett put her hand on mine. "They don't get to beat us."

"They don't get to win."

We spent the next hour in their room, talking about our individual deliveries and how we were sure Dr. Tan had a clone because she'd managed to be in both our rooms at practically the same time.

Then, as expected, the crew arrived, bombarding us with fresh flowers and more gifts and cigars for the new fathers. By the time lunch rolled around, I was exhausted, and when Leo informed the group we were kicking them out of our room, I gladly let him. We nursed the baby in privacy and laid her down, but the moment I closed my eyes, my parents arrived.

Dad was not happy to see Leo. He'd have to get over that.

Mom barely paid any of us attention, too happy to pick up Seraphina, holding her while she slept and gushing over her name.

"I need sleep." I sagged against Leo's side as Dad paced

the room. He'd smile at Mom and the baby, send a soft one my way, then glare at Leo.

"We'll get going," Mom said, reluctantly giving Seraphina to Leo an hour later. "Call tomorrow whenever you're ready for us to come get you."

"They're—"

I elbowed Leo in the ribs, earning a scowl. "Okay."

Leo walked them to the door, holding it open and closing it at their backs. Then planted his hands on his hips. "Are you going to tell them you're moving?"

"Yes. I'll call Mom later and tell her about the change of plan. Then she can tell Dad. Trust me, it'll be better that way."

Dad was going to freak out and I'd rather him not be here where there was a box marked SHARPS on the wall.

Leo came to the bed and lay down at my side, resting his head against the pillow. "About what Scarlett said earlier. About the basement. You got a look on your face. Want to talk about it?"

"Not today." *Not ever.*

He let it go, for now. Neither of us had the energy for a long discussion. But I doubted it would last and eventually, he'd bring up the kidnapping again.

It was not a worry for today. Today, we were going to relax here and revel in the birth of our daughter. And tomorrow, we'd go home.

For a fresh start.

For one last chance.

CHAPTER SIXTEEN

LEO

"How are you holding up?" Emmett asked from his seat on the opposite end of my couch. Between us, Seraphina was swaddled and sleeping on a pink, fuzzy blanket.

"I'm tired." I rubbed my face. "Remember those days at the clubhouse when we'd go on a bender? Ride and drink and get into fights and chase women, sleep for a few hours, then get up and do it all over again?"

He groaned. "Glad we grew out of that. It was exhausting."

"Nothing compared to this." I motioned to Seraphina. "She doesn't sleep at night. Maybe an hour or two at a time. Then conks out the second the sun comes up."

Which, after a week, had left Cass and me practically delirious.

She'd gone to lie down for a while, squeezing in a short nap after lunch and before the baby would wake up hungry. She'd told me to try and keep Seraphina awake but after an hour of playing with her toes and tickling her chin and doing whatever I could to entertain a newborn baby, I'd given up.

"Cass is drained." We both were.

I'd taken the past week off of work but I was already planning on telling Dash that I'd miss next week too. I just couldn't leave Cass alone to handle the baby on her own until she caught up on some rest.

Claudia came by every day, but it wasn't like she stayed the night, getting up with Seraphina to help with the midnight feedings and pace the halls with the baby in my arms so Cass could go back to bed.

"Not that I have any experience, but I'm guessing it's normal to be wiped these first few weeks," Emmett said.

"Yeah. I'm sure." I touched the tip of Seraphina's toes. It was nearly impossible not to touch her, especially when she looked so peaceful in her sleep. Her nose was the cutest nose in history, her lips a precious bow. Her closed eyes were two perfect crescents in a beautiful face. Open, they held a fist around my heart.

"You are smitten, aren't you?" he asked.

"Look at her." How could anyone not be totally enamored?

Emmett chuckled and tipped his beer bottle to his lips.

I mirrored the action, taking a long sip from my own Bud Light. It would be my only beer because if I had two, I'd be so tired I'd pass out. "How were things at the garage this week?"

"Normal. Pres is convinced Dash is going to screw every-thing up while she's on maternity leave."

I grinned. "Because he will."

"What the hell is he thinking? He hates office work."

"At least he hired someone to answer the phones."

Presley's baby was due any day now and while she was on leave, there'd be another woman working at the garage to help with the daily tasks. But Dash would cover the bulk of Pres's job duties as manager.

We'd see how long it lasted.

Not only did Dash hate that sort of work, especially when the rest of us were working on cars in the shop, but Presley wouldn't be able to help herself. I was giving her one month, then she'd probably be bringing her baby into the office while she made sure everything was in order.

Shaw was a damn movie star, worth millions, and when I'd asked if she was going to quit, she'd rolled her eyes and told me *hell, no.* Because to her, like it was to me, working at the garage wasn't just a job. Most of us would show up even if Dash didn't pay us. That garage was our family.

Until now.

Family meant more now than it had before.

Seraphina shifted, turning to face the other direction, and her eyes fluttered open. I put my hand on her belly, patting gently until she dozed off again.

"Good news on Tucker," Emmett said.

"I hope that son of a bitch gets shivved." The more I'd thought about Luke's update, the angrier I'd gotten. I wished that I had gotten my hands on Tucker before the FBI, because prison seemed too good a life for that miserable bastard.

He'd killed Emmett's father. He'd killed Draven. And he'd taken Cass. Tucker would have killed her or sold her into a trafficking ring, and the thought of her in the Arrowhead Warrior clubhouse made my blood boil.

"Think he'll come after us?" I asked.

Emmett nodded. "Eventually, yes. He might be in prison

but he's got connections to other clubs. Some of his own guys won't be put away for long. Part of me thinks that this sentencing will bring it all to a head, sooner rather than later. The other part thinks he'll wait until we've forgotten about him."

"We'll never forget." We'd never dismiss their threat. It meant a life of looking over our shoulders, but that was what we'd signed up for with the club.

My only regret was that Cass hadn't signed up for that. Neither had Seraphina. They'd be dragged into this because of me.

Emmett took another drink of his beer. "Luke thinks Tucker might go after Scarlett first, but he doesn't know about our history with the Warriors."

Luke didn't know how many Warriors the Kings had killed in the decades that our clubs had battled. Luke didn't see the blood on our hands.

"Yeah. He'll come after Dash, you and me. No question."

"What?" Cass gasped.

My eyes whipped to the hallway where she was listening, her eyes wide and her face pale. "Don't worry, babe. He might try but nothing will happen."

Emmett glanced over, his eyebrows coming together. He knew there was a risk here. Tucker had killed our loved ones and he wouldn't hesitate to do it again.

But Cass didn't need to know any of that shit. Maybe it was a mistake downplaying this to her, but she'd suffered enough at the hands of the Warriors. We had other things to worry about right now, namely keeping our daughter alive and our sanities intact. And before we ever talked about my past with the club, I needed to know how Cass felt about the kidnapping, something she avoided at all costs. I wouldn't tell her tales from lost days if they were going to hurt her in any way.

"I'm going to get out of your hair." Emmett pushed up from the couch, collecting his bottle and taking it to the trash can in the kitchen. Then he walked to Cass and wrapped her in a hug. "We're here if you need anything. Just a phone call away."

"Thank you." She gave him a weary smile.

Against his tall, broad frame, she looked so small and fragile. She looked twenty-four, something I forgot at times because though she was eight years younger, she had wisdom in her young face. More than I'd given her credit for over all these months.

Cass might be young, but she wasn't like other women her age, immature and prone to drama. She sure as hell wasn't like I'd been at that age, wild and reckless. It was a damn good thing too. Any other woman and she wouldn't have stuck with me. She wouldn't have forced me to stick it out too.

And I would have missed this. I would have missed my Seraphina.

Fuck, but I was a goddamn fool.

Emmett let Cass go, then smacked me on the shoulder as he passed the back of the couch. "I'm heading to The Betsy tonight in case you want to grab a quick drink. Get out of the house for a minute."

"'Kay. Thanks for coming over."

He smiled at Seraphina. "Not a hardship to hang with her for a few."

Emmett let himself out of the house as Cass came and looked down at our daughter.

"You didn't take a very long nap," I said.

"I can't shut my mind off. It's like I know it's daytime and even though I'm tired, I think I should be awake. I might take a long bath and read before she wakes up. Is that okay?"

"Of course. I've got her."

She reached out and ran a hand through my hair. "I know you do."

One touch was all I got before she disappeared to the bedroom.

Since she'd moved back in, we'd set up camp in the master. There was no point in sleeping—attempting to sleep —in separate rooms when we were together whenever Seraphina woke up. So we'd put the bassinet beside my bed and that was where Seraphina would stay until we were comfortable letting her sleep in a different room.

Cass had slept by my side every night, each of us face-planted into our own pillows. And other than the occasional kiss on her temple or forehead, I'd tried to give her space. Not force anything. Sex wasn't even on my radar right now— it wasn't about that. I simply needed to be close to her. To always be close.

The same was true with Seraphina.

The night she was born, those long hours I'd stayed up holding her, had changed everything. I'd stared at her precious face, lost in such a tiny person. My person. I'd imag-ined what Draven would say, wishing he had been around to meet her.

He would have kicked my ass for how I'd acted lately. He would have punched me in the face and told me to *man the fuck up, Leo.* As I sat in that hospital bed, his voice had rung so loud and clear in my head that I would have sworn it had drifted in from the hallway.

All this time, I'd been afraid I'd be my own father, a

selfish motherfucker who'd failed his kid. But he hadn't been a father.

Draven had filled those shoes.

I wouldn't be my own father. I'd be Draven.

It had taken this baby girl to open my eyes. If Draven was watching, I wasn't going to disappoint him.

Or Cass.

Carefully, I slid my hands beneath Seraphina, doing my best not to wake her as I walked down the hallway to the bedroom. Then I placed her in the bassinet, holding my breath as she squirmed for a moment before settling and staying asleep.

Not that I had anything to worry about. The sun was up, therefore, she'd sleep.

The faucet in the bathroom turned off and I walked to the doorway just as Cass sank into the white bathtub.

She stretched an arm over the rim, reaching for the book on the small stool beside the bath, but she couldn't quite touch it. "Ugh."

"I'll get it."

Her face shot to me as I came in and picked up the book, opening it to the page she'd saved with a bookmark.

"I didn't think this through." She held up her hands, both wet.

"That's okay. Just relax." I sat down on the stool and started at the top of the page, reading to Cass while she rested her head against the side of the tub.

The book was about World War II but as the pages passed, I didn't soak in the words like I would if I was reading it for myself. I was too busy trying not to stutter or rush through the words to absorb them.

This was her area of expertise. Books. History. Knowledge.

I was just a thug mechanic doing his best not to let the nerves creep into his voice or his hands shake as he turned the page.

Never in my life had I felt more vulnerable than I did in this moment, reading Cass's book to her while she listened on.

On the floor, her phone dinged.

Cass sat up straight, stretching for it, but I beat her to it, reading the text.

"It's your mom. She says they are bringing dinner over tonight. Around five."

"Okay." She relaxed into the water again, resting her cheek and hands on the edge. Those eyes met mine, the color as fine and smooth as the best whiskey. Her cheeks were flushed the color of the peach roses Emmett had brought her today. Her hair was tied up and only a few tendrils skimmed the water's surface.

"You're beautiful." I caught a droplet of water at her chin.

"I don't feel like it."

"Then believe me when I say you are the most beautiful woman I've ever seen in my life."

Her eyes welled with tears. There'd been a lot of tears, most ones of frustration and exhaustion during the late-night hours when Seraphina wouldn't sleep or struggled to nurse.

I picked up the book, reading a few more pages until she stopped me at the end of a chapter.

"You don't talk about your parents," she whispered.

"No." I closed the book and set it aside, leaning forward. "I don't have a close relationship with my mother."

"And your father?"

"Haven't seen or spoken to him since I was twelve."

"Oh. I'm sorry."

"Not your fault." I sighed, not wanting to get into this, but I also wouldn't deny Cass her curiosity. "My dad was a drunk and a womanizer. Guess the apple didn't fall far from the tree."

"You consider yourself a drunk?"

"No. But I doubt he would have either. He never lived with us so I didn't know him well. He and Mom weren't married. I don't know what their relationship was, but at times, he'd stay over. He'd be around for a week, then disappear for two months before coming back. Finally Mom had enough. When I was ten, she told him to get lost."

"And you never heard from him again?"

"He moved to California. Got tied into a club down there. He came back once or twice that following year. Mostly I think to see if Mom was serious. She was. The last time he came by, I was home. She doesn't know I was listening, but I heard her threaten to call the cops if he showed again. He didn't."

Cass stretched out a hand for mine, lacing our fingers together. "You're not him."

"I don't want to be him. I *won't* be him."

Her hand gripped mine tighter.

"I was on that path," I said. "I doubt my life in the club looked a lot different than his. The club was part of the reason Mom and I don't talk much. Not that we were ever close before. I think she looks at me and sees my father. After I graduated, she moved to Tucson and I joined the club. We talk a few times a year. Birthdays. Christmas. That's about it."

Mom had married a few years back. I hadn't gone to the wedding, nor had I been invited. She'd told me after the fact, promising it had been a no-fuss thing at the courthouse.

I'd called her earlier this week to tell her about Seraphina. She'd been surprised to say the least, especially since I hadn't told her about Cass or the pregnancy over our Christmas phone call. But Mom had been polite. She was always polite.

As a teenager, we'd argued. She'd get frustrated with me, wishing I'd been different. Wishing I'd cared more about school and my future than joining the local motorcycle club. *Exasperating.* That had been her word for me.

Our fighting had ended abruptly the day she'd moved to Tucson. Maybe she'd given up on me. Maybe I'd given up on her. Maybe we'd both exasperated each other.

I hadn't spoken to Mom long when I'd called. We didn't know one another and that wasn't going to change. Though I'd promised to send pictures of Seraphina. She'd invited us to Tucson, a trip we both knew wouldn't happen anytime soon.

Maybe one day my mother would meet my daughter. But in the past fourteen years, I'd seen Mom twice, so I wasn't going to hold my breath. Part of that distance was on me. I wasn't sure if there was a fix to be made or if it was best to simply acknowledge that my family lived here and was not related to me by blood.

Until now.

Seraphina was my blood. She was mine.

She'd always have Claudia and Dale as grandparents. She'd have a crew of aunts and uncles—Dash, Emmett, Presley and everyone else—who'd spoil her and shower her with affection. Cass and I had no siblings, but my Seraphina would have a big family.

"Does she know about Seraphina?" Cass asked.

I nodded. "I called her the day after we got home. You were both sleeping."

"You're doing a lot while I'm sleeping. Cooking. Cleaning. Walking the halls with her. You need rest too, Leo."

"I'm used to it. Years of long nights." A half-truth.

Cass's wasn't the only mind unable to shut down. The only time I could let myself relax was when both of them were sleeping, something that didn't happen often enough.

A squawk from the bedroom sent me to my feet. I grabbed a towel and held it out for Cass as she stepped from the tub and wrapped it around herself. Then she hurried past me to the bedroom, where Seraphina was ready to eat.

The three of us settled on the bed and once Cass was done nursing, I took over burping while she dressed in oatmeal sweats. Then we let Seraphina look around a bit before taking her to the living room, where we could set her in a swing.

"Want me to grab your book?"

Cass shrugged. "I don't know. I'm not really into it, which is strange because it was exactly the kind of book I would have devoured a year ago. Maybe my tastes are changing."

"To what?"

"Fiction." She grimaced and scrunched up her nose, something so cute I had to laugh.

"I've heard fiction is quite popular."

She groaned. "And I like it. I've always enjoyed historical fiction. But that was a distant second to nonfiction. Now they've seemed to swap. What's wrong with me?"

"Nothing, babe. Nothing at all."

"Everything is changing. Fiction feels like a betrayal to all the years I spent studying history."

"Why?"

"I don't know." She sighed. "I guess because I used to like real-life events. Now, maybe I just need to escape the real world, and fiction feels like the easiest route at times. And maybe because it hurts a little bit."

"Hurts?"

"Because as the days go by, now that she's here, I realize there's no going back. I won't get my doctorate like I'd always planned. It seems . . . unimportant. But it used to be so important."

"You might change your mind one day."

"True." She nodded. "But there's no school here, and I can't imagine moving away."

If she did, she'd have company.

"What do you miss most about school?" I asked.

"The library and the smell of old books. The discussions with professors. The debates with classmates. I loved how in a small group, we'd each like a different aspect of one particular story. That's what I like about history. We all see it through our own vantage point. And true stories are the most powerful."

This woman was fascinating. We hadn't spent nearly enough time getting to know one another, and as she spoke, I drowned in her every word. "How'd you get into it? History?"

"From books when I was young. And trips we'd take." She smiled and snuggled deeper into the couch, stretching out her legs.

I pulled them into my lap, massaging the arches and toes. "This okay?"

"I'll kick you if you stop," she said, making me smile. "My parents love to camp. When I was ten, Mom declared that she wanted to visit all of the national parks and picked Redwood National Park first. We drove down there that summer, making a three-week trip of it. Our station wagon didn't have a DVD player or anything, so I'd read. If we passed a town with a second-hand bookstore, we'd stop and I'd sell whatever book I'd finished reading and buy something new."

"I bet you read more books that summer than I've read my entire life."

Cass giggled. "I do read a lot. But after you read to me in the bathtub, I might have to make you do that with me all the time now."

I'd do anything she asked.

"There was no GPS then, so Dad taught me how to use a compass and read a map. When we got there, I was mesmerized by the trees and the forest. I couldn't believe they were so big."

"There's a picture of your mom hugging a tree at your house. In the hallway. Is it from that trip?"

Cass sat up straighter. "I didn't think you'd looked at those pictures."

"That one jumped out at me. So did the one of you with braces and bangs."

"No." She covered her face with her hands. "I was an awkward teenager. Please block that one from your mind forever."

"You looked cute."

"Liar." She laughed. "But yes, that was the trip. Before

we left the area, I bought a book about the park. How it was important to the American Indians. How it changed from logging after the westward expansion. How it was saved from destruction and turned into a national park. On the drive home, I read it twice. And it became a tradition for me. We'd go to a new national park every summer, and on the drive home, I'd have a new book."

"They're in the office?" I glanced down the hallway, picturing some of the books I'd helped her put in there.

"Yeah." She nodded. "I've kept them all. Mom and Dad still go camping all the time. As soon as the snow melts in the mountains, they disappear every weekend. But the national park trips were always for the three of us. I got so busy with school, and we haven't gone to one lately. I don't know if we'll go again."

"Someday."

Cass gave me a sad smile. "I hope so. I hope I can take Seraphina to some of my favorites one day."

"And maybe you'll let me tag along."

"If you want."

"I want." I relaxed deeper into the couch, trapping Cass's feet when she tried to take them away. Whatever I could do to prolong the touch and the conversation. "So those books from the parks are why you went into history?"

"Yes and no. They were the foundation. When other girls were reading Harry Potter, I was reading about the Romanov family and the fall of imperial Russia. Then when I was twelve, one of my aunts gave me two books from World War II. I've read them more times than I can remember. I fell in love with history and decided I never wanted to study anything else. Especially math."

"I wasn't into math either." I chuckled. "Do you still want to write books?"

"I don't know," she whispered.

It felt like another life when I'd been in her room, staring at her vision board and listening to her babble nervously and tell me that she wanted to write books.

"I was thinking about it a while ago," she said. "This transcription job has given me a new perspective. I could write from home in my spare time. But it would have to be"— her lip curled—"fiction."

"The horror," I teased.

She attempted a kick, but I held her tight, both of us smiling. "Before Seraphina was born, I finished transcribing this amazing book. It was historical fiction and made me wonder. What if? What if I tried it?"

"It's worth a shot, babe."

"You think?"

"Definitely. Try it. If you need to quit working, I've got you covered."

"Speaking of . . . I'd like to pay rent."

I scoffed. "Funny."

"I'm serious."

"This house is paid for, Cass. If you want to get groceries or whatever, great. But it's not necessary."

She blinked. "My parents' house isn't even paid for."

"I put money in the bank for a long time. I don't live on much. And I don't like debt so I paid off my mortgage the year I bought it. It's free and clear."

"Wow. I'm impressed."

"Don't be. I'm not the impressive one in this room. I barely graduated high school, let alone college and grad school. Told you before, but I hope she gets your smarts."

"And I hope she gets your art skills." Cass cast a glance at one of my drawings on the wall. "Your talent is remarkable."

I closed my eyes, resting my head on the back of the couch. "Tell me more about your camping trips."

We talked for hours about Glacier, Yellowstone, Grand Teton, Zion and Joshua Tree. I was so engrossed, I groaned when the doorbell rang.

"Eventually, you and Dad are going to have to come to a truce," Cass said.

That wasn't why I'd groaned, but now that she'd mentioned Dale, I swallowed another.

To say that he was pissed at her choice to move in here was an understatement. But he hadn't threatened to kill me again, so I was taking it as temporary approval.

Cass was right. Eventually Dale and I would have to hash it out, but at the moment, we were all focused on Cass and Seraphina.

"Stay here. I'll get the door." I slid free of her legs and went to let her parents inside.

"Hello!" Claudia swept inside like she always did, with a smile and a picnic basket full of food. "Where are my girls?"

"Living room." I took the basket from her, stepping aside as she kicked off her shoes.

Dale came in with a scowl, barely sparing me a glance as he took off his own shoes, then followed his wife inside.

Dinner was awkward but we all survived and seeing that Cass was exhausted, they didn't stick around for long. The moment Claudia had all of the dishes washed, she kissed us, me included, and said goodnight as they left.

"She needs a diaper change." Cass had Seraphina in her arms.

"I'll do it."

"Are you sure?" She yawned.

I kissed her hair as my answer and took our daughter to the nursery, where I struggled less and less with the diapers as the days progressed.

Her legs were so tiny, her toes like delicate flower petals. She whimpered at the cold until I had her snapped into her footie pajamas.

Then I sank into the rocking chair—my addition to the room, based on some eavesdropping of a conversation Presley'd had in the office one day about her list of nursery furniture. The sun was breaking on the horizon and the evening glow was fading through the curtained window.

"Just waking up for the day, aren't you?"

Seraphina cracked open her eyes and kicked her legs, learning how they worked.

"What are the chances you'll let us sleep tonight for more than two hours in a row?"

She kicked again.

"That's a no," Cass said from the doorway, walking into the nursery. "So . . . um, are you going to meet Emmett?"

"No. Why?"

"It's a Saturday. He said he was going to The Betsy. I thought you might want to get out of here for a bit."

I looked down at my daughter, then back at Cass. "Nah. I'm good here."

She studied me for a long moment, tilting her head in that curious stare of hers. Then it vanished and she took one more step, closing the distance to take my face in her hands.

And kissing me, wet and sweet.

CHAPTER SEVENTEEN

CASSANDRA

Scarlett swung the door open to her house and waved us inside. "Happy birthday!"

Luke was behind her with Mary in his arms. "Happy birthday, Cass."

"Thank you." I stepped inside with Leo following me close. He had Seraphina in her car seat looped on one arm and the diaper bag on the other.

She was kicking wildly, her eyes wide and bright. The color had changed some from when she was born, lightening and giving me hope that she'd have Leo's color. At two months old, she'd grown into this perfect baby with chubby cheeks and a happy smile.

"Come on back. We're all on the deck," Scarlett said.

"Sorry we're late." Leo set the car seat down and unstrapped the baby. "Someone had a blowout and we had to do a quick bath."

"I didn't even bother trying to save the outfit she ruined." It had been a cute green dress that was nearly too small for her. I'd hoped for one more wear, but after her diaper had exploded, I'd put it in the trash.

"That yellow shit doesn't come out of anything," Leo muttered.

"Been there." Luke chuckled. "Sounds like you've earned a beer."

We followed them through the french doors to their beautiful deck decorated with flowerpots, none of which had been planted yet. Though today was a warm spring day, Mom always said it was too risky to plant flowers in Montana before Memorial Day.

Scarlett must believe the same.

"Hi!" Mom and Dad were seated beside one another in a pair of matching chairs. She shot out of her seat, going straight for my daughter and practically ripping her out of Leo's arms.

"Hi, Mom."

"Happy birthday." She gave me a one-armed hug and went to her chair. When her favorite person was in the vicinity—Seraphina—the rest of us, even me, were ignored.

"Happy birthday, Buttercup." Dad pulled me into his arms and kissed my forehead. Then he let me go to shoot Leo a glare. "Leo."

"Dale," Leo clipped.

I rolled my eyes and frowned up at Dad. "Be nice."

"I'm trying."

"Try harder."

The two of them hadn't spoken about the animosity lingering, and with every encounter it seemed to get worse. Mostly because Dad hated to see that Leo was, in fact, a good father. Eventually, Dad would have to forgive Leo for his actions during my pregnancy.

Eventually.

Dad's tactic was to do his best to ignore Leo's existence.

"You look pretty today," he said.

"Thanks." I smiled and smoothed down the waist of my dress as he let me go.

"Beautiful." Leo's hand found the small of my back.

"Meh."

He frowned.

After two months, I was getting my body back, but the changes were harder for me to accept than I'd expected. The stretch marks bothered me the most. Along with those, there was a new fullness at my hips and breasts. I doubted my pre-pregnancy jeans would ever fit again and so I'd donned this dress today—a simple red print with small white dots, a tie at the waist and buttons down the skirt.

I didn't own a lot of red. For years, I'd thought the color was too much to pair with my hair. But I'd felt like a bit of bold today. And the way Leo's eyes had flared when I'd walked out of the bedroom, dressed for the party, had given me a boost of confidence.

Maybe he'd see me as a woman again, not just a mother.

Two weeks ago, the doctor had given me the all-clear to resume normal activities, sex included. And even though Leo had been in the exam room and had heard her every word, he hadn't touched me.

Maybe I've lost my appeal.

"Want a beer or something, babe?" Leo leaned in close, dragging in a long breath of my hair and stifling a pained groan.

Or maybe not.

"Sure. Whatever you're having."

"Be back." Leo grinned and walked for the cooler.

Beer, not a drink I'd enjoyed much in the past, had become sort of a treat these past couple of weeks.

Every few nights, Leo and I would cuddle together on the couch with a beer after Seraphina had her bath and was put in her crib. We'd watch a movie or he'd read to me, then sleepy and slightly buzzed, I'd fall asleep in his bed.

Our bed? Was it ours?

I hadn't slept in my own for two months and while at first, it had been a necessity to tag-team Seraphina during the night feedings, now it felt more and more confusing.

Were we friends? He felt like the best friend I'd ever had. He was there for me always. If I had a bad day or a good day, he was the first person I wanted to tell. When he was at work, he'd text often to say hello. He'd send me pictures of whatever he was working on. And when it came to writing, he was my champion.

His encouragement had given me the confidence to draft the first chapter.

My transcribing job was completely flexible. I hadn't taken on a new project since before Seraphina was born. Instead, during her nap times, I toyed with writing. Every night, I'd walk Leo through my story and where I wanted it to go next.

I'd dream aloud and he'd be there, listening intently while my head soared through the clouds.

I was undeniably in love with Leo Winter.

It had happened so effortlessly, like a yawn that comes over you in the middle of a lecture. No matter how hard you tried to smother it, there was no use fighting the inevitable.

"What's going on in here?" Dad asked, touching my temple.

"Nothing." I forced a smile and was mobbed by friends as he went to sit beside Mom and Seraphina.

Bryce and Dash and their boys each said hello before the kids raced away to play in the yard. Genevieve, due at any moment, waved from her seat while Isaiah wrangled a toddling Amelia. Presley hugged me hello, then disappeared inside to nurse her son Nico—just two weeks younger than Seraphina—as Shaw brought me the beer Leo had pulled from the cooler because Leo was too busy showing off his new tattoo.

"That's so cool," Bryce said as she leaned in to inspect the detail.

He'd gotten it nearly three weeks ago without telling me about it. That morning before work, he'd been in the office, rifling through paperwork from the hospital. Then he'd left that day and come home with Seraphina's newborn footprint stamped on his heart.

The piece was all black, much like the ink imprint they'd taken at the hospital. The artist had captured the indentations in her foot and the petite impressions of her toes.

As Leo pulled down his shirt, hiding those sculpted washboard abs, Emmett walked over to me. He slung a beefy arm around my shoulders and pulled me into his side. "Happy birthday."

"Thanks. How's your Saturday going?"

"Good food. Good friends. Nice day. Can't complain."

It wouldn't be a Saturday without Emmett. He came by every weekend to say hello. At first, I'd thought it was to try and drag Leo to The Betsy, but as the weeks had gone on, I'd realized his visits were like those an older brother would make to his younger brother.

They were family. And maybe . . . maybe Emmett was lonely.

"We've been taken over with babies." He chuckled as we both looked around the deck.

"But none of them are as beautiful as mine." Leo swept in behind Mom's chair and stole Seraphina right from Mom's hands, getting a huff from my mother and a coo from my daughter.

"How's my little?" He nuzzled into her neck, blowing a raspberry on her skin and earning the smile that stole my breath every time. That, and the words he'd say to her.

Every time he called her *little*, I melted.

"You get her every day, Leo." Mom stood from her chair and held out her hands. "Give her back."

He chuckled, kissed Seraphina on her wispy strands of red hair, then returned her to Mom.

"Can we play a game now?" Xander called from the yard.

Zeke nodded at his side, holding a yellow bocce ball.

"I'm in." Leo swiped up his beer, then joined the boys on the lawn, his swagger so slow and sexy it sent a shiver down my spine.

Emmett let me go to join the boys along with Dash, Luke, Shaw and Isaiah. And the ladies all settled around Genevieve so she wouldn't have to move.

We talked and laughed most of the day, eating more food than I'd consumed in weeks. And when the sun began to dip toward the horizon, the temperature falling with it, Scarlett brought out a white cake covered with twenty-five candles.

"Make a wish, Firecracker." Leo stood behind my chair, his hands on my shoulders.

I closed my eyes and wished.

I wish for you.

Silly, maybe. Probably. Definitely. Still, I wished, and when I blew out all of the candles, I glanced up to meet his gaze.

The heat in those bright irises made my mouth dry.

"We have presents." Presley rushed inside the house and brought out two boxes.

"You guys didn't need to do this." I tore the paper on the first, a boxed set of books that I'd mentioned offhandedly to Leo that I'd wanted. Then I opened the second box, this one a brand-new laptop.

I gasped. "This is too much."

"Nah," Dash said. "You're one of us now. This family is big on gifts."

"Leo says your laptop is a few years old," Emmett said. "If you're going to write a bestseller, we thought you'd need a new keyboard."

A sheen of tears filled my eyes and I blinked them away.

Family.

These people had pulled me into their world and made me one of their own.

I glanced up at Mom and Dad, both with smiles on their faces. Seraphina was asleep in Dad's arms.

We had a big family here. Mom and her sisters, my aunts. My grandparents on both sides. Dad had his brother too. But we had never done this type of regular family gathering, the barbeques and Saturday birthday parties. Often, my parents would choose to go camping instead. While they loved their families, we weren't close. They weren't . . . friends.

Here, it was both.

And there was safety knowing that, good or bad, they'd be here for me. For Leo. For Seraphina.

If the Warriors ever came after us, they'd have a battle on their hands.

Thankfully, news of the Warriors was limited and came directly from the FBI in the form of prison sentence updates. No one arrested had escaped incarceration, including the men who'd been involved in the kidnapping.

Bastards.

Shoving those thoughts aside, I focused on the box Mom set in front of me. I tore into the gold and silver paper, revealing a spa set for home and a gift card for the local spa in town.

"We should all have a spa day," I said.

"I'm in." Bryce raised her hand.

"Same here," Scarlett added.

Presley nodded. "Me too."

"I want a pedicure," Genevieve said. "I can't see or reach my feet."

"Tomorrow?" Mom suggested. "I'll call and see if they've got openings."

"That's good for me," I said as a whimper caught my ear.

"She's probably hungry." Dad brought Seraphina over.

"We'd better get her home," Leo said, already moving to collect our things.

Everyone must have had the same idea because we all shuffled out to the driveway and street, saying our goodnights and heading to our respective homes.

Leo drove us home in his truck with Seraphina temporarily satisfied with her binky. He had an arm draped over the wheel, and the other leaned on the console between us. It wasn't as sexy when he drove the truck as it was when he rode his bike, but when we rode together, I had the perfect view of his profile. Of the goatee he'd trimmed shorter just this morning. Of the strength in his sharp jaw. Of the soft pout of his lips and the small bump on the bridge of his nose.

His biceps strained at the sleeves of his shirt. The cotton stretched across his broad chest. Living together, I'd learned that he was religious about a daily visit to the basement gym, either to lift weights or box.

"You're staring, babe."

My cheeks flushed but I didn't look away. "Sometimes I have to look at you and remind myself that you're real."

That he was with me.

His mouth turned up and he reached for my hand, bringing my knuckles to his lips. He nipped at them, then kissed the spot where his teeth had grazed.

That single move and I squirmed in my seat, desperate for him to make a move. Any move.

Or should I? I'd kissed him months ago. He'd kissed me since, but it had always been like this. A chaste press of lips to my hand or my hair. A brush of his mouth against my cheek.

I didn't want gentle or reserved. I wanted him to kiss me like a woman he wanted to consume. A woman he craved.

The moment we parked in the driveway, he released my hand and then it was all about the baby. Seraphina nursed and had a warm bath. I rocked her to sleep, spending nearly an hour in the chair because she was overtired from the excitement of the party. Finally, those beautiful dark eyelashes drifted shut and she was out.

With her in the crib, I went to the bedroom and found Leo on the mattress, staring at the baby's video monitor. He'd kicked off his boots and socks. He'd yanked off his shirt and his jeans were unbuttoned, hanging low to reveal the tight waistband of his boxer briefs.

My pulse thumped in my veins. In my core.

"Hey." He caught me staring again and set the monitor aside. Then he jackknifed off the bed and padded across the room to the TV stand, picking up the small box on top. "One more present."

"You didn't have to get me anything."

"Of course I did. Open it." He crooked his finger, motioning me over.

I crossed the room, trying desperately to keep my breathing even. Taking the box from his hand, I pulled off the top, revealing a ring inside, resting on white padding.

My heart skipped, then I realized it wasn't that sort of ring. This was simply jewelry, not an engagement.

We weren't there. Maybe deep in my heart there was a pang of disappointment, but my rational side took over and reminded me that we weren't there.

We might never be there.

Leo dipped his pinky finger in to retrieve the ring and hold it up. "I got the idea from the book we're reading."

The wide, golden metal band had been etched with a series of lines and dots. It took me a moment, then it dawned on me. "That's morse code."

"Yeah." He took it off his finger and slid it onto my thumb. It fit perfectly.

"It's beautiful. And so unique. What does it say?"

"Firecracker."

I smiled and touched the piece with my other finger. "I love it."

"You do?"

"It's beautiful."

He sighed and took my face in his hands. "I want . . ."

"What?" I whispered when he trailed off.

Leo swallowed hard, his Adam's apple bobbing. Then he dropped a chaste kiss on my forehead and let me go. "Never mind."

My spirits crashed.

"You need rest," he said.

"I'm not tired."

His eyes flared and he took a step back.

Screw it. It was my birthday and what I wanted was to *feel* wanted. "Want to know what I wished for when I blew out my candles?"

"What?"

"You."

He gulped.

"D-do you want me?" It was the scariest question I'd asked in my life.

"Don't want to hurt you, babe."

"You heard the doctor. I'm fine."

"I don't mean physically. I mean . . ."

He didn't want to break my heart. Oh. My. God. That was why he'd held back. That was why he was putting distance between us, inching toward the bathroom.

"I'm not scared, Leo."

"I am."

He had no faith in himself. His confidence was shredded and there he stood, vulnerable and raw. The insecurities he didn't show anyone, he showed to me.

If I hadn't loved him before tonight, I would have fallen right here.

"I love you."

He froze and the color drained from his face.

Not exactly the reaction I'd expected. "Sorry. I . . ." *I don't know what the fuck I'm thinking.* Mortification spread across my skin, coloring it as black as the outlines on his tattoos.

I whirled around, ready to bolt for the door, but a strong hand gripped my elbow and forced me to stop.

"Cassandra."

God, how he said my name. Like a birthday wish of his own. A wish he wouldn't let himself make. I braced, ready for the rejection of my lifetime.

Why? Why had I said that?

Because he needed to hear it. The realization took a fraction of the embarrassment away. Leo needed to know who loved him. How many of us loved him. That he didn't need to feel lost or alone because he'd always have us.

"You never say what I expect." His arms snaked around me, wrapping around me and pulling my back into his chest. "And I love you."

My heart might have broken out of my chest if he hadn't been holding me so tight. I gasped. "W-what?"

His lips found the shell of my ear. "I love you. Didn't know you felt that way too."

"How could I not?"

"How could you?"

"Oh, Leo." I sagged into him, my head spinning. "Because you love our daughter. Because you treat me like I'm precious. Because you're a good man."

"I'm not—"

"You are a good man, Leo." I twisted, spinning in his embrace. "Whatever happened in the past is in the past. That's not the man you are now. The best stories in history are the true ones and they usually start with a string of mistakes. We're all flawed. We learn. But no matter the past, it doesn't mean you don't deserve my love. Besides, it's mine to give to who I choose. I choose you. And I chose you a year ago."

"Cass, you don't understand."

"I understand. I was in that basement. I knew what the Warriors would have done to me. I know what kind of men they are. I understand."

I understood that in a different lifetime, the Tin Kings hadn't been all that different.

He closed his eyes and dropped his forehead to mine. "You deserve better."

"Now you sound like my father."

"He's not wrong."

"Babe." I used his own word to get his attention. I loved my father, but in this, he was wrong. One day, he'd see it. He'd admit it.

I stepped away from Leo and walked toward the door to turn off the light. Then in the muted glow of the bedroom, I reached up and slipped free a strap from my dress.

Leo's eyes flared and he sucked in a sharp breath as I did the same with the other strap.

I slid the bodice from my torso and hips, along with my bra and panties, until I was standing in front of him, naked and vulnerable too.

My hands inched up to cover the stretch marks across my belly, but before they even reached my navel, Leo flew across the room and smashed his lips on mine.

His tongue swept inside my parted lips and I trembled as he delved into my mouth, devouring and tasting and worshiping.

"I love you." He spoke the words between licks. "I am so fucking in love with you, Cass."

"I love you too." My fingers fumbled to get his jeans off his legs.

Leo took over, stripping himself bare before picking me up and taking me to the bed. Then he slid inside me, joining us together. He made love to me, tender and unhurried, until we were both breathless and lost in each other.

When we came, it was together. When we fell asleep, it was together.

Right after he whispered, "I choose you."

And with his words, my birthday wish came true.

CHAPTER EIGHTEEN

LEO

"Goddamn it." I sucked in a pained breath and gritted my teeth.

"Call an ambulance," Dash barked.

"No." I stopped Emmett before he could take out his phone. "I'm fine. Just . . . give me a sec."

"I'm calling anyway," Presley said, moving out of the group of guys all standing around, staring at me.

I wasn't hurt, was I? My eyes were swimming in my head thanks to a massive jolt of terror and adrenaline.

"I gotta sit." I shuffled toward a rolling stool.

Dash kept hold of my arm, steadying me, then crouched in front of me. "Breathe."

I dropped my elbows to my knees and hung my head. When my heart finally stopped thrashing against my sternum, I shook my head. "Fuck."

Presley's hand landed on my shoulder. There were tears streaming down her face.

"I'm fine."

She nodded. "The ambulance is coming."

I scanned my arms and legs. They were whole and attached. Then I ran a hand through my hair, checking for blood. "I'm not hurt."

My shoulder had taken the brunt of the crash, but it would heal.

"You might have a concussion."

I didn't, but she wanted the ambulance, so I was going to let the EMTs check me out because it would make her feel better.

Every person in the shop looked pale faced and terrified. Tyler, one of our mechanics who did the routine work, was shaking. Behind him stood a customer who must have been in the waiting room. His dark hair was parted in a harsh line above his left eyebrow and like Tyler, his face was pale.

I didn't have time to worry about either of them because —*Christ*—I could have just fucking died.

What had just happened to me was a mechanic's worst fear. Equipment wasn't infallible. Tools were defective. Latches broke. Safety mechanisms failed.

I really couldn't die. I had things to live for.

The past month had been the best in my life. Seraphina was changing and growing. She'd started to coo and babble and damn it, I needed to hear her first word.

And Cass was a miracle. My miracle. Every day I loved her more. Every damn day. There was a future with her and damn it, I couldn't die.

I swallowed hard, the reality of the past five minutes sinking in.

"What happened?" Dash asked.

I sighed with the breeze drifting through the open bay doors.

June had brought green grass, sweet spring air and yellow sunshine. Cass wanted to plant flowers tonight after work in one of the beds in the front yard. I'd promised to help.

I could have died and missed the flowers.

Maybe I did have a concussion—I couldn't seem to organize my thoughts.

"Leo," Isaiah said, standing at my side.

Right. Dash had asked me a question.

"I don't know what happened. I grabbed the jack, the new one, and got it under the rear axle. It worked fine. I've been using it for weeks."

We had larger stations for the routine jobs, where the guys could pull a car inside, hoist it up and crank out an oil change or tire rotation. But for the Firebird, we'd been using the portable jacks, like we did all the time. This was a side project and not one that was going to disrupt the regular jobs.

"There was a strange noise. I was under the rear wheel, threading through the wiring for the air ride, and I heard a dribbling sound, so I slid out."

If I'd hesitated for another two seconds, I might have been crushed.

The jack had collapsed and slammed into the jack stand I'd put in as a safety measure. But the spot where I'd been lying was beside a piece of jagged metal that we'd yet to pull out because it was in a spot hard to reach.

That metal would have sliced open my throat.

On the concrete floor beside the Firebird and the jack was a pool of hydraulic fluid. That was what I'd heard dribbling. A seal must have blown.

"Think it wrecked the car?" I asked.

"Who gives a shit about the car?" Presley shrieked, then dropped her face into her hands as her shoulders shook.

Emmett went to her, tucking her into his side as she cried.

My chest tightened and I leaned forward again. Better to think about the car, the gift I wanted to give to Cass, than the fact that had I acted any slower, if that dripping noise hadn't alerted me to something being wrong, I'd be leaving the garage in a body bag.

The sound of a wailing siren filled the air.

Presley sniffled and pushed away from Emmett, then bolted for the bay door to meet the ambulance as its tires screeched into the parking lot.

I blew out a long breath, then stood, taking a moment before I attempted a step. Maybe Pres was right to have my head checked out. I was struggling to focus and my footsteps through the shop felt heavy.

The EMTs rushed to me, one of them taking an arm to help me to the back of the ambulance. They checked me out, head to toe, and when they deemed me fine, just shaken up, we all relaxed. Tyler returned to the garage to get back to work, and the customer disappeared to the waiting room.

"We could take you to the hospital, just in case," one of the EMTs said.

"Nah." I stepped down from the ambulance, feeling more like myself now that the adrenaline had ebbed. "Thanks."

Dash said goodbye to them as I walked toward Presley and pulled her into my arms.

She hugged me tight. "Don't ever do that to me again."

"Okay."

"You could have died." She started crying again. "What would we have done if you had died?"

"I'm not dead."

She squeezed, then let me go, swiping furiously at her face.

Then Dash was at her side, taking his turn to offer her some comfort.

Emmett and Isaiah surrounded me, our huddle close under the bright afternoon sun. None of us had much to say.

My eyes wandered down the parking lot toward the clubhouse.

It was there, always there. A constant reminder. For years, I'd pull into the parking lot and stare at that building, feeling like the reason I was so lonely was because of the boards on the windows and the chain padlocked on its doors.

Not anymore. It was just a building. It was the past.

Once, years ago, I'd made the offhand comment that we should burn the place down. It had been right after Draven's death. I'd muttered the words and instantly regretted them.

But they were true. I wanted to walk over, torch it and never look back.

Maybe that was just the accident taking its toll. The fear of death and a life cut short.

Whatever the reason, I wanted to take a chainsaw to the trees where I'd taken women and fucked them against the bark. I wanted to smash every fixture in the party room, blacking it out and with it the drinking and the drugs and the fights. I wanted to fill in the foundation with rubble and bury it in the earth, just like the bodies of the men who we'd killed in the clubhouse basement.

I wanted to come here and not see the reminder of who I'd been.

Cass deserved better than me and the sins I'd committed in that building. I hadn't had enough time with her. We hadn't had enough time for me to make good on her words.

She thought I was a good man and damn it, I wasn't.

But I wanted to be.

"Leo, you okay?" Emmett asked.

I blinked away the tears, suddenly realizing why the building looked so blurry, and shook my head. "We should tear it down."

"Huh?"

"The clubhouse. We should tear it down."

Dash jerked, his eyes widening. Then his jaw clenched.

That had been his home too. It had been his legacy and a place where Draven had once been king. My words hadn't just shocked, they'd slashed.

But I hated it. Today, I hated that building, dark as the stain on my soul.

"You should go home," Dash said, his voice carrying an edge. Yeah, he was pissed. I would be too if I were in his shoes. If I were thinking clearly. That was his father's building and I'd just told him to tear it down.

Shit. I nodded. "Yeah."

It was nonsense. Tomorrow I'd replay my words and realize that I sounded like a fucking asshole. Because there'd been good times in that place too. Brotherhood and family.

What the hell was wrong with me? My head hurt and I couldn't quite make sense of, well . . . anything.

"You shouldn't be riding," Presley said. "I'll call Cass and have her come pick you up."

"No. I don't want her to know about this."

Her eyes bulged. "But—"

"No one tells her."

Cass didn't need that kind of worry. I was fine. The jack would be replaced with one that actually jacked up a damn car, and we'd forget this happened.

"I'll follow behind," Emmett said before Presley could object to my decision.

"I'm fine." I started for the garage to get my keys.

He stayed behind me as we left the shop, climbed on our bikes and drove across town. But I didn't go home.

I couldn't go home yet. After that kind of scare, I wasn't going to put off the conversation that I'd been prolonging for a month. Besides, Cass would take one look at my face and know something wasn't right. I needed a little while longer to steady up.

The last thing I wanted was her worrying each day I walked out the door for work. I wasn't putting that on her for the rest of my working life.

I parked on the street outside of the county courthouse and when Emmett stopped behind me, I motioned for him to stay on his bike.

"What are we doing here?"

"I need to talk to Dale."

"Okay." He balanced on his bike. "I'll wait."

"You don't need to."

He pulled out his phone and gave it his attention. No discussion. He was waiting.

"Thanks."

"Good luck." He chuckled. "Never met a man so determined to get himself killed so many times in a single day."

I grinned. There was a chance Dale might murder me for what I was about to do. Some risks were worth taking. Leaving Emmett on his bike, I started up the wide, sweeping steps to the front door.

Dale worked as the director of Human Resources for the county. It took me a few minutes to navigate the labyrinth of hallways to find his office. With one fortifying breath, I shoved open the door.

"Can I help you?" the woman at the front desk asked.

"I'm looking for Dale Cline."

She gave me a sideways glance, her eyes raking over my tattoos.

It had never bothered me before, the careful looks and suspicious stares. The Tin Kings had caused a lot of chaos in Clifton Forge and I'd earned my reputation. *Fight first, talk later.* Anyone who'd lived here long enough knew who I was and if they had a problem with me, they could go fuck themselves.

But today, it bothered me. Maybe it was the accident. Or maybe it was because she didn't ask for my name.

Dale must have shared his disapproval of me around the office.

Hell, this is a bad idea.

I raked my hand through my hair and straightened my T-shirt. I'd gone for black today and it disguised a grease smudge on the hem.

"Leo." Dale's expression was stony as he came out of his office wearing a starched white button-down and pressed khaki pants. "Is something wrong?"

Other than the fact that I'd almost been crushed today? "No. Got a minute?"

He waved me back without a word, and when we got into his office, I closed the door. There was a small round table in one corner with four chairs. Behind Dale's desk there was a set of drawers and a bookshelf.

The bottom half was filled with books and binders, but

the top two rows had been reserved for framed photos. And in each one, Cass's face smiled my way. Even the one of her and Seraphina, taken at her birthday barbeque last month.

Dale moved behind his desk, taking a chair.

I stayed on my feet and got to the point. "I'm asking Cass to marry me."

"No." His fists balled on his desk.

"I'll ask her with or without your permission, Dale. But I'd like to have it."

"No."

A waste of my time. Damn it. I wasn't sure what to say to make him change his mind, other than the truth. "You told me months ago that I didn't deserve Cass. Maybe you're right."

"I *am* right."

"Fair enough. But the way I see it, she deserves me."

I walked to the bookshelf and picked up Cass's framed senior picture. She didn't look a lot different now. Yes, she'd grown into a beautiful woman, but she'd always have youthful features. Claudia was the same way. One day, I hoped to be the old man, weathered and gray, with the beautiful firecracker on my arm.

"I love her," I whispered. "I'll always love her. No man will fight for her the way I will."

Cass deserved me. No man would love her more.

Dale sighed. "My answer remains no."

I returned the photo to its shelf. I'd ask Cass anyway, with or without Dale's blessing. The ring was in my sock drawer at home, waiting.

I strode for the door, but the moment I put my hand on the knob, Dale stopped me.

"Leo."

I glanced back.

"Claudia's father told me no when I asked him for her hand. I was pissed about it for years. We have a good relationship now, but it wasn't always that way. I asked him once why he said no. He told me I'd understand it when Cassie was older. He was right. I understand. I'd say no to anyone because she's my daughter. Maybe you'll get it when Seraphina meets someone who loves her."

He swallowed hard and his eyes turned glassy. "If I say yes, that means I've lost her. I'm not the one who is in charge of keeping her safe anymore. Not that I kept her safe. Those bastards took her and . . . I wasn't there."

"That wasn't your fault."

"Do you honestly think I'll ever feel otherwise?"

"No." I hadn't even been a part of Cass's life at that point and I felt guilty for not having kept the Warriors out of Clifton Forge.

"My answer is no," he said. "I just . . . I can't say yes. To anyone. But if I had to, I'd say yes to you."

That was more than I'd expected today. "Thank you."

"Protect them."

"With my life." I nodded and let myself out of his office, leaving the courthouse to meet Emmett.

"How'd that go?"

I straddled my bike, breathing easier than I had ten minutes ago. "Better than expected."

"How are you feeling?"

"I'm all right."

"You sure?"

"Can't believe that happened." I shook my head, some of the fear creeping in. "Remember those days when we'd have a gun in our boot or holstered under our vest?"

He patted his boot, probably where he had a Glock stowed. Some habits didn't die just because we didn't pull on our cuts each morning and wear the patch around town. I didn't wear my weapons any longer, but there was a pistol locked in the compartment under my seat. Another was hidden in my truck. And I had a small arsenal in my home safe.

"It's one thing to face off with another man and know he might pull the trigger before you," I said. "It's another to trust in a machine that should work and didn't. That jack was new."

"I know." He shook his head. "It shouldn't have broken."

"Had to be faulty from the manufacturer. Shit happens, right?" I waved it off. "I'll be fine. But you aren't going to find me beneath a car anytime soon."

"Glad you're okay." He blew out a deep breath. "For what it's worth, I agree with you about the clubhouse."

I groaned. "I can't believe I said that out loud. Dash was pissed."

"He'll get over it." He turned the key to his bike. "See you tomorrow."

"Yeah." I nodded as the roar of his engine filled the air, then started my own machine, aiming it in the opposite direction, toward home.

Cass was going to find out about the accident eventually. As much as I wanted to keep it from her, I realized on the drive home that we couldn't have that kind of a secret. She'd have my balls when she found out, so I'd tell her what happened.

Just not today.

The house was quiet when I walked inside and keyed in the code on the alarm panel. I stepped out of my boots and padded to the nursery, finding Seraphina asleep in her crib.

My heart twisted as I took in her dear face.

I wasn't a praying man, but the fact that I'd survived today, maybe I'd have to start. Whatever angel was looking out for me, I owed them for making that noise and getting me out from under that car in time.

After one more minute with my daughter, I left her alone to sleep and searched the house for Cass, finding her in the bedroom.

Not sleeping peacefully.

Her beautiful face was twisted in pain. Her hand was strangling a corner of her pillow. I rushed to her side and shook her shoulders. "Babe, wake up."

She gasped, her eyes flying open. "Leo?"

"What's wrong?" I brushed the hair from her face as she blinked, coming out of her nightmare.

"Just a bad dream." She shoved up to a seat. "What are you doing home?"

"Missed you." I pulled her to me and kissed the top of her hair. "What was your dream about?"

"Nothing." She waved it off and stood, but I caught her hand before she could run away.

"It was about the kidnapping."

Her body tensed.

It had been over a year and from what I could tell, she hadn't talked about it. Not to me. To the girls. To Claudia or Dale. She was keeping it all inside and I hadn't pressed because so far, it hadn't seemed to bother her.

How long had she been hiding these nightmares? What other side effects was she suffering alone?

"You need to talk about it. At some point, you need to talk about it."

Cass's shoulders slumped but she allowed me to pull her onto my lap. "It's easier to pretend it didn't happen."

"Do you have these dreams a lot?" This wasn't something I'd seen at night, though I slept hard.

"Only when you're gone."

There was comfort there, knowing I kept the demons at bay. But I didn't want her battling them on her own. I knew the rough details from Scarlett, but I wanted Cass's story. I wanted her everything.

I'd promised Dale I'd protect her. Even if that was from herself.

"Tell me," I begged. "Please."

CHAPTER NINETEEN

CASSANDRA

"Tell me. Please."

No. My first instinct was to say no and bolt from this bedroom. But the plea in those beautiful green eyes was my undoing, so I stayed in Leo's arms.

"I don't like to talk about it."

"Babe, I get that, but it kills me that you're fighting this alone."

I blew out a long breath, sinking into his chest as his arms tightened around me. If there was ever a person to tell, it was him.

"It's not fair. I was in the wrong place at the wrong time. Nothing more. But . . ." God, I couldn't do this. I didn't want to go back to that basement and talk about this.

Leo didn't move. He didn't press or ask me to continue. He simply held me, wrapping me in his warmth. His cedar-and-spice scent had become my anchor.

"Why is this so hard?" I whispered.

"Because the low points are always the hardest to revisit."

Yes. Exactly. "I just . . . it's not fair."

"No, it's not."

"I was home to study. That was it. Just study and work on a paper. I'd come home to do that too the weekend we met at The Betsy."

For a time, I'd been so angry at myself for going to the bar. Even while pregnant, I'd regretted it to a degree. But I couldn't now. That night had changed my life. Without that night I wouldn't have Seraphina.

I wouldn't have Leo.

"Instead of studying, I got distracted by a hot biker."

He grinned. "That's your fault. You distracted me first."

I gave him a small smile and leaned on his shoulder. Such a strong shoulder it was. He'd raise Seraphina on this shoulder, and I loved that she could always depend on it. In the depths of my soul, I knew Leo would be a good father. The sins of his past didn't need to dictate his future.

These days, I think he realized it too.

It was like a switch had flipped after she was born. On to off, that night he'd held her in his arms. Or maybe he'd started to change when I'd moved out. Whatever the reason, I was grateful. Because Seraphina wasn't the only one who could lean on his strong shoulders. I could too, especially in this.

What was the harm in talking the kidnapping through? It had happened. It wasn't going to magically disappear the longer I ignored it. If anything, it was only getting worse. When he wasn't around, when I wasn't distracted by Seraphina, the memory would creep up on me, so fast and startling it was like a hooded figure jumping out from behind a corner to scare me into a scream.

So I took a deep breath. And let it out. All of it.

"I hate getting in my car, especially when I'm at Mom and Dad's. Every time I stand beside the door, I shake. I don't think I even realized it at the time, but that night you asked me to move in, part of me agreed just so I could escape that street."

"Babe." His hand rubbed up and down my spine.

"I either freeze and look all around, making sure I'm completely alone. Or I get in and slam the door shut so fast that one day, I rushed and slammed it on my foot."

I'd felt like a fool, terrified of nothing. Of everything.

"I'm glad that I never have to go anywhere alone," I said. The threat of danger with the Warriors had been a blessing. It meant I didn't have to walk out of the house alone. Someone was always with me or watching. "I don't think about it unless I'm alone."

"Then you won't be alone. Whenever you need me, just call. I'll drop everything and walk you to your car."

"Doesn't that sound ridiculous?" I sat up straight and stood, pacing the length of the bedroom. "We can't live like that, Leo. *I* can't live like that. It's been a year. Why won't it go away? I just want it to go away."

He stared at me with nothing but understanding on his face, then patted his knee.

I sank into his lap once more. "That's why I don't talk about it. Not even with my parents. I know they worry, but I just want it to go away. When that FBI agent called after it happened to check in, I started dodging her calls because I thought it would help make it go away. But it's not. It's still there. Every minute."

"Then let's walk through it. Start to finish. Tell me what happened."

I shuddered. "Do we have to?"

"Not talking about it isn't working, Cass. So let's talk about it. Once. Go from there."

"Okay." I blew out a deep breath. "I'd just gotten home from Missoula. Mom and Dad were off in the mountains. I'd brought a backpack full of clothes, my laptop and some junk food because I didn't want to raid Mom's fridge and have her come home to nothing after camping all weekend."

Pringles. Dr Pepper. Jelly beans. I'd planned to subsist on them and pizza delivery.

"I took everything inside but I'd forgotten my notebook in the car so I went outside to get it. That's when I saw Scarlett. She'd come out of Luke's house—I only thought of him as Chief Rosen then. She was wearing this backpack stuffed so full the seams stretched. I'd never seen her before, and my first thought was that she'd broken into his house and robbed him."

Leo chuckled. "Oh, she definitely robbed him."

I smiled. Yes, she had, hadn't she? She'd robbed him of his heart. "She was walking to the neighbor's house and I figured this was her plan. Rob all the houses while everyone was enjoying their Saturday afternoons away from home. Mom and Dad are part of the neighborhood watch and with them gone, she could have had free run of their house too. Scarlett even waved and smiled at me. I think if she hadn't done that, I would have called the cops right away. But she looked . . . nice. So I just stood there and watched her."

I'd watched her go to the neighbor's house and ring the doorbell. I hadn't known that neighbor. The family who'd lived there when I was in high school had moved the summer after my graduation. The house had been a rental and my parents hadn't tried too hard to get to know its various tenants.

Scarlett had waited on the stoop while my mind had volleyed back and forth between guilty and innocent. I'd actually landed on innocent, ready to leave her be. Maybe she'd gotten the wrong house. Maybe she was going door to door for her church. It was a safe street, right?

Silly me.

"The door at the neighbor's flew open. The guy who answered was so tall and Scarlett is so short that I saw his face. I saw the vest he wore. She spun away, her face twisted and mouth open like she was about to scream, but he hit her over the head with a gun and she collapsed. It happened," I snapped my fingers, "that fast."

I closed my eyes and it played in my mind like I was still standing there beside my car. "I should have been safe. I was at home. In the driveway. We lived on a safe street. Or maybe that's the biggest joke of all. Maybe there is no such thing as a safe place."

"Do you really believe that?" I opened my eyes. He reached up, cupping my jaw. There was pain on his face, almost like he feared the answer. But there was no reason.

"No, I don't."

Leo was my safe place. It was probably why I didn't have the nightmares when he was home. Because I knew he'd throw himself in front of a bullet to keep Seraphina and me safe.

"Good." He kissed the tip of my nose, then let go of my face so I could continue.

"I think I went into shock. I've never seen anyone hit before, not in real life. By the time I snapped out of it and scrambled for my phone to call the police, the guy had spotted me. There were three of them. I ran. I dropped my phone. But they caught me."

There were times I'd close my eyes and still hear the thud of boots pounding behind me. I'd feel that massive hand grip my arm and whip me around. I'd feel the same hand smash into my cheek.

"One of them hit me. No one had ever hit me before." Another shock. Another rude awakening for a girl who'd lived a privileged life. Hell, my parents didn't even believe in spanking.

Leo's frame tensed and the click of his jaw was audible. There was a flash of violence in his eyes and it made me love him just that much more. Because had the man who'd hit me stood in this room, I had no doubt that Leo would have killed him without hesitation.

"Things are fuzzy after that. It hurts a lot when you get hit in the face."

"It does." Spoken from a man who'd hit and been hit.

"I'd been so busy staring at Scarlett that I hadn't noticed a van, but one of the men, probably the one who hit me, picked me up and carried me to it. They'd already put Scarlett inside. She was unconscious in the back. They had her tied. They did the same to me and I was so out of it, I didn't even try to fight back."

"It would have only made it worse, babe."

"I still wish I had fought back," I whispered. A kick. A scream. Something. "Instead, I just lay there while they bound my hands, then slammed the doors shut."

The van's tires had whirled for what had felt like a year. The sun had streamed through the back window, bright and hot. The metal of the floor had dug into my shoulder as I'd tried not to roll and slam into a knocked-out Scarlett. Her blood had soaked the back of her blond hair, but she'd been breathing.

Then the van had stopped. I'd held my breath as the rear doors had been ripped open.

"When we got to the clubhouse, one of the men put Scarlett over his shoulder and carried her inside. The other two each took one of my arms and hauled me. I didn't know exactly where we were at that point. We went through an entrance and immediately down some stairs, straight to the basement. Then they tossed us in a cement room and locked us inside."

The sterile scent of bleach on the concrete had clung to my nose, and even now, a year later, there were days when I could smell that sterile, cold stench. There had been no windows and the only light had come from a flickering bulb dangling from a single black wire. The room had been pitched toward a floor drain in the center of the room.

That drain had been the scariest thing in the room. Because it didn't take much imagination to know what they rinsed away.

"I cried," I said softly. "When they shut the door on us, I was sure I'd die in that room, so I cried." For the pain my death would cause my parents. For the camping trips I'd miss. For the adventures I'd lost, all because I'd been in the wrong place at the wrong time.

Three hours away from home, I'd sat beside an unconscious Scarlett, a stranger at that point, and cried.

A river of tears had poured down my cheeks, but there were still days when I felt more coming. Like I hadn't drained the well. Maybe if we'd had to stay in that basement, I would have emptied it all out.

"Scarlett woke up eventually. After the music started."

"She said they had a party."

"Yeah. The music was so loud it shook the walls." But

thank God for that music. That party was likely the reason we were alive. "When Scarlett woke up, she told me where we were. One of my roommates at school is from Ashton. She'd tell me about the Arrowhead Warriors. I'd tell her about the Tin Kings. The rumors at least. The other girls we lived with thought it was so interesting that we each had a motorcycle club in our hometowns."

Leo closed his eyes, shaking his head. He was comparing himself and the Warriors. It was written on his face.

"You're not them."

"Cass—"

"Have you ever kidnapped two innocent women?"

"No."

"Because you're not them." I gave him a sad smile. "Maybe we shouldn't talk about this."

"No, babe. That's my own shit to work out. It's not going to happen today. Hell, it probably won't happen this year."

I'd be here, if he needed my help to work it out. For the coming year and all those after. I'd be here to show him that he was a good man.

"What happened after Scarlett woke up?" he asked.

"I tried to keep her awake because I knew she had a concussion. We talked for a bit and then *he* came in."

"Tucker."

I cringed at his name.

The FBI had told me about Tucker Talbot when I'd asked what was happening to the men who'd kidnapped us. Agent Brown had explained that he was the president of the Warriors and would be facing trial.

"He threatened Scarlett. He broke her phone. He said he was going to wait until after the party when things quieted down, then we'd 'have some fun.'" I shivered, burrowing deeper into Leo's arms. "I see his eyes sometimes in my nightmares. Dark and evil. He would have killed us with a smile on his face."

"He can't get to you," Leo said. "You'll never see his face again."

"Scarlett spit on him. I was so scared, I hadn't even had a chance to make sense of it. But now, looking back, I wish I had too."

"That's my girl."

"He would have killed us."

Leo nodded. "Yes, he would have."

"He would have tortured us and probably liked it."

He hummed his agreement.

"Still think you're like him?" I met Leo's gaze, daring him to agree.

He sighed and shook his head.

"No, you're not." I stood from his lap, feeling the sudden urge to move around.

Leo had been right, talking about it was freeing. Rehashing the kidnapping was almost like walking away from it. Seeing it through a mirror and picking it apart.

If I was lucky, I'd see it this once, I'd give it a long, hard stare, then move on. But if the nightmares didn't go away, if I still had a hard time leaving the house on my own or standing in my parents' driveway, then I'd get counseling.

I couldn't put all of this on Leo, time and time again.

This once was enough.

"I fell asleep at some point," I told him. "The adrenaline crash or fear, I'm not sure, but when I woke up, Scarlett was awake too. We talked for a little while about nothing. She asked me about school. Then this couple came in and they started having sex against a wall."

Another first. That night, it was like the blinders to real life had been ripped away. It hadn't been television. It hadn't been a book. My naivety had simply shattered, like a glass being dropped from a ten-story building. Only dust remained.

"Ghost." I grimaced. "That was his name or nickname, whatever. They kept calling Scarlett 'Goldilocks.'"

"Her nickname from the time she'd lived there with her ex."

"I guess. Ghost recognized her. He knew we were there, but he seemed to like having an audience. We were forced to do nothing but watch and listen. At first, the woman liked it. Then, she didn't."

When he'd slammed into her rear entrance, there had been nothing pleasurable about her scream. Her fingernails had scraped against the cement wall as he'd pounded into her.

If there was any justice in the world, Ghost would be sent to prison simply for how he'd treated that woman.

"Scarlett tried to take my mind off of it. She asked me about happy memories. I told her about camping with my parents. More about school. I don't really even remember what I told her. It was so hard to think."

At that point, I'd stopped feeling the tears as they fell. My body had gone numb.

I don't want to die here.

That was what I'd told Scarlett, the one sentence I remembered with perfect clarity. I didn't want to die in a basement. Not with people having sex at my side. Not without telling my parents how much I loved them.

"Scarlett promised we'd stay together. Until the end. And then the light went out. There was a loud crack and the music stopped. I was frozen, stuck there on the floor. And somehow, she thought to run."

The memories went in flashes from there. I'd clung to Scarlett as she'd led us through total darkness toward the door that Ghost and his companion had forgotten to close. We'd managed to get the door shut before he came after us. We'd made it to the stairs. Then Luke had been there with the FBI and I'd been swept away into the night.

"It was Scarlett who saved me," I told Leo as he sat on the bed, watching me pace. There was a stiffness to his posture, like he really wanted me closer, but he was fighting himself to let me have the space I needed. "I'm sure the FBI would have found us anyway, but she got me out of that room. She pushed me to keep fighting when I was ready to give up."

I hadn't admitted that to anyone, not even myself.

On that cold basement floor, I'd nearly given up. Maybe if I'd known I was pregnant, I would have fought harder.

"That's not how Scarlett describes it," Leo said. "She doesn't talk about it much either. I'm sure she does with Luke. Maybe Pres. But all I've ever heard her say was that if it weren't for you, she wouldn't have had the strength to get out of that room. And if you had stayed, Ghost might have killed you."

"It was dark."

"It only takes a moment. You both got out of that room on your own two feet. You fought for each other. From personal experience, it's easier to fight for someone else than it is to fight for yourself."

He was right. I would have fought for Seraphina if I'd known she was growing inside me then. Maybe the reason

I'd gotten to my feet wasn't because Scarlett had told me to run, but because we'd had to run together.

Whatever the reason, it was done.

The story was over.

"That's it." I shrugged, my feet stopping on the carpet in front of him. "I asked the FBI to take me to Missoula. I couldn't go home without my parents there. Then I came back after I found out I was pregnant."

Seraphina would likely never know that she'd saved my sanity. I'd let myself be consumed by the pregnancy, my anger and frustration with Leo, and ignored the kidnapping. Tucking it away. Now that it was free, there was a weight off my shoulders. A pressure off my chest. For the first time in a long time, I could breathe.

"You were right. I should have talked about it before." Then again, the only person who I wanted to have all of my past, present and future was Leo. "I love you."

His eyes softened. "Love you too."

"I don't want to be afraid. I don't want to live our lives always looking over our shoulders. I don't want to worry that one day, I'll go to pick up Seraphina from school and she won't be on the playground. They can't win, Leo."

"Hey." He stood and crossed the distance between us, taking my face in his arms. "They aren't going to win. They aren't going to touch either of you."

"They might."

"Yeah, they might. And we'll be ready."

I looked him in the eye, suddenly understanding why Dad had threatened Leo. No one fucked with our kid. "If they come after Seraphina, I'll kill them."

The corner of his mouth turned up. "Get in line."

CHAPTER TWENTY

CASSANDRA

"If that bitch keeps staring at you . . ." I fisted my hands. Leo and Emmett both burst out laughing.

"I'm serious." I elbowed Leo in the ribs.

"We're right behind you." Presley raised her glass, clinking the edge of it with mine.

"While you take care of her, I'll be dealing with the blonde who keeps eye fucking. My. Husband." Bryce shouted that last word at the woman who had the intelligence to shift her gaze toward the wall and pretend like the neon Miller Lite sign was the most exciting thing she'd seen since Dash's ass.

"Easy." Dash threw his arm around Bryce's shoulders, pulling her close.

"That is blatant." She glared at the blonde. "I'm standing right here. If she keeps it up, I'm clawing out her eyes."

"You remember that I'm the chief of police, right?" Luke asked. "And standing right here."

Bryce waved him off. "I'll just antagonize her until she throws the first punch. Then it's self-defense."

"Doesn't exactly work like that, baby." Dash chuckled.

"What is with these women?" Bryce scoffed. "Seriously. Why is it always like this?"

Because our men were the hottest in town. It was hard not to stare. Though they really needed to try harder.

"As the only single man here, I feel like it's my duty to defuse the situation." Emmett drained the last of his whiskey ditch, then winked at me and strode across the bar, taking the blonde under one arm and the brunette—who'd been drooling over Leo—under the other.

Both women seemed perfectly content to have won Emmett's attention as he steered them toward the door.

"What do you ladies want next?" Shaw asked.

"Lemon drops?" Presley asked Scarlett, Bryce and me, getting nods all around.

"Four lemon drops." Shaw signaled for the bartender—Paul, who I'd met when we'd come in earlier—that we needed another round of drinks.

The women were drinking tonight. The men had lost the coin toss.

Heads, the women drove the men home from The Betsy.

Tails, the men drove the women.

Except for Emmett, the guys were all nursing waters.

"You're going to be miserable tomorrow, babe." Leo pulled me into his side, kissing my temple.

"She's got age on her side," Dash said. "Remember how fast we'd bounce back after a bender at twenty-five? Now we're old and drinking too much actually hurts. For days."

"This has to be my last one," Scarlett said. "I don't want to be too late getting home."

Luke's dad was babysitting Mary tonight and, though the baby was likely sound asleep in her crib, I knew exactly how Scarlett felt. I was having withdrawals. And guilt.

Tonight was the first time we'd left Seraphina with my parents and it was beginning to gnaw at me. I'd called to check in twice and if I didn't think it would hurt Mom's feelings, I would insist that after we left the bar, we'd go pick her up and take her home.

"She's fine," Leo said quietly, reading my mind.

"I miss her."

"I miss her too." He pulled me close, trailing a hand down my spine. His fingers dove into a back pocket of my jeans. "But think of how much fun we can have at home."

"We have fun every night."

"Tonight I'm going to make you scream my name."

A thrill raced through my body, settling in my core with a low, dull throb. "One more shot, then we're out of here."

He chuckled and dropped his lips to mine in a kiss that was anything but decent. Good thing we weren't in a decent place. The Betsy was packed, like I suspected it was most Saturday nights.

In the two weeks since I'd opened up about the kidnapping, Leo and I had been closer than ever. He was there to hold me if I needed a strong embrace. He was there to make me smile or kiss a worried look off my face.

He was my safety net. One day, I hoped to be his.

He had secrets of his own. He had stories from life with the club that he hadn't shared with me. Maybe he never would. But if that day came, I'd be there to listen.

And if all I could do was be the example, then that was what I'd do. I'd made a silent promise to never keep a secret from him. Leo would always know my truths, no matter how ugly or insignificant.

"Okay, ladies." Shaw passed around lemon drops and when we each had one in hand, we raised our glasses.

"To Genevieve," Bryce said. Our friend was home with Isaiah and their two babies. Since Asher was so little, they'd declined the invite to the bar. "She can't be here tonight, so we'll take this one for her."

"Cheers!" I lifted the glass to my lips and let the cold, sour-sweet cocktail slide down my throat with a slight burn. My smile was wide and my laughter easy as I said, "We should do this more often."

"Totally agree," Presley said.

"Hell, yes." Bryce nodded. "And more spa days like the one we had after your birthday."

"And barbeques," Scarlett said. "I need everyone to come over again so I can justify the new deck furniture I just ordered."

Luke, who'd been talking with Dash, caught that and his face darted to hers. "What furniture? We just bought deck furniture."

"But not enough. When everyone comes over, it's already crowded. Think of how it will be once all the kids get older. We need more seats."

He looked to Dash and deadpanned, "We need more seats."

I giggled again and wrapped my arms around Leo's waist as the conversation drifted around us. Our friends loved to talk and laugh. Being a part of this group had become such an important part of my life.

These women would raise their children alongside mine. The men would be there to help us move furniture or work on a project at the house or cheer on the sidelines of football or basketball games. If this was just a fraction of how it had been with the Tin King club, I saw now why Leo had felt lost after they'd shut it down.

"What are you thinking?" he asked, bending to whisper the question in my ear.

"How lucky we are to have such good friends and family."

He kissed my hair. "I'm lucky to have you."

"Promise?"

"On my life." He let me go, his hand sliding down mine until he laced his fingers with mine. "We're out."

"Same here." Scarlett took Luke's hand.

After a few quick hugs and waves goodbye, we waded through the crowd for the door.

Leo and Luke shook hands. I hugged Scarlett once more, then as they walked to their truck, I climbed on the back of Leo's motorcycle. There wasn't much of a seat for me, but since I was small and had no problem snuggling close, it worked.

"Ready?" he asked with his hands on the handlebars. "Hold tight, okay?"

"Okay." I did as he ordered, my arms banded around his waist as he raced out of the parking lot and onto the street, earning a squeal.

My hair whipped behind me as we flew beneath the streetlamps. The summer air filled my lungs, and I closed my eyes and flew.

The machine glided across the pavement like a boat in the water, bounding between waves. When we turned, I leaned with Leo, fitting my body to his. One of his hands came to my thigh, stroking up and down the denim of my jeans.

I rested my cheek against his shoulder, savoring this. Us.

"Don't fall asleep back there."

I smiled and pressed a kiss to his spine, then held on and closed my eyes again.

I loved his bike. I loved riding. It was intimate. Exhilarating. Outside the bedroom, I'd never felt this connected to him.

The trip home was too short and when we pulled into the driveway behind his truck, I groaned.

"You like my bike, Firecracker?" he asked as he shut it off, turning to meet my gaze.

I leaned up and took his bottom lip between my teeth. "I do."

"We'll take it out again. Soon." He slammed his mouth on mine, his tongue diving in as he stood, lifting me off the Harley.

My legs wrapped around his waist and I clung to him as he carried me inside, kicking and locking the door behind us.

Leo carried me to the living room and stripped me to nothing, then dropped on his knees while I sagged against the back of the couch as he devoured me whole.

Then he made good on his promise at the bar. He made me scream his name.

After the first orgasm, thanks to his wickedly talented tongue, I returned the favor, stripping him bare and shoving him to the floor, where I wrapped my lips around his cock. He never came in my mouth and tonight was no exception.

He let me have my way for a while until it was time for him to take charge again.

It took hours for us to reach the bedroom and when we did, I collapsed onto my pillow, sated and blissfully happy.

He curled into me, nuzzling my hair. "You know I love you."

"I know you love me."

"Are you going to pass out?" He lifted my hand and brought it to his lips.

"That's the plan." My drunken buzz had faded after hours exploring Leo's body and licking his tattoos.

"Let me ask you a question first."

I cracked my eyes open. "Okay."

"Will you marry me?"

I'd been seconds away from sleep, but that one question had my eyes snapping open wide. "Huh?"

The magician that he was rolled a ring between his fingers. Where had that come from? When? "Marry me."

I scrambled to sit up, taking in the diamond as it caught the moonlight drifting in from the window. "Leo," I gasped.

"I choose you."

My eyes flooded. "I choose you."

He surged, crushing his lips to mine as his hand found my fingers and the ring glided over my knuckles.

I pulled away from him, taking in the princess-cut jewel and the smaller diamonds decorating the platinum band. "Am I dreaming?"

He wrapped his arms around me, holding me close. "If you are, don't wake up."

I closed my eyes and let him take us beneath the sheets, and I didn't let him go. Not until we'd exhausted each other once more and I knew that when I woke up, the dream was just beginning.

———

"I'M GOING to go rescue our daughter." I kissed Leo's head as the sun streamed through the bedroom window.

He cracked his eyes open. "I'll come with you."

"I'll be fine. You should sleep."

He shoved up on an elbow, the sheet falling down his naked, inked chest as he glanced at the clock. "How are you not tired? We only slept for an hour."

"Four hours." It was amazing how that might once have seemed like so little, but after having Seraphina, four hours was a huge chunk. "I'll take a nap later. I want to get her and go to the store."

"Not alone."

"My parents will come along."

"Why don't you wait and I'll go for you later?"

"I don't mind. Besides, we're almost out of formula."

"'Kay. As long as your dad goes too."

"He will."

Part of the reason I wanted to go alone to get Seraphina was because I wanted to tell them that Leo and I were engaged. Dad hadn't warmed to Leo and the last thing I wanted was for him to react badly and piss Leo off.

"I'll walk you out." He shoved out of the bed, shuffling to the walk-in closet.

I took a long look at the globes of his ass before he disappeared, returning moments later in a pair of unbuttoned jeans. "I don't have gas. Can I take your truck?"

He nodded and led me to the front door, handing over his keys. "Drive safe."

"I will." I kissed him and stepped outside into the beautiful morning, waving as he stood in the doorway.

He watched until I was in his truck and reversing out of the driveway.

The tinted windows didn't seem this dark when I was riding in the passenger seat, but behind the wheel, I sat ramrod straight, not quite comfortable in such a large vehicle. Leo wouldn't be angry if I ruined his truck, but he wouldn't exactly be happy either.

By the time I'd navigated the neighborhood and made it to the highway, I'd relaxed some in the seat. I pushed the blinker and turned onto the road, pressing the gas pedal until the fields beside the road streaked by in a green blur.

A white sedan came up behind me, going much faster. I glanced at it as it zoomed around me, then rolled my eyes. "In a hurry much?"

I expected it to continue on its race to town, but the brake lights glowed red as they slowed way down. So slow that I had to hit my own brakes as I glanced at the speedometer, dropping fast.

"Seriously? It's *sixty*-five, not thirty-five. What the hell? Why pass me?"

I held back, waiting to see if he or she would accelerate. I tried to look past the car, to see if they saw something I didn't, like a police car or an animal on the road ahead. But there was nothing.

Finally, deciding this driver was a lunatic and I wanted nothing to do with them, I checked for oncoming traffic and moved to pass.

With both hands clutching the wheel, I zoomed up beside the car, only risking a quick glance. Like mine, the car's windows were tinted dark. Plus with the height difference, I couldn't see inside to the driver's face. I hit the gas, wanting to get around this guy, but the front of their car lurched forward.

They sped up as I sped up.

"Asshole."

My heartrate quickened as I slammed my foot on the gas,

the needle on the dash diving toward sixty and sending me back into the seat. Sixty became seventy. Then eighty. For every boost I gave my engine, the sedan kept pace, not letting me pass.

My hands were sticky and I didn't breathe.

A car appeared in the opposite direction. My foot instantly came off the gas and toward the brake, tapping lightly.

I should have been able to ease into my lane, behind the white sedan. He should have zoomed away, the sick jerk. But as I slowed, he slowed.

"Stop." I clutched the wheel, slamming harder on the brake and ready to swerve into the right lane. There was just enough room to do it. Almost.

The car slammed on its brakes too, blocking me.

And the other car was coming down the highway fast.

What did I do? I hit the brake again, trying to swerve. The white car blocked me again, trapping me in the wrong lane.

"Stop!" Another swerve and another block.

I swallowed hard, realizing that I was going to have to run him off the road. I readjusted my grip, not sure I had the guts to slam into another car. But it was me or him. I wasn't getting in a head-on collision today.

I sucked in a breath, held it, ready to yank the truck toward his lane. I was braced for an impact that came from the wrong way. Maybe he'd known what I'd been about to do because he beat me to it.

The white car slammed into the truck's side, keeping me on the wrong side of the dotted lines.

"No!" I screamed, holding the wheel as tight as I could. "Stop!"

The white car slammed into me again, our tires screeching on the asphalt.

The oncoming car flashed its lights at me. The sound of a horn blared in the distance. But the white car wasn't letting me get over. So I did the only thing I could think of.

I yanked the wheel while slamming my foot into the gas and careened off the highway in the other direction.

The oncoming car's grill missed me by what seemed only inches. The truck dropped with a hard, jolting lurch into the ditch that lined the highway. A loud crunch filled the air, followed a split-second later by the pop of the airbags exploding.

The one that blew out of the steering wheel caught my face and shoulders, pinning me into the seat.

I gasped for air, trapped and terrified. My hands fumbled for the door handle, skimming along the window until I found it and shoved hard to escape. My entire body trembled as I squeezed out of the truck, falling too far to the ground. I collapsed onto my knees, close to the hissing engine.

Oh, God. I sucked in some air, my head spinning. Oh my God.

Leo. I needed Leo. My phone was on the floor of the truck. I shoved to my feet and stretched for it before crawling out of the ditch, my hands and knees dirty.

Other cars had stopped now. A man was jogging toward me while another flagged traffic to slow.

"Miss." He rushed to me, taking me by the elbow to help me to my feet.

I kept my back to the truck. I couldn't look at it. I couldn't see the damage. "He didn't let me pass."

"What?"

I cleared my throat. "The white car. He didn't let me pass."

"What white car?"

I glanced around, still not risking a glance at the truck, but out of all the cars parked on the side of the road, there was no white car.

"Call an ambulance," the man shouted.

A woman across the street beside a minivan nodded and pressed her phone to her ear.

I raised a shaking hand to my mouth, holding it there for a moment. Then I pressed my own phone to my ear and called Leo.

"Babe."

"I was in an accident." My voice cracked.

"What? Where are you?" There was a rustling sound, probably him crawling out of bed.

"On the highway."

"Don't move."

He made it to me a minute after the ambulance had arrived. The EMTs had just escorted me to the back of the ambulance when I heard the roar of his bike.

I spun away from the EMTs and ran down the shoulder of the road. I ran as fast as my weak legs could carry me, tears breaking free and falling down my face.

Leo parked and was off his bike in a flash, striding toward me with his arms outstretched. The second I hit his chest, he wrapped me up tighter than he'd ever held me before.

And I cried.

The adrenaline. The fear. It hit me like a tidal wave and if not for his arms, I would have fallen.

"Breathe."

I tried but it only worked another sob loose.

"You're okay."

Was he telling me? Or himself?

"You're okay." His hand stroked the back of my head. He kept it there, holding me to him like he did with Seraphina at times.

"Oh, God. Seraphina." She could have been with me. She could have been in her car seat.

"She's safe."

"I was going to get her," I cried.

"She's safe. So are you. Breathe, Cass. You need to breathe so you can tell me what happened."

I nodded and dragged in a breath. It took five of them until I could speak. Even then, my recount of what had happened came with hitches. By the time I'd explained it all, most of the cars that had pulled off the road were starting to disappear, people going on about their Sunday.

Two police cars were parked beside the truck where it rested in the ditch. The ambulance's lights were flashing and the EMTs hovered a few feet away.

"Did you get checked out?"

I shook my head. "No, but I'm fine."

"I'd like to hear that from one of them." Leo clasped my hand and led me to the ambulance. He helped me inside the back, where an EMT checked me over and, when she'd determined that I was fine, let me go to speak to the police officers.

I told them my story again, adding in details like the make and model of the car when asked and how fast we'd been going.

"You didn't catch the license plate, did you?"

"No." I shook my head. "Sorry. I just tried to pass him

and then he blocked me. Or she. I don't know. I couldn't see inside the car. They had tinted windows too."

"And you're sure they passed you first?"

"Yes. I'm sure. They passed me first."

The officer made a few more notes, then promised to call me if they found the white car. He didn't give me a ticket, though I suspected that was because Leo had made sure to drop Luke's name when the officers had introduced themselves. Maybe a reckless driving ticket would show up in the mail.

I didn't know how these things worked—I'd never gotten a ticket before.

We were done with our questions when the tow truck arrived, and as they winched the truck out of the ditch, I had no choice but to stand beside Leo and watch.

"It's totaled," I whispered, a new sheen of tears in my eyes. His brand-new truck, ruined.

"Not totaled." He clasped my hand. "It can be fixed. What matters is that you're okay."

The front was dented everywhere. The side where the white car had slammed into me was scraped and buckled.

"I'm sorry."

"Hey." He turned me into his arms. "I don't give a damn about that truck. You are all that matters. This wasn't your fault."

"No, it was that bastard's fault." I swiped my face, refusing to let any more tears fall. I clung to my rage instead, letting it keep me strong.

Leo nodded, his eyes narrowing on the truck.

"What?"

"This is too many accidents." He shook his head, running a hand over his goatee. "First, my brakes. Then that bitch at the bar who drugged me. Then the jack at the garage and—"

"Wait. What jack at the garage?"

"Fuck," he muttered. "I was going to tell you. It happened a couple of weeks ago."

My stomach dropped. "What happened?"

"There was an accident at the garage. A jack broke. I was under the car but got out in time."

All of the blood drained from my head and my knees gave out.

"Whoa." Leo caught me before I could fall. "Breathe, babe. Breathe."

So much for my anger keeping me upright.

I closed my eyes and breathed. When I felt steady again, I opened my eyes and swallowed hard, repeating what he'd just said.

"This is too many accidents."

CHAPTER TWENTY-ONE

LEO

"How are you doing?" Emmett asked.

I took a long look at Cass as she walked the length of the living room with our daughter in her arms. "She's okay."

It sounded more like a question than a statement.

"She's okay," he echoed.

"My truck isn't."

"Good thing we know how to fix those."

I rubbed a hand over my face and checked the clock. "Where are they?"

Emmett didn't have to answer. The rumble of motorcycles echoed down the block. Dash and Isaiah raced our way. Behind them was Luke in his police truck.

Shaw had volunteered to stay at home with Presley and Scarlett and their babies. Genevieve was at Bryce and Dash's place, where Bryce's father was coming over to stay.

"I'll get the door," Emmett said.

I walked over to Cass and put my arm around her. "You can sit this out."

"Never." There was a fire in her eyes. Ferocity. She'd been scared earlier. Now she was simmering rage.

When she'd told me about the kidnapping, there'd been regret in her voice for not fighting back. Cass wasn't the type to regret and stay unchanged. She'd fight anyone who came after her again. We all would.

"Let me take her." I reached for Seraphina but Cass shook her head.

"I've got her."

"Okay." I sighed. That baby girl was keeping her mama together. Though I was glad for Cass's anger, it would fade, sooner rather than later. And she'd have a well-deserved meltdown. The accident had scared her to the core.

It had scared me too.

My ride to meet her on the highway had been fast and frenzied. When my truck had been hauled away to the garage, I'd brought Cass home so we could exchange the bike for her car. Then we'd gone straight to Claudia and Dale's place to pick up Seraphina—the fuel light on the entire way. They'd asked us to stay for lunch, but we'd declined, getting out of there as quickly as possible without alerting them that anything was wrong. Cass hadn't wanted to tell them yet. There was another pressing priority today.

A meeting.

Christ, I was sick of these fucking meetings. We'd been having them periodically for years. Whenever trouble came, we'd get together, much like we used to as a club. We'd plan. We'd strategize. We'd act.

Except it wasn't Dash or Isaiah or Shaw or Luke whose woman was in danger this time. Though I loved the women in their lives, the danger to them wasn't the same as the accident with Cass. Until today, I'd been able to stay detached. Until today, I hadn't known true fear.

I understood now why they'd do anything for their wives.

Better to save Cass's life.

And sacrifice my own.

God, what if today had ended differently? What if she hadn't made it to the ditch? What if she'd had Seraphina in the truck? What if . . .

The *what ifs* would make me insane, so I shoved them away. I nursed my own black fury.

The guys walked into the living room and Luke walked straight to Cass for a hug. "That's from Scarlett."

"Thanks." She leaned into his side.

He squeezed her again. "That's from me. Glad you're okay."

"Me too." She gave him a sad smile and looked at Seraphina. "I'm just glad she wasn't with me."

Dash put his hand on my shoulder. "How are you?"

"Fucking pissed."

"Good." He nodded and took a seat on the couch.

"Come and sit, babe." I walked to Cass and took her hand, leading her to the middle seat beside Dash. Then we all gave her our attention as she went through what had happened earlier. Again.

"Damn it." Luke shook his head.

As a cop, he'd seen the fallout from accidents. How many people died on Montana highways every year? Cass could have been included in that number. Today could have been my own personal nightmare.

"You didn't notice anything about the driver," Dash said.

Cass shook her head. "Nothing. I was trying to keep my

eyes on the road and mostly just looked at the car."

"That was the right thing to do." He patted her knee, then looked at Luke. "Can you see if he rolled into town and got picked up on any traffic cameras?"

"I'm sure the officers who responded to the wreck will, but I'll call once we leave here and make sure it's a priority."

"This could have just been an accident," Isaiah said. "An asshole with road rage."

"He could have killed her." I shook my head, my throat clogging at those words. "That's some extreme rage."

"I know." Isaiah sighed. "I don't think so either but . . ."

"Wishful thinking," I finished for him.

We all knew that if it wasn't an accident, there was only one other explanation.

"The Warriors," Cass said, her voice low. "The accidents weren't really accidents."

"Let's walk through them," Emmett said. "First there were your brakes this winter."

"I shouldn't have trashed that truck," I said. "Fuck."

"Why?" Cass asked.

"Because I didn't check to see if the brake line had been sliced or tampered with. I assumed it was age and corrosion. I was pissed off, so I just let them junk it."

"Let's call the yard," Dash said. "See if they haven't crushed it yet."

"Yeah. I'll do it now."

"I got it." He stood, taking his phone from his pocket and going to the kitchen to make the call to the local junkyard outside of town. It wasn't a big yard but they'd take cars that had been in accidents. At times, they'd take spare parts and iron scraps from the shop after we were done with a remodel because they'd sell the metal or crush it.

As we waited, I put my arm around Cass's shoulder and kissed her temple. "You're okay."

"I'm okay." She leaned into me with a sleeping Seraphina in her arms. While Cass had been talking, the baby had dozed off. Content. Unburdened. Oblivious to the dangers of real life.

Exactly how a child should be.

"Want me to take her to her crib?"

Cass shook her head. "I just need to hold her."

"'Kay."

"That's a beautiful ring," Emmett said, gesturing to Cass's left hand. "Congratulations."

She smiled, the first one that had reached her eyes since we'd come home. "Thank you."

Isaiah and Luke offered their congratulations too, right before Dash came back into the room.

"He's going to go check and text me. We might have gotten lucky. He hasn't scrapped it yet."

Then we'd know. If my brakes had been tampered with by any tool, we'd know.

"I think that brunette might have been telling the truth after all," Emmett said. "About a man paying her to drug you."

"I think you're right, but why? What does drugging me do other than cause me to pass out at the bar?"

"Maybe he was hoping to take you somewhere," Cass suggested. "And the brunette beat him to it. I bet he didn't expect her to follow you after you brushed her off."

"That's a definite possibility."

"Or . . . maybe he thought you'd drive home," Dash said. "When you told me about it, you said the brunette caught you in your truck, right?"

"Yeah," I said. "She drove."

"But would you have driven if she hadn't been there?"

"No." I didn't drive drunk. Even smashed, I didn't drive. But I'd also never had anyone to come home to before. Cass had been here and I might have been stupid enough to drive so I could see her. That, and I'd been out of my mind. "Hell, I don't know. Maybe."

"Unless we find the mystery man behind it, we'll never know," Emmett said. "And he's a ghost. I went over the footage from The Betsy three times. It's anyone's guess."

"That whole thing sits funny with me," I said.

"Same." Dash nodded. "Has since it happened. You might not wear the cut, but people in this town know not to fuck with the Kings unless they want a beatdown."

Even without the club, we weren't afraid to throw punches. "For argument's sake, let's say I was drugged and whoever did it was hoping I'd wrap myself around a tree."

Cass flinched.

"Shit. Sorry."

"I don't want to even think about you getting hurt like that," she said.

Then she wouldn't like where this conversation was headed next. "Whatever the reason for drugging me, when that didn't work, he came to the garage."

"You think that jack was tampered with?" she asked.

I shrugged. "It looked fine to me. We'd been using it. There was no indication of a leak."

"Same here," Emmett said. "But I didn't exactly check it over thoroughly."

Dash sighed. "We shipped it to the manufacturer."

"Damn," I muttered. "Wish we had put this together sooner."

"There's not much to put together," Luke said. "If someone walked into the station and told me all of this, I'd have a hard time connecting the pieces. But . . . add in Cass's accident and it's suspicious."

"Knowing what we know about the Warriors and Tucker Talbot, it has to be them," I said. Yeah, we had made enemies over the years, but the club days had been a long time ago. For some random person to come after us now made no sense. Especially given how hard Dash and Emmett—and Draven, before his murder—had worked to become upstanding citizens.

Of the former Tin Kings, I was the only one who hadn't really changed.

Or hadn't, until Cass.

"Tucker's not going to spend his life in a prison cell without an attempt at revenge," Dash said. "It's why we've been so careful all these months."

"But accidents?" Emmett shook his head. "That's the only thing these incidents have in common. Minus Cass's crash today and the drugging, the other incidents were accidents. And accidents are not Tucker's style. He's not subtle. When he takes his revenge, he's going to want us to know exactly who's behind it."

Exactly the way he'd killed Stone, Emmett's father.

A bullet between the eyes wasn't subtle.

"He's in prison." Cass shifted Seraphina, sitting up straighter as she followed the conversation. "Could he orchestrate this?"

"It's possible." Dash nodded. "Getting information in and out of prison isn't hard. If he's got someone loyal outside, then yeah, he could do this."

"Any known associate of the Warriors is under FBI

watch," Luke said. "According to Agent Brown, they're watching closely. Unless someone snuck out of Ashton and ditched their tail, the Warriors are nowhere near Clifton Forge."

"That's a big assumption," I said.

My faith in the FBI wasn't as devout as Luke's. The feds had come sniffing around the Tin Kings years ago, trying to find something to pin on the club. Nothing had ever surfaced, and that wasn't just because we were good at covering our tracks.

Cops followed rules. Criminals didn't.

We'd always been one or two steps ahead. I hadn't had a lot of love for the police force before Marcus Wagner had tried to frame Draven for murder. After all Wagner had done, proudly wearing a badge, well . . . Luke was the only cop I trusted these days.

"It doesn't necessarily have to be a Warrior," I said. "Especially since Tucker has to know that we're watching out. And let's not forget that it was his dirt on his own men that will land some of them in prison. Not all of the Warriors will remain loyal."

"But some will," Emmett said.

"Yeah." Dash nodded. "Some will."

"What about family?" I asked. "Does he have anyone who's personally connected to him who could stage these accidents?"

"He's divorced. He's got two daughters in their early thirties," Dash said.

"What about the ex or his kids?" I asked.

Emmett shook his head. "All three live in South Carolina. Moved there after Tucker's ex divorced him. He doesn't seem to have much contact with them. His daughters are married with young kids. I watch their credit card activity and there's nothing showing they've come near Montana in the past seven years. Tucker's only relative who lives close is a nephew in Boise. Tucker's brother was in the club but the brother's dead now."

"Would the nephew do this?" I asked.

Emmett shook his head. "Doubtful. He's not in the life. His mother and father divorced when he was just a kid. Far as I know, he was never around the Warriors."

"You're sure?"

"From everything I've dug up, he's on the straight and narrow. He works as a credit officer at a bank. He's married and his wife runs a salon. He hasn't gone to visit Tucker since he was arrested. There are no phone records showing calls in and out of the prison."

"Um . . . how do you know all of this?" Cass's eyes widened.

Emmett grinned. "You're not the only one in the room who likes research."

"Don't let him fool you, babe. He's not as dumb as he looks." If there was a connection with the daughters, the nephew, or anyone else, Emmett would have a better chance than anyone to find it.

My friend flipped me off and explained to Cass, "When I was a kid, I got into computers. Really into them. Because my dad was in the club, I'd hang around the clubhouse a lot. One of the brothers was into computers too. He taught me some tricks and hacks. I've learned a few of my own over the years. It's a handy hobby to have."

"You're a hacker? You?"

Emmett grinned at the surprise on her face. "Learning about peoples' lives from what they do online is a lot less work than following them around. Besides, these days, you can tell a lot about a person by what they post on social media for all the world to see."

It was part of the reason that I'd never gotten social media accounts. Being around Emmett was . . . educational. For him, hacking was more than a hobby. It was an escape.

After his father had been murdered by the Warriors, Emmett had lost himself for a time. We'd all lost ourselves, but especially Emmett. To this day, I saw the differences in the man he was now compared to the man he'd been back when Stone was alive, working beside his son in the shop.

Emmett's smile wasn't as easy as it had been. There was an edge to his eyes that hadn't been around in our younger days. He'd probably say the same thing about me.

Maybe we'd both hardened with time. The two of us had grown jaded with the world together. Side by side.

If there was a brother of mine on earth, it was Emmett. He knew me better than I knew myself. Hell, the bastard had seen my love for Cass even before I'd realized it.

One day, I hoped he found that too. The woman who made him want to be better. Do better.

He'd find his own Firecracker.

I picked up Cass's free hand, needing to touch her.

She gave me a sad smile, then dropped her gaze to Seraphina.

"Are we being paranoid?" I asked. After so many years of warring with Tucker Talbot, maybe the only thing we were really fighting here was our own fear. "Could they be causing these accidents just because they know it will drive us fucking crazy not knowing what is going on?"

Emmett chuckled. "Tucker does love a good mind fuck."

"If it was the Warriors, they would have come after all of us. Especially you." I jerked my chin at Dash. He'd been the president of the club, his father a founder. If Tucker truly wanted revenge, Dash would be the target. "But they only targeted me."

"And me," Cass added.

"Unless they didn't know it was you driving the truck today. Those windows are tinted dark."

"Too dark," Luke said. It was the same thing he'd told me when he'd seen the truck for the first time. The tint wasn't exactly legal but when you were friends with the chief of police, why not push the boundaries?

"Dark enough that there's a chance that the driver of the car today couldn't tell it was you behind the wheel instead of me. You never drive it."

"Then you really think someone wants you dead." The pain in those beautiful eyes broke my heart.

"Maybe."

"And maybe it's the Warriors," Dash said. "I'm not ready to say these accidents aren't connected and that you aren't the target. We could all be targets and you were picked first. No offense, but you'd be the easiest."

"None taken. You're right." It wasn't like my habits were hard to pick up. Work. The Betsy. Come home alone. Repeat, repeat. If I were picking a King to fuck with, I'd pick me too. Dash had his family. Emmett wasn't as predictable, and he was more cautious.

"What now?" Luke asked.

"We watch our backs," Dash answered. "Same as we have been."

"I'll run through security footage from the garage," Emmett said. "If someone came in and tampered with the jack, we should have caught it on camera. I'm pissed I didn't think to look before."

I sighed. "How could you have known?"

"All right." Dash stood from the couch. "Stick close to your families."

"Always," Isaiah said, getting to his feet.

Luke nodded and stood too, leading the way to the front door.

Emmett was the last to leave, but he didn't go for the door. He strode across the living room to kneel in front of Cass and put a hand on her shoulder. "Glad you're okay."

"Thanks." She gave him a soft smile. "Have you ever hacked me?"

He winked and made her giggle.

"See you tomorrow," he told me, standing. "I'll call if I find anything on the tapes."

"Thanks." I stood and walked him to the door, locking it up. The mood was somber. Fear had tainted each of us, because if this accident could happen to Cass today, it could happen to anyone.

Thank you. I closed my eyes and sent that gratitude to the heavens. *Thank you.*

For saving her life today, for not having Seraphina in the truck with her, I'd become a praying man.

"Hey." Cass came up behind me, the baby still cradled in her arms.

"Hey." I pulled them both to my chest, never wanting to let go.

"Why is this happening to us, Leo?"

"I've made enemies, babe."

"Who? If this isn't the Warriors, who would do this to you?"

I blew out a deep breath, wishing I could explain it all. Maybe I would, in time. But at the moment, I didn't want to go back there. I didn't want to dive into the past and risk tainting what we had.

"You won't tell me." She stepped away and out of my arms.

I shook my head.

There was a flash of pain in her eyes before she turned and strode for the hallway, heading to the nursery.

I followed, giving her some space to set Seraphina in her crib.

Cass's face was the epitome of blank as she tiptoed out of the room and eased the door shut. Then there was the hurt again.

"I told *you* everything," she murmured, heading for the kitchen.

Damn it. I followed, finding her standing in front of the fridge, the door wide open as she stared inside. I doubted she was hungry, but for some reason, my woman stewed in front of the open refrigerator door. "I don't want you to know the truth."

"Why?"

"Because if you know the truth, all of it, then you might stop looking at me the way you do."

Her shoulders fell. "Right now, I'm looking at you like you're an idiot for thinking that."

I fought a smile. "Right now, you're looking at me like I'm an idiot and a decent man."

"Because you *are* a decent man."

"Because you don't know the truth. Please. If you beg me, I'll tell you. And I don't want to tell you."

She closed the fridge and walked over, putting her hands

on my hips. "Is it really so awful?"

"Yes."

Death. Drugs. Women. Drinking. Violence. Murder.

I'd pulled the trigger and watched a man's chest explode when the bullet had passed through his heart. I'd pounded my own two fists into a man's face until all that was left in the mush were skull fragments and teeth. I'd protected drug runs, making sure the goods got to buyers. Drugs I'd known would ruin lives. The list went on and on.

Cass studied my face, searching for the explanation I couldn't bring myself to give.

"I swear to you, Cassandra. I won't keep things from you. I swear it on my life. But you have to give me this. You have to give me this hope."

"Hope? What do you mean, hope?"

I took her face in my hands. "The hope that one day, I'll be the man I see reflected in your eyes. The hope that I can prove to myself that I'm not that man anymore. The hope that I actually have a shot in hell at deserving you."

"I could strangle my father for putting those thoughts in your head."

"He just voiced the thoughts that were already there."

She collapsed forward, her forehead resting against my heart. Her arms snaked around my torso, her hands splaying across my back. "I love you."

"I love you too."

"I won't ask. But know that I'm here. And know that my love for you won't ever change." The sincerity in her words nearly had me opening my mouth and confessing it all.

One day. But not today.

Today I was going to hold my girls and hold them tight.

And pray that tomorrow I could keep them safe.

CHAPTER TWENTY-TWO

CASSANDRA

You okay?

I rolled my eyes at Leo's text and typed back a quick reply.

I'm okay. You don't need to text me every fifteen minutes.

Leo didn't respond. Probably because he'd just keep texting me every fifteen minutes no matter what I said.

Over the past two weeks, life had returned to normal. Or as much normal as could be expected.

The day of the accident, Emmett had gone home and pulled the security footage from the cameras at the garage. An hour of looking hadn't shown anything on the day or night before Leo's incident with the jack. Even after his initial assessment, Emmett had kept going backward, but there'd been nothing to indicate foul play. It had likely been a faulty seal from the manufacturer.

The local junkyard owner had gone to look at Leo's old truck and examine the brake lines. He hadn't been able to tell, so Dash himself had gone out to inspect it.

Given that the truck had been built in the eighties,

cutting a single brake line wouldn't cause them all to fail—I'd learned more about dual master cylinders than I'd ever cared to know. The only way to completely disable the brakes would be to cut all lines, forcing the hydraulic fluid to rush out. The pedal would have slammed to the floor before he'd ever backed out of the driveway.

There'd been too much rust and age on the lines and hoses to tell for sure, but Dash thought it was possible someone might have caused a leak by puncturing them. He'd also thought it could have been natural corrosion, especially given the salt on the roads that time of year.

Two accidents with no explanation.

Doubt had been sitting on our shoulders like the devil, whispering in our ears.

We'd never know if either of Leo's accidents had been failed attempts to cause him harm. And we'd likely never know who had tried to run me off the road.

Luke's officers hadn't found a white car on any traffic cameras in town, probably because they had pulled onto a gravel road to flee after the accident. Maybe it had been someone with a serious case of road rage. Maybe not.

If Leo had been protective before, he was downright paranoid now. The fact that he'd actually let me stay home alone today was a miracle. For the first week after the accident, any time he'd had to go to work, he'd insisted that Seraphina and I go along too.

So we'd joined Presley and her son, Nico, at the garage. We'd crowded into the waiting room with Scarlett and Mary, taking over and creating a play space. Since Genevieve was on maternity leave from work, she'd joined us too. Bryce had commandeered Dash's office, using it to write for her newspaper.

Maybe a different set of friends would have grown sick of one another after two weeks, but it worked for us. We'd each pitched in to help with kids. The mom tasks had been shared and the girls had even given me an hour free each day to swap places with Bryce and write.

Today was the first day we hadn't gathered at the garage. Dash didn't work on Fridays, so he'd stayed home with his family. Presley had taken the day off to spend it with Shaw. Genevieve and Scarlett were at their respective homes on my parents' street.

Maybe everyone was having doubts about the accidents. Little by little, we were lightening up.

Leo had asked me to come to the garage but I'd craved a normal day at home. I'd wanted to spend time at the desk he'd built for me. He knew how much I wanted to make progress on this book. Today I'd planned to finish the chapter I'd been working on over the week, but between Leo's texts and the messages from the girls, each of us having decided that alone time was overrated, I'd written a whole ten words.

There was no deadline for this project, but I'd had an idea last night and my fingers itched to type it out. My parents had taken today off work to prepare for a camping trip over the weekend, but instead of packing, they'd begged for a few hours with Seraphina. This was their first camping trip of the summer—very unlike them—probably because they were soaking in as much time with the baby as possible.

I'd graciously accepted their babysitting, hoping that with a few hours free I could get the thoughts out of my head and into my document.

"Okay, no more phone." I set it aside, putting my fingers to the laptop.

Five words in and the phone rang.

"Seriously, Leo."

The alarm was set. I had a can of pepper spray on the desk beside my notebook and a pen. Leo had walked me through how to use it before he'd hemmed and hawed about leaving for the garage.

The ringing continued and if I didn't answer him, he'd worry, so I picked up the phone, only to find Olive's name on the screen.

"Hey," I answered, surprise thick in my voice. Olive and I hadn't spoken in ages, not since after my baby shower. We'd had a few texts here and there, the occasional photo of Seraphina, but otherwise we'd done exactly what I'd expected—drifted apart. "How are you?"

"Hey. I'm the worst friend ever for not calling. Things have been so busy here."

I laughed. "I haven't exactly called either."

"You have a baby. You have an excuse."

"You've got school. I know how consuming that can be."

For the first time, thinking about school didn't come with a twinge of envy. I ran a hand over the top of my desk. My favorite books sat on their shelves. And the laptop screen in front of me wasn't open to a paper or grueling assignment, but a book. My book.

Seraphina's nursery was across the hall. Leo's scent, cedar and spice and wind, clung to the air.

I wouldn't trade anything in this world, not an academic career complete with accolades, to sit anywhere else.

"What's new?" she asked.

"Oof." I blew out a long breath. Where to start?

Maybe a year ago, I would have told her everything about the stress in our lives. Maybe I would have told her about the accident. But too much had changed.

She didn't need details about the Arrowhead Warriors or the Tin Kings.

It was best that way.

"Seraphina is getting so big," I said. "She's almost sleeping through the night, which is basically a miracle. I'm biased, but she's perfect." Even thinking of her face made me smile.

"Of course she's perfect," Olive said. "How are things with Leo?"

"Good." Another smile. "We're getting married."

"What?" Her shriek pierced my ear. "Congratulations!"

"Thanks." The ring on my finger was more beautiful than I'd imagined. Maybe because I hadn't imagined one. While I was in school, thoughts of marriage and babies had been as foreign to me as another language.

Mom was thrilled at our engagement, because over the months since Seraphina had been born, Leo had won her over simply by being an amazing father and partner. Dad was struggling but it was with sadness, not anger. I was grown up, not his little girl anymore.

Seraphina was doing a fine job filling part of that hole.

"Have you set a date?" Olive asked.

"No, not yet." Leo and I had talked about it just last night, but he was so fearful at the moment. I was nervous too. So until more of the Warriors were sentenced and this string of unlucky accidents passed, we were going to forgo planning.

We'd have a wedding when it was time.

"Are you going for a big affair or small?"

"Leo and I both want something small and intimate," I said. "I'd be okay getting married at a park or in my parents' backyard. I don't know. Originally I was thinking of throwing the whole fancy party, and then I got tired just thinking about the flowers and cake."

Olive laughed. "That doesn't surprise me at all. You love simple."

"I do." I smiled. "I've missed you."

"I've missed you too. My roommates here are no fun."

I laughed. "Tell me everything about school."

We talked for thirty minutes about her classes and professors. I waited, wondering if I'd feel that sting of regret, but as she talked, all I felt was relief not to be balancing university stress with Seraphina.

Olive would make a brilliant PhD one day. Her dream was to work at a museum, and I hoped that we remained in touch long enough so I could see her achieve that goal. Only time would tell.

"How is transcription work going?" she asked.

"It's actually quite enjoyable. But I haven't taken a job since Seraphina was born. I've actually been, um . . . writing. Fiction. Historical fiction." I held my breath. Outside my group of friends here, Olive was the first person I'd told.

"Fiction." She seemed to ponder it for a moment. "Oh, I love that for you. I mean, you always said you wanted to write a book. And let's be honest, nonfiction can get a little dry if that's all you are reading—hello, that's my life right now. Why not infuse some imagination in there? Can I read it first?"

Relief washed over me. If Olive was supportive, maybe I hadn't completely sold out my dreams. "Second. I already promised Leo that he gets it first."

"I'll take it whenever you're ready to share. What's it about? Where'd you come up with the idea? Tell me everything."

I opened my mouth and when I finally stopped talking, another thirty minutes had passed.

"This is brilliant," she said.

"You think?"

"I love it."

"Even if I do nothing with it, writing it has been fun."

My story was set in the late 1800s in what would become the Redwood National Park. Since our trip there, that place would always hold a special piece of my heart and I couldn't imagine setting my first book anywhere else.

The tale was of two sisters, Helen and Ruth, coming of age at the turn of the century. Helen, the oldest, was kidnapped, taken from her own garden by a man who lived in a remote area of the forest. He'd seen her and wanted her as his bride.

And men, now and then, took what they wanted from females, with or without their permission.

I hadn't written much more than the beginning yet, but the bulk of the story would be about Ruth's journey to rescue Helen after everyone in her family had grieved and dismissed the loss as if there were no other action to be taken. Ruth's travels would take her five years; meanwhile, Helen would fall for her captor.

I wasn't sure how the book would end yet. At times, I wanted Helen to return to her family. Others, I wanted her to stay where she'd made a home. In today's society, readers might think her weak for not attempting escape or letting hatred fuel her actions. Or maybe they'd see her how I saw her—strong.

It took strength to make the best of a bad situation. It took endurance to survive the hard moments and find happiness at the end of a cruel journey.

Writing had been therapeutic and giving Helen the fears from my own kidnapping had helped me channel those emotions. That, and giving her the love of a man who was misunderstood by most.

Whatever her ending turned out to be, the real victory in this story was not for Helen or Ruth.

But for me.

"When you finish, I want to come and visit," Olive said. "And I claim the second signed copy because I'm guessing Leo will get the first."

"You'd be guessing right."

"What else is new? Is that hot guy still around? Leo's friend?"

"Emmett?"

"Emmett. That was his name. When I come to see you, I might have to see him too."

"Um . . . sure." Why did that bother me?

Olive was my friend, but a protective urge for Emmett came out of nowhere. He was my friend too and I didn't like the loneliness in his eyes. It was the same loneliness I'd seen in Leo a year ago. Emmett was the only one of our group not in love. Did that bother him? If it did, I doubted he'd ever admit it.

"Well, I'd better let you go," she said. "It was great catching up."

"You too. Study hard."

She groaned. "It is hard, but I love it."

We said our goodbyes and when I set the phone down, I stared at it for a long minute.

Would I talk to her again?

The visit she'd mentioned probably wouldn't happen. And if that had been the last phone call, I'd miss Olive but wouldn't be heartbroken. Our lives had headed in opposite directions.

She was living her next chapter.

This was mine.

Leo had texted twice while I'd been talking to her and I'd given him a quick reply each time. My writing day had been a bust, and in an hour, Mom and Dad would be here to drop off Seraphina.

I stood from my desk and walked to the window just as a familiar rumble filled the street. A smile tugged at my lips as I walked to the front door, disengaging the alarm and flipping the deadbolt.

Leo pulled into the driveway, looking as handsome as ever and sexy as hell on that bike. "Hey, babe."

"Hey." I smiled, going out to meet him in the sunshine. "You're home early."

"It's too nice to be inside. Emmett and I bugged out of work early. Want to go for a ride with us?"

"Yes." We hadn't been on a ride since our night at the bar. I stood on my toes, letting him brush his mouth to mine. "Seraphina is at Mom and Dad's, so we've got about an hour before they're bringing her back."

"Perfect." He ran his hands up the bare skin of my arms. "Let me get you a helmet from the garage."

"We didn't wear a helmet when we went to the bar."

"We're going to go a lot faster today."

"Oh. You don't wear one?" I'd gladly wear the helmet, but why didn't he?

"Your brain is a lot more important to protect than mine."

I rolled my eyes. "That's the dumbest thing I've ever heard."

He chuckled. "Fine. I'll wear one. Let me go change my shirt."

"What's wrong with your shirt?"

He raised his arm, revealing a gaping hole in the armpit. "This one died today."

"Okay." I giggled. "I'll attempt to find the helmets."

"Right behind you." He kissed my forehead and smacked me on the ass as I went one direction while he went inside the house.

The garage was a bit of a mystery. I'd only been inside once and that had been just last week with Leo. He'd needed the owner's manual for his truck, which was currently at the garage, scratched and dented, awaiting new parts from the factory.

Painted the same navy blue as the house, the garage had a wide, wooden door, unlike most of the white garage doors in the neighborhood. It had been stained to match the posts and accents on the house. A bird's nest was tucked into the elbow of the small gable ornament in the pitch of the eaves.

The inside of the garage was exactly as I'd expected, dark and full of tools. It smelled of oil and metal and paint. The helmets were probably on one of the sturdy workbenches he'd built along the windowless walls.

I strode across the lawn with electricity in my step. A ride on a hot summer afternoon, just Leo and me, sounded amazing. There was a keypad on the garage door and I realized as I was halfway there that I couldn't remember the code.

Seven-five-three-two. Or was it seven-five-two-three?

I spun around and jogged to the house, where the remote opener was hanging from the key holder in the entryway. With it in hand, I retraced my path, stepping over my newly planted flower bed, and pressed the single button on the garage door opener.

A gust of wind slammed into my face.

A loud boom pierced my ears.

The air picked me up, my toes inches above the grass, and threw me backward so fast, I didn't have time to blink or brace for impact with the ground. I hit hard, my lungs instantly empty. The smell of fire singed my nose. The sting of wood splinters jabbed into my skin.

My ears were ringing, my head spinning and my throat burned.

The garage. The wind had come from the garage.

I looked up, fighting the haze and fog clouding my mind.

Where the garage should have stood was nothing but a ball of fire.

"Not wind," I murmured before blackness crept at the corners of my consciousness.

Not wind. The garage had exploded.

CHAPTER TWENTY-THREE

LEO

"Cass!" I stumbled to my feet, my boots crunching on broken glass as I sprinted through the front door for the lawn.

She was lying on the grass, right beside her new flower bed. Pink and yellow petals were strewn around her hair.

"Cass!" My legs wouldn't go fast enough as I raced. The heat from the garage fire carried on the air as I collapsed at her side and gripped her shoulders. "Cass, wake up. Wake up!"

She groaned. "Leo."

"Come on." I scooped her up, surging to my feet and pulling her farther away from the garage to the opposite side of the driveway.

The explosion had spattered the yard and driveway with debris. The windows on the house were shattered. My bike was lying on its side beside Cass's car.

The neighbors who'd been home on a Friday afternoon came rushing outside, and in the distance, someone shouted, "Call 9-1-1!"

But my focus was on Cass.

"Talk to me," I ordered as I carried her toward the next-door neighbor's property, laying her down the second I found a patch of clean grass.

"Cass, talk to me." My hands roved over her body, feeling for blood. My eyes followed the path, sure I was missing something when I came up empty. Her chest had no gushing wounds. There were small cuts on her arms and tears in her black tee, but nothing else.

"Can't. Breathe." She panted, her eyes squeezing shut as she struggled to take a breath.

A row of faces and people hovered around us. "Call an ambulance."

"They're on the way."

I ran my hands over her again, unwilling to stop touching her. To feel her heat under my palms. The tension of pain in her chest. Pain was good. Pain meant she was alive. "You'll be okay. You'll be fine."

She winced as she tried to breathe, her hands coming to her sternum where she clutched her heart.

"What do I do?" My eyes blurred with tears. "What do I do? Be okay. Please be okay."

She didn't answer. She didn't open her eyes. She just clung to her chest as her face twisted in agony.

"Cass, please. You gotta breathe, babe." I shook her shoulders gently. "Breathe."

Years ago, in the days when violence had been part of our everyday lives, we'd had a run-in with a meth dealer. The crazy son of a bitch had wanted to join the club. Draven had told him no, but he'd come around often enough that we'd let him party with us.

Then one day, he'd stopped coming by. He'd been

cooking meth in his house and the place had exploded. Only he hadn't died in the explosion. He'd been outside in his yard. According to the reports, the shock wave had ripped the air from his body and his internal organs had failed.

The way she was holding her chest. The way her face contorted in sheer pain.

Please, God.

"Don't leave me, Cass. Please. Breathe."

A drop of water landed on her cheek. A tear. My tear.

"Cassandra." I bent low, dropping my forehead to hers. There was barely a breath on her lips. "Please. Stay with me."

I clung to her, and when I looked up, the faces of my neighbors, people I barely knew, were full of shock and fear. "Where's the ambulance?"

No one answered me.

"Where's the fucking ambulance?" I screamed.

An older woman wearing a green dress flinched and took a step back.

A man, the guy who lived three houses down and mowed his lawn at seven in the morning every Sunday, held up his phone. "They're on the way."

"Cass. Firecracker." My fingers pressed into the skin of her face. "Breathe."

A moan escaped her mouth. I leaned in close, my fingers shifting to her pulse. It thrummed beneath my skin. "You'll be okay."

She nodded, her hands lifting as her fingers searched for mine.

I clasped them between my palms, squeezing tight. "You'll be okay."

Her eyes cracked open and she winced, then she rolled

away from me, curling into the fetal position. And that was when she finally managed to draw in a breath.

As she filled her lungs, the air rushed out of mine. Fucking thank you.

Cass tried to shove up on an elbow, cringing with the slightest movement.

"Let me help." I pulled her gently to a seat, then wrapped her in my arms, holding her against my chest.

Her breaths were labored but with each one, she seemed to find the next more easily.

"God, you scared me." I peppered her hair and forehead with kisses. My hands roamed over her back and shoulders and ribs, just to feel her alive.

"W-what happened?" she slurred.

"The garage. It . . . exploded." My gaze shifted to the place where my garage had once stood.

Flames licked and clung to the skeleton of the building's frame. Smoke billowed into the blue summer sky, coating the sun above in a haze of gray. What remained of my workbenches were black and on fire.

"Fuck." I raked a hand through my hair.

Cass had gone to get the helmets. Had she not turned back . . .

"Leo." She clung to me, her gaze worried as she glanced up.

"Yeah. Another accident."

She shook her head.

No, this hadn't been an accident. And the doubts I'd had about the others all vanished. Someone had meant to kill me, because Cass never went into the garage. She had no reason to. That bomb had been meant for me.

I scanned the street, taking in the neighbors who were

still hovering close. One had crossed the driveway and was staring at the blaze with a hand over her mouth. The piercing wail of sirens sounded in the distance.

The faces were familiar. The men. The women. There weren't many—most people were probably still at work on a Friday—but each person here lived on the street. I knew these faces.

Except . . .

There was a man standing beside a car two houses down. While everyone else had rushed outside and toward the explosion, he had hung back.

I knew his face but not from the neighborhood. He was a customer at the garage. The day of the jack accident, he had been there for an oil change. He'd hovered over Tyler's shoulder to see if I was alive.

"Babe, I need you to stay right here." I shifted, moving slowly away when she stiffened and sat straight.

"Leo."

My eyes were locked on the man. It couldn't be a coincidence that he was here, at yet another accident.

"Leo," Cass's voice cracked.

"Wait here." I stood and the moment I was on my feet, the man turned and began walking the opposite way down the sidewalk.

The neighbors tried to talk to me, to ask me where I was going, but I blocked them out and started running. I hit the street and broke into a dead sprint, my boots pounding and my lungs burning as I tore down the street. The man was walking even faster.

He must have heard my steps because he glanced back and when he spotted me running, he took off, darting into a yard. Except the yard he'd chosen had a tall fence. He bounced off the boards and scrambled to pull himself over the top.

Maybe it was the adrenaline, maybe it was the fury—maybe both—but my legs had never moved faster. My hands fisted, my arms pumping. The man hadn't had enough of a head start.

The moment he was within reach, I stretched, catching a handful of his jeans. Then I yanked him off the fence, the movement making us both stumble.

He tried to get up, to get away, but I found my balance first and leapt on him, tackling him to the lawn. Our bodies thudded on the grass and he let out a yelp.

It was the only sound he made before my fist raised above his face. "Who the fuck are you?"

He brought his hands up, blocking his nose, so I slammed a fist into his kidney.

"Ah!" He screamed, thrashing and writhing beneath me, trying to get free, but I just kept punching, hit after hit until he dropped his arms.

Mistake.

My hands found his throat and wrapped tight. "Did you do this?"

He clawed at my wrists and forearms but it only made me squeeze tighter.

"Did you do this?"

He gurgled, his mouth opening and closing as he tried to get some oxygen.

"Did you do this!" I roared.

A pair of hands wrapped around my bicep, yanking hard, but I didn't move. "Let him go."

Another person tugged at my shoulder.

I was a mountain, not to be moved. And I'd choke the life

out of this motherfucker for nearly killing Cass. An innocent man would have shaken his head. He would have gone wide-eyed and afraid. But this son of a bitch was guilty.

It was there in his dark gaze.

"Let him go!" The voice barely penetrated the blood roaring in my veins.

An arm banded around my waist and I was ripped away, pulled back with such force I didn't have to turn to know who it was.

"Calm down, brother," Emmett said.

"Fuck that." I shook my head and surged forward, but his hold on me was firm. "He almost killed her."

The two cops who'd tried, unsuccessfully, to pull me off the man were hauling him to his feet.

He doubled over, coughing and gasping as he braced his hands on his knees.

"You have no options here," Emmett said, his voice low in my ear. "Calm down before you land yourself in jail. Think of Cass and Seraphina."

I sucked in a sharp breath, letting the rage burn for another second.

An ambulance whipped past us, hauling ass down the street.

"Let me go." I shook Emmett off and stepped away, pointing to the man the cops were standing beside. "He was at the garage the day of the accident. He was here today. It can't be a coincidence."

"Go." Emmett jerked his chin. "I'll stay here."

"Don't let them release him."

"Go."

I nodded and turned, taking off down the street toward home, running as fast as I had before.

The group of neighbors who were crowded around Cass broke apart as a couple of EMTs rushed toward her. One of the EMTs was the same woman from the truck accident.

"Move," I barked, pushing my way through the people to Cass's side.

She spotted me and looked down the road. "Did you catch him?"

"Yeah," I panted, kneeling at her side.

Her shoulders sagged. "Now what?"

"Now we go to the hospital." I looked to the EMT, who gave me a small nod. Then she let me pick up Cass and carry her to the ambulance.

"I love you," I whispered against her hair as we walked.

"So much for our ride." Her gaze tracked to the bike in the driveway.

"There will be others." I hugged her tighter.

We'd have a lifetime of rides together.

———

DASH CAME STRIDING out of an open bay door at the garage as I climbed out of Claudia's car.

I hadn't expected anyone to be at the garage since it was long after closing time, but he must have had a project to work on. Or, like me, he needed a little time alone to get his head around all that had happened in the past three days. After dinner at Dale and Claudia's tonight, I'd told Cass I'd needed to run a quick errand.

Really, I just needed a few minutes to think.

Three days and I was still struggling to make sense of it all.

"What are you doing here?" he asked. "Thought you were at the Clines'."

"Claudia's car needs an oil change and Dale's tools are shit. I came to steal some."

"You've got her car here. Why not pull it in?"

"I want to stick close to Cass, and I need something to do tomorrow." Pacing the hallways wasn't working to burn off my nervous energy.

Dash nodded. "Take whatever you need."

Raiding the tool chests didn't take long. Neither did taking a few quarts of oil from the supply room.

"How's Cass?" Dash asked as he helped me load it all into the trunk.

"She's all right. Pissed. Scared. Grateful. It swings back and forth."

"Know the feeling. How are you?"

"Pissed. Scared. Grateful."

He nodded. "She'll be okay."

"Yeah."

The doctors had kept us at the hospital over the weekend to make sure Cass didn't have any delayed symptoms from the blast. We'd been lucky that the worst of her injuries were a few cuts and some soreness in her ribs from being tossed to the ground.

They'd discharged us this morning and we'd gone straight to Dale and Claudia's place.

My bike would need repairs. All the glass in her car was wrecked. Our house needed new windows and new siding. While I'd been with Cass at the hospital, Emmett and Dash had arranged for a contractor to come over and get replacements ordered. They'd also taken care of boarding up the house so it wouldn't be full of animals and bugs when we were finally able to go home.

My garage was another story.

The area had been roped off until Luke could close the investigation on the explosion. But even with the case open, we all knew what had happened.

Tucker Talbot's nephew had done his best to kill me and make it look like an accident. The coward hadn't wanted to land in prison beside his beloved uncle.

We didn't know, probably never would, why he'd targeted me alone, but my theory was that I'd been the easiest and therefore the first. Had he succeeded, I had no doubt he would have gone after Emmett and Dash.

The bomb had been planted in the garage while Cass had been quietly working in her office. The nephew had rigged it to the door so that when opened, it would detonate.

Had Cass not opened the garage from close to the house, she would have been caught in the explosion. Had the bomb been larger, the blast wave would have killed her. It might have killed us both and made Seraphina an orphan.

Since I was the only one who went into the garage, maybe he'd hoped it would be me. Maybe he hadn't cared that it could have been Cass.

That bastard had almost cost me everything.

Emmett was the one who'd discovered it was Tucker's nephew. After I'd choked him, the nephew had refused to talk—either faking a damaged voice box or because he'd known he was fucked. Luke had arrived seconds after Emmett, who'd been on his way over for our ride.

Luke had taken the liberty of getting the nephew's wallet and ID.

Doug Hamilton.

Emmett had recognized it immediately and told Luke he was Tucker's nephew.

Doug was currently in custody for attempted murder. Yesterday, one of Luke's officers had found an abandoned white sedan on a county gravel road. The registration was to Doug's wife and the paint scratches and dents matched those on my truck. He'd also purchased the chemicals for the bomb on his personal credit card. The dumb motherfucker.

I'd been busy with Cass, but Emmett had taken a photo of Doug to the brunette's house—the woman who'd drugged me. He'd asked her if Doug was the man who'd paid her, and she'd confirmed it though wouldn't agree to tell the police.

We'd never know for sure, but I assumed his plan had been to drug me, get me out of the bar and drive me somewhere my body would never be found. It was just a guess.

Not that it mattered. We had him on enough.

Doug's free life was over.

We couldn't prove he'd tampered with the shop's car jack. There was no sign of him on the security footage at the garage, but we typically shut the cameras off during the day when we were there working. Maybe he'd snuck in over the lunch hour, but I was certain that had been no mechanical failure.

"Is this ever going to end?" I asked Dash.

He blew out a long breath. "Fuck, I hope so."

"Listen," I slammed the trunk, "about what I said a while back. About the clubhouse."

"Forget it." He waved it off. "That was a stressful day."

"I shouldn't have said it."

"I understand why you did." He sighed, turning his gaze down the lot. The grass around the clubhouse had been cut, something he did at night when the rest of us were gone.

Dash tended to the place, even though he didn't set foot inside.

"There have been times when I've wished the same," he admitted. "That I've wished Dad had never started the club in the first place. Some days, I think you're right and we should demolish it. Others . . . we might not be a club anymore, Dad might be gone, but I can't bring myself to tear it down."

That building housed more than one of my sins.

And one day, I might need that building again.

"From the outside, the nephew wasn't a threat," I said.

He had no affiliations with the Warriors or with Tucker. But we'd missed something.

Clearly, the nephew had enough of a connection with his uncle and that club to come after us. Maybe he'd been promised money, a huge payday that would set him up for life. All he had to do was take out three men.

Maybe Doug had been a Warrior and we hadn't even realized it. His wife was currently being questioned by the FBI to understand her involvement, if any.

Emmett was pissed off at himself for not finding it. Though I suspected there wasn't anything to be found. He'd since redoubled his efforts to ensure that Tucker's ex-wife and daughters weren't involved.

Luke had confirmed that they were all on the FBI's watch list too.

My only hope was that Tucker's daughters hated him as much as we did. That maybe they were glad he'd spend his life in prison.

We were all clinging to hope.

"We underestimated Tucker's influence," Dash said. "I

think there were more members of his club than we or the FBI ever knew about."

"They will come for us."

Dash nodded. "They will."

"What do we do?"

He kept his gaze locked on the clubhouse. "What we've always done. We protect what's ours."

"At all costs."

Dash put his hand on my shoulder, giving it a squeeze, then left me and returned to his garage. Draven's garage.

And I went to my family.

Dale was sitting outside the front door when I pulled into the driveway. His eyes were fixed firmly on the yard.

Leaving the tools and oil in the trunk, I joined him, sitting on the step at his side. The smell of cigarette smoke clung to the air. "Didn't know you smoked."

"I don't often. Just one here and there. I'll have to take a shower before Cassie wakes up. If she smells it on me, she gets upset."

"And Claudia?"

"Oh, she does too. But Rose Petal will grant me this one without comment."

The two of us sat in silence, the unspoken words heavy between us. We'd been avoiding them for days, too busy making sure Seraphina was cared for and fussing over Cass at the hospital.

We both could have lost her. There was no avoiding it here, where the summer air was warm and the evening quiet.

"I'm sorry," I said, my voice hoarse.

"It's not your fault."

"Swore to you I'd protect her."

He turned, giving me a sad smile. "The way I see it, you

340

chased down that man before he could escape. He would have kept coming."

Dale and Claudia didn't know all of the details. They never would. But Cass and I had been honest with them that the explosion hadn't been an accident. One mention of the Warriors and both had gone pale.

"I wish none of this had happened to her," I whispered. My former club had put Cass's life in danger once again. When would it stop?

"So do I."

"I can't walk away from her, Dale. From them. I know it's the right thing to do to keep them safe, but I can't."

"I disagree. If you leave her, you'll break her heart. I don't want that for my daughter. Or my granddaughter. The right thing to do is stay, son. Stay and do your best."

Son. "No one has called me son in a long time." The last man had been Draven.

"You're part of this family now."

"Does that mean you don't plan to murder me?"

"Not today." Dale chuckled, then blew out a long breath. "I suppose I'd better mow the lawn. That's what I came out here to do though it's getting late."

"I'll do it for you tomorrow."

"You know, I think I'll let you. Make use of my soon-to-be son-in-law's free time."

Mowing was the least I could do. Until our house was put back to rights, Cass and I were staying here. Once the repairs were done, she could decide if she wanted to return home. If she didn't feel safe there, then we'd sell and find a new place.

"Where's Cass?" I asked.

"Asleep. Seraphina was fussy after you left so Cassie did

her bath early and put her to bed. Then I think she went to lie down."

I stood, opening the door to disappear inside, but paused on the threshold. "Thanks, Dale."

He nodded once, then returned to staring at his yard. Maybe he was keeping watch. Maybe he was about to have another cigarette before his shower.

I left him alone and went inside, toeing off my boots before walking to the guest bedroom. Seraphina was asleep in her portable crib, her arms raised above her head. Her eyelashes fluttered, and her tiny mouth pulled at the corner into a smile.

Sweet dreams, little.

I left her sleeping and went next door to Cass's room, finding her, like our daughter, curled up in bed. Her eyes opened when I climbed onto the mattress behind her.

"Hey, babe."

"Hi." She snuggled into my chest as I wrapped my arms around her.

"I love you."

"I love you too."

Her love intertwined with the threadbare strands of my soul.

A miracle. A miracle I hadn't earned, but one I'd be grateful for each and every day. A miracle I'd cling to for the rest of my days.

My Cass.

My Firecracker.

EPILOGUE

CASSANDRA

O *ne month later . . .*
        "Well, there's one advantage to living with Mom
and Dad," I said as we walked down the sidewalk toward
Genevieve and Isaiah's house. "Short commute to the
Saturday barbeque."

Leo nodded. "This is true."

But our living arrangement was about to change.

Next week, we were going home.

The construction project would be done in a week, with
new windows and siding. Since the garage had been
completely destroyed, we'd decided to rebuild it twice as big
and attached to the house so that we could each park inside.

Leo had asked me if I wanted to move and I'd told him
no. If I could get through being kidnapped from my parents'
driveway, I'd work through the explosion. I'd keep talking it
through, like I had the abduction. With Leo. With Scarlett.
Even with my parents. Each time, it was easier to process.

I didn't want that bastard to win and chase me out of our
home.

I loved our house. There were more happy memories there than sad. It was ours, the place where we'd fallen in love. The place where we'd brought Seraphina home from the hospital. And one day, maybe we'd do the same for a sibling or two.

"Goo ahh eee," Seraphina babbled, grabbing at Leo's face.

He tickled her side, earning the smile that conjured my own. Then he smooched her cheek and shifted her to his other arm. She'd left a drool spot on his white T-shirt and the wet spot allowed the orange, red and black of the phoenix tattoo on his shoulder to show through.

At five months old, she was gnawing on everything as her first tooth attempted to work free. The slobber was nearly impossible to contain. The cute pink dress I'd put her in this morning was in the hamper and now she was wearing a marigold romper adorned with ruffles. I had another change of clothes in the diaper bag.

"Now that the house is almost done, we should host the next barbeque," I said.

"Uh, yeah. Sure, babe." He shifted Seraphina again. And even though he smiled at her, his shoulders were bunched tight. He dragged in a long breath, held it, then blew it out, like he was forcing himself to relax.

"Are you okay?"

"Yeah. Course."

"Leo."

He looked at me and there it was. Nerves. "I'm good."

"Do you not want to go today?" I slowed, pointing back to Mom and Dad's. "We can stay home."

He shook his head, took my hand and clasped it tight. "I'm good."

"Okay." I didn't believe him, but maybe after we got to Genevieve and Isaiah's, he'd chill.

In the past month, we hadn't had a group gathering. The men had been scared to have us all in one place. But we couldn't live in fear forever.

Doug Hamilton was no longer a threat. Just this week he'd been convicted of attempted murder. Maybe the dumbass shouldn't have charged the makings of his bomb to his personal credit card. Or maybe he should have used a car not registered under his wife's name when he'd tried to run me off the road.

Either those mistakes had been made from sheer stupidity, or he'd been so arrogant that he hadn't fathomed being caught. He'd really thought it would be easy to kill Leo and make it look like an accident.

Whatever his motives, I was giving Doug less and less headspace as the days went on.

We weren't sure exactly how he'd been connected to the Warriors. No matter how deep Emmett dug, there was no electronic link between Doug and Tucker Talbot. From the outside, it appeared as if he had been estranged from his father, not even taking the Talbot last name.

The mystery would likely remain that way. Though he had pleaded guilty, Doug hadn't confessed how or why he'd come after Leo.

Though we all knew it was because Tucker had ordered it.

Luke had requested the visitation records for Tucker, and he'd had no visitors besides his lawyers. But Luke was a good cop and when that hadn't panned out, he'd called the FBI and requested the records for every Warrior serving sentences at the Montana State Prison.

According to the records, a Henry Williams had visited two of the senior members of the Arrowhead Warriors a year ago. Agent Brown had confirmed that, based on security footage from the penitentiary, Henry Williams was in fact Doug Hamilton.

Maybe Doug had been Tucker's last shot. Maybe not.

Leo and I were both doing our best to live life to the fullest each and every day while maintaining caution.

He went to work at the garage. Some days, Seraphina and I went with him. Others, we stayed home or spent the day at Scarlett and Luke's. I squeezed writing into little moments and otherwise my days revolved around a growing baby girl who was changing too quickly.

Seraphina's hair, a lighter shade of red than mine, was growing in small wisps that curled at the ends. Her eyes were slowly shifting toward what I hoped would be Leo's pale green. One day, when she was a grown woman, I'd tell her how she'd forged my path. Because of her, I'd found the place where I'd always been meant to be.

At Leo's side.

I gripped his hand tighter as we reached Genevieve and Isaiah's place. "This will be fun."

He nodded and forced a smile.

"We'll be fine."

"Yeah," he muttered, raising a hand to ring the doorbell.

Isaiah opened it with Amelia on his arm. "Hey. Come on in."

I smiled, but when I went to step inside, Leo cut in front of me, going first.

Ohh-kay.

"How are you guys?" I asked Isaiah, tickling Amelia's arm.

"Good." He led the way to the living room. "You?"

"We're good. Leo's a little edgy about this."

Isaiah dropped his chin, hiding a grin that was more suspicious than happy. For a man who didn't smile often, it was a lot like he was in on a secret.

"Is something—"

The sliding door to the patio opened, and Scarlett slipped past the curtains, her cheeks flushed. "You're here!"

Presley was right behind her, making sure that as she came inside, the curtains stayed fixed over the door's glass. She gave Leo a single nod as she came over and took Seraphina from his arms.

Then everyone disappeared. Scarlett, Isaiah and Presley scurried away to the backyard with my daughter, leaving Leo and me standing in the quiet house.

"Okay, what's going on?"

His Adam's apple bobbed as he swallowed, then he took my hand and led me toward the door, pulling the curtain away.

I gasped.

"What—" The words died on my tongue.

An altar stood in the yard, its circular wooden frame decorated with pale pink and ivory flowers. Greenery crept through the buds, contrasting with the sheer white curtain that had been hung behind the structure.

Rows of galvanized buckets, each filled with the same flowers as the altar, created an aisle on the lawn. Between the buckets, rose petals adorned the path. And a crowd had gathered, all eyes fixed on me.

Mom leaned into Dad's side, dabbing at her eyes with a tissue.

"They left to run errands." I blinked, sure that this was a

dream. Beside Mom stood Pastor Parsons from my church. "What is this?"

"Marry me," Leo said. "Today."

"Today?" I gaped, unable to take my eyes away from the yard.

They'd planned this. They'd all planned this. The decorations had Scarlett's name written all over them.

"Today." Leo took my face in his hands, turning me from the glass. "I don't want to wait for you to be my wife."

Tears flooded my eyes. That's why he'd been nervous on the walk over. He'd planned our wedding.

I glanced down at my outfit of shorts and a plain black tank top. This was not the outfit I wanted to get married in. "My clothes . . ."

"Scarlett picked out a dress. If you hate it or want to wait, we can wait."

"No." I shook my head, the word rushing out so fast it surprised me. "Today."

"Oh, thank fuck." Leo smashed his lips on mine, banding his arms around me as his tongue dove into my mouth. And I clung to him, kissing him with everything that I had.

When he pulled away, the smile on his face was blinding. He threw his head back and laughed, the excitement radiating off his body palpable. "I was sure you'd say no. But you always surprise me."

He turned to the glass and whipped the door open, then whooped at our friends. "Let's do this!"

A chorus of cheers carried over the air as everyone sprang into action.

Scarlett, Bryce and Genevieve raced for the door, all of them rattling off details as they took me to a bedroom where a beautiful ivory dress was laid across the bed.

"Oh." My hand came to my heart.

"Like it?" Scarlett asked.

I could only manage a nod, then stripped out of my shorts and tank top. They'd thought of everything. Jewelry. Undergarments. Shoes. The gown itself was a dream.

The torso was simple, with thin straps and a slight V at my breasts. The back laced up so it fit perfectly. But the skirt made the dress magic. I swished it, letting the ethereal fabric brush the tops of my bare toes.

"What about my hair and makeup?"

"Your mom brought some makeup if you want to freshen up, but you look beautiful," Genevieve said. "And with the way Leo toys with your hair, I think you should leave it down."

"Okay." A laugh bubbled free. "He did all of this. How?"

"The club might be gone, but that doesn't mean you aren't a Tin King," Bryce said. "We're there for each other. Leo wanted to surprise you today. We all made sure it could happen."

A Tin King.

One year ago, that would have terrified me. Now, I couldn't imagine my life in any other place or with any other people.

The club wasn't gone. It just looked different now.

I walked down the aisle to Leo, who'd changed into a white button-down shirt and dark jeans. We exchanged vows. He kissed me—his wife—as our friends applauded.

It was twilight by the time the excitement settled down and the caterer had cleaned up what was left from the food.

"I've got a present for you, Mrs. Winter," Leo said, stroking my arm.

I was sitting on his lap in the chairs Isaiah and Dash had hauled out after the wedding. "More?"

He grinned and gave Emmett a nod.

"Where's he going?" I asked as Emmett jogged around the yard toward the front of the house.

Leo stood, taking me with him and setting me on my feet. Then he took my hand and we all meandered to the front yard, following the path where Emmett had disappeared.

The rumble of an engine caught my ear. "I'm not getting on a bike with this dress."

"It's not a bike." Leo dropped a kiss to my neck as our group congregated on the sidewalk.

The cement was warm on my bare feet. Down the road, lights glowed in the windows at Mom and Dad's, where they'd taken Seraphina after she'd fallen asleep.

A flash of color caught my eye from Luke and Scarlett's driveway. A shining, flaming-orange car rolled down the street, the fading rays from the sun catching the flecks of gold on its hood.

Emmett sat behind the wheel.

"He got a new car?"

Leo shook his head. "No. You did."

I blinked. "Huh?"

"She's yours."

"No. It's too much." Not with what we were paying for the house and garage, plus the repairs on his truck. I wasn't exactly bringing in a lot of money to contribute to household income at the moment. My student loans needed to be repaid.

"No arguments." Leo brought my knuckles to his lips. "I want you to have a car that's for fun. One that you feel safe inside. We restored it at the garage. And you can sit behind the wheel and know that from the moment I saw her, I knew she was yours."

"Leo, I'm . . ."

"I love you, Cassandra."

I met those beautiful green eyes and fell a little more in love. Every day with him was like swimming deeper into an ocean of stars, its tides pulling me under to the rhythm of my heart. "I love you too."

He gave me a chaste kiss as Emmett stopped on the street. Then Leo tugged me toward the driver's side, opening the door and helping me in.

It smelled of leather and paint and Leo.

"Where are we heading, babe?" he asked, settling into the passenger side.

I glanced at the backseat. "Somewhere secluded."

He grinned.

And with a *Just Married* sign in the back window and soup cans tied to the bumper, we set out into our forever.

———

NOVA

"I told you it wouldn't work."

Across from me, Tucker Talbot bristled. He didn't like that I was right. He didn't like failure. But he shouldn't have trusted something like this to Doug, a man who lacked both the brains and the motivation to see it through.

Tucker's dark hair had more gray streaks in it these days. These past months in prison had aged him. His goatee was as white as the hair at his temples. Others might see a man beaten but if they met his dark eyes, they'd see the warrior.

"Are you ready to do this my way?"

He shook his head. "No."

"Fine." I stood, shoving away from the metal table in the dull, windowless room. A guard watched us from a single window in the steel door.

"Wait." Tucker clenched his jaw and nodded for me to sit.

I resumed my seat, leaning close.

"What's your plan?" he asked.

My gaze flicked to the camera mounted in the corner. It was illegal for them to record this conversation, but I wasn't taking a chance. "You'll have to trust me."

Tucker met my gaze, studying my face. We didn't need to voice our desires because they were one and the same.

To ruin the Tin Kings.

To get our revenge for the lives they'd stolen.

My brother's.

My father's.

Tucker gave me a nearly invisible nod. "Be careful."

"I will." I stood again, collecting my briefcase and signaling for the guard to unlock the door.

"Nova," Tucker said, his voice barely audible. "I love you."

Words—fuel—for what I was about to do.

"I love you too, Dad."

BONUS EPILOGUE

LEO

"Lift up your arm," I told Seraphina as I held her on my lap.

"No." She crossed her arms over her chest, holding tight.

"Do it."

"No." She shook her head, her hair falling across my jeans. The braid Cass had done in the tent this morning had worked its way free.

"Do. It." I poked at her ribs. "Lift up your arm."

"No." She giggled as I poked her again. "Stop, Daddy."

"Come on. You know you'll like it."

"Nu-uh. I hate it." Her smile said otherwise. And that smile melted my heart.

"Just lift up your arm and take your tortures."

"No!" She laughed. "No way."

"Okay, fine. I'll help." Peeling her arms free, I pulled one above her head and dove in, delivering today's tickle tortures until she squealed and howled and squirmed to be set free.

"See? Told you you'd like it." I picked her up and set her on my lap, then touched the tip of her nose.

She shook her head, panting as she caught her breath.

Then she huffed, put her small hands on my face and squeezed my cheeks together as hard as she could until I had fish lips. "No. I. Don't."

I stood in a flash, taking her with me. Then I launched her into the air, catching her as she came back down.

"Again!"

I did it again, tossing her even higher.

Four years old and she was fearless. Or maybe she just knew I'd always catch her.

Two more *again*s and finally I set her on her feet.

The zipper to the tent clicked open and Cass stepped out with the baby in her arms. "You two are loud. But at least we know the bears will be scared away."

Seraphina's smile dropped as she stared up at me. "Bears?"

"She's just joking." *Sort of.* I ruffled her hair and reached for the baby.

Farah Mae Winter was two months old today. Much like we had with Seraphina, Cass and I hadn't discussed a name until we were at the hospital, holding our newborn daughter. Then I'd pulled up my list of top names, hitting the winner with the first choice. Farah, meaning happiness, was named for the life Cass and my children had given me.

"Where did Mom and Dad go?" Cass asked, looking around the campsite.

"Just for a walk. They should be back soon."

"Okay." She sighed and went to our circle of camp chairs, relaxing under the shade of the trees.

We weren't at a famous national park, just a campsite on forest service land, but the Montana mountains had their advantages—fresh air, beautiful meadows teeming with summer wildflowers, and we were close enough to home that if camping with an infant turned out to be a disaster, we could make it back to town within an hour.

"Mommy, can I have a snack?" Seraphina flashed Cass those pretty green eyes—my eyes—which usually got her whatever she wanted.

"Sure, honey. Do you want to pick it out?"

She nodded and raced toward the truck on the other side of our tent, climbing up onto the tailgate and popping open a cooler.

"How are you doing, babe?" I sat beside Cass, propping Farah into the crook of my arm.

"Good." Cass relaxed deeper into her seat. "I'm glad we came out here this weekend."

"Me too." We'd needed to get away.

No cell phones. No laptops. No work. Just family, cooking over a fire and exploring the woods for two days.

Camping had become a regular family activity. If their destination wasn't too far, we'd tag along with Cass's parents. Other weekends, we'd meet up with our friends at the lake, enjoying the boat Dash had bought a couple years ago.

Before Cass, I hadn't camped much. Certainly not as a child. Dale and Claudia were firm believers in their tent, and though it worked for us too, next year, I was buying Cass a camper for her birthday.

"When I was nursing Farah, I had an idea for another book," she said.

That got my attention. "Yeah?"

"Yeah." She nodded and the smile that stretched across her face was full of relief.

Cass's first book had been published about three years ago. Her second had come not long after. But with the drama that had happened during that year, followed by another pregnancy and life with a toddler, she hadn't started a third book, even though her publisher was clamoring for one.

She'd simply stopped writing.

When I'd asked her why, she'd told me she was waiting for the right idea.

"I needed this weekend." She tilted her head to the sky and the white clouds stealing the occasional ray of sun. "To get away. To disconnect. I needed the headspace to let my mind wander."

"I'm proud of you." So damn proud.

She blushed and closed her eyes. Her talent was a gift but she'd never been one to boast, no matter how successful her books had become.

I'd asked her years ago if she wanted to go back to school. I'd told her I'd move wherever she needed to be, but she'd promised the only place she wanted to be was in Clifton Forge. That writing books and raising our daughter was more than she'd ever hoped for.

"Seraphina!" Claudia emerged from the tree line, her hands cupped to her mouth.

"What, Nana?"

"We found some pretty flowers."

"I wanna see!" Seraphina scrambled down from the truck with a pack of crackers in her fist. Then she was a blur of fiery hair and a delighted smile as she ran.

That kid ran everywhere. Dale joked that she'd walked just long enough to learn how to run.

"She's going to sleep so well." I ran a thumb over Farah's face. "What about you? Gonna sleep all night?"

Farah blinked.

"That means no." Cass laughed.

I stretched out my legs, then turned my attention to my beautiful wife. "Tell me about your idea."

My firecracker emerged, her caramel eyes dancing as she explained what she wanted to write. It was brilliant, like Cass, and I had no doubt that it would be wildly successful.

"I get to read it first," I said.

"That's a given."

"When your publisher invites us to New York, we're leaving the girls at home."

"They might not pick it up."

"Please." I scoffed. "We're going, whenever that happens, and we're going alone."

The two of us were insatiable and even with the girls' crazy sleep schedules, our sex life was phenomenal, but a vacation in a New York hotel could mean a lot of fun.

Maybe even a son.

"What is that look for?" Cass's eyes narrowed at my profile.

"Huh? Nothing."

She shook her head. "She's two months old and you're already thinking about a third, aren't you?"

"Maybe." I chuckled, loving how easily she could read me after our years together. Though she'd always been able to read me, usually understanding what was happening in my head before I'd made sense of it myself.

"If we do have a boy one day, I get to pick the name," she said.

Hell, no. She'd want to name our kid Dale after her father. And though I loved and respected Dale, my kids had badass names. We could do better than Dale. "I love you, babe. But picking the names is sort of my thing. I mean . . . I'm kind of great at it."

She smirked. "We'll see."

———

Two and a half years later, sitting in a hospital bed with our son in her arms, Cass ran a fingertip down the bridge of his little nose. "Leo. I want to name him Leo."

The phone in my hand, open to my list of names, slipped from my grip. "You do?"

"Yes. Seraphina means fire. Farah means happiness. And to me, Leo means love."

Well, damn. If she wanted to name our son after me, I'd be honored. "Okay."

"You like it?"

"Yeah. But it was not what I was expecting. I had a whole speech planned."

"A speech for what?"

"I was sure you were going to want to name him Dale."

ACKNOWLEDGMENTS

Thank you for reading *Fallen Jester*! I'm beyond grateful for all of my incredible fans who have fallen in love with this world and come along with me on this adventure in Clifton Forge.

An enormous thanks to my editing and proofreading team: Elizabeth Nover, Julie Deaton, Karen Lawson and Judy Zweifel. Thank you to Sarah Hansen for Leo and Cass's breathtaking cover.

Thank you to all of the amazing bloggers and incredible readers who have followed me on this Clifton Forge journey. I can't believe there is only one book left. It will be bittersweet to leave this world, but because of your love and support, it has been such a fantastic journey. So thank you for loving these characters as much as I do.

Lastly, thanks to my family and friends. You know who you are, and I hope you know how much I love and appreciate you.

ABOUT THE AUTHOR

Devney Perry is a *Wall Street Journal, USA Today* and #1 *Amazon* bestselling author of over forty romance novels. After working in the technology industry for a decade, she abandoned conference calls and project schedules to pursue her passion for writing. She was born and raised in Montana and now lives in Washington with her husband and two sons.

Don't miss out on the latest book news.
Subscribe to her newsletter!
www.devneyperry.com

Printed in Great Britain
by Amazon

40524694R00209